A STRANGE SENSATION

"I'll think on what you've said, Mr. Cameron," Jessica said in her most businesslike tone, "and get back to you tomorrow with my answer. Now I believe you have work to do."

"That I do," he agreed easily, and just when she dropped her guard, thinking the skirmish was over, he leaned forward. "But not before I get a good-bye kiss from my wife."

"You most certainly will n—"

His kiss cut her off.

Jessica tried to push away, but in her position leaning backward over the table her attempts were futile. It was like trying to push against solid rock. His hand slipped up her back to support her head as his lips moved slowly, languorously over hers. His kiss was as warm and soft as before—and it stirred the oddest tingling down her arms. In her wonder over this strange sensation she soon forgot about struggling altogether.

When Luke pulled away her eyes were still closed, and having his fair share of male ego, he grinned.

Unfortunately, Jessica chose that moment to open her eyes, and her fury exploded. "Get out!" she snapped, eyes flashing with embarrassed indignation. "And don't you ever try that again or I'll—I'll tell Sheriff Davis I made a mistake and let him hang you after all!"

Cynthia Strickland

The Deal

LEISURE BOOKS　　　　**NEW YORK CITY**

A LEISURE BOOK®
May 1997
Published by

Dorchester Publishing Co., Inc.
276 Fifth Avenue
New York, NY 10001

Printed in the United States of America.

I dedicate this story to...

The family and friends, too numerous to name, who believed. Thank You.

The memory of my grandparents, who filled my life with unconditional love.

My parents for instilling in me the courage and tenacity to dream, then giving me the love and support to follow those dreams.

Michael, for being the joy of my life. Always remember, you can do anything if you want it badly enough.

But above all, this is for you, Steve. You were willing to keep your feet planted firmly on the ground so that I could fly. For that alone I will always love you. You are much more a hero than any I could create.

Chapter One

The pungent scent of freshly cut pine rose to assault Luke Cameron as he slowly climbed the twelve steps to the newly constructed platform. At the top he paused to look out over the heads of the crowd gathered below, out past the shops and houses that lined the main street through town, out to the sun-washed prairie that had been his only home for the last six years. As if in answer to his longing gaze, a faint breeze stirred the early morning air, sifting through his hair like a lover's caress—and setting the rope swaying that waited to end his life.

A nudge from behind set his feet in motion once more, and squaring his shoulders, Luke crossed the platform to stand beside the noose. A stark scarecrow of a preacher dressed in somber black stepped forward eagerly, and in his best Sunday sermonizing voice began to expound on the wages of sin, exhorting Luke to repent of his evil deeds while he still had the chance. It was evident to all listening, however, that the reverend thought the condemned man better prepare himself for an afterlife in a much warmer climate.

Luke let the man's words pass over him. He wasn't the least bit sorry for what he had done to bring himself to this end. He was also sure in his mind that even if he could be given the choice he knew he'd do the same again. If that meant facing the punishment the preacher was ranting on about with such relish, then so be it.

With detached interest Luke's gaze scanned the crowd below him. Morbid bunch, he thought with distaste at seeing the excitement on their faces as they anxiously awaited the spectacle. You could tell a lot about a person from their eyes. What was that saying about the eyes being a window to the soul? If that was true he saw a few souls standing before him that maybe should start being a little less concerned about his final destination and a little more concerned about their own.

Take that old gray-haired biddy sitting over there in her buggy, a parasol shielding the glare so she wouldn't miss one grisly second of the action. Her clouded blue eyes were fairly glittering as the preacher's words worked her into a self-righteous frenzy. She looked for all the world as if she hoped to see the ground open up at any second and the fires of hell start licking at his boots. And then there was the guy in the blood-stained butcher's apron. Didn't the man see enough of death without stopping his work to come to a hanging? And the banker standing over there holding his little son's hand. Yeah, this was sure a sight no kid should miss seeing.

And over there was . . .

His angry inventory of the faces came to an abrupt halt on a black veil. The woman hung back from the crowd, seemingly nervous to be among them. Now why on earth would a woman in mourning want to come to a hanging? Unless, of course, Luke had been the one to bring about her condition. That seemed unlikely this far north of where most of his "evil deeds" had been committed.

Still, he couldn't help but wonder who she was. Maybe it was just that with his own life rapidly slipping away, the widow's presence reminded Luke painfully that there would be no one to mourn his passing.

He had tried not to think of this void in his life as he'd sat on the narrow cot in the jail during the last few days, listening to the insidious sounds of sawing and hammering as the gallows was erected across the street. He had told himself that he really didn't care. Since he had finally completed his sworn vendetta six months ago, he had been left without a purpose to live, with only the memories. And death had to be better than the living hell of remembering.

But standing on the gallows now, listening to the preacher winding down, Luke suddenly realized that life hadn't seemed so precious until this moment, when he was just seconds away from losing it. Or maybe it was just the dying part he wasn't ready for. There was a mystery that shrouded death. Would he burn forever in hell, as the preacher predicted, or was God a merciful, loving Father, as Royce and Delia Cameron had taught their son?

It seemed he was about to find out, for the good reverend snapped his Bible shut and stepped to the far side of the platform. The pious look on the man's face showed that he had no doubt this sinner was going to fry in hell despite his best efforts to save Luke's soul.

The sheriff stepped forward then, and for some reason Luke's eyes went to the widow. He found himself wishing she would remove the heavy lace veil so he could see her face, wishing she were here to mourn him, wishing someone in this world would care that he was about to die.

"Got any last requests, son?" the sheriff asked, rousing Luke from his musings.

"A fast horse and a head start?"

Wilford Davis almost laughed at the fatalistic attempt at humor, but given the circumstances he could only shake his head. He had to hand it to the gunslinger, he had guts. Wilford had actually grown to like the young man over the last three weeks, which made it real hard to hang him now.

"Sorry, son, but I can't do that," Wilford answered in a tone of sincere regret. "Anything else?"

Looking out toward the open prairie one last time, Luke felt his stomach begin to knot. "Just get it over with, Sheriff," he said for the man's ears alone. Davis seemed to be the only person in the God-fearing town who wasn't enjoying this spectacle. "Let's just hope God has a hell of a lot more mercy than these good Christian folks."

The graying lawman nodded his agreement to that, and with a sigh of regret turned to take a dark burlap bag from his deputy. He then reached for Luke's Stetson. "I truly am sorry about this, son. If it was up to me—"

"Sheriff Davis."

All eyes turned at the strained voice, and Luke looked down

Cynthia Strickland

in surprise to find that the widow had made her way to the foot of the steps. He wondered if he was the only one who noticed how tightly her hands were clenched in front of her. She looked neither right nor left as the crowd behind her erupted into curious whispers.

''May I speak to you a moment, Sheriff?''

The man was obviously taken aback by her request. With a perplexed frown he walked over to the top of the steps and stooped down to speak to her. ''Can't it wait, Ms. Randall?'' he asked quietly. ''I mean, at least 'til after—well, 'til after we're finished here?''

''No, it can't,'' she persisted. ''It's important that I speak with you right now. *Please.*''

Looking back over his shoulder in indecision at the man standing beside the noose, watching them, Wilford rose and reluctantly walked down the steps, muttering under his breath all the way about the eccentricities of females. He took the lady's arm and led her well away from the gallows. In his wake he left a crowd of avidly curious onlookers, not the least of whom was Luke Cameron.

When Wilford found a spot out of hearing range of the crowd, he turned on the widow, trying to overcome his impatience with her untimely request by reminding himself of the recent cause of her state of mourning. ''Now, what is it, Jessica?'' he asked calmly.

Jessica Randall took a deep, steadying breath, clenching her hands until the knuckles turned white. It had taken every ounce of courage she possessed, along with the loss of all common sense, to make her come here today. It was beyond belief that she had even conceived of this plan, much less had the fortitude—or stupidity, she corrected mentally—to carry it out. The man was a gunfighter! A killer!

Unfortunately, that was just what she needed.

''Please, Jessica,'' the sheriff prompted, losing some of his patience as she stood wringing her hands silently. ''That man may be a gunfighter, but I don't think he should have to stand there lookin' at that noose and thinkin' about what's to come while we stand here talkin' about something that can surely wait.''

After a long moment of continued silence that he took for agreement, Wilford said gently, ''Go on over to my office. I'll be there in a few minutes and we can talk all you want.''

Jessica was chewing the inside of her lip now, trying to force the words past the knot in her throat. But she had to get them out. After Sheriff Davis's ''few more minutes'' it would be too late. Even now he was turning away.

''Sheriff!''

He turned back with an impatient snort, and Jessica hurried forward before she completely lost what little nerve she had dredged up. ''Sheriff, isn't there a law in effect that a woman alone can save a condemned man if he agrees to marry her?'' she blurted out in a rush.

Wilford couldn't have looked more surprised if she had asked if it were possible for her to save the Devil from sinning. ''Jessica, surely you can't be thinkin' to—''

''Is that the law?'' she cut him off, trying to put a sense of conviction in her voice that she was far from feeling.

Wilford hesitated a long moment before answering. ''Well— yes, it is. But John ain't been dead more'n four months! If it's help you're needin' then—''

''May I speak to the man?'' Jessica interrupted again, more calmly now that she had committed to her course.

There was no argument Wilford could offer in the face of her stubborn resolve. She was right about the law. With so many men killed during the War Between the States there had been a law enacted in these parts that a widow could save a condemned man if he agreed to marry her. Much as he didn't want to see Jessica take up with the man, Wilford still couldn't help the small part of him that hoped he wouldn't have to hang Luke Cameron after all. There was something about the young man that didn't fit with the usual gunslingers Wilford had dealt with, something in the eyes.

''All right,'' he finally relented at her waiting silence. ''But I don't think you want to talk to him in front of that crowd.'' He nodded his head in the direction of the gathering. ''And I can't leave you alone with him.''

''If you put him back in his cell, I should be perfectly safe talking to him—alone, please.''

He thought on that a long moment. Spending some time alone with the man might be just what she needed to change her mind about this insane notion. ''Okay,'' he finally answered with obvious reluctance. ''You go on to the jail and I'll bring him right over.''

Releasing the breath she had unknowingly been holding, Jessica nodded. She didn't know whether to feel relief that he had given in to her wishes, or stark raving terror. She turned, and with deceptive aplomb crossed the street to the jail, feeling the curious eyes of the crowd staring holes in her back every step of the way.

Somehow she held on to that outward calm through the long walk from the empty lot where the gallows had been erected to the jail across the street. It was only after the door had shut behind her that Jessica finally gave in to her quaking knees and sagged against the oak panel for support. Wrapping her arms across her stomach against the tight knot that had formed there, she closed her eyes and forced her lungs to take in several deep, calming breaths.

It had been this way as long as she could remember. She had no trouble whatsoever dealing with people one on one, or even two or three at a time, but put her in a crowd and her stomach suddenly clenched up, her heart started pounding like a runaway mustang, and she couldn't seem to get her breath. And today, nervous as she was already over this insane scheme, it had felt as if some huge unseen hand was clutching her insides trying to squeeze the very life out of her as she stepped forward to call up to the sheriff, gaining the avid attention of the entire town. Only the greater fear of what she stood to lose if she didn't follow through with this plan had forced her toward those gallows, and the man who stood atop them waiting to be hanged.

After a few more breaths Jessica felt the knot in her stomach slowly begin to untangle until she could think again. She now realized she should have handled this situation differently. She

14

should have come here to the jail privately, *before* the gun-fighter was led to the gallows. The common sense she usually possessed—which she had battled against since first concoct-ing this plan nearly a week ago—wouldn't seem to let her commit to the folly until the last second, though. Maybe it was the fear that if she saw the man up close, saw his rough ap-pearance and looked into the cold eyes of a dispassionate killer, she knew she wouldn't be able to go through with it.

So she had stood rooted to her spot at the edge of the crowd, waiting. A small wave of relief had rippled through her when Sheriff Davis had finally led the prisoner from the jail. The man certainly didn't fit her idea of a ruthless gunslinger. She had always pictured them as dressed all in black, with shiny boots, silver spurs, and an aura of death surrounding them like a pall.

Thankfully, Luke Cameron looked nothing like that percep-tion. Instead he looked for all the world like any of the cow-boys that worked on her ranch, with his snug-fitting denims, cotton shirt, and well-worn boots. The collar of his shirt was as far as she had allowed her gaze to travel upward, afraid that if she saw the coldness in his killer's eyes she would surely lose her resolve.

She couldn't let that happen, Jessica reminded herself once more. The Circle R was her home, the first real home she had had since her mother died all those years ago and her father had . . .

No! She wasn't going to think of that now. The coming minutes were going to be hard enough without waking the sleeping demons of the past. Everything she loved, everything she held dear in life was at stake, and if it took making a deal with the Devil himself, she swore she would do it.

The thud of booted footsteps on the sidewalk outside shook her out of her thoughts, and Jessica whirled to stare at the door, her heart pounding once more from its place lodged in her throat. Backing away, she locked her eyes on the doorknob as it began to turn. There was an ominous creak as the door slowly swung open to admit the brilliant sunshine, silhouetting a tall, broad-shouldered form that took up nearly the entire doorway. Jessica swallowed hard. Surely it was only a trick of her taut-nerved imagination that made that shadowy form look just as she had always pictured Satan himself.

From the way he was squinting, she could tell that the gunfighter was trying to adjust his eyes to the dim interior of the jail after the blinding sunshine outside. The brief moment gave her a chance to collect her careening fears and study him objectively, without being subjected to his own scrutiny. She found herself surprised by what she saw.

He had replaced his Stetson—tan, not black, she noticed. Tawny hair with just the slightest curl fell past his collar, matched by a beard and mustache that nearly covered the top half of a pair of firm lips. The nose was straight, tilting downward a bit at the tip. Not so bad really, Jessica thought with a sigh of relief as she finally worked up the courage to look into his eyes. He might even be considered nice looking if—

A gasp caught in her throat as Jessica was suddenly subjected to the full force of eyes more frigid than any ice could hope to be. A shiver ran down her spine as she looked into the coldly emotionless blue eyes, and at the moment dealing with the Devil seemed preferable to dealing with the man standing before her.

Sheriff Davis took Luke's arm, breaking the frozen tableau as he led his prisoner back to the cell he had so recently vacated. As he turned the key in the lock with a sharp click, his eyes held Luke's. "I'll be just outside the door if you need me, Ms. Randall," he said, though Luke realized the words were more for his benefit than the lady's.

Having given the warning, Wilford left, and Luke's eyes returned to the black-draped form who was now pacing a safe distance from the bars. He wondered again who she was and why he was here. There had been no one more surprised than he when Davis had returned from talking to the widow and had taken him by the arm and led him back down the steps toward the jail where the lady in black had just disappeared.

Maybe she did know him. Maybe he was the one responsible for her state of mourning. The thought gave his conscience a brief twinge, but he quickly pushed the feeling aside, reasoning that, if so, the lady should have chosen more wisely when she married. The men he had killed were all spineless bastards, worthy of death.

Still, that didn't explain why he was here now instead of swinging at the end of a rope. If he had been the one to make her a widow, then surely she would have cheered his hanging, not postponed it. Unless she wanted to be the one to exact her revenge. He watched her carefully for any sign that she meant to pull a derringer from that little reticule she was carrying. But she only continued to pace silently, making no move to shoot him or to give an explanation for this short reprieve.

Luke was notorious for his nerves of steel, but being dangled over the jaws of death, then brought back here to watch a widow pace back and forth in silence, succeeded in wearing those nerves to the breaking point. Uncharacteristically, he made the first move. "Take your time, ma'am," he offered with mock levity. "I'm in no hurry to get back to the party, for all that it is in my honor."

The first words caused Jessica to jump nervously. She caught the mocking tone, yet underneath she thought she heard bitter regret tinge the words as well. And why wouldn't it? Of course the man didn't want to die. The thought gave her hope, and surreptitiously she glanced at him once more. He stood at the barred cell wall, leaning against it with one knee bent slightly forward. His arms were linked negligently through the bars as if he were totally at ease with the situation, which made Jessica totally *un*easy.

He was bigger than he had appeared on the gallows, both in height and in brawn. The blue cotton shirt he wore was rolled up at the sleeves to reveal sinewy forearms. Her gaze traveled up those arms now to a thick expanse of chest.

Gritting her teeth, she tossed her head back and defying her fear, again met those ice-blue eyes.

His gaze seemed to bore through the thick protection of the veil to see into her very soul. Like a great, tawny mountain lion surveying its prey he watched her, deceptively calm, yet ready to spring with lethal force should she unwisely venture too close to the bars that separated them. Swallowing nervously at the thought, Jessica had to wonder if she was completely insane to still be considering this scheme.

Luke felt her gaze, and saw the almost imperceptible shudder as she watched him quietly. He would concede that he wasn't the picture of a gentleman right now, but this dowdy little crow hardly had room to be criticizing appearances. He was about to tell the woman just that when she spoke.

"Mr. Cameron?" Her voice was softer here in the silence of the jail and it flowed over him like the smoothest silk. "I know you must be wondering why the sheriff brought you here."

At the moment Luke was too busy trying to see past the veil to wonder why this woman wanted to see him, for that honeyed voice had aroused his male curiosity. This was no *old* widow.

The fact that he remained silent did nothing to bolster Jessica's already flagging confidence, and she went on to fill the silence nervously. "I don't know if Sheriff Davis explained why I asked to see you."

"He didn't."

Some of her nervousness abated now that he had finally chosen to speak. She tried to tell herself that any man would be wary in his situation, and that was the only reason he seemed so tense. But surely no man in his right mind would turn her down. Would he?

"Mr. Cameron, I've come here today to offer you a business proposition."

A tawny brow went up as morbid amusement overtook curiosity for a moment. "Ma'am, I don't know if you understand what you just interrupted out there but I can assure you I'm not the best choice for a business partner right now."

His demeanor suggested that he thought she might not be playing with a full deck, an attitude to which Jessica took offense. "You are a gunslinger and you were about to hang for it," she bit out succinctly. "Fortunately for you, that makes you *just* the business partner I need."

Now it was becoming clear. "You want someone killed, is that it?" Luke asked, shaking his head in disgust. She was just like all the others, assuming that because he was a "gun-fighter" he went around killing people indiscriminately.

"Well, I'm sorry to disappoint you, lady," he went on sca-thingly, "but I doubt ole Sheriff Davis is gonna let me go shoot someone for you, even if I do promise to come back afterward. But then I guess you figure since they're hanging me anyway it wouldn't hurt to add one more notch to my gun before I go, huh? Keeps your own hands nice and lily white."

This wasn't going at all like she had planned, Jessica thought with a frown. He was supposed to be on his knees thanking her right about now, not verbally attacking her. "I am not asking you to kill anyone, Mr. Cameron," she tried to explain. "And if you agree to my proposal you won't be han-ged."

That got his attention, and he straightened with interest. "What do you mean by that?"

"I mean, you have the ability to handle a gun, which I need. In return, I have the ability to see that you walk out of this jail a relatively free man, which you need. My proposal is that we help each other."

He was visibly skeptical. "Unless you're God or the gov-ernor, lady, I don't see how I can be set free just on your say-so."

Here it was, the moment of truth. Once she stepped over this verbal line there would be no turning back. Jessica took a deep breath, and before she could let reason convince her to shut up and go home, she took the step.

"I don't know if you're aware of it or not, Mr. Cameron, but there is a law in this part of the country that states that a condemned man can be redeemed by a widow if he—ah—agrees to—marry her."

A heavy silence followed her words.

"You're kidding, right?" Luke asked with a snort of dis-belief when he finally found his tongue again. "No woman in her right mind would be so desperate as to want a convicted murderer for a husband!"

Jessica's teeth clenched at his tone. It was one thing for her to question her own sanity, but the fact that this gunslinger kept doing so was starting to get on her nerves. "I don't want or need a *husband*, Mr. Cameron. I need a hired gun. Unfortunately, the price I have to pay to hire you is marriage. Believe me, this deal will be strictly business!"

The way she stressed *strictly* left no doubt in his mind what she was talking about. As if there was a snowball's chance in hell she had to worry about that, Luke thought with a shudder as he eyed the black lace skeptically. There seemed only one plausible explanation for so heavy a veil, and it wasn't for the element of intrigue.

Still, against his better judgment Luke found that he was curious about the widow. She needed him for some reason, and that need had brought her to offer marriage not only to a complete stranger, but one who was a convicted killer. He always had admired courage, especially in a woman.

And too there was that softer-than-silk voice that was teasing his curiosity.

"Well, Mr. Cameron? Do we have a deal?"

"Take off the veil."

Of all the things he could have said, this was the one she hadn't expected. "I really don't think that's necessary. It has nothing to do with—"

"Let's just say I like to see what I'm bargaining for."

Jessica could only stare in disbelief for a moment at the incredible gall of the man. "You're bargaining for your life!" she reminded him baldly when she found her voice once more. "I hardly think you're in any position to make demands."

Luke was getting more than a little irritated himself trying to figure out what kind of game she was playing. "Look, lady, you need my gun, badly enough to marry a condemned killer to get it. I think you should understand my havin' a few questions about what you're wantin' to get me into."

Put that way, Jessica began to understand why he hadn't jumped at her offer immediately. It was only natural that he would want to know something about her and her reasons for hiring him. Well, maybe it was best to lay her cards on the table and find out if he was willing to do the job.

"I own a small ranch just south of town," she began, and

in her agitation over the subject, didn't realize that she had begun pacing once again, her graceful strides distracting Luke somewhat from her story. "Four months ago my husband, John, was killed. The sheriff looked around for a while, then finally determined it must have been done by outlaws. I agreed with him at first, but now I'm not so sure. Less than a month after John was killed, one of our neighbors suddenly asked me to marry him."

"Maybe he likes veils," Luke threw in dryly.

Jessica glared at his attempt at humor from behind the mentioned covering, but went on. "When I refused to marry Benjamin Mateland, he became angry and told me I would change my mind after I saw what it was like to try to run a ranch without a man around. I didn't think much about it until later when several . . . things began to happen."

"Things?" Luke questioned, unable to help himself. It was that blasted male response to the damsel-in-distress scenario.

"It wasn't much at first—a few missing cows, a shed burned. But lately someone has been taking potshots at some of my hired hands. It was obvious they didn't mean to actually shoot anyone, but a couple of the men have quit just the same."

"And you think this rejected suitor of yours is to blame?"

"Ben Mateland is not my suitor!" Jessica snapped, angry that he saw her problem as frivolous, as if it were no more than some lovers' spat. "He wants my land, though God only knows why when he owns over five thousand acres now. You would think my eight hundred wouldn't be worth his time, yet I know he wants it because three weeks ago he offered to buy me out. When I refused, he very subtly implied that my troubles are going to get worse."

"Why don't you just sell?" Luke offered the obvious solution.

"Because I won't be run off my land!" It was the only answer Jessica felt he deserved. "Now you know why I need you, Mr. Cameron. Do we have a deal?"

Luke studied her for a long moment, then said, "The veil."

"I told you that's not necessary. This is business."

"Do you want your hired gun?"

He was being infuriatingly stubborn on this point. "I could walk out of here right now and let them hang you," she challenged.

"You could."

There wasn't the least trace of concern in his voice. He was so confident she wouldn't do it, it showed in that cocky, self-assured smile that barely tilted the corners of his mustache. Oh, but she wanted to turn her back and walk out the door, to hear him call to her and beg her to come back and save his worthless hide!

But would he? Luke Cameron didn't look like the kind of man who would beg for anything, especially from a woman. And Jessica couldn't afford to test that assumption. It had taken nearly a week to work up the nerve to come here. Only the scheduled hanging this morning had finally pushed her to act on this insane plan. If she walked out now she might as well ride over to the Bar M right now and hand Ben Mateland the deed to her land.

Luke saw by the slight slump of her shoulders the moment she admitted defeat. "Well?" he questioned expectantly.

"Well what?"

He grinned at her pique. "The veil."

"This is ridiculous!"

"Humor me."

When she still stood stubbornly motionless, Luke lost his amusement as well as his patience. "What is it with you and that veil anyway? Do you break mirrors or something?"

Jessica plain hated giving in, especially given the situation. But it actually seemed as if he might consider refusing her offer if she didn't comply, incredible as that seemed.

With an angry snort that nearly blew the lace covering from her face, she reached up and snatched off the hat with its attached veil. "There!" she snapped. "Are you satisfied, Mr. Cameron?"

Chapter Two

Luke stood motionless for several seconds, just staring. He had expected plain, or even downright, mud-fence ugly. What he hadn't expected was the woman who stood before him, eyes flashing defiantly as she angrily met his gaze. Now he understood perfectly why she chose to wear the heavy veil. It was to keep from being crushed by a stampede of zealous suitors!

With the hat and its concealing veil gone, he was left to stare in awe at the thickest mane of honeyed-brown hair he'd ever seen. It hung in luxuriant waves nearly to her waist, and Luke found himself wondering how that slender neck could support so much weight without breaking. She obviously felt his interest, for she took a protective step backwards, stepping into a shaft of sunlight that streamed in through the window to her left. The golden rays seemed to ignite hidden strands within her hair, turning them to shimmering flames until the entire mass warmed to rich auburn.

Shaking himself mentally at the trail his thoughts were taking, Luke dragged his gaze away from her hair to her face. But that was no help in regaining his senses, for his eyes now wandered over creamy skin that provided the perfect backdrop for features any angel would envy. From the thickly lashed golden-green eyes that continued to shoot angry sparks at his intense perusal, to that intriguing beauty mark just to the right corner of a pair of lips that begged to be kissed, her face was as near perfection as any woman could hope to come.

At the uncomfortably familiar feelings of insecurity that washed over her as he continued to stare, Jessica mentally chastised herself. Why should she care what this gunfighter thought of her looks? She was asking him to work for her, not court her!

"I think you've stared quite long enough," she bit out. "Unless you find me too ugly to work for?"

Luke managed to hide his enthusiasm well. "No, ma'am."

"Then do we have a deal?"

Of a sudden he was strongly beginning to consider it. "We'll have to marry, you say?"

"Yes, but as I said before, it won't be a real marriage. I'm just hiring you for protection until I find out who killed John. If I prove it was Mateland, or his men, then he won't be able to harass me anymore. I'm asking you for one year, Mr. Cameron, or until I get the proof I need, whichever comes first. When our bargain is met, I'll give you enough money and time to disappear. The marriage will be annulled and we'll both have what we want: me, my ranch, and you, your freedom."

Luke studied her for a long moment, using the lengthening silence to his best advantage. He had already made up his mind, now he just wanted to see how desperate she was. "So you save my life today, and in return I spend the next year layin' it on the line for this ranch of yours. Then, if I live through the year, you give me a few dollars and send me off to Mexico. Is that about it?"

Put in those terms, the deal did sound a bit one-sided. "But at least you'll have a chance this way," Jessica pointed out to him.

"It just seems if I'm going to put my life on the line for this marriage I ought to at least get a little more out of it than what you're offering. Don't you think?"

The smile that lurked beneath that mustache made Jessica decidedly uneasy. "Just what is it you want, then?" she asked warily.

Those mesmerizing blue eyes seemed to imprison hers as he answered in a low, husky tone, "What if I said I want you, Ms. Randall? Would you still make the deal?"

Caught off guard by the unexpected—and totally disgraceful—suggestion, Jessica was rendered speechless for a moment. It was only for a moment, though, and then she found her tongue quick enough. "You can hang, Mr. Cameron!" she spat, turning toward the door. She would just find some other way to—

"You can't blame a man for tryin' to negotiate for the best of a bargain." His call stopped her before she reached the door. "I wasn't really serious anyway. I just needed to know how serious *you* are before I get in the middle of this." It was only a small lie. "You have yourself a deal if you're still interested."

Jessica took a deep breath, counting to ten as she fought the urge to keep right on walking out the door. But blast it all, she needed this provoking man! Had it only been his way of testing her resolve? Gritting her teeth against offended pride, she slowly turned back to face him. "You'll sleep in the bunkhouse?" she asked to clarify his acceptance of the terms just in case he had been serious earlier.

"I'll sleep in the bunkhouse," he confirmed, and only after she had jerked a nod of acceptance and stepped out on the sidewalk to talk to the sheriff did Luke quietly add, "for now, my fiery little widow."

Being the small town that Langly was, Wilford Davis served as both its sheriff and justice of the peace. Still, he seemed taken aback when Jessica asked him to perform the service that would unite her and Luke Cameron in holy matrimony. At his surprised look she glanced nervously at the groom, then stepped closer to Wilford to quietly explain, "Under the circumstances, I don't believe Mr. Cameron would care to have Reverend Phillips perform this marriage."

Thinking of how the good reverend had been committing Luke's soul to the fires of hell only a half hour ago, Wilford was inclined to agree. After calling his deputy in as a witness, Wilford reluctantly began. He pulled the small book out of his desk that held the marriage vows and wiped the dust off the cover. Standing before the two, he opened it and cleared his throat to begin. It all seemed to pass as a blurred dream to Jessica until she noticed that the sheriff had stopped talking and everyone was looking at her.

"Are you sure this is what you want, Jessica?" Wilford asked with a worried frown. When she nodded, he hesitated, then finally asked his question again. "Do you, Jessica, take Lucas Royce Cameron to be your lawfully wedded husband?"

"I do." Was that reed-thin reply really her voice?

"Where's the ring?"

A ring! She had completely forgotten they'd need one. Chewing at her lower lip as she thought quickly, Jessica finally came up with a solution, but it was one she didn't care for. Still . . .

Taking off her gloves, she looked down at the slim gold band she now wore on her right hand. John's ring. Would he understand?

Taking a deep breath and hoping he wasn't watching her from wherever he now was, Jessica slipped the ring off her finger and handed it to the man who stood watching her in thoughtful silence. He took it, turning to face Wilford once more.

The rest again passed as a blur for Jessica until she heard a deeply voiced "I do" and felt the warm golden band being slipped onto her left hand. As if through someone else's eyes she looked down at her small hand nearly swallowed up by the larger male one.

"You can—uh"—Wilford looked to Jessica uneasily before forming the last as if it were a question—"kiss the bride?"

The dreamlike haze evaporated quickly. Jessica opened her mouth to protest, but before she could utter a word, Luke had pulled her into his arms. "Don't mind if I do, Sheriff."

Fighting down panic at the memory of his earlier words, Jessica felt suddenly paralyzed as she waited helplessly for the ravaging kiss of an outlaw. Only now was she fully beginning to realize the consequences if he had been serious! As his ruggedly handsome face drew closer, her eyes squeezed shut, her lips clamping together into a thin line as she prayed mentally that this would be over quickly. She swore that if he ever let her go she was—

The soft tickle of his mustache beneath her nose startled

Jessica out of her thoughts, and her lids popped open to find the blue eyes smiling into hers almost as if in amusement. In wonder at the change in those eyes, her lips relaxed unknowingly so that when his mouth closed over hers she gave a tiny gasp of surprise. His lips were warm and surprisingly soft, and instead of ravaging her mouth as she had expected, his kiss seemed more a gentle caress.

When he finally pulled away, Jessica remained rooted to the floor, staring at him dumbly as she tried to connect the tenderness of that kiss to the ruthless outlaw who had so frightened her with that icy blue stare.

Luke read her thoughts easily, grinning at the stupefied look on her lovely face. "Now that's the way to seal a deal, Mrs. Cameron," he said in a husky whisper.

The name snapped Jessica out of her stupor, and clearing her throat in embarrassment as she remembered the sheriff close by, she stepped away from the disturbing man she had just . . .

Oh, Lord, I've just married a gunslinger! she thought with the dawning panic that one usually experiences with the sudden return of sanity. *What am I going to do?*

But God didn't answer, probably, Jessica thought with a stab of guilt, because of that "till death do us part" vow she had just made with no intention of keeping. She was more than likely on her own now.

Their ride down Main Street was much like a one-buckboard parade. With Luke Cameron's saddlebags thrown in the back of the wagon and his flashy gray stallion tethered to the back, they passed the gawking townspeople who made no attempt to hide their curiosity. Luke mockingly tipped his hat to the gray-haired biddy who had shown such anticipation at his supposed hanging. With a contemptuous huff she snapped her parasol shut and turned her back on them.

Jessica saw the exchange and heard his humorless chuckle, and unexpectedly her heart went out to him. She didn't know exactly why this man had turned to the life he had led, but she did know what it felt like to be an outcast. But even at that she realized she couldn't begin to know how it must feel to have people so eagerly await your death, then show such obvious disappointment to be deprived of watching you hang.

She wanted to give some word of comfort but didn't know what to say. "Thankfully we don't have to come into town very often."

Luke misread her meaning completely. "There's still time to save your reputation, Mrs. *Cameron*." He stressed the name snidely, unreasonably stung that she felt embarrassed to be seen with him. "You can always say that your grief over losing dear John caused a momentary lapse of sanity. I'm sure these good Christian folk would welcome you back into their *self*-righteous bosoms."

There was such contempt in the words, such anger in the rigid set of his broad shoulders that Jessica again had to wonder at her sanity in marrying this volatile stranger.

Reminding herself that he had cause to be angry, she tried to remain calm. "You misunderstood me, Mr. Cameron. I didn't mean that I regret our—deal, only that I don't like to come to town. I don't care for crowds."

He still wasn't buying it. "You mean you don't belong to the Ladies' Society, or go to teas, or belong to a sewing circle?"

His voice dripped with sarcasm, but Jessica remained calm. It would be better for him to get the resentment out now rather than allow it to fester. "I don't care for such things. And even if I did there's no time for them, running a ranch."

"Well, how ever do you keep up with the latest gossip then, dear?" he asked in a mockingly high-pitched female tone.

Jessica was dealing with her own painful memories now, and didn't realize how soft her voice had gotten as she answered, "I don't care for gossip. It's cruel and vindictive, and in my experience it is always exaggerated, if not an outright lie."

Luke studied her profile for a long moment, some of his anger draining away as he thought on her words, and on the telling pain in her tone as she'd said them. Suddenly it occurred to him that he might not be the first to experience the harsh hospitality of the good people of Langly.

Chapter Three

An hour after they left town the buckboard passed beneath a wooden crossbeam that held an iron R enclosed in a circle. The house lay directly ahead of them, flanked by a barn on the right and a bunkhouse on the left. While those two buildings were a weathered gray, the house was painted white and had a wide porch that ran the length of the front. The windows were open to catch the afternoon breeze, and lace-edged curtains fluttered at each.

Multicolored flowers grew in beds along the front of the porch and lined a walkway that led to the gate of a short white picket fence. The little fence that enclosed the front yard didn't serve any real purpose, but was the kind of thing a man would indulgently put up for the woman he loved.

The hominess of the place brought back painful memories, and Luke quickly looked away. "Just what is it you expect of me?" he asked, hoping to drag his mind out of the past. "Besides, of course, to shoot this neighbor of yours."

Jessica glanced at him sharply, wondering if he was still nursing his anger, since he hadn't spoken another word after that scathing retort about keeping up with the local gossip. From his tone now it sounded as if the silence hadn't improved his temper.

"I didn't hire you to shoot anyone, Mr. Cameron—unless they shoot at you first."

"You didn't *hire* me," Luke reminded, his gaze dropping to her lips meaningfully.

Jessica looked away nervously at the reminder of that kiss. "We made a business deal," she stressed, lest he had read

29

more into that kiss than he should have. "This will benefit both of us."

"And since we're on the subject"—Luke's curiosity finally won out—"just why did you have to marry a gunslinger? Couldn't you just hire one?"

If possible, Jessica looked even more nervous as she tried to explain. "If I hired a man, he could be run off. You—ah—" her gaze dropped away as she finished quietly—"you can't leave."

She looked so guilty Luke nearly laughed. Could she possibly be so naive as to believe a condemned outlaw would actually feel bound by a marriage such as this? Why, he could be long gone by morning if he wanted to, leaving her with worse problems than before. It was just lucky for her that he wasn't ready to leave just yet. Something about her problem had him intrigued.

Yeah, right, Luke, he told himself as he watched the sun reflect its fire through that thick mass of curls. *Admit it. It's not the lady's problem that has you intrigued.*

A short, red-haired man emerged from the barn just then and, with obvious reluctance, approached the wagon. Without a word he reached up and helped Jessica alight, then turned to stare up at Luke the way a mother grizzly would when defending her only cub. The challenge was clear.

"Zeke, this is Mr. Cameron." Jessica made the introduction she had been dreading. She could feel the tension radiating from her longtime friend like heat from a red-hot cook stove. "Mr. Cameron, this is my foreman and dear friend, Zeke Furguson."

Neither man would be the first to extend his hand.

"Zeke and his wife, Frannie, have been with us for five years now," Jessica explained, trying to fill the awkward silence. It was like watching two roosters sizing each other up. "They came to work for us just a year after John and I settled here."

Silence.

"Frannie helps me in the house."

Silence.

Finally Jessica threw up her hands in irritated defeat and glared at both men. "I have work to do. When you two are finished trying to stare each other down, Zeke, you can show Mr. Cameron where to stow his gear in the bunkhouse." That said, she turned and strode off toward the house.

A bushy red eyebrow raised in question. "The bunkhouse?"

"That's what the lady said."

This seemed to unruffle some of the old man's feathers, though his tone was still gruff as he said, "Come on, boy, I'll show ya where ta bed down."

Luke held out his hand in invitation, "After you," and as the Scotsman turned away he couldn't resist adding, "old man."

"I never thought ya'd go through with it," Frances Furguson said as she peeked out the kitchen window at the new arrival. "I thought fer sure yer good sense would come back or I'd never've let ya go ta town. An' the deed's done, ya say? Ye're actually married to a gunslinger?"

"I am," Jessica answered with a tired sigh as she removed her hat and pulled off her black kidskin gloves. "And you know why I had to do it. Bobby Daniels and Mike Kinston quit just this morning. If I don't do something I'll soon be running this ranch all by myself. Wouldn't Ben love that?!"

The older woman straightened to her entire height of five feet one inch. "Is that ta say you think me an' Zeke'll be desertin' ya in yer time o' need?" she asked in an offended tone.

Jessica crossed the room to wrap her arms around the woman who had virtually become a mother to her over the last five years. "You know I don't think that. In fact, you and Zeke are the only thing in my life I *can* count on."

This seemed to mollify Francis. "Then why him?" she returned to her earlier line of questioning as she jerked a thumb toward the bunkhouse.

"Because he knows how to deal with people shooting at him. Because I need someone to help us stay in business until

I can find out if John's death and all these troubles we're having really are accidents. And because he can't run out on me.''

Frances gave a snort to that. "An' who says he can't? You think a piece o' paper's gonna hold a man like that? I'll lay odds he won't be here come mornin'.''

Jessica opened her mouth to answer, then slowly closed it. She hadn't even considered the possibility that he wouldn't feel honor bound to see their deal through. Thinking about it now, she suddenly felt an almost hysterical urge to laugh at her own naive stupidity. *Honor bound*? She was talking about a man who killed people for a living! An outlaw! He had no honor!

"He will stay!" Jessica stated firmly, but they both knew her words were merely an attempt to convince herself that she hadn't just made one of the biggest mistakes of her life.

Luke looked around the bunkhouse. Eight bunks were lined up down each side of the long room. At the end of each bunk sat a trunk for the cowboy's belongings. An open kitchen with a large cook stove took up one end of the room; two tables separated the kitchen from the sleeping area. On each table sat an oil lamp, and beside one lamp a deck of cards lay neatly stacked awaiting the cowboys' return.

Looking down the two rows of bunks, Luke noticed that only eight seemed to be in use, one of those being his own. It seemed that Mrs. Randall—*Cameron*, he corrected—hadn't been exaggerating her troubles.

"Supper's at seven," Zeke informed him gruffly. "Get settled in an I'll tell ya what'll be expected of ya tomorrow. Ya ever worked cattle before?"

Luke couldn't resist. "Only at night," he answered, fighting to keep a straight face.

"Figured as much," the Scotsman grumbled contemptuously. "Think ya can learn how ta do it in the light o' day like an honest man?"

"I might can manage it."

"We start at sunup—if that ain't too early for ya."

32

The Deal

That said, Zeke turned and left the room, intending to go and add his own "I told you so's" to those he knew his wife was already heaping on Jessie. The idea! Marrying a gunslinger! And one that practically admitted being a rustler to boot!

None of the other hands were told that their lady-boss was, in fact, married to the newest arrival. To them he was just another hired hand like the rest of them. He might be here for the next year or he might get the itch and move on by next week. The only constants in their lives were the land, the sky, their horse, and the freedom to move on whenever the urge struck. It was why most of them had chosen the life of a cowboy.

So, not being appraised of the situation, the other men accepted Luke with typical occupational comradery. Zeke had warned him to go along with the deception, and though it went against the grain for Luke not to defy that warning, he played along, mostly because he enjoyed the easy acceptance he received as a mere hired hand.

Also, he found he learned a lot more about the true situation he faced than he ever would have as the "new boss." For instance, the men informed him that whenever they visited Langly's saloon, the Watering Hole, they could be assured of a fight, instigated by someone from the Bar M ranch; Ben Mateland's men. He also learned that those "potshots" someone had been taking at the hands had spooked a horse, causing it to throw its rider, breaking the cowboy's arm. More shots had been fired, causing a stampede that nearly killed two other men. It would seem his new wife hadn't been completely honest when making her deal.

During the first three days he was on the Circle R, Luke got to know the men he would be working with as they began preparations for the fall roundup. Since he had a rather cynical view of humanity, his first suspicion was that this Mateland character who was giving Jessica such a hard time would most likely have thought to plant one of his own men on her ranch as a saboteur. He soon found, however, that all of them had been with Jessica since well before her husband's death. They also all seemed to have a surprisingly strong sense of loyalty toward their lady boss. But then he reasoned that most men seemed to become blind idiots when it came to a pretty face.

Thinking of the pretty face in question, Luke had come to the conclusion after the third day of not seeing her that his new wife was purposely avoiding him. She didn't leave the house before he rode out with the men in the mornings, and she had retreated to its safety again by the time he returned each evening.

After three days of this routine, Luke was positive she meant to avoid seeing him altogether. Being of a perverse nature, he decided to make a game of the situation. On the morning of the fourth day, he stood before the mirror in one corner of the bunkhouse and carefully plied a razor to the beard that had been growing since his arrest three weeks ago. That done, he pulled on a tan cotton shirt and tucked it into the waistband of his denims. Rolling his shirtsleeves up to the elbows, he settled the tan Stetson over his freshly washed hair and sauntered out onto the porch of the bunkhouse.

It was still dark out, but a light shone from the kitchen window of the house, and seeing it, Luke grinned. It seemed about time to share his first breakfast with his elusive wife.

Jessica answered the knock on the back door with a smile, assuming that Frannie had come early to visit over coffee. Instead of the plump Scotswoman, she found herself face-to-face with the one person she was least prepared to see, her husband. But this wasn't the rough, bearded outlaw she had married standing on her doorstep, and her breath caught in surprise at the face he had kept hidden behind that beard. The word *handsome* came to mind, but she discarded that as not quite accurate. *Rugged*? *Masculine*? *Breathtaking*? There, that was a literal description of the man standing before her.

Swallowing hard, she tried to unobtrusively block the doorway. "Is there something I can do for you, Mr. Cameron?"

Luke hid his grin. He could tell by her voice that she was shaken at seeing him cleaned up. He hoped he knew why. "I just thought it might be nice to have breakfast with my wife," he said, taking a step into the room.

Jessica had the choice of either taking a step backward or being pressed against that broad chest. She chose retreat. "You can't! I mean—the men don't know we're—married," she offered lamely.

"And you think they're not going to eventually find out?" Luke asked, taking another step forward. "Come on, Jessica, the first time they go into town they're gonna hear the whole sordid story. Don't you think it would be better if we tell them now rather than have them find out later and wonder why we lied?"

She knew he had a point, Jessica just didn't want to concede it. She quickly searched her mind for a reason to keep him just where he was. "We could . . . tell them you're sleeping in the bunkhouse because you want to get to know them better," she offered, in what she felt was a burst of inspiration.

The expression on his face looked as if she had just suggested he grow another head. "There is no way in hell I'm gonna tell a bunch of men I'd rather sleep with them than with my new wife!"

When she realized just how that sounded, Jessica had to bite her lip against the sudden urge to laugh at his offended male ego. She felt she did an admirable job in hiding her amusement, too.

Unfortunately, Luke saw the sparkle in the golden-green eyes. So she thought the situation was funny, did she? She felt powerful being able to relegate him to the bunkhouse. Well, it was about time he let the lady know just how much power she really did have over Luke Cameron!

Like the mountain lion Jessica had imagined him, Luke slowly moved toward her. His eyes locked with hers and he grinned, a slow, sexy grin that succeeded in wiping the amusement out of his prey's eyes. Becoming decidedly nervous, she began to back away until the kitchen table stopped her retreat. Her eyes were large, and he could see the pulse beating rapidly at the slender column of her throat. Good, she was learning.

His gaze traveled over her face, ending once again on that intriguing little beauty mark. It had an almost hypnotizing way of drawing a man's attention to those full, trembling lips, tempting him with the urge to kiss her thoroughly. And Luke never had been one to resist temptation.

As if she read his thoughts, Jessica's lips parted and her tongue moved to moisten them nervously. "Don't you have to get to work now, Mr. Cameron?" she asked, leaning backward to put more distance between them.

Planting his hands firmly on the tabletop, Luke imprisoned her hips between his forearms. "We still have the problem to solve of where I'm gonna sleep," he said in a low, husky tone that seemed to envelop Jessica.

She suddenly found it hard to swallow and told herself it was fear. She was alone in the house with a convicted killer. "We've settled that issue once. You sleep in the bunkhouse," she stated firmly, though not very convincingly since her voice cracked.

"The men are eventually gonna find out we're married, Jessica. And everyone—including your friend Mateland—is gonna expect a husband and wife to sleep in the same house, if not the same bed."

She knew he was right, and from his words an idea began to form. "It might be possible for you to sleep in the downstairs guestroom," she reasoned aloud. "I'll have to think on it, though."

With a little planning she should be able to avoid seeing him just as much as she did now, yet put up a good front. Besides, there was a lock on her door if he decided to try anything.

Luke saw her mind churning and knew exactly what she intended. What this little manipulator didn't realize, however, was that he had a few plans of his own. All that remained to be seen now was which of them would find *her*self outmaneuvered in this game they played.

"I'll think on what you've said, Mr. Cameron," Jessica said in her most businesslike tone, "and get back to you tomorrow with my answer. Now I believe you have work to do."

Luke mentally shook his head. She still thought she could take control. "That I do," he agreed easily, and just when she dropped her guard, thinking the skirmish was over, he leaned forward. "But not before I get a good-bye kiss from my wife."

"You most certainly will n—"

His kiss cut her off.

Jessica tried to push him away, but in her position leaning backward over the table her attempts were futile. It was like trying to push against solid rock. His hand slipped up her back to support the back of her head as his lips moved slowly, languorously over hers. His kiss was as warm and soft as before—and it stirred the oddest tingling down her arms. In her wonder over this strange sensation, she soon forgot about struggling altogether.

When Luke pulled away her eyes were still closed, and having his fair share of male ego, he grinned.

Unfortunately, Jessica chose that moment to open her eyes, and her fury exploded. "Get out!" she snapped, eyes flashing with embarrassed indignation. "And don't you ever try that again or I'll—I'll tell Sheriff Davis I made a mistake and let him hang you after all!"

He had kept the grin until that last part. Now Luke's eyes froze to chips of blue ice as he straightened to look down at her coldly. "You might as well learn right now that I'm not one of your hired hands to be bossed around, Mrs. Cameron," he bit out. "And I don't take threats. You make your decision right now whether you want out of this deal or not. If you do, let's see if you can get me back to Langly. If not, I don't ever want to hear that threat again. Understand?"

This was the Luke Cameron who had killed men, Jessica thought, trembling at the fierce anger in his eyes. Was she completely insane threatening such a man? She swallowed hard and braced herself, fully expecting him to strike her in his rage.

But then the strangest thing happened. She knew he saw her fear—it would take a blind man not to—and when he did, the anger seemed to drain out of him as quickly as it had come. He lifted his hand, and still expecting violence, Jessica flinched. She saw a look much like pain cross his face, and with a gentleness that she never would have thought a man such as he could possess, he brushed a stray curl over her shoulder, letting his fingers softly graze her cheek.

"I'm sorry. I didn't mean to frighten you," Luke apologized, but to make sure she got the point he finished gently but firmly, "but I did mean what I said. I won't have you throwing that threat at me every time I do something you don't like. So decide now what it's gonna be; do I stay, or do I go?"

She noticed he didn't say "hang." They both knew there was no way she could make him return to town. Even if she could, Jessica realized she wouldn't do it. He could have run out on her at any time in the last three days, but he hadn't. True, she had been frightened just now facing his wrath, but she was honest enough to admit that he had a right to be angry at her cruel threat.

"If you're still willing to honor our deal, then so am I," she offered finally, forcing down her earlier fear with a tremulous smile.

The corners of his mustache lifted in a lightning change of mood. "Shall we seal it again?" he asked, his eyes growing warm at the thought as he leaned forward with obvious intent.

But, nervous at her disturbing memory of their recent kiss, Jessica quickly stuck her hand out between them. "I believe a handshake will do just fine," she offered hastily.

With a lion's smile that showed flashing white teeth, Luke took the hand she offered. Instead of shaking it, though, he turned it over to caress the sensitive palm with his thumb before raising it to place a lingering kiss there. "It may do," he said in a husky whisper against her skin as his eyes locked with hers, holding her captive with some strange, hypnotic intensity, "but it's not nearly as pleasurable."

She stood for a long moment, mesmerized by the twin blue flames she stared into. Then suddenly realizing what was happening, Jessica shook herself and jerked her hand back, rubbing the palm against her skirt to still the tingling sensation his kiss had evoked.

Before she could deliver the stinging reprimand he so deserved for his outrageous remark, he turned and without another word was gone. Jessica was left in his wake, staring at the door in the dazed state of one who has just weathered a storm and isn't quite sure how, or even *if*, she survived.

Chapter Four

Throughout the morning and into early afternoon Jessica's emotions vacillated between confusion and anger. Things were supposed to have worked out so easily. She would save the gunslinger's life, and out of an overwhelming sense of gratitude he would provide protection for all those here. Meanwhile, Jessica would discover if Ben Mateland was responsible for John's death and the subsequent troubles she had been having. It was as simple as that. *She* held all the cards. *She* was in control.

The only problem was, Luke Cameron didn't seem to know that. He walked in here bold as brass and told her he wouldn't be told what to do. He had even had the gall to suggest he move into the house with her! At the memory, Jessica shivered, but told herself sternly that it was only at the memory of his fierce anger, and not his kiss. Yet even as she tried to remember the fear, her thoughts kept straying to that strange way her arms had tingled as he kissed her. And that tingling hadn't felt anything like fear. So what *had* it been?

Thinking hard, Jessica tried to remember if she had ever felt that way when John kissed her, and quickly realized she hadn't. But then John had always been a gentleman, so sweet and considerate. Maybe it was the danger this gunslinger represented. Maybe it was unconscious fear that had made her react as she had. That had to be it.

She was also troubled at his request to move into the house. Why had he done it? She discounted lust out of hand. Oh, he had kissed her, true, but that was probably just to intimidate her. Men often used their strength and power over a woman for just that purpose. Besides, she had seen him staring at that blasted mark on her face. She had been terribly self-conscious about it ever since she was fourteen and some of the girls her age had made fun of her, telling her it was so ugly that only a blind man would find her attractive. Being young, she had believed the malicious words.

Deep inside, she still did.

Frances appeared in the doorway of the kitchen to interrupt Jessica's musings. "Jessie, hon, I'm through in here. If ye've got nothin' else for me ta do, I'll be goin' on home ta fix Zeke's dinner." She nodded toward the window. "The boys come in early today. As hot as it is, I expect they'll be headin' for the creek."

"Go on, Frannie. I can finish what little there is left to do in here."

Frances frowned slightly. "Don't ya be overdoin' now. It's hot as the devil out today."

"I won't," Jessica promised with a smile. "I may just make some lemonade and sit out on the porch."

When the older woman was gone, Jessica stepped over to the window. The men were walking their horses toward the barn, and she told herself it was only the beautiful smoky-gray Appaloosa that drew her attention immediately to Luke Cameron.

As Frances had predicted, the men didn't waste any time seeking out the cool water of the creek about a half mile away. With Zeke and Frances at their house, everything soon grew quiet. It was a peaceful interlude for Jessica, who decided a glass of lemonade was just what she needed. Alone, she walked out onto the front porch and sat in one of the rocking chairs, laid her head back, closed her eyes, and just enjoyed the silence.

But it was a peace that was soon broken by the sound of several horses approaching. Jessica opened her eyes as they rode under the crossbeam, and she stiffened as she recognized the man who led the group. Ben Mateland.

"Wonderful," she said under her breath as she slowly stood and crossed to the edge of the porch.

Cynthia Strickland

To look at the man's physique no one would guess that Ben Mateland was pushing sixty. Years of carving an empire out of the harsh, unyielding land had left deep lines on his face in testimony, yet his body was as hard and strong as that of a man half his age. He held himself like a king surveying a much lesser domain as he rode his buckskin stallion up to the gate and waited imperiously.

It was obvious he wasn't going to dismount, and Jessica refused to make a fool of herself by yelling across the yard. Showing an outward calm she was far from feeling, she stepped down from the porch and walked to the gate, hating that their positions made it necessary for her to look up at him.

Ben's smile told her he was enjoying the situation immensely. "Afternoon, Ms. Randall," he said, barely touching the brim of his Stetson. He leaned forward to brace one arm on the horn of his saddle as he looked down on her. "Hot day, ain't it?"

Seeing his eyes lock on her bodice, Jessica remembered too late that she had undone the buttons at her throat. She knew she was still decently covered, though the look in Ben's eyes made her feel as if she were standing before him completely naked. Instead of fumbling with the buttons, though, she met his gaze and stared back with such icy reproof that he finally looked away to scan the yard again.

"I just rode over to see for myself if that wild gossip flyin' 'round town is true."

The icy look remained. "I wouldn't know, Mr. Mateland. I make it a point not to listen to gossip."

"Usually don't myself," he claimed. " 'Specially when it's so farfetched as this was. But then the man didn't hang, and folks saw him ride outta town with you. They say you actually married that murderin' piece of s—"

"Mr. Mateland!" Jessica cut him off frostily. "I'll thank you to watch your language!"

Ben grew red with anger that the little chit had the audacity to take him to task for his manners. He didn't have the answers he'd come for yet, though, so he backed down. "Pardon, ma'am. I got carried away thinkin' of folks sayin' such a thing about you. I know you must be lonely, what with John gone— God rest his soul—but I told everyone you weren't so desperate you'd sink that low.''

Jessica had to grit her teeth against the rage that comment kindled. She almost expected to see lightning come down from heaven and strike Ben dead for such blatant hypocrisy. But instead of an outright challenge she chose a more subtle retaliation for his implied insult. Looking at him meaningfully, she responded, ''I guess there's only so low even a desperate woman will sink in marrying a man, isn't there, Mr. Mateland?''

He sat up at that, his face turning hard with rage, telling Jessica that her arrow had found its mark. Good. Let him remember that she had refused *his* offer of marriage.

All pretense of civility was gone now. ''You seem to be all alone, Jessica,'' Ben commented, swinging down from his horse to walk up to the gate. ''Has your *husband* run out on you already?''

Jessica knew he meant to intimidate her, and she swore that no matter what she wasn't going to back down from his bullying tactics. ''He's working,'' she spoke the lie calmly. ''We do have a ranch to run.''

''Well now, I'm truly surprised he'd be out workin' cattle when he's got a pretty little thing like you at home,'' Ben said suggestively. The men behind him made several lewd sounds of agreement at that as Ben reached for the gate. ''Why, a pretty woman alone could face all kinds of—''

''That's far enough.''

Jessica had to mentally force herself not to sag in relief as all attention focused on the man coming up behind her. Luke Cameron came to a halt at her side. Watching the two men size each other up was like watching two grizzlies preparing to battle over territorial rights.

''Aren't you going to introduce us, sweetheart?'' Luke asked levelly, and Jessica didn't even care that he slipped his arm around her waist so familiarly.

''This is our neighbor, Mr. Benjamin Mateland,'' she informed him, unnecessarily she was sure. "Mr. Mateland, this is my—husband, Lucas Cameron." She cursed herself for the way her voice faltered.

The two men refused the hypocrisy of shaking hands.

"I see the gossip's true," Ben said to Jessica, intentionally ignoring the man at her side.

But before she could reply, Luke answered. "Yep. She married the gunslinger. So you won't have to be so concerned that Jessica's all alone anymore. I intend to take very good care of my wife."

The tension was so thick between the two that Jessica, standing in the middle, could almost feel herself being crushed by the animosity. Ben looked angry enough to strike, yet somehow Luke looked as composed as if he were at a Sunday picnic—except for his eyes, which glittered like chips of ice.

"I'm surprised the sheriff let you keep those," Ben said, motioning with his head, and for the first time Jessica looked down and had to control a gasp at the sight of the two Colt revolvers riding low on Luke's hips.

"I guess he figured I might need 'em," Luke returned with a challenging smile. "For *snakes* and such."

Ben stiffened at the implied insult. "Yeah?" Well, you better keep 'em close, boy. You never know what can happen out here."

"I'll take that warning to heart," Luke returned. "Now if you've finished congratulatin' my wife and me on our marriage . . ."

Jessica saw Ben's hands clench as if he was itching to go for his own gun, but again his eyes slipped to the pearl-handled Colts on Luke's hips and he backed down. "I got to get back to my own place now," he said gruffly. "I just came over to check on Jessica."

Luke's brow arched in obvious disbelief. "And we appreciate your concern, don't we, sweetheart?" he asked the woman at his side, squeezing her waist for an answer.

Jessica met Ben's gaze. "Yes, thank you, Mr. Mateland." And she couldn't resist adding, "But as you can see, I'm well protected now. There's no need for you to worry about me being all alone anymore.''

Ben's irritation was obvious as he whirled angrily and jerked up the reins to his horse. He swung up into the saddle, glared at the couple behind the gate for a moment, then turned his horse and rode off, his men following behind.

When the cloud of dust that marked their departure had finally settled, Jessica released a tremulous sigh, then, remembering herself, quickly stepped away from her husband. "So, now you've met Benjamin Mateland," she said, turning to face him. "What do you think?"

"I think he's a son-of-a—" Her raised brow censored his words. "I think I'm glad Sheriff Davis let me keep these for snakes."

"You know you didn't endear yourself to the man," Jessica informed him without the slightest trace of regret. "I'm sure you just made an enemy."

"The way I see it, it's better to know who your enemies are up front. It keeps you from wonderin' when your back's to them."

"You made him very angry. Ben isn't used to anyone standing up to him."

Luke shrugged her concern away. "An angry man is more likely to make mistakes."

Looking down to pick at a place where the paint was chipped on the gate, Jessica finally said what she felt she had to. "I—uh—appreciate your help just now." But then she looked up as she quickly added, "Though I could have handled the situation by myself if I'd had to."

The corners of his mustache quivered suspiciously. "I know you could have. I just thought reinforcements couldn't hurt."

He could feel amusement now, but the truth of the matter was that when Luke had come around the corner of the house and seen all those men on horseback, and the one advancing on Jessica, he had flashed back to another time, to another woman who had faced a gang of men alone. With that image burning in his mind, his hands had instinctively gone for the Colts. Only the threat to Jessica had made him hesitate long enough to get his initial rage under control.

Seeing the cold look pass across his face, Jessica had to wonder at it, for she was sure he had been fighting a grin only seconds before. Still, she appreciated the fact that he didn't openly dispute her claim of bravado, even though they both knew there was no way she could have handled Mateland and his men alone. She had never in her life been more relieved to hear another's voice as she had Luke Cameron's when he stepped around the corner of the house.

"I must admit your timing was excellent," she conceded. "I don't think he would have harmed me. I think he just meant to frighten me."

"And did he?"

Jessica opened her mouth with a ready denial, but looking into his eyes she couldn't voice the lie. "Well, maybe a little," she admitted reluctantly.

Instead of gloating as she expected, he surprised her by saying, "That just shows you're not stupid. Only a fool wouldn't feel fear at such uneven odds."

"You didn't seem afraid."

He gave her an almost self-mocking smile. "Life's taught me how to deal with uneven odds."

There was so much implied in those few words that again Jessica found herself wondering what had happened to make Luke Cameron into the man he was. Surely a gunfighter wasn't born, but made out of circumstances. What horrible thing had happened to make him take a gun and kill people?

Seeing the wary fear in her eyes, Luke gave a tired sigh. It was always the same; either women avoided him out of fear of his reputation, or they were attracted to him because of it. For some reason, though, Jessica's fear bothered him more than usual.

Hoping to ease her mind, he made his tone teasing. "What were you expecting me to use to protect you? A stick?"

"No . . . I just . . . it was just seeing them for the first time I . . ."

Gently Luke placed a finger beneath her chin, lifting it until she was forced to meet his gaze. "I'm not some crazed maniac that shoots down people for the fun of it, Jessica. The men I've killed deserved it.''

That was the opening she needed, and hoping to find some noble reason for what he had done, Jessica took it. "Why? Why did the government consider it murder?"

The look in his eyes became icy. "Sometimes a government sees things differently."

"But surely if those men did do something horrible, then you can—"

"Drop it, Jessica!" Luke saw her flinch at the harsh command and he tried to control his anger to explain. "Sometimes justice is blinded by the prejudices of those who sit in judgment. All I can tell you is that you can be sure you'll never have cause to fear me."

Yet I do fear you when you look like that, she thought uneasily as she remembered the fierce rage that had filled his eyes just moments before. She prayed he was telling her the truth, that he would never turn that rage on her.

"Jessica?"

The soft word drew her attention and she met his gaze, hoping her fear didn't show. It did.

Luke raised his hand to gently stroke her cheek, wanting to somehow convince her that she had nothing to fear from him. "I've never touched a woman in anger," he said softly. "In fact that's why I was so angry earlier. I thought Mateland intended to hurt you."

She relaxed a little at the explanation, giving a laugh that still held a tinge of apprehension. "You take your job seriously."

"I take any man bullying a woman seriously," he corrected.

Jessica could see the truth of the claim in his eyes and she relaxed even more. "Then it seems I hired the right man."

"You didn't *hire* me," Luke reminded. "Which brings us back to our unresolved conversation of this morning."

She really didn't want to get into that again. "I need to be—"

"I'm moving into the house."

The pronouncement successfully brought her to a halt.

"You what?" she asked in a carefully controlled tone, turning back with a look of astonishment. Surely she hadn't just heard him *tell* her he was moving into *her* house.

"You heard me. This morning it was a suggestion. Now, after meeting Ben Mateland, I don't want you alone in the house at night. I wouldn't put anything past that bas—that snake." He could see she was about to argue and quickly continued. "We're not talking about a tea party here, Jessica. I've dealt with men like Mateland before. You already suspect him of murdering your husband. You're scared, or you never would have married a gunslinger."

She was about to dispute that opinion but he cut her off. "You want me to protect you, woman, so let me do it. I'm not suggesting you stoop to taking me into your bed. I intend to sleep downstairs where I'll be some good to you if he tries anything."

Jessica saw the bitterness when he said she wouldn't have to "stoop" to sleeping with him. She didn't want him to think she was like the townspeople, that she thought herself so much better than him. Couldn't he understand that she didn't know him? She was a woman who had just lost her husband. She didn't want any man in her life right now.

But she did need him.

"You're right, of course," she agreed, and saw a look of surprise cross his face. "I can't ask you to do a job for me and then tie your hands because of some ridiculous sense of propriety.

"We both know I could have been in serious trouble if you hadn't shown up when you did." She bit her lower lip. "Until I can prove whether or not that . . . snake had anything to do with John's death, I need your protection, Mr. Cameron."

Luke knew it had taken a lot for her to make that admission. The only thing that bothered him now was that, despite how he knew she felt about him personally, it still felt good to hear her say she needed him.

It felt too good.

Chapter Five

From his place beside the house Zeke had seen and heard everything. He had been washing up at the well behind his home when he heard the horses ride by on their way to Jessie's place. Seeing who it was, Zeke had hurried up the path to warn her. He had rounded the corner to find Cameron watching Mateland and Jessica, his hands hovering dangerously over the guns that rode his hips. Afraid any sudden noise would spook the gunslinger, endangering Jess, Zeke had frozen.

He heard Jessie's insult and grinned at the thought of how the old buzzard would take that. Then there had been a mumbled reply, and before Zeke knew what was happening, Cameron had stepped around the corner, and the force in his command had even made Zeke freeze for a second. Slowly, Zeke had made his way to the front corner of the house, his hand on his own gun should he have to protect Jessie from either man.

Zeke had stood there listening until well after Mateland and his men rode off. There was a war raging within him. From the first he had tried to talk Jessie out of her insane plan, thinking it was like asking the Devil himself to guard your back. He didn't trust the gunslinger. He didn't like him!

But, an insistent voice intruded, *there's no way you can deny what just happened. The man just let Mateland know in no uncertain terms that he was going to be here now to protect Jessie.*

Yes, but he also just told her he was moving into the house with her, Zeke argued with his conscience. *And I'll lay odds I know why. And it sure isn't to protect her!*

With a decisive nod, Zeke turned to leave. He'd give Cameron time to go about his business, then he'd come back later to talk to Jess. One thing was sure in his mind, though; there was no way on earth that gunslinger was going to move in with Jess.

When Zeke was finally able to corner Jessica alone, he first tried to reason with her, but soon his Scot's temper took over, and the glass in the windows nearly shook at the sheer volume of his dire warnings. "I'm tellin' ya that gunslinger's got nothin' good in mind, wantin' ta move in here!"

Jessica made a futile attempt at reason, but when nothing she said by way of explanation seemed to penetrate that Scottish obstinacy, she resorted to raising her own voice. "And I'm telling you I know what I'm doing! Don't think I'm fool enough to trust him completely. I do intend to lock my door. Right now, though, I think the threat from Ben Mateland outweighs the threat Luke Cameron poses."

"Move in with Frannie and me if ye're scared, girl, but don't invite the Devil hisself in ta guard ya from harm!"

Jessica calmed herself, realizing that the older man's anger was really just concern for her. She crossed to stand in front of him, taking his big, callused hand in hers. "You know why I won't do that, Zeke. You and Frannie need your privacy, as I need mine."

"But for a little while—"

"I won't let Benjamin Mateland run me out of my own home," Jessica stated firmly, hoping to bring an end to the argument.

"But you'll let 'im make ya take a gunslinger into it?"

"For the time being, yes. Besides, the men are going to find out sooner or later that we're married. It's best they believe it's a real marriage."

"You could tell 'em the truth," Zeke offered helpfully.

"And have them know what I suspect Mateland's capable of? The bunkhouse would be deserted come morning. Then where would we be? Three hundred head of cattle to round up and bring down to the lower pastures and no hands to do it with is not a situation I want to face."

Zeke saw the truth in what she was saying, though he was loath to give in. "I want ya ta keep a gun ready beside yer bed for *whoever* decides ta try anythin'," he admonished sternly.

"I will."

"And you'll lock yer door?"

"I'll pull the armoire in front of it if it will make you feel better," Jessica offered with an exasperated smile.

"I know I'm soundin' like a mother hen, but I worry about ya, darlin'."

"And I appreciate it, Zeke. But I can take care of myself."

She looked so sure of herself, standing there with her shoulders squared and a look of resolve burning in those golden-green eyes. Only Zeke saw past the facade. He had grown to love this young woman like the daughter he and Frannie had never been blessed with, and for what must be the thousandth time he cursed the man who had hurt her so badly, the man who had made it necessary for a child to have to learn to take care of herself.

Angry as he was, Zeke realized it was probably a good thing he didn't know any more than John had been able to tell him and Frannie. If he knew the full extent of the heartache his Jess had been put through, he would most likely have gone after her father with a gun long ago. But John hadn't known more than just the barest details. And Jessie closed up like a clam whenever anyone mentioned her past.

Before he could grow any angrier, Zeke got back to the subject at hand. "Ya can't stop me from worryin'. I don't trust that gunslinger any more than I do Mateland."

Pride wouldn't let Jessica admit she didn't either, really. "Right now Mr. Cameron is the lesser of two evils. And besides, he did get Ben to leave."

The older man gave a snort at that. "No fox wants competition in the henhouse."

"Zeke! The man intimidated Ben into backing down after what I consider was an obvious threat. He's doing the job I hired him to do. We should at least give him that."

"You didn't hire him."

Jessica was really getting tired of hearing those words, especially since they weren't accurate. "He's just another hired hand to me," she corrected, taking the older man's hand once more and smiling in an attempt to reassure him. "A year from now he'll be gone, and so will my problems with Ben Mateland."

She looked so sure of that fact that Zeke didn't have the heart to disillusion her with the truth. Luke Cameron would be gone from here long before the bargained-for year was up. And if the man had his way, he'd surely leave Jess with more problems than she had now!

That afternoon Luke moved into the guest bedroom. Jessica couldn't remember later just what they had told the men in explanation of their bizarre marriage. She could remember Luke saying something about her being a guardian angel, that she had snatched him from the jaws of death. By mutual consent they didn't mention the real reason they had married, or that it was only temporary. It seemed best to keep those reasons to themselves. Besides, Jessica didn't see any need in letting the hands know that she was . . . concerned.

The men took it much better than she had assumed they would. Oh, a couple of them had looked angry at first, but they had evidently gotten over it, for when Luke came out of the bunkhouse a half hour later after packing up his belongings, the men had followed him out onto the porch. There was a strange silence, and watching from the parlor window, Jessica had expected them to bid him an angry good riddance. It came as some surprise when one of the men called to Luke when he was halfway to the house, telling him that they'd see him at first light to start the roundup.

It had been said with a note of comradery, and Jessica wondered at it—but not enough to question the darkly brooding man who stepped through her front door. Besides, what did it matter to her whether the men did or did not make Luke Cameron feel welcome? He was here to do a job. That was it.

Jessica reminded herself of just that fact when she went to the door of the guest room later to announce supper. She realized that, living in the same house, they would have to take their meals together. That fact needn't encroach on their individual privacy, however, or alter in any way their business relationship. This could still be a very civilized arrangement between two adults.

With that thought firmly in mind, and seeing his door standing wide open, Jessica assumed it was safe to step to the doorway and let him know by invitation that he could eat in the house from now on.

"Mr. Cameron, supper is rea—"

The words died in her throat. Or more precisely, they were choked off by a gasp as Jessica came to a dead halt in the open doorway. He stood at the washstand by the window wearing only his boots and pants. She was unable to stop her gaze from moving up long muscular legs encased in snug-fitting denim, past trim hips and a narrow waist, to incredibly broad shoulders. His tawny hair was freshly washed, and lather covered half of his face where he was now plying a razor. Her eyes clashed with his in the mirror, and he flashed her a wicked grin that said he thought she was actually *admiring* him, the conceited lout!

"Supper is ready," she finished in her frostiest tone.

The grin remained. "I'll be right there, ma'am."

"And in the future I think you should keep your door closed when you aren't decent."

She was trying to seem so unaffected, but Luke had watched her eyes slowly travel up his body. "That may be hard to do," he said in a voice that sent tingling sensations straight to her knees. "Most folks say there's nothin' decent about me."

Jessica was determined she would die before she let her gaze drop below his eyes again and risk fueling his incredible conceit. "No doubt they're right," she answered haughtily. "I'll make my request simpler for you to understand then; unless you're fully clothed, I'll thank you to keep this door closed."

Her face was such a becoming shade of pink. "Yes, ma'am."

"Do I need to remind you of the terms of our arrangement?"

"No, ma'am."

"Even though we're living in the same house, we must still hold to propriety."

"Yes, ma'am."

The corners of that mustache twitched as if he wanted to laugh at her, but Jessica couldn't be positive given the thick layer of shaving lather that coated that part of his face. "Just so you understand me," she stressed her point authoritatively. "Now hurry before the food gets cold."

The door shut, and Luke was finally able to let go of the laughter he had been holding back. Thinking of her reaction if he had laughed in her face made him shake his head in amused appreciation. She turned into such a feisty little thing when she felt cornered. With that rich auburn hair and those wary eyes, she reminded him of a fox caught in a trap. She knew she needed his help, but her entire body tensed whenever he came near.

But then that hadn't been fear he'd seen in this little vixen's eyes as she let her eyes roam over his body just moments ago, Luke reminded himself with a wide grin. No, he didn't believe the lady's sensibilities were nearly as offended as she'd claimed.

In a much better mood now, Luke went back to shaving, whistling softly as he suddenly remembered just how much he used to enjoy hunting fox.

Chapter Six

Every year since building the Circle R, John and Jessica had held their fall roundup the first week in September. Now, as she pulled on her clothes in the gray predawn light, Jessica was assaulted by the memories this tradition brought back. Unlike most men, John had never forbade her to go along on the trip into the surrounding mountains to cut out their cattle from those of the neighboring ranchers and bring them down to the lower pastures for the winter. Once that was done, two-thirds would be sold to buyers from back East, with the remaining third kept to replenish the herd for the next year. It was a practice that had worked well for them.

To face the ritual now without John at her side sharply curbed Jessica's usual excitement. With a bittersweet smile she remembered that first roundup when she had learned right along with her husband how to cut Circle R cattle out from the many others that grazed on the open range. Rather than resent her for becoming an accomplished ''cowgirl'' as he had called her, John had instead bragged on the fact. That considerate, understanding, tolerant nature was only one of the reasons she had cared for him so.

Shaking off the memories before she could become too melancholy, Jessica finished buttoning her shirt and tucked the tail into her denims. Pulling on the boots that waited beside her bed, she was now ready to join the men and get the day started.

The rich aroma of brewing coffee hit her halfway down the steps, followed quickly by the smell of bacon frying. Slowing her steps with a puzzled frown, she reached the doorway to the kitchen to find Luke Cameron standing before the cook stove, a fork in his hand as he turned the bacon in a large black-iron frying pan.

"Just what do you think you're doing?" Jessica asked, irritated that he felt comfortable enough with his situation to take over her kitchen.

Luke heard the irritation in her voice and grinned. He turned with what he was sure would be an inflammatory remark to his little fox on the tip of his tongue. It stayed there, however, as he was hit full force with the sight of Jessica Ran—Cameron in snug-fitting denims. Not sure whether to frown or leer at her choice of attire, Luke settled for a look that was carefully blank. Some might condemn her for the manly garb, but then those would be women who were jealous of the fact that Jessica looked anything but manly in those britches. And that thought brought a sudden scowl as Luke remembered that he wasn't the only man who would see her looking this good.

"Do you intend to wear that today?" he asked, letting his eyes run over her in a look he hoped would pass for disapproval and not lust.

All set to take him to task for his preemptive behavior where her house was concerned, Jessica was struck silent for a moment, astounded that this gunslinger would have the gall to question the propriety of her clothing. It was almost laughable. "Cows are unimpressed by a lady's attire, Mr. Cameron," she informed him in her haughtiest tone.

"But men are, Mrs. Cameron," he came right back. "I hope you don't intend to let the hands see you like that."

"Unless they intend to ride all day with their eyes closed, I don't see how it can be helped."

The look in his eyes almost made Jessica take a step backward. "And just what do you mean by that?" he asked in a tone that was ominously low.

Was it possible he didn't know she was going with the men? "I mean that this is what I always wear on roundups. The men realize it's necessary."

"I guess I could concede that point—if you were going."

Jessica could only stare at him in openmouthed disbelief at what she thought he had just said. "I beg your pardon?"

she asked a growing knot of anger forming in her throat.

Luke could see the storm clouds gathering in those golden-green eyes. "It's too dangerous for you to be out on the open range," he explained. "There's a thousand places a man with a rifle could hide. It'd be impossible for me to protect you."

Even seeing the reason in his words, Jessica still could not believe he would tell her she wasn't going on her own roundup. "Mr. Cameron"—she stressed each word carefully—"I have not missed a roundup of Circle R cattle in six years and I do not intend to start now. I am going."

Luke's brow rose at her temerity. "Is it necessary for me to point out that those roundups were before your husband was shot?" he asked, knowing that the brutal reminder was necessary. "Mateland has tried to marry you, buy you out, and scare you out. Are you willing to gamble that it wasn't him that had John killed, or that he won't resort to the same method of dealing with you?"

That thought had crossed her mind, but Jessica wouldn't admit her fear to the man standing before her with his *male* frown of disapproval. "I won't hide behind closed doors because Ben Mateland might try something. Besides, how better to get my proof if he is the one?"

Luke's jaw nearly dropped. "A hell of a lot of good that proof will do you when you're dead! Is that the reason you're so fired up to go, so you can play bait for Mateland's gunman? What kind of a fool notion is that?"

Jessica's chin came up at his implication that she was foolish. It might sound that way, but it wasn't any of his business why she was determined to do this. He only worked for her. She was the boss around here.

"*I* am going on this roundup because *I* am the owner of the Circle R, Mr. Cameron," she stated as calmly as possible. "*You* are going because *you* were hired to protect me and my men while we do our jobs. Do you have any question about our roles?"

It was an open challenge. Luke had seen this same look in the eyes of those who fancied themselves as fast guns. He had faced them in practically every town, men who were sure they could outdraw the infamous Luke Cameron. But where he knew how to play this game to perfection, the young woman who faced him now was obviously a novice. He took a step closer, and smiled when her eyes told him about the battle within her not to retreat. Another step brought him to within inches of her tense body.

"I don't have any questions, Jessica. But I do have an answer or two for you." His gaze pinned her to the floorboards. "First of all I'm gonna tell you for what I hope will be the last time necessary, I do not work for you." She opened her mouth to argue, but his look stopped the words in her throat. "Secondly," he went on, "I agreed to protect you, and to do that, you're gonna have to do what I tell you or else I ride outta here right now. Understand?"

Jessica stood her ground mutinously. "I have to go on this roundup. This is my land, and I won't let Ben Mateland or anyone else take it away from me!"

The emotion she tried to hide took Luke by surprise. This wasn't just a show of power or stubbornness on her part. He paused for a long moment, torn between common sense that told him not to give in, and an unwillingness to deny her something that seemed so important to her.

"What if I offer a compromise?" he asked finally. "Would you agree to my terms?"

The wary look was in her eyes again. "What sort of terms?"

"You stay beside me. You don't go riding off by yourself. And if I suddenly tell you to do something you might not understand, you'll do it quickly, without questions."

It seemed reasonable, since protecting her was why she had hired him in the first place. And even though he had been difficult at first, it seemed that his only real concern was being able to do that job. It said something that he was willing to compromise. Wasn't it only fair she do the same?

"A compromise then," Jessica offered finally. "I'll go on my roundup, but I'll trust your instincts to protect me from danger. Agreed?"

Any other woman he had ever known would have pouted,

or gloated that he had given in somewhat. But not Jessica. She was willing to be reasonable and meet him halfway. Looking at her standing there in those snug denims with her hand held out and a warm smile lighting those eyes, Luke suddenly wondered if he could protect her from the most imminent danger she faced: himself.

Still, he took her outstretched hand. "Agreed."

The seasoned mare moved like an extension of Jessica's body as she maneuvered to cut a steer with a Circle R brand away from those of a neighboring ranch. She worked the steer toward those that she and the hands had already collected, then took her place beside the herd once more, totally unaware of the man who watched her with growing admiration.

"Hard ta believe, ain't it?" Luke heard from beside him, and turned to find one of the hands, Hank Fields, grinning at him. "That Mrs. Ran—uh, pardon, Mrs. Cameron is shore good on a horse."

Luke nodded. "She's a lot better than good. Probably the best woman rider I've ever seen—other than Jane Canary, that is."

"You know Calamity Jane?" Hank asked, clearly impressed.

"I wouldn't say I know her," Luke corrected. "I saw her in Laramie a few months back with her beau, Bill Hickock. Him being a marshall, I didn't think I should walk up and introduce myself."

Hank chuckled. "Don't guess you would at that. Still, I heard Bill Hickock's a fair man. If you'd've explained the way things was, then surely—"

"I quit explaining a long time ago, Hank," Luke interrupted in a tone that told the other man not to continue. "I only told you and the others so you wouldn't have to spend the next few months watching your backs."

"Hey, most of us are from the South, Luke. You don't need to tell us how blind Yankee justice can be. Ain't a one of us wouldn't have done the same as you if it'd been us."

At that statement the two men rode in silence for a few

minutes, each becoming lost in private memories. Life had changed for everyone with the War Between the States. Seemingly overnight a way of life had been lost. And not a family, Southern or Northern, seemed to have escaped unscathed. But no one could dispute that those in the South had seen the worst of it. Many had lost their family, their home, their livelihood—their heritage. It was no wonder so many had come West searching for a new life.

But although men like Hank were free to live here in peace, Luke had lived the last six years constantly looking over his shoulder, always keeping just one step ahead of the lawmen and bounty hunters. Always, that was, until four weeks ago when his luck had run out and Wilford Davis had recognized him coming out of Langly's general store.

Luke thought back on that day now. He'd been wearing the Colts and could have easily outdrawn Davis, but there had been women and kids around who could have been caught in the crossfire. Luke had given himself up without a fight, knowing it meant he would hang. Funny thing was, he had almost looked forward to the thought. He had finished what he'd set out to do, and with the driving need for revenge gone, there had been nothing left but remembering. With the reputation he had built over the past six years, the future that lay before him was a constant line of up-and-coming gunfighters until he finally met that one who would be faster. Not a very bright future, that. Maybe it was why he had let Davis take him so easily. Maybe death had seemed preferable to the continuing hell of living.

But death hadn't come, thanks to Mrs. Jessica Randall, now Cameron. He looked at her, riding her horse as expertly as any man in those tight denims with that thick braid of sunlit auburn hair hanging to her waist. She was a living, breathing contradiction, all soft and womanly to look at, yet as prickly as a cactus when you got too close. Or at least when *he* got too close, Luke reminded himself with a rueful grin.

The lady saw him as nothing more than a guard dog until she could prove that Mateland had killed her beloved John. For some reason that thought made Luke clench his fists, making the horse beneath him sidestep nervously at the unfamiliar pressure on the reins. Luke loosened his grip, quietly speaking to the stallion in a soothing tone.

"It's gettin' near dark, Lu—ah—boss," Hank said, stumbling over his uncertainty of just where Luke stood. "There's a good place ta camp a little ways up ahead if'n that's okay with you."

Luke understood the questions the men had. "Sounds fine to me," he answered amiably. "And Hank? I like the sound of 'Luke' better."

The cowhand gave him a grin and rode off to tell the others where they were going to make camp. There, Luke thought, he hadn't actually come out and told Hank this marriage was a sham. It would be easier this way for the hands not to have to switch back to looking to Jessica as their boss after he left if he didn't completely take over the role now. She was lucky as it was to find men willing to take orders from a woman.

Within twenty minutes they came to the spot Hank had spoken of. The fertile valley stretched before them like an oasis after a long day of breathing the cloud of dust stirred up by the herd. The sun was hanging low over a mountain ridge to the west, bathing the valley in mottled shadows and turning the creek to a pale pink ribbon that ran the length of the valley to disappear at the far end.

The tired riders urged the cattle through knee-high grass toward the creek where the thirsty animals could drink their fill. The cattle taken care of, the herders could now set up camp. Luke, who had spent hundreds of nights camped out under the stars, listened to the frogs croaking softly down by the creek as the last shade of magenta faded to deep purple. Stopping to take a deep breath of the heavy night air, he suddenly realized that he hadn't felt such a sense of peace in a very long time.

Leaning against a pine, he watched Jessica as she knelt by the fire slicing bacon to add to the pot of beans Zeke was stirring. She leaned forward and a waterfall of honey-brown hair cascaded over her shoulder, seeming to draw life from the fire as it turned to shimmering auburn. Without thought

61

she reached up with one hand and gathered the entire mass at the back of her neck and twisted it a few times, then tucked it into the neck of her shirt before going back to work on the slab of bacon.

Luke grinned at the action. It was refreshing to see a woman who wasn't constantly fretting over her appearance. Hadn't he known enough women who spent the majority of their lives looking in mirrors? But that wasn't Mrs. Jessica Randall Cameron. She camped out under the stars to drive cattle. She stepped down off her porch and walked right up to Benjamin Mateland rather than running into her house to hide. And she made a deal to marry a gunfighter rather than be run off her land. Yes, there was a lot more to this woman than just a beautiful face, and fiery hair, and eyes that haunted a man's dreams, and a body that made him want to . . .

The fine hairs on the back of Jessica's neck rose with the feeling that she was being watched. Very calmly she picked up the chunks of bacon and dropped them into the pot simmering over the fire, then casually leaned back on her heels to surreptitiously survey the darkening woods at the edge of camp. When her gaze came to a halt on a tall form standing in the shadows, she nearly let a gasp of fear escape before her eyes adjusted and she made out the now familiar tan Stetson. Relieved that it was only Mr. Cameron watching out for her, and not one of Ben's hired henchmen sent to shoot her, Jessica gave him a smile before going back to work.

It was funny, but all day she had felt safe knowing he was there watching out for her. Maybe it was just the knowledge that with all his experience in avoiding danger over the years, she could relax and trust him to look out for her. But then that very thought was beginning to worry Jessica, for even though she had hired Luke Cameron to do a job, past experience had taught her not to trust any man.

Unwillingly a memory returned of a little girl who stood clutching the tiny doll her mother had given her as she watched her father walk away, ignoring her pleas for him to come back. He had kept right on walking, and Jessica had never seen Anson Stanford again since that day he had left her on the steps of that gray, forbidding orphanage, crying and tugging with all her might to escape the restricting hold of the headmistress.

Swallowing hard, Jessica bit down on her lower lip until the knot in her throat finally eased. She would not dwell on the past. It was over and done. Besides, hadn't her father's desertion taught her some very important lessons? She had learned to stand on her own two feet. She could make her own place, her own life, in this world. And lastly, but most importantly, she would never, *never* let herself care for another man so much that she would be devastated if he walked out of her life!

Squaring her shoulders at the reminder, Jessica carefully locked the memories away in that dark corner of the soul where ghosts from the past are kept, and with a smile that was a bit too bright, she looked toward the men who were shaking out their bedrolls. "Supper's on! Come and get it before Zeke and I eat it all!"

The hungry cowboys didn't have to be called twice. They descended like a swarm of locusts around the campfire to set in on the beans, biscuits, and coffee. Watching them, Jessica had to smile fondly. There was Hank Fields, and Clayton Reeves. They had been with her the longest, nearly four years now. Allen and Sam Fisher were brothers who had hired on two years ago from Texas. And rounding out the group were Billy Lewis, Lee Stark, and Tim Weston, all hired on within the last year.

Then of course there was Zeke. With Frannie at home these people made up Jessica's family—an untraditional one, she would admit, but she cared deeply for all of them just the same.

And now there was . . .

That was who was missing, Jessica realized as her gaze did another quick inventory of the faces gathered around the campfire. Not finding the one she sought, her eyes scanned the shadows surrounding the camp. She found the dark form standing just where he had been earlier, watching over her.

Fixing a plate, she walked over to join him. "I'm glad that

you take your job so seriously, Mr. Cameron,'' she said with a greeting smile as she stopped in front of him. ''But surely you can at least take time out to eat.''

She held out her offering, and after a moment's hesitation Luke accepted it.

How long had it been since anyone cared whether he was hungry or not? How long since a beautiful woman had brought him a plate of supper at the end of a long day?

Closing his eyes briefly against the memories that threatened, he ate a spoonful of the beans. The second was halfway to his mouth when he realized she was just standing there, watching him.

''Aren't you gonna eat?''

''Yes, but—well—I need to talk to you about something.''

He ate another bite, and when she didn't say anything Luke laid down his spoon. ''Well?''

Picking at a loose thread on her shirt sleeve gave Jessica a good excuse not to have to meet his gaze as she voiced her concern. ''About tonight. Not understanding the way things are, the men might expect—um . . .''

The light blush that crept further up her cheeks with each word caused Luke to smile. ''They might expect me to want to sleep with my wife?'' he finished helpfully.

She wouldn't meet his gaze, but nodded.

''You know, I've been thinkin' about that too—and I think it's a pretty good idea.''

Her head snapped up so quickly that Luke wondered how the movement didn't break her slender neck. At the stunned look on her face he couldn't control his chuckle. ''Can I take heart that your silence means you agree?''

''Hardly!'' Jessica hissed quietly.

''But what will the men think?''

She was so angry that she didn't recognize the teasing sparkle in his eyes. The trouble was that part of the reason she *was* so angry was that standing here in the enveloping darkness, listening to his husky voice speak of such intimate things, had suddenly sent gooseflesh crawling up her arms that Jessica knew she couldn't blame on the balmy night air.

"I don't care what they think!" she whispered, conscious of the men who stood only a few yards away. "Besides, they wouldn't expect us to—well—to . . ."

When she stuttered into embarrassed silence, his brow went up questioningly. "To what?" he asked innocently.

"You know!"

The corners of that mustache twitched. "Tell me."

"You're despicable!"

"I agree."

"A total scoundrel!"

"I've been called a lot worse."

"I'll just bet you have!" Jessica ground out, trying to hold on to her anger. She should slap him. She really should. But that mischievously handsome smile made it nearly impossible to stay angry with him. The—*scoundrel*!

Luke saw the reluctant softening in her eyes and grinned. "But I'm useful to have around," he offered.

Jessica gave a skeptical snort at that. "Maybe."

"Which brings me back to why I want to sleep with you tonight. Shall I tell you?"

Her raised brow dared him to.

For a brief moment his grin was downright wicked before he finally relented to explain. "If someone's gonna try something they'll most likely do it at night. I want you to sleep close by so I can keep an eye on you. That is, if you think you can keep your hands to yourself," he couldn't resist adding.

"Believe me, that *won't* be a problem!"

She seemed so sure of the fact that Luke could only take it as a challenge, kind of like waving a red flag in a bull's face. Setting the plate down, he took a step closer, trailing one finger down her arm from shoulder to wrist. He smiled inwardly when he saw the change in her eyes. "Are you sure of that, Jessica?" he asked in a voice so husky it sent a shiver down her other arm.

Her chin came up, and Luke saw the battle she fought not to retreat. It was the one time her obstinance was going to work to his advantage. "It'll be chilly tonight. We could share our body heat."

Why was it that instead of giving him the stinging set-down he deserved, all Jessica could think of was the way he had kissed her yesterday morning, the way those eyes had turned to twin blue flames just before his mouth captured hers? Maybe it was because he had that same look in his eyes right now, like some dangerous predator attempting to mesmerize its prey before devouring it. "We have a fire for that," she got out in a choked whisper, fighting to break her gaze from his.

At some point, Luke wasn't quite sure when, this had stopped being just a game. He found himself remembering yesterday's kiss, and the sweet taste of those inviting lips. Looking at them now, seeing her face tilted up to him and the confused look of blossoming passion in her eyes, he couldn't resist any longer. Sliding his hands up her arms, he gently pulled her forward against his chest, nearly groaning at how good she felt in his arms. He paused a brief instant, giving her the opportunity to pull away. She didn't. And slowly, so as to savor each delicious second, he lowered his head to claim her lips.

Jessica had known what was coming from the instant his hands touched her arms. She also knew she had the power to stop it. What troubled her was that she just didn't seem to want to stop it badly enough to pull away. So many emotions washed over her as his warm, firm lips slanted across her mouth—wonder at the new feelings that fluttered through her body, guilt that she had never felt like this with John, and fear at what these feelings could do to her life.

That last was the thought that finally made her pull away. "We can't do this," she whispered quietly, almost desperately, as she took a protective step away from him. "We know this isn't a real marriage."

It was on the tip of his tongue to tell her it could be, but Luke knew it wouldn't be his *brain* talking. She was right. Much as he wanted to find a quiet spot near the creek and make love to this flaming-haired angel all night, he knew it wasn't right. That inherent sense of honor his parents had worked so hard to instill in him—which at times like this he almost regretted—wouldn't let him take advantage of her vulnerability.

Taking a deep breath, he clenched his hands against the urge to pull her back into his arms, and nodded. "You're right. The only defense I can offer is that moonlight and a beautiful woman make a mighty big temptation." Giving her a smile of reassurance, he went on, "You go get something to eat, then bed down near the fire. I'll be there in a little while. And I promise to keep my hands to myself." With a soft grin he added, "if you will."

Jessica tried to act casual as she joined the men by the fire. *It was only a little kiss*, she told herself. *It meant nothing to either of us.*

So why, her conscience asked with its typical demand for honesty, *are you still trembling?*

Chapter Seven

Jessica lay watching the rosy fingers of dawn stretch slowly above the horizon to the east. The smoke-gray sky had gradually been getting lighter for the last half hour. She knew because she had been watching the sky for what seemed the entire night, praying for dawn.

Truth to tell, Jessica couldn't remember if she had slept at all since seeking out her bedroll last night. This she blamed on the man who lay so close to her that she could reach out and brush that tawny wave of hair out of his eyes—eyes closed in blissful sleep, the wretch!—if she wanted to. As if she wanted to touch Luke Cameron!

Six years she had come on this roundup. Six years of riding with only men, eating with only men, crouching beneath tarps while the rain soaked everything in the camp with only men, and yes, bedding down within arm's reach of a half dozen or more men, and never had she lost a second's sleep over the fact—until now.

But last night, with a cool breeze to chase away the insects, and the frogs croaking a lullaby down by the creek, she hadn't been able to sleep a wink. And it was all his fault, Jessica thought irritably, wanting to reach over and punch the man sleeping so peacefully beside her.

A muffled cough caught her attention, and Jessica gave a relieved sigh as she rolled over to find Zeke carrying the coffee pot toward the creek. Pushing herself up on one arm, she raked the fall of hair back out of her eyes to look around the camp. The rest of the men were beginning to stir. Grumbling beneath her breath about men in general, and gunslingers particularly, she rose to make her way to the creek, hoping the cold water might revive her until the coffee was ready. Rounding up steers all day was hard enough after a good night's rest, but with no sleep?

It was going to be a long day.

After six hours of riding they stopped for lunch at a ford in the creek where the cattle could drink their fill. Jessica ignored the men's surprised looks when she suggested they stay here for an hour or two. It had been a long morning. She was hot, she was dog tired, and her head was pounding as if the cattle had been driven through it. She didn't really care right now what anyone thought. All she could think of was finding a quiet place to lie down and die.

Finding a spot away from the others, she stretched out in the mottled shade beneath a tree. The gurgling creek combined with the gentle breeze that wafted over her tired body like a tender caress soon worked their magic on her heavy eyelids, lulling her into the beckoning arms of sleep.

Jessica had no idea how long she'd slept, but when her eyes finally opened she frowned, unsure just what had awakened her. And then the noise came again, a distant popping sound, almost like . . .

Before she could finish the thought, Luke appeared on Shiloh, pulling back on the reins as the stallion danced impatiently at the abrupt halt.

"I want you to get back over there with Zeke and the men and stay put 'til I get back," Luke ordered, looking down at her before his gaze quickly went back to the direction from which the popping sounds had come.

"But—"

His gaze snapped back to hers. "This is one of those times when you do what I say without any questions, Jessica! Now go!"

Two more pops, and Jessica suddenly realized what they were. "That's gun—"

"Yes, it is!" he cut her off impatiently. "Now move!"

The headache was gone, and Jessica found that the nap had

restored a more charitable attitude toward her protector. But before she could caution him to be careful, he was gone.

Four years of fighting in the war had taught Luke the benefits of stealth when it came to staying alive, but it was the six years of avoiding lawmen and bounty hunters that had caused that skill to evolve into what was now finely honed instinct. With the silent tread of a stalking cat he crept along the creek bank where the thick moss muffled his footsteps.

The shots had come from only a mile or two up the trail they followed, and after riding Shiloh as far as he thought was safe, Luke had left the stallion tied in a grassy spot and come the rest of the way on foot. At the sound of voices just through the trees to his left he paused to listen.

"Twenty dollars!" a man's voice said in disgust. "All this trouble for twenty damn dollars and a wagonload of furniture."

"Told ya we should've found more stagecoaches instead of robbin' dirt farmers," another spoke up. "Hell, *we* got more money than they had!"

Luke crept closer until he could see, and immediately wished he hadn't. His fists clenched in rage at the sight before him. A man and woman lay close together beside their wagon, blood seeping from wounds in their chests as the four men standing nearby casually discussed the merits of one form of robbery over another.

"It's just like you to kill the woman, Clem," one of the men complained. "Look at 'er! Least she could'a made this a little more interestin'."

"She was reachin' behind the seat," the one named Clem defended. "Would you rather I'd let her pull out a rifle an' plug ya between the eyes?"

"Shut up, both of ya!" the first man ordered. "Get to lookin' through this wagon an' see if there ain't somethin' to make this worth our trouble."

Luke had heard enough. He stepped through the trees, the Colts clearing their holsters with the fluid speed of a striking rattler. In the time it took to blink, two of the bandits lay dead.

"What the—"

The one named Clem spun in surprise, and his eyes widened on seeing the man standing by the trees, the look in the ice-blue gaze promising death. Clem's gaze dropped to the smoking Colts and he fumbled for his gun. Luke dropped him where he stood with a clean shot through the heart.

That was all it took for the remaining bandit to turn tail and run. Crouching low, he raced for his horse, swung up on the nervously prancing animal, and kicked it into a run. The man seemed to develop a burst of courage once on the animal's back and he pulled his gun, turning in the saddle to fire toward the man who had thwarted his plans. Luke stepped from the cover of the trees and slowly brought his arm up to take aim. The man fell dead, his horse racing on without him.

The first shots after so long a pause made Jessica jump nervously. Raising her head, she met Hank's gaze, then looked around to see the same question mirrored in each of the men's faces. None of them felt right to be sitting here while Luke faced whatever was ahead of them alone. Another shot brought Hank, Sam, and Allen to their feet, and they looked to Jessica expectantly. She bit her lower lip in a second's hesitation of whether to obey Luke's order or not.

The fourth shot made up her mind.

"Let's go!"

"Jess!"

Jessica turned on a frowning Zeke. "You may not care for him, Zeke, but he's doing this for us. I won't leave him out there to face who knows how many gunmen alone!"

The other men were already mounted, and Clayton handed Jessica the reins to her mare. As they rode out, she looked back to promise Zeke she'd be careful, but found him swinging into the saddle of his gelding. With no more thought for anything save the man who she had let ride alone toward possible death to protect her, Jessica pushed the mare into a full run.

The scene they came upon as they rounded a curve in the trail brought all of the riders to a quick halt. Four bodies lay strewn along the trail leading to a wagon. The only person left alive amidst the carnage was a man who whirled, and with a draw that was an indistinguishable blur, now leveled two deadly Colts at them. Seeing who they were, he replaced the guns in their holsters, but Jessica felt only slight relief, for his eyes blazed with an anger as intimidating as the lethal Colts.

"What the hell are you doing here?" Luke growled, walking over to grab the mare's bridle. "I thought I told you to stay put!"

"It weren't her fault, boss," Clayton spoke up quickly, hoping to deflect Luke's anger. "We all wanted to come. You really didn't expect us ta just sit back there an' let you get shot up, did ya?"

Clayton looked around him at the four dead outlaws, then back to the man left standing. "Don't guess we should'a been worried, though, huh?"

Jessica wasn't too happy at hearing Clayton refer to Luke as his "boss," but that thought quickly fled when she took in the scene before her. "What happened?"

Luke's voice took on a hard edge as he described what he had come upon, leaving out the one outlaw's intentions for the woman out of consideration for Jessica—and because if he thought about it he would most likely shoot the man again for good measure.

Dismounting, Jessica stepped to the rear of the wagon to check on the settlers, but Luke's hand on her arm stopped her. "Don't," he said quietly, and she looked up to find that the anger had been replaced by a sadness that seemed at odds with the cold rage he had just displayed.

"But they could still be—"

"They're dead, Jessica. Take my word for it."

She swallowed at the implication in his tone, but squared her shoulders. "Then they'll need to be buried."

"The men and I can see to it."

He was trying to spare her this horrible scene, and Jessica would have gladly let him, if not for the woman. "I appreciate what you're trying to do, but I think that woman would have preferred that I see to her instead of men she didn't know."

He hesitated for another moment, then released her arm.

Taking a deep breath in preparation, Jessica stepped around the wagon. Her stomach lurched at the sight of so much blood, but she clenched her teeth against the nausea and moved forward. She felt Luke's presence behind her as she knelt beside the dead woman. Looking into the still face, Jessica felt her eyes fill with tears. "She's not much older than me," she whispered quietly as she brushed a strand of wheat-gold hair from the young woman's face. Then, clearing her throat, she said to the man behind her, "Would you look in the wagon and see if you can find two quilts, please?"

He didn't answer, but she felt him turn and leave.

"I'm so sorry," Jessica whispered to the dead couple. "What dreams you must have had when you left—"

"Jessica?"

At the soft but urgent call she looked over her shoulder to where Luke stood motionless at the back of the wagon. "What is it?"

"Would you come here, please?"

His voice was so gentle that she frowned in confusion as she rose to join him. When she stood beside him, he nodded toward the inside of the wagon, and Jessica looked inside. "What is it? I don't see any . . ."

And then she spotted what he did, a pair of frightened brown eyes peeping out from beneath the wagon seat.

"After what just happened, I think it would be best if you go in," Luke said softly.

She nodded, and moving slowly so as not to frighten the child further, Jessica crawled into the wagon. "You don't have to be afraid of us, sweetheart," she said gently. "We're here to help you."

The child crouched farther beneath the seat.

"Can you come out here?" Jessica coaxed. "It must be terribly cramped under there."

The brown eyes looked enormous in the ashen little face as the child shook its head.

"Did your mother and father tell you to stay there?"

A nod.

73

"You're a very good little—child, then." She still couldn't tell if it was a boy or girl. All she could see was the fear in those eyes. Jessica felt her heart contract. "It's very good to obey, but sometimes things happen and you have to do otherwise." She ignored the soft snort behind her and went on, "Please come out. I promise you won't get into trouble. I'll take the blame."

The eyes showed indecision, and Jessica searched her mind for something that might entice a frightened child. "I could let you ride my horse."

"Horsey?"

The tiny voice made her heart lurch, but Jessica smiled coaxingly. "Yes, horsey. She's very pretty too. Her name is Belle."

There was a rustling sound before a dark head appeared. The sight of the little girl, who couldn't have been more than three or four, brought fresh tears to Jessica's eyes. She held out her arms and smiled encouragingly. The little girl hesitated only a moment, then trustingly walked into the open arms.

Rocking gently, Jessica held the child tightly, forcing the tears down as she whispered, "It's all right, sweetheart. Everything's going to be all right."

"Jessica?"

The suspiciously hoarse voice brought her head around, and Luke continued, "Keep her in here for now."

He was turning away when her call stopped him. "I don't think so. Do you really think we can show her two mounds of dirt and then ride away, expecting her to accept that her parents are gone and she'll have to go with us?"

"You can't mean to let her see them," Luke said, keeping his voice calm for the child's sake.

"Get the quilts and wrap them until only their faces show," Jessica instructed gently. "Try to make them look as peaceful as possible. I'll try to explain it to her."

Hesitating a moment in indecision, Luke finally gave a reluctant sigh. "I'll come get you when we're ready."

Twenty minutes later Jessica stood beside the carefully wrapped couple, holding tightly to the hand of the little girl who looked down at her parents with a confused frown.

"Mama an' Papa s'eepin'? "

From behind them Jessica heard several throats being cleared. She stooped down to place her arm around the child, praying for the right words as she tried to explain. "It's a kind of sleep, sweetheart. They've gone to be with God."

The little girl seemed to think on this for a moment, then said, "My grampa went to be wif God, in heaven."

There were several distinct sniffs now. All Jessica could think, though, was that she would much rather be standing back watching this heartrending scene than be the one trying to explain to this little girl that her parents were gone. What did you say to comfort a child after this kind of tragedy? Jessica racked her memory, trying to remember what had been said to her after her own mother's death.

"I hear it's a lovely place," she attempted weakly.

The troubled brown eyes turned up to her. "But—they forgetted me."

The words hit Jessica like a blow to the chest, and the tears she had held at bay threatened to spill over as she hoarsely tried to explain, "They can't take you, sweetheart. It isn't time for you to go yet."

The little lower lip began to tremble as the child suddenly began struggling to pull away. "I wanna go wif my mama an' papa!"

Losing the fight against her own tears now, Jessica pulled the little girl against her chest, hugging her tightly as the tiny shoulders began to shake. "You can't go. God didn't take you. He wants you to stay here."

It was all she could think of to say, and, unable to stand any more Jessica stood with the child still in her arms. Turning her head to nod blindly at the men who waited behind them, she walked briskly toward the creek, the little girl's heart-wrenching sobs trailing pitifully behind them.

Chapter Eight

They made camp at the spot where they had stopped for lunch. It had been late in the afternoon when they finished burying the unknown couple, and having no heart to go on with the roundup so soon after, they rode back to the still grazing herd and made camp.

Feeling both physically and emotionally drained, Jessica sat on a quilt rocking gently back and forth as she held the now sleeping little girl. She looked up as a tall form blocked out the waning rays of the sun.

"How is she?" Luke asked quietly, looking sadly at the small face before his gaze rose to meet eyes that were suspiciously red.

"She cried herself to sleep."

As if to confirm the words, the child gave several jerking sobs before settling down once more into fitful sleep. Luke watched her silently for a long moment, wondering why it seemed that life was always the most unfair to the innocent. "Did you ever find out her name?" he asked, wondering what was going to happen to the child next.

"From what I could understand it's Heather."

Another long moment passed while Luke decided whether he wanted an answer to another question that had been bothering him. "Do you think she saw what happened?"

Jessica looked up at the worried tone. "I don't think so," she answered, feeling the strangest urge to reassure him. "From the way I had to coax her out from under the seat, I hope she hid there through it all."

"Good. We buried the bastards," Luke said, his voice suddenly turning cold, "much as I'd have liked to leave them for the buzzards."

Jessica couldn't condemn him for the gruesome thought, for she felt much the same way. The outlaws had behaved like animals, killing without the least trace of mercy.

"You know we're going to have to report this to Davis," Luke said slowly, "He'll have to know about her."

Jessica's arms tightened protectively around the sleeping child. "Heather is staying with me!"

"I didn't say she wasn't," Luke soothed, surprised by the wild look. "In fact, I was hopin' you would feel that way. I don't think she needs the added confusion of being passed around between strangers after all she's been through."

Jessica's hold loosened somewhat at his words. "If we had found anything to tell us who she was or if she had family who really wanted her, I'd see that she got back to them," she offered defensively.

"I know you would."

"But I won't let her be put where she's not wanted."

"I won't let that happen either."

There was wary hope in the golden-green eyes now. "So you'll help me convince Sheriff Davis that she belongs with me?"

"The man probably doesn't set much store in my opinion," Luke answered, trying to coax a smile from her, "but I'll do whatever I can to help."

"She's a sweet child," Jessica offered, content now in the belief that all would turn out well.

"She seems to be. A good little girl too," Luke added pointedly. "Obedient when she's told to do something. Unlike others I could name."

At his stern frown Jessica's eyes guiltily slipped away.

"I told you to stay put," he went on, growing angry as he thought of the consequences her action could have caused. "You could have gotten yourself and the men shot by riding up like you did."

"But you were alone! We were worried when we heard the shots."

Luke wasn't swayed by her argument. "I thought you chose me because you trusted me to be able to take care of situations like that."

"But there were four of them! And there could have been more!"

"And it could have just as easily been a trap set up by Mateland. And you would have ridden right into it like a sheep to slaughter, woman! If you want me to protect you, then you better do as I tell you from here on out. Understand?"

Jessica's chin came up at his high-handed manner. "I think you're forgetting who's in charge here, Mr. Cameron," she said haughtily.

"I swear if you dare say you hired me again I'm gonna turn you over my knee, *Mrs.* Cameron. I don't work for you, and I thought I'd already made it clear I don't take orders. We're partners in this deal, and if you want me to keep my end, then you're gonna have to do what I say when it comes to things like this."

"Tell me if I have this right," Jessica asked with biting sarcasm. "We're partners, so I can't tell you what to do, but you can order me around however you please. Is that about it?"

She looked so furiously outraged that Luke suddenly had to fight the urge to grin. "That sounds about right."

Seeing the infuriating twitch at the corners of his mustache, Jessica's eyes narrowed dangerously. "I'm glad you find this amusing," she spat. "Maybe you'll find it so funny you'll be able to laugh outright when I tell you what you can do with *your* orders!"

"Uh, uh, Jessica," Luke chided, his eyes gleaming. "You're a mama now. And mamas aren't supposed to show their tempers."

"They can when they're dealing with unreasonable gunfighters!"

"Gunfighters who they've asked to protect their life?"

That silenced her for a moment, then, "What if we make another compromise?"

Crossing his arms, Luke gave her a skeptical look. "Such as?"

"I will take your suggestions very seriously, and concede to them in most cases."

He straightened slowly, his look turning from amusement to rising anger. "In other words, I'll never know for sure if you're going to *concede* to my *suggestions* when I'm risking my life to save yours, and possibly Heather's now as well? Is that about it?" he echoed her earlier question mockingly.

"It's not like I'm going to do something stupid!" Jessica defended. "But I can't make you a promise I can't keep. If circumstances change and I think your orders will endanger someone's life—even if it is yours—I'll have to trust my own judgment."

Luke wanted to argue with that, but it just sounded too logical. But he had to be able to know that she wouldn't ride into something thinking she was helping, like today, and endanger them all. "I understand what you're saying," he allowed softly, "but you're going to have to trust my judgment in cases like this. I can see past the surface of how a situation looks to what could actually be going on. Like I said before, today could have easily been a trap. There could have been men hiding, ready to shoot you and your men when you came riding in to the rescue."

He was right, and Jessica hated it because now she was going to have to admit it. And there was nothing a man liked better than to hear that he was right. "Okay, so I could have made a mistake today." His brow raised at "could" but she went on before he could comment. "At the time our only thought was that you were outnumbered."

"I appreciate your concern." And he did. It had been a long time since anyone had worried about him. "But you have to trust me to know what's best. And I have to be able to trust you to stay put when I tell you to."

"What if I promise to do as you say as long as the circumstances don't change so drastically that it would be dangerous to do so?"

It was a wordy question and seemed to give her a lot of

leeway to do whatever the hell she wanted. "That's not very reassuring."

"Maybe not," Jessica agreed. "I guess it comes down to whether or not you credit me with good judgment."

"It comes down to whether I want to stake my life, and yours, on your good judgment."

"So are you saying you trust me?"

"I'm saying we'll see if I come out of my association with you alive, Mrs. Cameron."

Jessica shook her head, smiling at his pained expression. "You make me sound absolutely dangerous to be around, Mr. Cameron."

His eyes darkened to smoky blue as he met her smiling gaze, and in the barest whisper Luke admitted, "More than you realize, Jessie."

She swallowed against the pounding pulse in her throat, and remembering how easily things had gotten out of hand just last night, Jessica quickly sought a topic to avoid another such scene between them—for her own sanity. She chose the safest, closest topic at hand. "I'll need to take Heather home tomorrow."

Luke knew what she was doing, and the sensible part of him appreciated it, even if the rest of him didn't. "We'll leave at first light. We should be able to make the ride in one day without any cattle to worry about."

"We?" Jessica questioned, trying to keep the nervous edge out of her voice. "I thought maybe Zeke could ride with me."

"Zeke knows how to round up cows. I know how to look for danger. Now, which one of us should stay here and which should go along to protect you and Heather?" Luke questioned archly. "In your *good judgment*?"

Drat, but why did he have to always be right?

"You," she answered with an ungracious snort of acceptance. There seemed to be no escape from being forced into constant contact with him. "We'll be ready to leave at sunup."

* * *

"I don't like it!"

Jessica looked around at Zeke's outburst to see if the whole camp had stopped to listen. When she found, thankfully, that they hadn't, she pulled the frowning Scot further into the trees. "He made a very good point, Zeke. What am I supposed to do, leave him to round up the rest of the herd?"

"Probably steal 'em," the old man grumbled. "But better that than you ridin' off alone with 'im."

Sighing impatiently, Jessica asked, "Why do you still not trust Mr. Cameron? Hasn't he proved himself? Didn't yesterday show you what kind of man he is?"

Zeke eyed her curiously. "You sure are singin' his praises. Could it be ye're takin' a likin' to him?"

"Certainly not!"

Several of the men looked their way, and Jessica lowered her voice. "I hired him to protect me. It only makes sense that he would ride back to the ranch with Heather and me. Besides, we should be there by nightfall—that is, if we can leave right now," she added pointedly.

"I still don't like it."

"Frannie will be there."

"At the house maybe. But she won't be with ya between here an' there," Zeke pointed out.

"You just will not credit the man with a shred of decency, will you?!"

"Not where ye're concerned. I'd be hard pressed to trust a saint ta look after ya proper, Jess. And Luke Cameron is fer sure far from bein' a saint."

With a smile filled with exasperated affection, Jessica laid her hand on the gruff old Scotsman's arm. "I love you too, Zeke," she said softly. "But you have to trust me in this. Mr. Cameron will protect me out of honor."

"Ain't that kind of protectin' I'm worried about," Zeke answered, covering her small hand with his large, callused one. "What worries me is who's gonna protect you from him."

A half hour later Luke, Jessica, and Heather left camp heading home. Heather rode in front of Jessica, and at the early hour it hadn't taken her long to fall asleep once more to the rhythmic sway of the horse's footsteps. Her little head rested on Jessica's shoulder, and to accommodate her Jessica leaned back in the saddle.

"I can carry her with me," Luke offered as he saw her trying to find a comfortable position while cradling the girl.

"No, I'm fine. Besides, you need to have your hands free if something happens."

He nodded.

"You know, it's really starting to make me angry, this constant looking behind every rock for somebody who might want to shoot me," she complained.

Try doing it every second of your life for six years, Luke thought tiredly, but said, "Maybe it'll be over soon. Mateland sounds anxious."

"Which still puzzles me," Jessica said with a frown. "What could there possibly be to the Circle R that makes him want it so badly? We're a small operation compared to what he owns."

Luke gave a shrug. "That's what I'm here to find out." He wouldn't voice his thoughts on the most obvious thing Mateland could want, and that sure wouldn't necessitate killing Jessica.

But then the man had tried to buy her out, then scare her off, so lust didn't seem to be his motivation. What else did that leave as far as what drove a man? Revenge? He'd have to see if John Randall had ever done anything to anger Mateland. Greed? Like Jessica said, she was small time where a man like Benjamin Mateland was concerned.

Lust. Greed. Revenge. That about covered the reasons that led a man to the point of killing. And even though Jessica could inspire lust in a eunuch, Luke had to discount that as the driving force behind what Mateland was doing. So it was either greed or revenge. Now all he had to do was give ole Ben a nudge to find out which one it was.

Chapter Nine

Frannie, who had never had a child of her own, was delighted to hear that Heather would be staying at the Circle R. She cried over the heartrending story of how the parents had been killed, then looked at her young friend searchingly when Jessica went on to tell her how Luke Cameron had singlehandedly faced down the outlaws, and how gentle he had been later when talking to Heather. The glowing words of praise told much more than Jessica realized as she tried to convince Frannie that Luke was actually a very honorable and trustworthy man. She was sure that whatever he had done in the past was for a good reason. Once they were able to straighten things out and offer proof to a judge, she was sure that all charges against him would be dropped.

Frances watched her young friend's eyes closely. "Could it be ye're comin' ta care fer the gunslinger?" she asked worriedly.

At the familiar question Jessica gave an exasperated sigh. "Why do you and Zeke both have to think I care for Mr. Cameron just because I'm willing to admit that we were wrong about him? He's proven to me that he isn't a cold-blooded killer. Is it so strange that I hate seeing someone accused of being something they're not?"

"He was tried by a judge an' found guilty."

"Well, maybe he couldn't produce the evidence for his defense. If he's as wicked as you and Zeke want to paint him, then why has he stayed here this long? Why didn't he ride out of here that first night?"

"I don't know," Frannie confessed. "Why do men do any-

83

thing? I just don't want ya gettin' yerself hurt by fallin' in love with an outlaw.''

"I'm not falling in love with him!" Jessica stressed each word. "I'm simply saying he's a better man than we thought. I'm giving credit where it's due. That's all!"

"Hmm."

Jessica threw up her hands at that. "Okay. I'm madly in love with Luke Cameron and we're planning on running off to Mexico together. Is that what you want to hear?" she asked sarcastically.

"Ya don't have ta get snippy with me."

"Then stop acting as if I'd be foolish enough to fall in love with any man!"

Understanding the reason for the pain that had flashed through her young friend's eyes, Frances stepped forward to slide an arm around Jessica's waist. "There, now, I didn't mean ta fuss. It's just that I worry about ya, darlin'."

"Well you don't have to," Jessica assured her. "My life is perfect the way it is—or it will be once Mr. Cameron takes care of my problem with Ben. I don't want or need a man in my life; not Mr. Cameron, not anyone."

Luke turned away from the open window where he had stood listening and walked back toward the barn. He was glad she was such a sensible woman, he told himself as he pushed open the barn door with a little more force than necessary. It could sure make things a lot more difficult when he had to leave if she were to be so foolish as to start caring for him.

He picked up a pitchfork and climbed the steps to the hayloft. Stabbing the tool into a mound of hay, he heaved up a forkful that was large enough to fill two stalls and threw it down to the floor below. It would be the height of foolishness for either one of them to start thinking there could ever be any more to what they had together than just a business deal. And what had passed between them two nights ago? Well, that had only been a moment of madness brought on by the moonlight, he decided as he stabbed the pile of hay once more, viciously.

* * *

The Deal

The weeks passed in relative quiet. The men came back from the roundup with 287 head of cattle. The workings of the ranch helped Heather keep her mind occupied on something other than her loss, and she quickly became the darling of the Circle R. Jessica kept herself busy painting one of the upstairs bedrooms and sewing curtains and a spread to decorate the room for Heather. Luke, meanwhile, left early each morning, not to return until the last red fingers of sunset faded from the sky.

That left only the evening hours when Jessica was hard-pressed to find something to do to keep herself from having to spend so much time in Luke's company. It wasn't that she disliked him, just the opposite. When he let down that icy barrier and let his sense of humor show through, he was really quite enjoyable to be with.

Which was the exact reason she had avoided him. It was too enjoyable spending time with him. Sure, she liked talking to all the men who worked for her. She considered them friends instead of hired hands. But it was different with Luke. She never felt her heart race with Billy or Lee like it did when Luke spoke to her in that husky, totally *male* tone. And none of the others would even dare to kiss her, much less look at her as if they wanted to devour her!

Certainly it hadn't been like that with John.

Dear, sweet John. He had given her so much. Jessica hoped she had given him some happiness in return. If it hadn't been for him and Alicia, she would probably still be in Kentucky, scrubbing floors in some Yankee carpetbagger's home right now.

At sixteen she had had enough of the orphanage and had run away, hoping to find a way out west—to the land where dreams came true. Fate had smiled down on her that day. Intent on finding a job and saving the money for passage, and to get her started in her new life, Jessica had gone into the local mercantile and had chanced to overhear a middle-aged couple talking to the owner. The lady was expecting, and they were interested in hiring a young woman to make the trip to California with them to help care for her.

85

Jessica had stepped up immediately and *accepted* the job. The husband had been reluctant since they didn't know her, but the woman had looked deeply into Jessica's eyes for a long moment, then told her she had the job. A week later Jessica had left Lexington, Kentucky, as the hired companion of Alicia Randall.

Two months into the journey Alicia had fallen ill, along with several others in the wagon train. Unwilling to stop, the wagon master had insisted the train move on, and, fearful of being attacked by Indians or outlaws if they lagged behind, John and Jessica moved on with it. They took turns driving while the other nursed Alicia, who grew weaker with each passing day. As is usually the case, out of adversity a deep bond grew between the three. Nights would find Jessica sitting at Alicia's bedside with John as he talked of the ranch they were going to build. On that last night Alicia had taken Jessica's hand and asked her to stay on and live with them on that ranch.

The next morning Alicia Randall was dead.

Jessica hadn't known such grief since her mother had died. And John, who had suffered through the horrors of four years of fighting and come out of it with his sanity still remarkably in tact, nearly lost his mind with grief. Having become close friends over the past two and half months, and sharing a love for Alicia, it was only natural that John and Jessica turned to each other for comfort. It never entered their minds that anyone would even consider the possibility that they were anything other than friends who grieved together over their loss.

It didn't take long, however, for the ugly gossip to start about the recent widower and his beautiful young employee. Jessica first heard of the stories when the young preacher who was traveling with the train came to tell John what was being said. The people felt it their Christian duty to see to the situation. Therefore, they informed John and Jessica that they could not remain together, not being married.

Not one of the good ladies would allow her husband to offer the solution of taking in Jessica. She and John both knew that to leave the train would be tantamount to suicide. So with no other option open, and still too filled with grief to fight back, the two had allowed the preacher to marry them that afternoon.

There had been no intimacy between them for the first year, for John was still mourning the loss of the woman he had loved so deeply, and Jessica was filled with resentment toward the ''good people'' of the wagon train who she felt had forced her to betray her friend's memory. She and John had never resented each other, though. They had always been good friends, and as time passed the bond of shared grief turned to one of good memories of the woman they had cared for so much.

Jessica wiped a tear that threatened at the corner of her eye. Alicia had accepted her without reserve, offering friendship, and later, a place in their family. As important as the need to belong somewhere was within Jessica, she would have flatly refused that offer if she had seen the least trace of pity in Alicia's green eyes. But what had shown there was a love that had grown between them over the weeks to that of what sisters would feel.

It was strange that they had become so close so quickly, for Jessica had learned not to allow herself to love easily. Children came and went in the orphanage. A friend here today could be gone next month. When she ever did love, however, it was complete and unconditional, with a loyalty that bordered on obsession. Over the years she had grown to love John that deeply, not in a romantic sense, but as a very good friend.

When the wagon train had stopped in a small town named Langly in Wyoming Territory four months after Alicia's death, John and Jessica had both had their fill of the pious, holier-than-thou people who could only see the worst in others. Looking around them at the verdant grasses and rolling hills, they decided this was the place they would build Alicia's dream.

Jessica felt a sharp pain that neither John nor Alicia had survived to enjoy their dream. Gritting her teeth with renewed determination, she again vowed to see the man who had killed John hanged for his crime. Maybe then she could return all her energies to running the ranch and making a home for her "family."

With the roundup complete and the cattle sold, the hands found themselves growing bored with the sudden lack of activity. With nothing else to do, they rode out one day in pursuit of a herd of wild mustangs Clayton had seen roaming in the hills.

It was late in the afternoon when Jessica heard the excited whoops of the returning cowboys. She stepped out onto the porch to see a cloud of dust rolling up the road leading toward the house. The thundering of hooves reached her ears long before she saw the mustangs break through the billowing cloud of dust with men riding on each side, waving their hats and urging the sweat-glistening horses toward the split-rail corral on the far side of the barn.

Sam and Allen Fisher took up their posts at the entrance to the corral, and the brothers worked as a team to herd the dozen or so wild horses through the gate. Sam quickly closed it off before the nervous animals could break free.

Feeling nearly as excited as the triumphantly smiling men, Jessica lifted her skirt and ran across the yard to join them in looking admiringly over the wild-eyed animals. "They're so beautiful," she whispered in awe.

"Sure are, ma'am," Allen agreed with a wide grin. "Clayton was right. They're some of the best-lookin' mustangs I ever seen."

"Wish we'd'a got the leader, though," Clayton said, joining them by the fence. "He's black as sin an' smarter than any horse has a right to be."

"Not smart enough ta keep us from takin' half his harem," Sam interjected. "I bet he's watchin' us right now, mad as a hornet."

The rest of the men agreed in amused tones that told how much they had enjoyed outsmarting the black. Jessica smiled at their amusement before turning once more to watch in appreciation as the horses pranced nervously around the confines of the corral, so beautiful because of their untamed spirit. If she didn't know that a lot of the range horses wouldn't make it through the harsh winter, she would be disinclined to let these wild creatures be tamed. At least none of these animals would face starvation this winter.

"We'll start breakin' some of 'em tomorrow," Hank said with obvious anticipation. "An' I know just the one I'd like to tame." He eyed a sleek mare that was cutting back and forth, eyeing the corral fence as if she was contemplating jumping it. "That little lady runs like the wind."

"Sure wish I'd'a had her back in Tennessee," Tim said, stepping up beside Hank to watch the mare. "Could'a made me a bundle racin' her. It took me and Hank both to keep her with the pack."

"She was wantin' ta get back to Diablo for sure," Hank agreed.

Jessica's brow furrowed questioningly. "Diablo?"

"The black," Hank explained. "Clayton calls him that 'cause he's mean as the Devil hisself."

"Maybe he's only mean to men who take his lady away from him," came a deep-voiced response behind them, and Jessica frowned at the unwanted leap in her pulse.

She wouldn't turn to look at the man who stepped up beside her, but every nerve in her body suddenly seemed aware of his presence.

"Can't say as I blame him," Hank offered. "She's a beauty. That red coat of hers gleams just like fire in the sunlight."

Luke let his eyes slip to the woman beside him. She was watching the horses intently, so he was free to let his gaze slide leisurely through the thick mane of hair that hung loose to her waist. Like fire in the sunlight. It seemed that color attracted all males like moths to a flame.

"You ever broke a horse, Luke?" Sam asked, gaining his reluctant attention.

"Now and then."

"See any fillies that interest you?"

Luke hid a grin at the question and turned to survey the mares. "Hank's already spoken for her."

Cynthia Strickland

"Rules are she goes to whoever tames her," Sam supplied with obvious relish. "Hank's called for first crack at her. You get second try if he don't do it."

Hank gave Luke an amiable nod to let him know there would be no hard feelings. "I'll wish ya good luck. Don't think you'll be needin' it, though, 'cause I intend to tame that little lady."

Luke returned the smile. "If you don't, then I will."

That was just what Sam had been waiting for, and he immediately instigated a round of good-natured betting on who would actually tame the spirited mare. Hank was favored, as most of the men had seen him break horses before, but Sam chose to lay his money on Luke.

Suddenly Billy Lewis turned to Jessica. "You want in on this, ma'am?"

All eyes turned to her at the question. It was a measure of how relaxed the men were with their boss lady to ask a woman such a question. It wasn't that they didn't have the greatest respect for her; any of them would cut the tongue out of the man unwise enough to even hint at an insult to the lady. Most of them, even though they worked for her, came to quickly feel the affection of a protective big brother toward the woman who tried to make this feel like a home with the little things she did, like nursing them when they were sick, or remembering every one of their birthdays with a cake or pie. That kind of thoughtfulness to these men inspired unconditional loyalty. That was why most of the men who ever hired on at the Circle R, unlike other ranches, stayed on for years rather than moving on. Ms. Jessica made this home.

"Yeah, who do you think's gonna tame the mare?" Tim asked.

"She's got ta pull for her own husband," Clayton said in a tone that said he thought that fact should be obvious.

"I guess so," Billy answered in a resigned tone of regret. "Guess loyalty's more important than money anyhow."

Looking around at the expectant faces, Jessica knew they were waiting for her to agree. The only gaze she couldn't bring herself to meet was that of her husband, though she felt it intensely.

"I say she'll get both," Sam piped up. "I got ten dollars says Luke'll be the one to tame the mare."

That started another chorus of bets, and in the loud chorus of voices Jessica finally chanced a look at the man beside her. His gaze was so intense it nearly took her breath. "You can bet on Hank," he offered in a tone that said it didn't matter one way or the other to him. "I'll understand."

Jessica knew she should do just as he suggested and place the bet that would be safest for her emotionally. That voice of reason within screamed that she needed to do everything possible to distance herself from this man who was affecting her in ways that were far too dangerous to allow.

Make a bet on Hank! Pull away before it's too late!

"I've got twenty dollars that says my—that Mr. Cameron will tame that mare."

Sam whooped his agreement with her bet. "There you go, ma'am. We're gonna clean up on this one."

The good-natured arguing went on around them, and Jessica finally made herself meet that ice-blue gaze. She nearly sagged against the fence in relief when he chose not to ask the question that was clearly written in his eyes, for she was too afraid to consider the answer.

Chapter Ten

Jessica finished drying the breakfast dishes and put them away in the glass-fronted cupboard. Hanging the drying cloth on a nail by the back door, she took off her apron and laid it neatly over the back of a chair, then went in search of Heather. She didn't have far to go, finding the little girl perched on the end of Luke's bed.

Reluctant to enter the lion's den, Jessica paused at the door. "And just what are you doing, Miss Priss?" she asked in a light tone, trying to avoid looking at the man who sat in a chair pulling on his boots. The muscles in his upper arms flexed at the movement, and Jessica couldn't halt the memory of how those same arms had felt pulling her close to his chest. She swallowed with some difficulty past the dryness in her throat to speak to Heather. "Why don't you come on out and let Mr. Cameron finish—ah—getting ready?"

Luke met her gaze and his eyes twinkled devilishly. She was almost certain he was remembering the last time she had walked in on him getting dressed. Her face flushed at the memory of that broad, muscular back and the way it narrowed to a trim waist and . . .

She swallowed again and looked away. "Come on, Heather," she urged, holding out her hand.

"Yuke's gonna ride de horse!" the little girl offered with an enthusiastic grin. "He's gonna win lots of money!"

Jessica's brow raised at that and she forgot her embarrassment for a moment. "You've explained gambling to this child?" she asked with a censorious look.

"Not in detail. I just told her I was going to win. And she

agrees. Don't you, puss?" he asked, turning to smile at Heather as he ruffled her soft, dark brown curls. She grinned back, nodding vigorously.

Seeing him like this, smiling so openly at the child sitting on his bed, it was hard for Jessica to imagine him as the hardened gunfighter. But she had seen the other side, the one that could kill with the lethal speed of a striking rattler, the side that kept most people a safe distance away.

"Yuke's gonna name our horse F'ame," Heather said, breaking into Jessica's thoughts, " 'cause her hair yooks 'ike yours."

For the first time since she'd met him, Jessica saw a look almost like embarrassment quickly cross Luke's face. "I said her coat is about the color of your hair when the sun hits it," he explained gruffly. "Kinda like fire."

Even though she was sure it wasn't meant to be a compliment, Jessica felt a strange warmth in her chest, one that she quickly chided herself for.

"Yuke said I could ride F'ame."

"You left something out there, puss," Luke said at the concern on Jessica's face. "I said when she's tame I'd let you ride her with me."

The little girl gave a disgruntled frown, then with the lightning-quick mood change of youth, a brilliant smile lit her face. "You gonna watch Yuke ride, Jess'ca?"

Those blue eyes were watching her again. She could feel them. "I thought I might."

"She has money ridin' on this too, puss," Luke said with a grin for the child. "We'd better make sure I win or Jessica is gonna be mad. She might even make me sleep in the barn tonight."

Heather gave him a look that said she knew he was teasing her, and in a very well-informed tone she argued, "Hun uh. Mamas an' papas are spose to s'eep together."

Against her will, Jessica's gaze flew as if by instinct to Luke's face. As she had feared, that blasted mustache was twitching.

"They are?" he asked, as if this were news to him.

93

"Uh huh. That's what makes 'em be mamas an' papas."

Jessica nearly choked. Surely the little girl couldn't possibly know what that statement implied. She wouldn't let herself look at Luke this time, but she could hear the amusement in his voice as he said, "Ya don't say?"

Heather's face reflected how seriously she took this responsibility of instructing him. "Uh huh." Then her head cocked to one side and she looked at Luke curiously. "Are you and Jess'ca gonna be a mama an' papa, Yuke?"

That was it! This conversation was giving Luke Cameron far too much enjoyment, Jessica realized, growing angry at herself for actually blushing. "We need to go now and let Mr. Cameron finish getting ready, Heather," she said firmly.

The little girl scooted down off the bed obediently. "Okay. I gonna go see Hank now," she called as she scampered out the door.

Jessica turned to follow, hoping to make her own escape before that grinning gunfighter could embarrass her further, which she could tell he was itching to do.

"Interestin', the things kids say, isn't it?"

She hadn't made it. Turning, Jessica resigned herself to brazen this out. "Things are simple to children. She wouldn't understand our special circumstances."

"I thought she had a pretty good idea."

Even though she knew he was teasing, Jessica felt a shiver run down her body at the way he was looking at her. "Are you forgetting the terms of our deal?" she asked with an arched brow, hoping to intimidate him into dropping the subject.

But you didn't intimidate Luke Cameron. He crossed to stand directly in front of her, so close that they were nearly touching. "Terms can be broken if you want 'em to be, Jessica," he whispered in that husky tone that always made it hard for her to breathe.

Desperately her mind screamed in protest against her weakening will. *And then what? Are you ready to give him your heart, then stand on the porch and watch him leave too?*

When she looked up to refuse, the heated promise in his

eyes froze her tongue. Was he actually suggesting something permanent, or did he expect her to open herself up to care for him, only to watch a few months from now as he walked out of her life forever, without so much as a backward glance? Well, she had done that once for another man and she didn't intend to make that mistake ever again.

The painful memory of that day long ago was what finally helped to break the hold of his spell, and Jessica took a step backward. In a voice she was relieved didn't shake tellingly she said, "The terms stand just as they are, Mr. Cameron."

The heat in his eyes cooled instantly. Shrugging to show he really didn't care one way or the other, Luke stepped over to the dresser to pick up his Stetson. He turned to look in the mirror, dismissing her as he settled the hat on his head. "Then I guess I might as well go break that mare."

It was said so casually, as if he really didn't care that she had refused the offer he made. Jessica turned to leave, unreasonably hurt by his cavalier attitude. She willed herself not to run from the room as she so wanted to do. She would not let herself care! She would not let Luke Cameron hurt her!

Luke watched as the door closed behind her. Only then did he let himself feel the disappointment of her rejection. It was doubly hard to take because for a brief instant she had let her guard down and he had seen a matching desire flare to life in those green eyes. She had wanted him as badly as he wanted her. Hadn't she? Or was that only wishful thinking?

Several of the hands sat perched along the top rail of the corral, arguing over who was going to tame the mare. Sam had pulled Lee Stark over to Luke's side, since Lee had never seen either man ride. Now the rest of the men were trying to convince him that he was throwing his money away. Heather was sitting on Clayton's shoulder as he stood beside the fence. Her high-pitched voice could be heard over the many masculine ones as she argued in Luke's behalf.

Hearing their conversation, Jessica walked up to the assembled group. "You men haven't tried to convince this innocent child to take up gambling, have you?" she asked with a mock frown, though her eyes were sparkling with humor.

"No, ma'am," Hank assured her. "I don't believe I could stand havin' both you ladies bettin' against me."

"You know I don't like to choose between any of you men," Jessica said, hoping he wasn't hurt by her choosing to bet on Luke.

"I know ya had to bet on your own husband," Hank said with a look that told her he wasn't. Then he grinned. "I just hate to see ya lose your twenty dollars because of it."

"We'll see about that, Hank," came a familiar voice from behind them, and all the men turned with a friendly greeting for Luke, saving Jessica the need to face him.

"How ya feelin' this mornin', Luke?" Sam wanted to know.

"Good enough to tame a mare," Luke answered with a grin as he turned to Hank. "How about you, Fields?"

"Good enough to deprive you of the chance," the cowboy returned jovially.

"Then let's get to it!" Sam said, rubbing his hands together eagerly. He pulled a pocket watch from the front pocket of his denims. "You'll each get thirty seconds, alternatin' till one of you tames 'er. Hank gets first ride since he called for 'er first. Then Luke'll ride 'er second—and tame 'er."

A chorus of objections went up at that while the two opponents shook hands and headed over to the narrow stall where Allen held the mare. A cloth covered her eyes in an attempt to calm her. It wasn't working, for she fought against Allen's hold for all she was worth.

Hank climbed onto the stall, then gingerly lowered himself onto the mare's back, planting his feet firmly in the stirrups. After taking a deep breath, he looked over at Allen and nodded.

The second the gate opened, the furious mare shot out into the open corral. Her eyes rolled wildly now that the cloth had been removed, and a high-pitched whinny accompanied her vigorous efforts to dislodge the unaccustomed weight from her back. She came off all four feet at once, arching her back, then kicking her hind feet out before landing again with a spine-snapping jolt. Hank hung on tenaciously, as if trying to ride a tornado.

"Thataboy, Hank!" Billy called out. "Ride 'er just like she was a two-dollar—" The rest was cut off by a sharp elbow to his ribs, and he looked at a frowning Clayton, then up into the inquisitive eyes of Heather, who was looking down at him. Red-faced, Billy looked past Clayton to Jessica. "Ah—pardon, ma'am," he apologized.

Jessica fought a smile. "That's all right, Billy. I'm sure you can find a way to finish that sentence that's fit for little ears, though."

"Yes, ma'am."

At twenty seconds the mare finally gave a twisting leap that dislodged her rider. Allen and Sam were off the fence immediately to corner the nervous animal. Between the two of them they finally got her back into the stall, while Hank dusted off the seat of his denims and limped stiffly over to crawl between the rails to join the others. "Your turn, Luke," he offered with a pained grin. "And let me warn you in case you didn't notice, the lady ain't wantin' to be tamed."

Luke gave him a conspiratorial wink. "Those are the ones worth the effort, my friend."

For some reason Jessica found that innocent comment vastly annoying. It didn't help her pique any when she looked up to find his eyes locked on her. His grin grew downright devilish. With a toss of her head she looked away dismissingly, then gritted her teeth when she heard his grating chuckle.

"Come on, Luke," Sam called. "Time to show these guys how it's done."

Taking one last, amused look at the feminine back turned to him, Luke climbed over the fence and walked over to the holding stall. The mare's ears went straight back and she tossed her head angrily, reminding him of another spirited female. With slow movements Luke reached for the horse's halter, and though she fought him, he gently pulled her head down, speaking soft words no one else could hear. Despite her anger Jessica found herself watching him.

"Trying to use charm on 'er, Luke?" Clayton called in amusement.

Luke didn't answer. He pulled the mare's head closer, and it looked almost as if he was blowing softly into her velvety nostrils.

"You gonna ride 'er or kiss 'er?" Lee asked, and the others joined in his laughter.

Running his hand down the sleek neck, Luke slowly stepped over the top rail of the stall and gently eased onto the mare's back. The second his foot stepped into the left stirrup she begin to prance nervously, but a few soothing words in that soft tone from Luke seemed to calm her, for she settled down.

The men sitting on the fence stopped laughing.

Luke looked over at Allen and nodded, and it took the impressed cowboy a moment to remember that he was supposed to open the gate. The sudden movement of the gate swinging open, combined with the loud cheer that went up from those watching startled the mare and she shot out into the corral, coming off her feet with a mighty buck. Luke held on, and when her feet hit the ground once more, instead of using his left arm for balance, he stroked the mare's sleek neck and leaned forward to say something to her that was lost to the cheering cowboys. To their amazement the mare quieted almost immediately, and after tossing her head with one last show of spirited defiance, she calmed under her rider's gentle hand.

Tim looked suitably impressed. "Would ya look at that?"

"I'll be dogged if he didn't charm her!" Clayton agreed. "I wouldn't't'a believed it if I hadn't seen it with my own eyes."

Billy shook his head, still watching mare, who now circled the corral in a showy trot. "I seen it with my own eyes an' I still don't believe it."

Heather was clapping her hands in worshipful approval as Sam walked up the fence where the other men stood in awe. "Yuke ridded de horsey! He winned!" she announced unnecessarily.

The grin he wore nearly split Sam's face. "He sure did,

sugar,'' he agreed with obvious relish as he turned to his friends, rubbing his hands together in anticipation. "Time to pay up, boys!"

When all the debts were collected, Sam handed Jessica a stack of bills. "I told ya we'd clean up, ma'am," he claimed happily. "Wasn't that an impressin' sight? I never in my whole life seen anything like it."

She had to give credit where it was due. "It was something to see all right."

Looking over, she saw Luke throw his leg over the mare's neck and slide to the ground. He stepped to the animal's head, and the mare nuzzled his hand like a tame kitten as he stroked her velvety nose.

"You sure got a way with the ladies," Jessica heard Allen compliment Luke.

Before she could look away, Luke's gaze caught and locked with hers. He ran his hand down the mare's nose slowly, and his eyes remained imprisoning her as he answered Allen. "I've found they all respond better to a gentle touch."

Cursing herself for the tingle that ran through her body at his statement, Jessica tore her gaze away. She turned to take Heather from Clayton's shoulders and gave a quick farewell to the men before escaping to the safety of the house, telling herself all the way that it was only anger that made her heart pound so.

Chapter Eleven

With reluctance Jessica laid out a skirt of deep emerald green, then went back to the armoire to find the matching green and gold striped blouse. She dressed slowly, not so much to fuss over her appearance as to put off what must come when she was finally ready. She had been avoiding this for over three weeks now and she couldn't put it off any longer. She had to go into town.

Never enjoying the trip to begin with, Jessica now dreaded it because of the confrontations that were sure to come. Trying to be charitable, she decided that most of the folks of Langly just must not have much of a life of their own. Surely that had to be the reason they were always sticking their noses into someone else's.

For the last five years, since most of the ladies of the town had come to know their newest ranching neighbor, their conversation had centered around speculation—concerned of course—as to why she hadn't been able to conceive a baby. There was no way Jessica was going to tell anyone that the one attempt she and John had made at consummating their marriage had ended in. dismal failure. It was none of the townspeople's business in the first place. And secondly, she really didn't give many of them credit to understand the reasons why she and John had chosen not to have that kind of relationship.

Truth be told, Jessica hadn't been able to handle intimacy between them any better than John had. Alicia had been so good to her, had grown to be so much like the sister she had always wanted so badly, that Jessica couldn't bring herself to betray her friend. The loyalty she felt would never let her take her friend's husband, even though Alicia was dead.

Jessica shook her head as she thought about trying to explain that to the ladies of Langly. By experience she knew what the rumor mill would churn out: either that she refused her husband her bed, or that he was unable to perform his husbandly duties. Not wanting to put either one of them through another round of vicious gossip, she had lied. She had finally gotten so fed up with the constant, meddling questions that she told them she had had an accident as a child and couldn't conceive. Now the good ladies felt sorry for her, in a superior sort of way.

But now Jessica had no doubt the questions would start again. Of course, this time she had to admit they had a right to be curious. It wasn't every day a widow of four months rode into town to snatch a gunfighter off the gallows, marry him, then ride out again without so much as a how-do-you-do to anyone. She had to chuckle dryly at the bizarre picture. The townspeople must surely think she'd lost her senses.

Which is exactly what Jessica wondered herself, more so as the days went by.

She slowly walked down the stairs and crossed to the kitchen door. Frannie was standing at the table, flour covering both arms to the elbows as she kneaded bread dough. Perched on a chair beside her was Heather.

"I'm leaving now," Jessica called out to the engrossed pair.

Heather's head came up at that, and her eyes clouded for a brief instant with fear. She jumped down out of the chair and ran over to throw her arms around Jessica's legs, looking up pleadingly. "P'ease yet me go wif you, Jess'ca. I promise I be good."

"You're always good," Jessica said with a bright smile as she smoothed a stray lock from the worried little brow. "But this is going to be a quick trip. And besides, Frannie needs you to help her with the bread."

A look of understanding passed between the women. "That's right, pumpkin," Frannie piped up cheerfully. "I need someone ta help me put in just the right amount of raisins.

Can ya imagine how disappointed the boys'll be if they don't get the raisin bread we promised 'em?''

The little girl gave a reluctant nod. "You be back soon?" she asked, looking up at Jessica for reassurance.

"As soon as I possibly can," Jessica promised, hoping that time and a lot of love would eventually diminish the demons the child was having to deal with.

"Out with ya now," Frannie broke in lightly as she saw her young friend's eyes begin to tear up. "Heather an' I've got work ta do an' the day's awastin'."

Jessica stooped down and pulled Heather into her arms. "You help Frannie with that bread and I'll be back before you know it. And I may just bring you a surprise," she added with a mysterious smile.

When Jessica looked up again, she found Frannie frowning at a point behind her. She didn't have to turn to find out what—or rather *who*—the woman was frowning at.

"Hank asked me to tell you the wagon's ready," his voice came from the doorway. "Now you want to tell me what the wagon's ready for?'

It wasn't a question.

"It's ready for me."

The flippant answer made Luke scowl. "For what purpose?" he asked with deceptive calm.

She hadn't wanted to argue, not here in front of Heather, but it seemed she wasn't going to be able to avoid it. With a resigned sigh Jessica rose to her feet and turned to face him, almost losing her calm reserve at the building anger in his eyes. "I have to go into town." She saw an emotion she wouldn't attribute to pain flash briefly in his eyes, then it was gone.

"Okay."

That was easy. Too easy. "Okay?"

"I'll get Shiloh saddled and be with you in a minute."

She knew it had been too easy. "Zeke is going with me."

"I think we've had this discussion before. Zeke's forte is cattle, mine is—protection."

Shooting people! Your forte is shooting people! Jessica

wanted to correct, out loud, so he could hear it, so she could hear it, so she could remember the only reason he was here. But Heather was listening intently.

"I'm only going into town," she explained instead.

"You take Yuke, Jess'ca. He take care of you," Heather piped up, jerking on Jessica's skirt to get her attention.

Jessica looked down at the worried little face, thinking how unfair it was that Heather couldn't understand the complexities of—

"Out of the mouths of babes."

Jessica's head snapped up at the sarcastic remark, and before she could think to curb her tongue she snapped back, "I guess I just figured you wouldn't care to go back to Langly after your last experience there!"

A deathly silence fell over the three adults at the vicious remark.

When he finally did speak, Jessica almost cringed at the icy steel in Luke's voice. "Be in the wagon in five minutes."

He turned his back on her with that and walked down the hall, the echo of his boots on the polished wood floor the only sound to fill the silence left in his wake.

Jessica held the reins loosely, staring at the dusty backs of the horses as they pulled the wagon along. She hadn't meant that comment to come out like it had. Actually, she had meant to spare Luke a return to Langly, and the reception he was bound to get. Only his sarcasm had made her own response come back as a taunt. She regretted that now, immensely. It wasn't like her to intentionally hurt someone's feelings. She looked over at the man riding in stony silence beside her. His face was a chiseled, emotionless mask. That hurt more than if she had seen pain, for she knew he must be hurt. Wouldn't she have been by such cruel words?

"Mr. Cameron?"

He didn't show the least sign of having heard her.

Jessica hesitated. "Luke?"

That got his attention. He turned, nearly freezing her on the spot with the chilling blast from those ice-blue eyes. "To what do I owe the honor of finally hearing you deign to call me by my name, Mrs. Cameron?''

He could speak well when he chose to. And he seemed to choose to when he wanted to put her in her place, like now. ''I wanted to apologize.''

A tawny brow went up at that. ''Whatever for? Telling the truth?''

It was said with such lack of emotion that it was far more successful in hurting her than if he had broken down and cried. As if Luke Cameron would ever do such a thing.

''I meant what I said earlier, only not in the way I said it,'' Jessica tried to explain. ''I truly didn't think you'd want to ever go back to Langly again after what you went through there.''

''They were hanging a murderer.''

That shut her up for a moment. Then hesitantly she asked, ''Would you like to tell me what happened?''

Silence was his only response.

Jessica tried again, ''I don't know whether you did what they accused you of, but—''

''I did.''

She swallowed, but didn't give up. ''Do you want to tell me about it?''

''Not particularly.''

''You had a reason.''

It was a statement, not a question, and Luke turned his head to look at her again, a bit less hostilely this time. ''What makes you say that?''

''I've seen the way you are with Heather. No one can be so gentle with a child and shoot innocent people down in cold blood.''

''The Territorial Governor said I did.''

''Government officials have been know to be wrong before.''

Some of the defensiveness left his eyes. ''What makes you think they were this time?''

She answered with a question of her own. ''Were they?''

The Deal

He met her look for a long moment before answering. "I think they were."

"Do you want to tell me about it?"

"No."

"Then I'll accept your word for it."

And she intended to, he could see it in her eyes. That was the reason why, after a long pause, Luke began to speak. "I rode with General Bedford Forrest during the war. Our outfit was a thorn in the side of the Yankees from the word go." He smiled softly in memory. "That had to be the bravest man I've ever known. Did you know he had thirty horses shot out from under him, and still he kept coming back, giving the Yankees hell till he about drove 'em crazy thinking he was some sort of invincible war god? It got to the point that every Union commander south of the Carolinas was obsessed with wiping us out."

His jaw clenched as the memories began to change. "The bluecoats finally got a spy into our outfit. He found out what he could about us, personal things about our families, and sent it back to his commanding officer, Captain Harold Drake." The name was said with such venomous loathing that Jessica felt a shiver run up her spine.

"Drake was determined to exterminate us, and since he couldn't do it honorably, on the field of battle, he chose to do it like the coward he was, by striking from behind."

He stopped talking here, and at the haunted look that came into his eyes Jessica thought he wasn't going to continue. She wasn't sure she wanted him to.

"I was given a weekend pass to go home," Luke finally went on, more to himself than to the woman who listened intently. "I hadn't seen my wife for nearly six months."

Wife! The word hit Jessica like a blow to the stomach.

But Luke wasn't paying any attention to her look of astonishment. He was lost among the ghosts of the past. "I didn't see them until it was too late. Drake and fifteen of his men ambushed me a mile from my home. They beat me until I was unconscious. The next thing I knew, they were throwing water in my face and I was tied to a tree in front of my house."

Jessica swallowed against the lump of dread, knowing she didn't want to hear what she feared was coming. Her voice was a bare whisper. "You don't have to go on."

But Luke was beyond hearing her now. "Drake told me he wanted me to give a message to Forrest—to tell all the men in my outfit about what the Yankees did to troublesome Rebs. They torched the house, and in the light of the flames they held Melinda down on the ground in front of me and . . .'

After several seconds of wrestling down those demons, he continued, his voice hoarse. "Melinda somehow managed to get one of their pistols, but before she got the chance to defend herself against those bastards they shot her."

Jessica's stomach convulsed at the horrible picture his words portrayed.

When Luke continued, his voice had turned to ice. "After that, Drake had two of his men beat me until I was just this side of death. Then, satisfied they'd done about all they could do and leave me alive, they rode off. That was their mistake."

She didn't have to ask what he meant. "So you killed Captain Drake?"

"I killed all of them." The sheer lack of emotion in the statement made it that much more frightening.

"But you were justified. They raped and murdered your wife."

"What they did was considered an 'act of war.' By the time I had healed up enough from their beating to go after them, the war was over. And besides, an ex-Reb doesn't shoot down a captain in the Army—who by then had been sent out West to deal with the Indian problem—even if it is in a fair fight. And you especially don't get away with it when the Territorial Governor happens to be a personal friend of Drake's."

What could she say? *I'm sorry* seemed trite given the pain and injustice he had faced over the last six years. It was no wonder he could be so coldly emotionless sometimes. The rest of the ride passed in silence.

They rode into town to every bit of the curiosity Jessica had expected. The word spread before them like a prairie fire, and people stepped out of stores on both sides of the street to gawk openly as they passed. She knew this must be hard for Luke, and for some ridiculous reason she felt an urge to protect him surge up in her chest. Her protect Luke Cameron! Now, there was a ludicrous thought.

As Jessica pulled the wagon to a halt in front of Langly's mercantile, Luke swung down from the saddle and tied Shiloh to the hitching post. Solicitously he stepped over to help her down from the wagon seat, removing his hands quickly as soon as her feet were on the ground. People gawked, Luke was stonily silent in the face of their censorious stares, and Jessica fumed.

"Thank you," she said sweetly, and when Luke's eyes snapped down to hers in surprise at the words, Jessica smiled.

"I'll wait here," he offered quietly as he glanced at the people who still stood on the boardwalk.

It was then that Jessica realized he thought she was ashamed to be seen with him. The thought filled her with righteous anger against the townspeople, especially after the tragic story she had just heard. She smiled again, holding out her arm. "It's customary for a man to escort his wife," she said softly, for his ears alone.

Luke stared at her arm for a moment as if afraid to touch her.

"You wouldn't want these people to think you regret marrying me, would you?"

The warm, coaxing smile and words did it. Luke took her arm, and together they climbed the steps and passed through the rudely staring crowd to enter the store.

A tiny bell jingled to announce their entrance, and Byron Jessup turned with a welcoming smile on his face that froze when he saw his newest customers. "Mornin', Ms. Randall— ah—I mean . . ." He stuttered into silence at Luke's raised brow.

"It's Mrs. Cameron now, Mr. Jessup," Jessica corrected before Luke had a chance to. He looked at her questioningly, but she merely smiled coolly at the nervous shopkeeper.

Cynthia Strickland

"Uh—yes, ma'am," Jessup answered. "What can I do for you this mornin'?"

"Here's a list of supplies I need," she answered in a too sweet tone, handing him a piece of paper. "And also I'd like you to add ten cents' worth of this candy, please," she went on, gesturing to a large glass jar of peppermint sticks on the counter.

"That for that little girl y'all found?"

Gossip traveled fast. "Yes."

"Heard her parents were ambushed," Byron Jessup said as he took the top off the jar and measured out the candy into a small paper sack. He glanced up at Luke. Jessica's teeth gritted at the implication, and though she usually wouldn't have bothered to respond to such hateful speculation, she did now. "Unfortunately so. They were attacked by outlaws. Only by the grace of God and my husband's intervention was he able to save Heather before they killed her also."

The man's bushy black brows raised nearly to his receding hairline. "Didn't hear about that part of it."

Jessica looked around at the other customers, who were trying to pretend they weren't hanging on every word. Her gaze came back to meet Jessup's and her voice was frosty with disdain. "No, I expect you didn't."

She paid for the purchases without another word, furious at the unjust attitude of these people toward Luke. If they only knew the circumstances, if they only knew him, they'd change their opinions quick enough. She didn't stop to ask herself why she was suddenly being so defensive on his behalf. She simply knew that she hated injustice of any kind.

So caught up in her righteous indignation that she forgot Luke was standing behind her, quietly listening, Jessica whirled and stalked right past him, failing to see his look of amusement mingled with disbelief. Her temper was just to the simmering point as she caught the door with the heel of her hand and pushed it open, stalking out onto the sidewalk—and right into the arms of Benjamin Mateland.

"Whoa there!" Ben said, putting his arms up to steady the female who had just plowed into him. When he saw who he held, his arms remained around her longer than was necessary. "Hello, Jessica."

Recognition had come at the same instant for Jessica, and she quickly disengaged herself from his arms. "Excuse me, Mr. Mateland," she said in a voice that was barely civil, and then only because they were being watched by others on the sidewalk. Didn't these people have lives of their own?

"You seem flustered," Ben pointed out, smiling a crocodile's smile.

Jessica didn't answer, but tried to step around him.

Ben matched her move. "But then a lot of things can happen to fluster a woman alone." He looked around meaningfully. "That murderin' outlaw you married left you already, huh?" he asked quietly, his smile still in place for the benefit of their audience.

Pushed beyond caring by his act, Jessica opened her mouth with a scathing retort, but had it cut off by the deceptively emotionless voice behind her.

"I'm still here, Mateland."

Hearing his booted heals stop behind her, Jessica gave a smile of her own now. "You remember my husband, don't you, Mr. Mateland?" she couldn't resist goading.

Ben scowled blackly. "Figured you'd'a been halfway to Mexico by now, boy."

Luke stepped away from Jessica. "Now, that wouldn't be a very nice thing for a husband to do. Would it? That'd leave my wife all alone to be flustered by bas—"

"As you can see, my husband is still here," Jessica cut in quickly as it suddenly hit her just why he had stepped away from her. The move left a clear path between the Colts on his hips and Benjamin Mateland. "Now, if you'll excuse us, Mr. Mateland . . ."

Turning to Luke, Jessica's eyes pleaded with him not to make a scene in front of the gawking townspeople. He hesitated for a long moment, looking at Mateland, then back to Jessica. The look in those golden-green eyes finally made Luke do something he wasn't accustomed to doing—he turned to walk away from a confrontation.

"Take care, Jessica!"

She grabbed Luke's arm as it came up, and to anyone watching it looked as if he had simply made the gesture of offering her his arm. Only Jessica knew the truth, that she had stopped his hand just short of reaching its goal—the Colt.

Chapter Twelve

For some reason that neither of them questioned, Luke had chosen to make the ride back to the ranch in the wagon. Complete silence had accompanied them for the past mile since they had left Langly, a silence that Luke reluctantly broke now. "I wasn't really going to shoot him, you know," he admitted grudgingly, his eyes locked on the dusty backs of the team.

Jessica turned to stare at his profile. "Then would you care to tell me what that action I prevented was?"

"Reflex."

Was that a smile lurking at the corners of that mustache? Surely not. Surely he couldn't find what they had just gone through funny! "If you didn't intend to shoot him, then may I ask what you did intend to do once your reflex had you aiming a gun at him?"

"Scare the hell out of him, I imagine."

He was smiling! He still wouldn't turn to face her, but that was definitely a smile. Jessica shook her head in utter disbelief. "You really don't mind frightening people, do you?"

The smile faded. "I've found it comes in handy when you're dealin' with bullies."

"Isn't that like bullying a bully?" she asked, fully expecting him to deny the charge. But he said nothing in defense.

They rode in silence for several minutes before Luke finally asked the question that had been eating at him since they arrived in town. "What made you do it?"

She turned to look at him questioningly, but again found him staring at the backs of the horses. "Do what?"

111

"Take up for me with old caterpillar brows."

Jessica had to hide a smile at the apt description. "You mean Byron Jessup?"

He nodded.

"I simply told him the truth, an insignificant matter that gossip usually overlooks."

"But you didn't have to."

You didn't have to take my arm either, Luke thought, wondering why the simple gesture had meant so much to him. *You didn't have to act like you weren't the least bit ashamed of being seen with me. So why did you?* He wanted to ask, but couldn't bring himself to voice the words.

"It was something they didn't want to hear," Jessica was explaining as the question rolled through his thoughts. "Maybe I just wanted them to know what you truly are."

"They know what I am. I'm a murderer."

"No, you're not."

Luke still wouldn't look at her. "What would you call it then?"

"Seeing that justice was done."

Unable to accept her unconditional pardon, he argued, "I hunted down sixteen men and killed them."

She didn't bat an eye. "All in fair fights. And all of whom should have been standing on a gallows instead of you."

Land sakes, but he should have had her at his trial as his lawyer. With her calm conviction he would have walked out of that courtroom with a medal of honor! Still, it was hard to let down his guard and allow someone to defend him. "I don't want your pity," he said gruffly.

"You don't have it," Jessica returned calmly, "at least not in the way you mean. If I felt pity for anyone it would be for the sixteen men who had to face you after what they did. But they deserved it, so I have no pity for them either."

Luke rode in silence for a long while, digesting that. If not out of pity, then why had she defended him so staunchly?

They pulled to a halt in front of the barn, and Luke looped the reins over the brake handle and jumped down. Before he could round the wagon to help Jessica down, Zeke was at her side. "We got a problem, Jess," the Scotsman said without preamble. "Lee come up on someone cuttin' a section o' the fence. They shot 'im."

Jessica's face had lost all color before Zeke realized what his words implied, and he quickly rushed on. "He's not dead. Just took a bullet in the leg is all."

She was already on her way to the bunkhouse before he finished speaking. "Have you sent for Dr. Andrews?"

"Sam's gettin' his horse saddled now. Tim was out with Lee. He'd stopped to mend a slack place in the wire when he heard a shot up ahead. He just got Lee back here a few minutes ago."

Jessica pushed open the door to the bunkhouse, and the men gathered around Lee's bunk looked up, then moved to make a place for her. Allen pulled a chair beside the bunk and she sat down, lines of concern edged deep on her face.

"Lee?"

He opened his eyes and tried to smile, but it came out more as a pained grimace. "I'll be just fine, ma'am," he assured at her frightened look.

Glancing at the bloody cloth over the wound, Jessica went pale once more, and thinking she was close to fainting, Tim quickly spoke up. "It ain't serious. I seen him hurt a lot worse when a bronk near ta kicked his ribs out down in Abilene a couple o' years back."

That didn't reassure her any. "Can I do anything for you until the doctor gets here?" Jessica asked gently, taking his hand in hers.

Lee managed to make the smile a little more convincing this time. "I'm fine, ma'am. Really. Like Tim says, I've had worse."

"Did you recognize the man who did it?"

At the deep-voiced question, Lee's eyes went past Jessica to Luke, and self-consciously he pulled his hand away from hers before he answered. "He was wearin' a bandana over his face. But I'm purty sure I knowed the fella. I seen him at the Waterin' Hole a time or two with . . ." His words trailed off as he looked up at Clayton as if in question.

Luke followed the look between them. "Who was it, Lee?"

Clayton nodded slightly, and Lee's eyes came back to Luke's. "I think I seen him a time or two with the men from the Bar M."

Mateland's ranch.

"Are you sure?" Luke asked.

"Can't be fer sure positive. He pulled his gun when I rode up behind him. I think I spooked him more'n he planned on shootin' me."

There wasn't much difference, in Luke's opinion. Shooting was shooting, no matter the intention. He turned for the door.

Jessica caught up with him on the porch. "Where are you going?"

"Where do you think?"

She grabbed his arm when he would have kept walking, forcing him to turn and face her. "I'm angry too, Luke. But there's no proof Ben was behind this, or that he even knew what was going on if that was one of his men. He was in town when it happened."

"Yeah. Convenient, wasn't it?"

Jessica tried another argument. "What can you do without proof?"

"I can let him know I intend to start shootin' back."

"And they'll shoot back at us, and it will keep going until eventually someone is going to be killed!"

Scowling down at her, Luke demanded, "So what do you suggest we do? Nothing, and hope Mateland decides to leave you alone? It could be you they shoot at next!"

His eyes flashed so dangerously at that thought that Jessica nearly took a step backward. "Lee could tell the sheriff what happened," she offered. "If it could be proved—"

"It can't be!" Luke cut her off. "You heard him say he wasn't positive."

"But you're positive enough to confront Ben?"

"Damn right I am!"

"Why?"

Luke ground his teeth in silence. What could he say? That he hated the man because of the way he looked at Jessica?

Because he wouldn't stand by helplessly again and let another woman he—another woman be hurt, perhaps even killed?

"Please, Luke," Jessica was saying, drawing his attention back to her.

"Let's report it to Sheriff Davis. Even if nothing is found out now, it could help us later when we do find proof against Ben. A string of coincidences can raise some valid doubt."

When she saw that he was starting to waver, she pushed her advantage. "Besides, wouldn't it be better if he doesn't know we're on to him?"

He grumbled an unintelligible reply.

"Please, Luke."

She was still holding on to his arm, looking up at him with a soft, pleading look in her eyes that wiped Benjamin Mateland clear out of Luke's thoughts. Angry at himself for being so susceptible to her pleading, Luke growled, "I'm not accustomed to backin' down from a threat, Jessie. This is twice today I've done it for your sake."

"And I really do appreciate it," Jessica assured him quickly, her breath coming out in a sigh of relief. "Now I'd better get back inside and check on Lee. Will you make sure Frannie keeps Heather in the house until I can explain that everything's going to be all right?"

She was gone before he had a chance to answer, sure he would do anything she asked of him, no doubt. Watching the bunkhouse door close behind her, Luke frowned. He hadn't backed down once in the past six years. Now he had done it twice in one day. Twice! And why? Because he couldn't say no to those pleading golden-green eyes. Because he cared what Jessica thought about him. He cared about her!

Damn!

The doctor arrived an hour later, and close on his heels, Wilford Davis. While Lee was being patched up, the sheriff questioned Jessica and the men on what had happened. They told him everything Lee had said, but as Luke had pointed out, without a positive identification there was really very little Wilford could do but question the man Lee suspected. Luke was sure that Ben's cowhand would have a dozen witnesses at the Bar M willing to vouch that he was nowhere near Circle R property at the time of the shooting.

The graying lawman seemed somewhat surprised when Jessica walked him out onto the porch of the bunkhouse after he had spoken with Lee and quietly asked him not to question Mateland's hired hand.

"Can I ask why not?" Wilford wanted to know.

"I have my reasons, Sheriff. I just ask that you write this down so I'll have it later—if I need it for any reason."

He frowned at that, having heard the gossip of the run-in between Luke and Ben in town. "Is there anything goin' on I should know about, Jessica?"

"No."

"Things goin' okay with you an' the—your husband?"

"Things are going fine, Sheriff. Why do you ask?"

"Oh, I don't know. Maybe because you come into town an' married a gunslinger right off the gallows, a man you hadn't ever laid eyes on before that day. Then there's a scene in town between him an' Mateland when the two of 'em shouldn't even know each other. Then one of your hands gets shot by a man he's purty sure is one of Mateland's men. Then you ask me not to question the man, but to write it down so you'll have it later. Now, you tell me why I'd be questionin' a situation like this?"

He was looking at her probingly as he finished, and Jessica couldn't quite meet his gaze. "What would you say if I told you it was all coincidence?"

Wilford snorted. "I'd say—with all due respect to you as a lady, of course—that you were lyin' through your teeth. I'd also want to know why. Is that gunslinger causin' you trouble, Jessica? Cause if he is, I can—"

"No!" Jessica replied quickly, meeting his gaze now to assure him that she was telling the truth. "Lu—Mr. Cameron has done nothing but help me. I told you how he saved Heather when you came out here last week."

Wilford studied the young woman in front of him for a long

moment. She was so defensive of her husband he had to wonder . . .

"I'll be goin' then—for now," Wilford said after a long pause. "But I'll warn you to let me know if any more *coincidences* happen out here."

"Yes, Sheriff."

She stood on the porch as the frowning lawman swung into the saddle. He looked at her one more time, then tipped his Stetson and turned to ride off. With a heavy sigh Jessica crossed the yard to her house, hoping fervently to never see another day like this one.

In the next few days it seemed that Jessica's wish was to be granted. There were no more incidents, Lee was mending well, and everything on the ranch ran smoothly. Besides that, the tension that had existed between her and Luke before they went into town had thawed considerably, a situation everyone noticed. But while the hands seemed relieved at the change, Zeke and Frannie couldn't hide their concern. Jessica found herself taking a defensive pose more than once with the older couple. It seemed she could find no peace either, for if she left the house to escape Frannie's dire predictions, she was invariably cornered by Zeke, who lit into her on the folly of trusting an outlaw.

Finally, on the morning they joined forces to attack her in her own kitchen over what was supposed to be an amiable start to their day over coffee, Jessica had had enough. "That's it!" she broke in on Zeke, slamming her coffee cup down on the oak table with an angry thump. "I've heard all I'm going to hear of your dire warnings about Luke Cameron. Now it's my turn to talk, and I think what I have to say just might change your opinion of the man."

The couple looked surprised at her outburst, but Jessica refused to apologize as she went on, "I usually don't repeat what someone tells me, because I figure it's their business and they'll tell who they want to know. But in this case I'm going to break that rule. I assume neither of you know why Luke was to be hanged?"

117

"He's a murderer," Zeke answered gruffly, hurt by the thought that his Jess was taking sides with a gunfighter against himself and Frannie.

"No, he's not! At least he's not what you think. I believe that when you hear what happened you'll change your minds quick enough."

Zeke's look was belligerent, and Jessica threw up her hands in exasperation. "Are you going to listen, Zeke? Or are you going to close your ears and continue to judge him by what you think, instead of by the truth?"

Frannie reached over and took her young friend's hand in a calming gesture. "We're gonna listen, darlin'. Just remember we're only worried about you."

"I know you are," Jessica said with a long sigh. "But I'm trying to tell you that you don't need to be. Luke is a good man."

Slowly, with more emotion than she thought she would feel, Jessica began to relate the story Luke had told her. She watched the faces of her friends, seeing the belligerence give way reluctantly as they listened to the sad story.

Zeke, who loved his dear Frannie, couldn't help but be moved by the thought of how he would have reacted under those same circumstances. Grudgingly he felt distrust melt away, to be replaced by a growing respect for the man he hadn't cared a lick for just a few short minutes ago. He could understand the injustice of it also. Hadn't the Scots fought for centuries against the English and their weighted sense of justice? How many of his own ancestors had become outlaws simply for trying to protect their families against British soldiers?

"Don't you think so, Zeke?"

Shaken from his thoughts Zeke looked up at Jessica's question. "What did ya say, darlin'?"

She frowned but asked her question again. "I said, don't you think we could be a little more welcoming? He could be the difference between Ben getting away with trying to run us off the ranch, or putting a stop to it."

"I say we help the man," Zeke answered, giving a grin as

Jessica's jaw nearly dropped to the tabletop. He couldn't control the laugh at her reaction to his words. "After all, Cameron is a good Scottish name."

Jessica could only shake her head in disbelief at the turnaround in his attitude. She turned to her other companion, hoping for the same change. "And what about you, Frannie? Will you give Luke a chance?"

The older woman was less willing to do the about-face her husband had, probably because her concerns in this matter were different from his. Zeke had worried about Luke taking advantage of Jessica physically. But Frannie saw with a woman's eye her young friend's reaction to the gunfighter. Her fear was that Luke Cameron was going to steal Jessica's heart, then ride out of her life. Knowing most of Jessica's past, through what John had been able to tell her, Frannie was afraid her friend couldn't survive another heartbreak such as she had suffered at her father's hands.

"Frannie?"

Looking into the hopeful eyes, the older woman finally relented a bit. "I'll admit we misjudged him." But at the relieved look that told Frances she was justified in her concerns, she went on, "But I hope you won't go givin' him all yer trust too soon."

Jessica frowned at the strange look. "But he's proved I can trust him."

"Aye, you can trust him to do his job here. Just don't you be forgettin' that when it's over and done with, he'll be ridin' away."

Jessica was about to assure the older woman that she could hardly forget the terms of her own deal with the man, but for some reason when she thought about Luke actually leaving, she remained silent. With a catch that came dangerously close to her heart, she wondered just how she was going to react when it came time for Luke Cameron to ride out of her life, forever.

Chapter Thirteen

With all the cattle sold except for those to be kept as breeding stock, the work on the ranch decreased considerably for the cowboys. The hay had been cut and was stored in the hayloft above the barn. The mustangs had all been broken, with half being sold to the livery owner in Langly, and supplies had been bought and stored for the coming winter. Jessica and Frannie had picked the last of the vegetables from the garden, and with Heather's help had put up everything they could. Now came the time of year when long days of hard work gave way to shortening days that left more leisure time for everyone.

The men whiled away the hours between chores playing cards or practicing rope tricks that Sam and Allen taught them from their days in Texas. Zeke and Frannie spent more time at their own home, preparing for the coming months of frigid temperatures. Jessica worked on teaching Heather her alphabet by the song she had learned from her own mother so many years ago. Still, while everyone else went about their everyday lives, Luke waited for Benjamin Mateland to make his next move.

It had been three weeks since Lee had been shot. The men rode out in threes now to check the fence line each day, but so far there had been no further trouble. While everyone else on the Circle R enjoyed the peaceful interlude, Luke saw it as just that, a passing reprieve that would soon be broken. Ben wanted them to become complacent. He was hoping the incident with Lee would be put down to rustlers. He was wisely biding his time so that his next move wouldn't cause suspicion with anyone outside the Circle R.

Waiting had always been the hardest part for Luke. Timing was an element Bedford Forrest had utilized to his full advantage, and a young and impatient Luke had often had to grit his teeth when faced with hours, and sometimes days, of waiting for just the right moment to strike.

Luke had learned a lot from his commanding officer's experience, however. It had given him the patience to spend five years traveling all over this country and Mexico as well, following every lead to track down Drake and his men. Purposely, Luke had saved the captain for last as he methodically sought justice on those who had raped and murdered Melinda. Because Drake had ordered the acts, Luke held him the one most accountable for them, and had dealt with him last. Through those long years it had taken to exact his revenge, Luke held on to the hope that the final act of facing Drake, of looking into the man's eyes as he died for his sins against Melinda, would finally release him from the nightmares.

He had finally caught up with Drake over six months ago in Texas. From the start, Luke had been adamant that all sixteen men would face him for what they had done. He wanted to look into their eyes and see fear, a fear like that Melinda had suffered at their hands, before they died. Methodically he had hunted down all fifteen men who had ridden with Drake, no small feat since with the end of the war they seemed to have scattered to the four corners of the country. But each one in turn had paid for his part in Melinda's murder, until only the captain was left. And even though the man didn't deserve it, Luke had walked into the saloon in Austin and challenged him to a fair fight.

It was a testament to Drake's cowardice that he had drawn as Luke turned toward the door. Only a gilt-framed mirror hanging beside the door had given away the captain's intent, bringing Luke back around in time. Even then the federal government had considered it murder that an ex-Reb had killed the captain they had sent out West to handle the escalating Indian troubles. It was only after his arrest in Langly that Luke found out that Wyoming's Territorial Governor had been a close personal friend of the late Captain Harold Drake. When the sharp young lawyer did some investigating and found out about the demise of the other fifteen men who had ridden with Drake in similar gunfights, fifteen more counts of murder were tacked on to the charges.

Luke had to smile as he thought of the impotent rage the Governor was going to feel when he discovered, if he hadn't already, that despite his railroading tactics, Luke hadn't been hanged after all, that one of his government's own laws had saved him from their so-called justice.

Jessica was being held in Luke's arms as he kissed her tenderly. Her hands moved up that muscled expanse of chest to twine behind his neck as the kiss deepened. But then suddenly, like trying to catch a wisp of smoke, he was gone. She opened her eyes to see only his back as he walked away. She called out to him, begging him to come back to her, but he kept walking. His image began to waver. He wasn't as tall anymore. His tawny hair darkened to burnished brown. And now Jessica stood on the stone steps outside a huge, depressingly gray building as she fought the hold of a stern-faced woman who held tightly to her shoulders. She clutched a tiny doll in her arms as she watched the man who slowly disappeared into a thick fog, still ignoring his six-year-old daughter's cries to come back for her.

Jessica tossed on the bed, still hearing the cries of a little girl. In the drowsy state between sleep and wakefulness she shook her head to clear away the last remnants of the dream, but still she couldn't silence the pitiful cries. She finally woke fully enough to notice that the cries weren't coming from her dreams, but from the bedroom next door. Throwing the covers back, she hurried out the door.

This wasn't the first time Heather had experienced the nightmares, and as with the previous ones, Jessica sat down on the side of the bed and pulled the trembling child into her arms. "Another one?" she asked softly.

The dark head beneath her chin nodded.

"Was it the same as the others?"

Again a nod.

Jessica held her close and gently rocked back and forth, rubbing the little back soothingly. She had hoped the nightmares would go away eventually, since Heather had told her that first night when she woke crying that she hadn't seen what happened. But the child had heard everything. She had lost both parents in one cruel twist of fate. Even at so young an age, when the daylight hours might convince them she was healing from the blow, the nighttime hours told Jessica it would be a long while before the little girl fully dealt with her loss.

"Wi' you sing to me, Jess'ca?"

At the muffled request Jessica began to softly sing the song she had sung for Heather on those other nights, the one her own mother had sung so long ago when she would wake from a bad dream. The memory of those few happy years made her hug Heather closer, and her voice became hoarse.

"Where's your mama, Jess'ca?"

For a moment Jessica wondered if the child could read minds, but decided it was an understandable question given the circumstances. Clearing her throat, she said, "My mama is dead too. She died when I was only a little older than you."

Heather pushed away to look up at her, concern filling her dark brown eyes. "Did bad men kill your mama too?"

"No, sweetheart. My mama got very sick. She got so weak finally that she couldn't fight anymore to breathe and she died."

"But you still had your papa," the little girl tried to console innocently. "God makes sure to yeave us wif someone to take care of us, just yike you said."

Jessica didn't say anything to that, but simply pulled the little head back to her chest and resumed rocking, as much for her own comfort as the child's.

"Jess'ca?"

"Um hmm?"

"I g'ad God gived me to you."

Tears flooded Jessica's eyes until she could barely see through the shimmering veil. "So am I, sweetheart," she answered in a choked whisper. "So am I."

A board creaked in the hall and they both looked up to find a large, shadowy form step into the doorway. "You ladies all right?"

Jessica relaxed at the familiar voice. He sounded a bit hoarse, but she put that down to interrupted sleep. They had all had a long day and he had probably been sleeping soundly. But then if that was the case, how had they awakened him? And just how long had he been standing there?

"I had a bad dream," Heather was explaining.

He took a step into the room and the moonlight shining through the window fell across his face, showing the concern in his eyes. "Are you all right now?"

There was a slight hesitation. "Uh huh."

He looked up to Jessica for confirmation, and she wondered again that a man who could be so emotionless at times could be so caring over a child's nightmare. She nodded at the question in his eyes. "I'll sleep here with her for the rest of the night. You go on back to bed."

He hesitated, then turned to go.

"Yuke?"

Turning back with a gentle smile for the child, he asked, "Yes, puss?"

"Wi' you s'eep wif me too?"

Complete silence filled the room for the space of several seconds. Jessica wouldn't dare meet his gaze as she tried frantically to think of some reason the child would accept as to why Luke couldn't share this bed with them. But the little girl was already in motion. Pressing Jessica down on one side of the bed, Heather snuggled down in the middle and held the corner of the covers up on her other side invitingly. "Come on, Yuke."

Luke looked to Jessica, who had finally worked up the courage to meet his gaze. Her eyes reminded him again of a trapped fox. "I don't think—"

"P'ease," the tiny plea cut him off.

The Deal

This wasn't exactly the way he had pictured his first time sharing a bed with Jessica. And he had pictured it in his mind—every night as he lay alone in his bed downstairs, staring at the ceiling and thinking of his delectable wife so close at hand. But never in those fantasies had he believed their first night together would find a child snuggled contentedly between them. Crossing to stand beside the bed, he looked at Jessica questioningly.

He would put the decision on her! Jessica thought desperately. He stood there wearing only his denims, the moonlight on the broad, bronzed, naked chest making him look like some marble statue of every woman's dream. Worse yet, his tawny hair fell softly across his forehead so appealingly as his eyes asked her permission to join her in bed. It wasn't fair for Heather to put her in this position!

"Darling, Luke is very tired. He could sleep much better in his own—"

"I won't bover him," Heather cut in with quick assurance. "P'ease."

Jessica couldn't find it in her heart to refuse. Swallowing with some difficulty, she looked up at Luke and nodded, looking much as if she were giving him the okay to shoot her.

Heather was the picture of contentment as Luke eased into the bed beside her. She looked up at the two adults with a bright smile, innocently unaware of the maelstrom of emotions churning between them. "G'night," she said happily as she snuggled down between them and immediately closed her eyes.

Luke met Jessica's nearly panicked gaze over the tiny head between them, and the situation suddenly struck him as very funny. It had taken a child to get past Jessica's defenses and get him into her bed. If he knew his fiery little fox, she was caught somewhere between panic and thwarted anger right now at being manipulated, however innocently, into this position. At the thought, he grinned as he said, "Good night, Heather." Then, when his eyes rose once more to meet Jessica's, they were gleaming like sun-washed ice as he added devilishly, "Good night, Jessica. Sweet dreams."

125

Grinding her teeth in the face of that infuriatingly knowing grin, Jessica angrily rolled away from him to stare at the wall. It was obvious this situation didn't trouble him at all. He wasn't the least bit uncomfortable about spending the night in the same bed. The thought angered her, while at the same time it stung her feminine ego that he could be so unaffected by her while she was so excruciatingly conscious of him! Fighting hard to think of something—*anything!*—other than the man beside her, Jessica sought an elusive sleep.

It would have eased her mind considerably if she could have read Luke's thoughts at that moment. Then again, maybe it wouldn't have, for he was exceedingly conscious of how very close she was. He was remembering every detail of how she had looked sitting curled up on the bed in the moonlight with her hair hanging in an unbound mass of curls to her waist with that soft, innocent cotton gown teasing him to explore the feminine secrets it hid. His hands were fairly itching to do just that, and he had to forcefully remind himself of the child that lay like an impenetrable fortress wall between them.

Stifling a groan, Luke turned away from the temptation that lay just inches away yet was as far from his reach as ever. He suddenly realized that Heather really hadn't done him a favor after all by committing him to spending a night so close to the temptation of Jessica's warm body. Punching the pillow up beneath his head, he tried to find a comfortable position, though he really didn't know why. It was a sure bet he wasn't going to get any sleep this night.

Luke woke near dawn to a small pair of knees pressed into his back, and it took his sleep-fogged brain a moment to remember where he was. Carefully he rolled over. The picture that met his gaze in the pale gray light coming through the window caused him to pause a moment in appreciative silence. Jessica lay on her side facing him, her hair spilling across the pillow to surround that exquisitely lovely face, flushed now in sleep. The dark head of hair snuggled into the hollow beneath her chin framed a face of nearly equal feminine beauty in miniature. They were cuddled together, with Jessica's arm wrapped protectively around the child. The picture caused Luke's heart to ache with want.

For a brief unguarded moment he let himself dream. He imagined that this was his home, that this beautiful woman and child were his family. He conjured up an image of those thick black lashes fluttering open to reveal golden-green eyes that would smile a sleepy smile of love on seeing him. They'd quietly climb out of bed and tuck the covers around their sleeping child, then sneak away to their own room for a leisurely hour of early morning loving to start the day.

But reality quickly intruded to ruin the golden glow of his dreams. Jessica may understand now why he had done the things he had, but that didn't mean she would ever let herself care for a man like him. Luke knew well enough he couldn't ask her to take on the kind of life being his wife would entail. As long as he wore the label of gunslinger, there would always be some up-and-comer looking to prove himself. With resigned certainty, he knew that the day would eventually come when one of them would be that split second faster. It wasn't fair to ask Jessie to wait for that day. It wasn't fair to ask her to continue to live with the condemnation of the townspeople either. Still, knowing all that didn't make it any easier to accept the bleak future that stretched before him.

With a deep feeling of regret, Luke allowed himself a few more minutes to look longingly on the one thing he wanted above all else, but could never have: a family.

When he finally moved to ease out of bed he heard Jessica stir. He turned to see her eyes flutter open just as he had imagined they would, and for the briefest instant, caught between dreams and reality, she smiled. Luke felt his heart tighten painfully. Dear God, what he wouldn't give to have the life that smile promised.

"Go back to sleep, Jessie," he whispered finally, his voice sounding a bit hoarse. "It's still early."

The door closed behind him before Jessica surfaced from sleep enough to realize he hadn't been a dream. Snuggling back down in the warm covers, she pulled a still sleeping

Heather closer into her arms. With a puzzled frown, she lay there for several minutes just staring at the closed door wondering why, after so many years of sleeping by herself, the sight of that closing door suddenly made her feel so alone.

Chapter Fourteen

When Jessica came downstairs an hour later, she found a pot of coffee sitting on the back of the stove and an abandoned cup on the table. Trying not to recognize her reaction to the empty kitchen as disappointment, she began to set out the ingredients for Heather's favorite pancakes. Unfortunately, the activity of making breakfast didn't keep her mind from wandering back to last night.

She had only been intimate that one time with John, and that had ended with both of them racked by guilt. He had left her room without a word, and by silent, mutual consent they had never shared a bed again. Jessica had never really had the desire to share her bed in that way with a man—until Luke walked out this morning. What probably troubled her the most was that she didn't even know *why* she seemed to want that with him, not if it would be anything like it had been with John. Not that John had intentionally hurt her. She had realized then that it was only the combination of whisky and grief that had made him come to her at all that night.

Some small voice told her now that it wouldn't be the same with Luke. There was that strange tingling she'd felt on those two occasions when he kissed her that Jessica still couldn't explain. Then there was the warm weakness that seemed to afflict her knees when his voice took on that husky tone that always accompanied his teasingly suggestive remarks. If it weren't for the fact that she only felt these disturbing feelings when Luke was around, Jessica would be concerned that she had developed some strange illness. Knowing that it wasn't an illness made her even more afraid when she considered what

Cynthia Strickland

the reason could be for her reactions.

Setting the bowl of batter on the counter to rise for a few minutes, she poured herself a cup of coffee and stepped over to the window. Leaning against the frame, she took a sip of the steaming brew and looked out over the yard toward the barn, only to find the object of her disturbing thoughts talking to Sam and Allen. The three of them were preparing their horses to ride out and check the fence line, but her eyes were only for the man in the blue cotton shirt and snug-fitting denims.

He wore the familiar tan Stetson, but all Jessica seemed able to see was the memory in her mind's eye of how his tawny hair had looked this morning, all sleep-tousled as he softly whispered for her to go back to sleep. How would it feel to have Luke as her husband in fact? Jessica let herself wonder for one, dangerous moment. How would it feel to be loved by such a man? To be looking out at him now and know he would be coming home to her tonight? That he would always be coming back home to her?

From experience Jessica knew it was a dangerous path her imagination traveled, for down this road lay pain such as she never wanted to experience again. Before she could weaken further to his undeniable pull, she turned away from the window just as the three men mounted up. For some reason she didn't want to watch Luke's back as he rode away.

By the time the black-iron frying pan was hot enough to start cooking the pancakes, Frannie was tapping on the back door. At Jessica's call the older woman came in and immediately crossed to stand beside the cook stove. "There's a definite nip in the air this mornin'," she said with a slight shiver as she held her hands out to the welcoming warmth of the stove. "Won't be too much longer 'til we'll be gettin' snow."

That was another thought Jessica tried to avoid. How was she going to handle the long months ahead when she would be virtually trapped in this house with Luke for days at a time because of the snow? Maybe it would be better for all of them if she asked him to move back into the bunkhouse soon.

"Frannie?"

The older woman was sipping coffee now. "What is it, darlin'?"

Jessica didn't look up as she poured a ladleful of batter into the sizzling butter in the pan. "How did you feel when you first met Zeke?"

Frannie had been watching the pan, but at the question she looked up, worry filling her eyes. "Why do you ask?"

"I'm just curious," Jessica answered lightly as she watched the bubbles pop up on the frying pancake.

She didn't fool the older woman. "Curious why?"

Heather came in at that moment rubbing sleep from her eyes with one hand as she pulled on the side of her little cotton nightgown with the other. "Jess'ca, where'd Yuke go? Ya'll yeft me ayone in bed."

Frannie's brows nearly disappeared into her fading red hair as her gaze swung back to her friend.

"Luke had work to do, sweetheart," Jessica explained, concentrating her gaze on the sleepy-eyed child. "You go on back upstairs and wash your face and comb your hair now. Breakfast is just about ready."

The muffled sound of little bare feet had barely disappeared up the steps when Frances couldn't hold the question back any longer. "*Ya'll* left her alone in bed?"

"She had another nightmare. I went in to comfort her, and Luke heard voices and came to check on us."

"And so he spent the rest o' the night in bed with ya?" Frannie asked sarcastically. "How good o' him."

"Yes, it was!" Jessica defended angrily. "He was on his way back downstairs when Heather begged him to stay with her too. She slept between us all night—without any further nightmares, I might add!"

"Ye're bein' defensive again."

"I have to! You're accusing me of—of—"

"Of maybe feelin' like I did when I met Zeke?" Frannie asked shrewdly.

Jessica looked back to the stove as she flipped the pancake over. Her shoulders sagged. "I don't know," she answered so

131

quietly that the older woman had to strain to catch the words. "I don't know how I feel. He's so different than I expected when I came up with this ridiculous plan. He was supposed to be a conscienceless gunfighter. He was supposed to stay in the bunkhouse and do his job and then go away. He wasn't supposed to be decent and honorable and . . ."

"And you weren't supposed to care for him?" Frannie asked softly.

Jessica silently nodded, then sighed. "I know you don't like him, Frannie."

"I don't want you gettin' hurt, darlin'," the Scotswoman corrected as she slipped her arm around her young friend's waist and hugged her. "Ye're like a daughter to me an' Zeke. Neither of us wants ta see ya come ta care for the man an' then him ride out on ya."

So Jessica wasn't the only one who saw the possibility of just that happening. "But how do I keep from—caring? He's a good man, and I know he means to help me with Ben for just that reason."

"Are ya sure it's not just gratitude ye're feelin'?" Francis asked hopefully. "Ya know how ya take ta all the boys that come through here like a mama hen to her chicks. Are ya sure it's not the same ya feel fer Luke?"

Jessica met the older woman's gaze thoughtfully. "I don't know. He's—well—he's kissed me—twice." Frances gasped indignantly but Jessica rushed on before the woman could interrupt. "And, Frannie, I felt the strangest tingling down my arms. And sometimes—I get weak in the knees just hearing his voice."

Frances's face paled. "Is that all?"

There was a hesitation. "No."

The Scotswoman looked as if she didn't want to hear any more, but Jessica went on anyway. "I can't understand it, but I get railing mad whenever someone says or does anything that I think might hurt his feelings, even madder than when they do things to hurt me. I know it's crazy, but I want to protect him. Can you imagine that?"

The Deal

Francis turned away to look out the window for a long moment in silent contemplation.

"Frannie?" Jessica asked hesitantly. "What does that sound like to you?"

When the older woman turned to face her young friend, she gave a very long sigh. "Much as I don't like sayin' it, it reminds me of exactly how I felt when I met Zeke."

Allen frowned at his brother, who shrugged in return at the silent question. Allen tried again. "Luke?"

Just realizing he had been spoken to, Luke looked over at his companions. "Sorry, d'you say something, Allen?"

"Yeah," Allen answered with a laugh, "but you were a hundred miles away. Problems?"

Yes, he had problems. He couldn't get the picture of Jessica lying there in that white gown, holding Heather close while they both slept, out of his mind. It worried him more because he was picturing the little girl too. That proved that it wasn't simple lust he was feeling. The alternative, he didn't even want to think about.

"Luke?"

At the amused call he looked over again to find both men grinning.

"You were smilin' so I guess we don't have ta ask who you're thinkin' about," Sam said.

"Yeah, you're a lucky son of a gun," Allen agreed. "I had me a woman like Ms. Jessica I'd be smilin' too. Might even be tempted ta marry her."

Luke didn't take offense, knowing how all the men felt about Jessica. "She's a special lady all right."

"Ain't many women like her," Sam put in his opinion. "She's a lady through and through. But she don't turn up her nose like she's better'n anybody else. Treats us hands like we're family too. That's why most of us hang around through the winter 'stead of driftin' on down south."

Allen nodded his agreement. "Guess you weren't expectin' ta get a family this soon, though. But I tell ya, that Heather can sure wrap a man around her little finger. 'Nother ten or twelve years, she's gonna have the boys followin' around behind her like bees after honey." He grinned. "Ya better keep them Colts close at hand, *Daddy*."

Luke forced a smile for his friends' benefit, but inside he felt a sharp pain that he wouldn't be around to watch Heather grow into the beautiful young lady she promised to be. He could almost picture himself standing on the front porch wearing his Colts as he faced down yet another beau, putting the fear of God into the boy before he stepped aside to let Heather join her young man to go to a barn dance or picnic. He'd be hell on the boys, but only because Luke could remember all too well what he had been like at that age!

And while he was trying to scare off Heather's latest unworthy beau, Jessica would probably be inviting the boy in through the back door for cake and lemonade, Luke thought with a wry grin. That woman took in folks who came to her house like anyone else might take in stray animals.

But then he remembered their trip into town. Jessica didn't take to everyone. In fact, she could get downright icy when someone did something to rub her the wrong way. With a strange feeling in his chest, Luke remembered what Jessup had done that day to anger her. It was the first time in his life Luke had ever stood back and let someone else take up for him, and the main reason he had done it then was out of pure shock. She had looked like an indignant avenging angel as she frostily stared down everyone in the store before turning on Jessup to put him in his place.

It still puzzled him as to why she'd done it. The only answer he could come up with was that, like Sam said, she treated everyone on the Circle R like family. She probably felt it her duty to defend him out of loyalty. Or maybe she just did it to make herself look better in the townspeoples' eyes, like she hadn't made such a horrendous mistake in marrying a "murdering gunslinger."

Whatever the reason, Luke wasn't going to see her defense of him as anything more than what she would do for any of the men who worked for her. And no matter how many times he pointed out differently, Jessica still only saw him as someone who worked for her.

"You think Lucinda Phillips'll be there?"

Sam's question brought Luke from his thoughts to the conversation going on between the men who rode beside him. "Don't see why not," Allen answered his brother. "Everyone always goes to the McCalisters' shindig."

"Yeah, but Reverend Phillips acts like anytime a person's havin' fun they gotta be sinnin'," Sam complained. "I don't know if he's gonna let his daughter come to a *dance*! It plum puzzles me how such a ornery, ugly old scarecrow like him made such a sweet, purty little thing like Lucinda."

Luke was in full agreement with Sam's perception of the good reverend, but right now something else had caught his attention. "Dance?" he asked curiously.

"You been off daydreamin' again?" Allen asked with a laugh. "We been talking about the McCalisters' big barbecue an' barn dance for the last five minutes. It's the biggest event around these parts. Everybody goes."

"Ms. Jessica always enjoys it," Sam added. "She an' Ms. McCalister are good friends."

Luke felt a second's dread at the thought of an entire day spent forcing himself to be civil to some of the people who only a few short weeks ago had been so eager to hang him. He would have to, though, for Jessie's sake. These people were her neighbors, her friends. He couldn't expect her to turn down their invitation just because he wasn't thrilled with their guest list. Jessie needed a little fun in her life after what she had been through in the past few months, and he wasn't going to be the one to keep her from it. Besides that, putting up with a few glares from the holier-than-thous seemed a small price to pay for an entire evening of holding his beautiful wife in his arms.

At about the same moment Luke was planning their evening together, Jessica was answering the knock at the front door. A cowboy she recognized from the Rocking M stood on the porch, his Stetson held respectfully in one hand, an envelope sealed with a red wax rose in the other.

"Hello, Jud," Jessica greeted the man warmly. "Won't you come in?"

" 'Preciate it, ma'am but I can't today. Ms. McCalister's got me deliverin' the invites," he said with a good-natured shake of his head as he handed her the envelope. "Like word don't spread faster'n I can ride all over the countryside givin' out these fancy little envelopes to folks. Don't know why she bothers anyway. She always invites ever'one for a hundred miles around."

Jessica smiled at that. "Ruth just likes to do everything properly, Jud."

"Guess I can understand that," he answered, but it was plain from his perplexed expression that he didn't. "Anyway, I better be goin'. I got a bunch more of these things to deliver." .

When she had closed the door again, Jessica stood staring at the envelope for a long moment. Even though she had been expecting the invitation, she still wasn't sure quite what to do about it. James and Ruth McCalister were the only true friends she had, outside of the people on the Circle R, and as such, she had always made it a point to attend their annual barbecue and barn dance. But that had been when John was still alive. This year things were very different.

Leaning back against the door, Jessica couldn't help but smile at the memory of her first meeting with Ruth McCalister. It had been only two weeks after she and John had left the wagon train and picked out the land where they wanted to build their ranch. Jessica had been riding along the creek that separated the land they had just purchased from that of the neighboring ranch when the sound of pounding hoofbeats from across the creek drew her attention.

A few hundred yards away a cow broke into sight over a hill, but it had been the sight behind the running animal that captured Jessica's full attention. A woman with shoulder-length blond hair was riding hell bent for leather, her slim, denim-clad thighs hugging the horse beneath her as she raised a lasso over her head. With an expert flick of her wrist she sent the rope sailing through the air, snagging the fleeing steer.

It must have been a full minute that Jessica sat there with her lower jaw sagging, nearly to the saddle, she was sure. And it was only the sharp, masculine whistle of approval that came from a dark-haired man who came over the rise then that dragged Jessica from her state of awe. He rode up beside the woman and said something, then the two leaned over to share a kiss that had Jessica looking away in embarrassment at its intimacy. She was about to turn away, hoping that they wouldn't notice her, when they did.

The woman raised a hand and motioned for her to cross the creek, and caught in the act of spying, Jessica could hardly refuse. Whatever she had expected after the scene she had just witnessed, it wasn't the woman she met. In a cultured voice that would have graced the best parlors of the South, Ruth McCalister introduced herself and her husband, James. She seemed to be not the least bit embarrassed at her earlier unladylike display, nor was her husband for that matter. Their very unconventional attitudes endeared them to Jessica instantly.

Over the years Jessica had seen Ruth often, and the two women had become good friends. It had been Ruth who taught her how to guide a horse with her knees, leaving her hands free when herding cattle. She had also been the one to convince Jessica of the necessity of wearing denims, and had even presented her with a pair made by Mr. Levi Strauss. John had just shaken his head and laughed with James over their "cowgirls."

Drawn away from the memories and back to the issue at hand, Jessica tapped the invitation against her chin, thinking. If she went to the barbecue, everyone would naturally expect her husband to attend with her. She knew that James and Ruth would be kind, it was just their way not to be judgmental of others, but she wasn't sure how the other guests would react to "that gunfighter" in their midst, socializing with them.

Jessica gave a derisive snort. Who was she trying to kid? Most of the people who would be there were the same ones who had so eagerly attended Luke's scheduled hanging! She knew *exactly* how they would treat him. Which was exactly why she was so adamant that she was going to deny them the satisfaction.

Chapter Fifteen

Two days went by during which Luke waited for Jessica to tell him about the upcoming barbecue and dance. He'd given her ample opportunity, lingering over his coffee in the morning while she was clearing away the breakfast dishes, finding chores to do that would take him into the house for something, but still she'd made no mention of it. It was Friday afternoon now and the barbecue was to be Sunday, which could only mean one thing. She didn't intend to go.

As he worked in the barn repairing a frayed cinch on a saddle, Luke thought of all the reasons Jessica could have for not attending an event that Allen said she wouldn't have dreamed of missing in the past. Always he was brought to the one reason that made sense: she was ashamed for her friends to see how low she had sunk in marrying noose bait.

Tying off a knot with an angry jerk, Luke told himself it was just what he ought to expect. He wouldn't recognize the pain he felt in finding out that Jessica was ashamed to be seen with him. Facing a few self-righteous gossips in town was one thing, but introducing him as her husband to her friends was another. These McCalisters had probably been good friends with John as well. They'd probably gotten together at their barbecues and church socials and talked about roundups and the price beef was bringing on the hoof and whether it was going to be a long winter, or a dry summer, or whatever the hell ranchers talked about.

He could picture the McCalisters now. Why he could almost see the oh-so-proper Mrs. McCalister swooning when she was introduced to the ''murdering outlaw'' poor Jessica had been forced to marry. Of course, it seemed doubtful the lady was going to get the opportunity to swoon, for it was more than evident that Jessica had no intention of being seen with—

"Luke?"

It was probably the worst moment Jessica could have chosen to appear in the doorway, for Luke had worked his temper to the boiling point and he just needed one small thing to give him cause to vent his rage. Unfortunately for Jessica, she was much more than *one small thing*.

Luke turned on her, his eyes like twin blue flames. "And what brings you out to the barn with the hired help, boss lady?"

Jessica could only blink in confusion at the unexpected attack. "What?"

Turning back to the cinch so he wouldn't have to look at her beautiful, heartless face he growled, "I asked what you wanted."

She took a hesitant step forward, wondering why he was in such a foul mood. "I—have something I need to talk to you about."

His hands stilled for a second, then went on tying off another knot. "Go on," he said with less hostility. Had he been wrong about her? Was she going to tell him about the dance after all?

"I was thinking we ought to tell the men about what's going on with Ben. After the incident with Lee, I think they need to be aware of the danger when they see the men from the Bar M at the . . . in town," she quickly amended.

Luke spun on her so suddenly that Jessica jumped back a step. "Go ahead and say it!" he ground out angrily. "When they see them at the barbecue Sunday. That was what you almost let slip, wasn't it, Jessica?"

"You know about that?" she asked quietly.

"Of course I know about it! It's being given by your good friends the McCalisters, isn't it? You are planning on going, I assume?"

Jessica's gaze fell to the hay at her feet. "Well—no—I thought I might—skip it this year."

He was standing in front of her before Jessica could even think to retreat. "Surely not!" he bit out sarcastically. "Why, the boys tell me it's *the* event in Langly. They say you *never* miss it. Now, why on earth would you want to break with tradition this year, pray tell?"

His eyes were glittering like chips of ice by the time he finished, but Jessica couldn't understand for the life of her just why he was so angry. "I just don't—feel like going this year," she tried to explain calmly.

He took a step that brought him so close she could feel the warmth of his body radiating through his shirt front. "You're lyin', Jessica! Why don't you tell me the real reason? Why don't you admit I'm good enough to protect your precious ranch, but you don't want to remind everyone you were so desperate that you had to marry a condemned gunslinger?"

She could only stare for a moment in disbelief. "That's what you think?"

"What's the matter, Jess? Your friends don't know about Mateland? You afraid they'll think you were just desperate for a man? After all, good old John's been gone for months now. You've been a long time without—"

The crack of her palm against his cheek cut him off.

"You can rave like a lunatic all you want," Jessica spat out, angry now herself, "but don't you ever bring John into it again! He was a good man!"

In Luke's present frame of mind, that was about the worst thing she could have said. He grabbed her by the shoulders and jerked her hard against his chest, his arms going around her to lock like steel bands. Jessica struggled against his hold but it was useless. Still, she met his blazing gaze defiantly.

"Let go of me, Luke, or I swear I'll scream this barn down around your ears."

Driven by an emotion he wouldn't admit to as jealousy, Luke's tone became biting. "I want to hear more about *good old* John," he said, tightening his arms until she stilled. "I want to know what he did to make you think he was such a *good* man. Was it this?"

His mouth descended like a red-hot brand on the spot where

141

Jessica's neck sloped into her shoulder, and she gasped at the tidal wave of sensations that washed over her. She knew she should struggle, should curse him with every foul name she had ever heard for the way he was talking so disrespectfully about John's memory, but her throat had suddenly gone dry.

"Did he make you feel this?" Luke was asking as his hand came around to close with insistent pressure over her breast. At her moan he loosened his grip slightly, sliding his palm, then thumb, over the sensitive crest in a caressing motion that had her trembling.

The anger that had boiled within him was quickly turning to desire as Luke felt the resistance draining from her body. She was actually pressing against him now, and he released his punishing hold to let his free hand wander over the soft curves hidden beneath her skirts.

As if they had a will of their own, Jessica's arms crept up and around his neck. Her fingers sank deeply into the tawny hair that fell below his collar. Somewhere in the back of her mind it registered that his hair was as soft as she had imagined it would be, but then his lips started blazing a trail of liquid fire up her neck that instantly incinerated all thought, leaving only sensation.

"Your skin tastes so sweet," Luke whispered huskily against her shoulder. "Like sun-warmed honey."

Her head tilted to one side to allow him better access to the slender column of her throat as each kiss sent a fresh wave of heat coursing through her body. She gave a deep moan of pleasure that registered in the pit of Luke's stomach.

"You like that, don't you, Jessica?"

Another moan was all she could manage in answer.

"I make you feel good, don't I?"

"Yes." It was a breathless sigh.

He pulled away slightly and waited until her eyes fluttered open. "I can make you feel a lot better," he promised in a husky growl. "But not here where we might be disturbed. Come with me to the house."

The spell was broken by his words, and Jessica's face suddenly flamed with embarrassment as she looked around the barn to make sure none of the men had witnessed her wanton behavior. She stepped back so quickly that Luke was taken off guard and didn't have time to think of stopping her. Straightening her dress kept her from having to meet his gaze. It was the hardest thing she had ever done, but Jessica brought her pounding heart under control enough to mask her tone with an indifference she was far from feeling as she said, "I believe we were discussing the barbecue."

Now it was Luke's turn to blink in surprise. Just seconds ago she had been clinging to his neck as if her legs wouldn't hold her up. Her ability to be so indifferent now kindled his anger anew.

"What?"

"The barbecue. Sunday. We were talking about—"

"I remember what the hell we were talking about!" Luke cut her off with an angry growl. "You were going to admit the real reason you don't want to go!"

"No, I wasn't."

He took a threatening step forward, suddenly deciding he might just put her indifference to the test. "If that's the case, then you won't mind the alternative—going to the house with me."

Jessica retreated from the heat of his gaze as much as from the threat his words held. She couldn't let him touch her again or she might lose what little common sense she had held on to a moment ago and give in to his suggestion. "I'm not staying home for the reason you think," she said quickly, retreating a step to match the one he took toward her.

Luke gave the slightest grin. Good. The intimidation was working. "Then you shouldn't mind telling me the real reason you don't want to go."

"Does it really matter?" Jessica asked, blanching at the note of desperation that came through despite her efforts to sound calm.

He shrugged. "I guess not." Her shoulders sagged in relief before he finished. "If you don't want to talk, then we'll just get back to what we were doing. And come to think of it, the house is too far away. I think the hayloft will do just fine."

Jessica retreated another step, coming up against a stall as she held both hands up protectively. "You made a deal," she reminded quickly. "Strictly business. Those were the terms."

"I'm changin' the terms," Luke said, stepping forward until her palms pressed against his chest. "That is, unless you want to start talkin'."

"That's blackmail!" Jessica gasped in outrage.

"I prefer to think of it as persuasion," he answered in that husky tone that threatened to make her knees buckle.

"I don't want to go!"

He leaned closer until his lips were a hairsbreadth from hers. "Try again, Jessie."

"I don't!"

"Why?"

Land sakes but he was more stubborn than any mule ever thought about being! If she didn't give him some answer to appease him, though, she was afraid he might make good his pro—*threat*—to carry her up into the hayloft. A shiver ran through her at the thought even as she told herself she couldn't let that happen. "I just don't like the guest list," she tried.

Frowning at the desperate look in her eyes, Luke suddenly realized there was one other possibility he hadn't considered for her not wanting to go. "Are you afraid Mateland will try something?" he asked, softening at the thought that she might be frightened. "I'd be there to protect you."

The tender promise had a more devastating effect on her than his kisses, for it struck dangerously close to her heart. "It's not Ben," she answered honestly. "You've proved you can protect me from him. I just don't care to spend the day with some of the people that will be there."

Luke stiffened. "Because of the way you think they'll treat you?" he asked, his tone growing harsh once more.

Closing her eyes, Jessica shook her head. He just wasn't going to let this go until he had the truth, and he would continue to attack her until he had it. With a sigh of resignation she finally met his gaze again. "No, Luke. It's not because of the way I *think* they'll treat *me*, it's because of the way I *know* they'll treat *you*."

144

The Deal

It was the last answer he had expected, given the way his earlier imaginings had so blackened her intentions. He wasn't ready to admit he may have been wrong either. "So without even asking me, you presumed to decide we wouldn't go?"

Jessica was really getting tired of the injustice of his verbal attacks, especially since she had made the decision only to spare his blasted feelings. "Excuse me!" she bit out sarcastically. "I guess I should have come to you and said, 'Hey, Luke, want to go to a party with the same folks who were so eager to watch you hang just a little while ago? Surely they'll feel differently toward you now.'"

Even as she was saying it Jessica couldn't believe those cruel words were coming out of her mouth. Why was it he was always able to bring out the very worst in her?

Luke's eyes narrowed. "Yes, you should have, 'cause then I could have told you I don't give a royal damn what those folks think of me. I could have told you one of the greatest pleasures in my life is buggin' the hell out of people like that by showin' up at their little soirees."

"And that's why you want to go? To irritate everyone there?" Jessica asked, trying hard to control her mounting rage. She had actually worried about his feelings! What a laugh! "The McCalisters are good friends—the only ones I have outside of Zeke and Frannie and the men—and I won't let you go to their barbecue with the sole intention of ruining it!"

She had turned with an indignant huff to walk away, but Luke grabbed her arm and spun her back around to face him. "You won't *let* me go?" he asked in a dangerously quiet tone.

Jessica might be furious, but she wasn't stupid. The look in his eyes made her swallow the biting retort that was pressing to get out. Instead she answered, "You know what I meant. I'm not going if it means ruining Ruth's party. She's too dear a friend."

"And what if I promise I won't do anything to ruin it? Would you go then?"

She eyed him suspiciously. "Why would you want to go if not to irritate people?"

145

Because he wanted to see if she actually would go with him. He wanted to see if her earlier words that she was only concerned about his feelings had been the truth or simply a good-sounding excuse. And because he couldn't get the idea of an entire night of holding her in his arms, even if it was only to dance, out of his mind.

But Luke wasn't going to tell her any of those reasons. "I didn't say I wasn't going to irritate anyone," he offered with a devilish grin. "I'll just do it in ways that your friend won't even notice."

"Because you've mastered the art, I'm sure!" Jessica claimed from her own most recent experience.

The grin broadened. "Of course. But you'll get to see first-hand Sunday."

"I already have!"

"Now, now, Jessica, you don't want to hurt my feelings, do you? I thought that was what you were trying so hard to avoid."

She gave an angry oath and jerked her arm from his grasp. "Don't think I'll ever worry about that again! You don't have any feelings!"

His laughter followed her out the barn door, which Jessica turned to vent some of her anger on with a satisfying slam. Luke Cameron was without a doubt the most irritating, arrogant, infuriating human being she had ever met!

Chapter Sixteen

When Sunday morning dawned it was as if the day had been created especially for a barbecue. The sky was a vibrant blue, the sun was shining, and there was a slight, but refreshing, nip in the air as a reminder that fall was here. Everyone was in high spirits as they rushed around to get chores done so they could start donning their very best party clothes. While the men headed for the creek to bathe, Jessica was busy in the house trying to get herself, as well as Heather, ready.

The little girl was a bundle of excited energy that could hardly be contained long enough for Jessica to dress her. Together they had chosen a flouncy green gingham dress trimmed with yellow ribbons from the trunk of clothes Hank had thought to retrieve from the wagon. The men had quietly brought in the trunk the night they returned from the roundup while Heather was asleep. Luckily the child hadn't questioned how it came to be in her room.

Watching the little girl scamper off at a run, Jessica stood and smiled fondly after her. In just these few short weeks she had come to love Heather completely, and she truly felt the child had come to love her, as well as everyone else on the Circle R. The thought wasn't completely comforting, however, and it brought a slow frown as Jessica thought of how the little girl had come to think so much of Luke. She had become a short little shadow who followed his every move, especially over the last two weeks. That fact was beginning to worry Jessica.

At her young age, it was only natural that Heather would look for two people to fill the void left by losing her parents.

Jessica wanted desperately to accept the role of mother, for she wanted to shower the little girl with all the love she herself had missed out on having. Jessica's only fear was that Heather was starting to look to Luke as a substitute father. She knew all too well the hurt the child would suffer when the day came for Luke to ride out of their—her life. But try as she might, none of her covert attempts to keep them apart had worked so far.

Jessica continued to puzzle over just what she could do about the problem as she climbed the stairs to get dressed. Crossing to the large armoire, she opened the doors for the final decision between the three gowns she had narrowed her choice to.

Over the last few years, since the ranch had started turning a moderate profit, Jessica had allowed herself one concession in spending money in a way some might consider frivolous. Clothes. Growing up in the orphanage, she had always worn someone else's castoffs, dresses that rarely fit and were more often than not nearly worn out by the time she got them. Through those years of growing up she had often watched the carriages ride past the home holding families out for a ride around the city's park. Those young girls had worn beautiful new dresses with matching ribbons in their hair. Jessica's dreams had come to center around someday having a carriage of her own, of riding in the park with a family of her own, and wearing beautiful gowns that were new and belonged only to her. She had never explained any of this to John, but then he never questioned the money she spent on cloth, or even the ready-made dresses she sometimes bought. He seemed to accept it as the simple fact that all women loved pretty clothes.

Dragging her mind from gloomy thoughts of the past, Jessica focused instead on the long day ahead of her. She intended to eat and talk and laugh and dance and generally enjoy herself. And she all but convinced herself her gaiety had absolutely nothing whatsoever to do with the fact that she was going to be doing all of this with Luke Cameron.

Standing there, hanging her hands on the open doors of the armoire, Jessica chewed at her bottom lip in indecision. The green was nice, and it would somewhat match Heather's frock. But then the yellow was so bright and festive, like she was feeling. Then there was the sapphire muslin. She kept coming back to it, as it was one of her favorites. Trimmed with yard upon yard of frothy cream-colored lace, the gown always made Jessica feel so feminine and—well—almost pretty when she wore it. She wouldn't allow herself to think that those were the exact reasons she decided to wear it today.

Luke was lifting the heavy picnic basket into the back of the wagon when he heard a hush fall over the men who stood beside him. He figured it was because Jessica had finally come out and silenced the typical male jokes about women always taking so long to get ready to go anywhere. The cowards were just afraid to keep voicing those sentiments now that she had joined them.

With a teasing remark on his lips, Luke turned, and suddenly saw the reason for the men's silence. The vision standing behind him was one to strike a man speechless. The blue gown had a rounded neck trimmed in lace that showed just enough creamy skin to whet a man's imagination. From there it hugged her slender body to the waist, then fell into a full skirt holding a wide scallop of the same creamy lace near the bottom. That thick mane of burnished hair was piled loosely on top of her head with a few stray wisps left to fall temptingly against her slim neck. The excitement she felt was mirrored in her eyes, making them sparkle like sunlight reflecting off a moss-banked pool.

Luke knew he had never in his life seen anything more beautiful than Jessica at this moment. She was a vision. The kind of woman every man dreamed of—the woman who was married to him yet he couldn't have. It was that thought that made his voice curt now as he growled irritably, "It's about time. We've all been waiting for half an hour!"

The smile faded. The sparkle in her eyes was extinguished as if the inner sun had suddenly been choked out by great black clouds, and seeing the change, Luke felt like a man who had just kicked a puppy. Looking around guiltily at the faces

149

of the men standing beside him, he could see they held about the same low opinion of him.

Clayton cleared his throat in the uncomfortable silence. "If you don't mind my sayin' so, ma'am, it was well worth the wait."

Jessica tried to smile despite the hated sting of tears behind her eyes. What did she care what Luke thought anyway? Probably red satin and black lace garters were more to his taste in a woman's apparel. Her chin came up. "Thank you, Clayton," she said with a bright smile as she swept by Luke without a glance to survey the men around him. "And may I return the compliment? I can't make up my mind which of you is going to break the most hearts tonight."

They all preened at the comment like a bunch of schoolboys that had just impressed a pretty young teacher, Luke thought in disgust. Besides, Clayton was too old to be giving compliments like that. *It was well worth the wait.* That was the kind of thing that—well, hell, it was the kind of thing *he* should have said! Maybe if he had, instead of letting his darn temper speak for him, she might be smiling up at him now instead of acting as if he didn't exist.

"Zeke said to stop by and he and Frannie would follow us," Luke said lightly, hoping to patch things up for his churlish remark. She wouldn't even look at him, but gave a cool nod and turned to Clayton to help her into the wagon.

Lee came out of the bunkhouse then, limping only slightly on his mending leg as he walked beside Heather. The smile on his face was in direct contrast to the serious expression of the child walking beside him. Jessica forgot her own disappointment for a moment and was about to ask what was wrong when Heather's words explained the situation.

"I gonna ride wif Yee. His yeg is't all better yet so I gonna he'p him wif his horse."

Jessica hid a smile as she met Lee's laughing eyes. She looked back at the serious little face. "It's nice of you to take care of Lee, sweetheart. You can help him as far as the gate to the Rocking M, but then you need to ride the rest of the way in the wagon. A lady doesn't arrive at a party riding astride on a horse."

The little girl frowned at this. "But I don't wanna be a yady! I wanna be a cowboy!"

There were a few muffled coughs.

"Girls are supposed to be ladies," Jessica mimicked the words she had so hated hearing as a child, and wanted to shake her head at hearing them come out of her own mouth now.

Heather frowned in confusion. "But you're a cowboy sometimes," she pointed out with childlike simplicity.

Eight pairs of eyes swung back to Jessica at that, and there were several distinctly muffled coughs this time. "I herd cattle when I need to," Jessica tried to explain. "But when I go to town or to a party I try to conduct myself like a lady."

Heather was still frowning.

"Be a cowgirl when no one's looking and a lady when they are," Luke simplified, earning a glare from the woman sitting beside him.

"That's not what I—"

"You want to sit here another hour tryin' to explain it to her?" he asked, a tawny brow arched challengingly.

Grinding her teeth, Jessica jerked around to stare ahead in silent dismissal. The chuckle he gave fueled her anger, but she stubbornly refused to speak. In her present mood she wasn't sure she would ever speak to him again!

When they arrived, the yard at the Rocking M was already filled with people. The men stood in one group by the barbecue pit, passing an earthenware jug between them which they quickly hid whenever Reverend Phillips came within sight. The younger children played together, while the older youths broke up into groups of boys and girls, each pretending they weren't the least bit interested in the other. Meanwhile, the women were unpacking the food they had brought and arranging it on the long tables set up in front of the house.

When Luke pulled the team to a halt, the noise slowly died away and all eyes turned to stare. Even expecting just such a reaction, Jessica still felt her stomach knot at being the center

Cynthia Strickland

of such intense curiosity. It was as if the world had suddenly frozen as everyone just stood, silently staring. She could feel the condemnation in their gazes, and even though she really didn't care about these people's opinion of her, it was still difficult to try to calmly accept their rudeness.

"We can leave," Luke offered for her ears alone, feeling a sudden wave of guilt for putting her through this. He was used to silent hostility, but he could well imagine how it would hurt a tender-hearted woman like Jessie.

The tired resignation in his voice was what finally brought Jessica out of her stupor. It also did a lot to melt her earlier anger—or rather, her anger transferred from Luke to the rudely staring townspeople. "And let them win?" she asked incredulously. "I don't think so. In fact, I suddenly have the urge to give your hobby a try. I'm going to see just how much I can irritate these people."

Luke chuckled, but deep inside he felt his chest swell with unreasonable pride at her squared shoulders and raised chin. She looked so beautifully proud and defiant at this moment that it was all he could do to curb the impulse to pull her into his arms and kiss her, thoroughly. Instead, he settled for merely encouraging her defiance. Or he would have if the call hadn't cut him off so abruptly.

"Jess!"

Luke stiffened at the sight of the man who had broken away from the others and was now making his way toward the wagon. He was tall, and Luke figured most women would consider the man handsome, but the smile he was flashing Jessie now was just too damn warm in Luke's opinion. He was about to tell Jessica just that when he suddenly noticed she was smiling back at the man just as warmly.

"James! It's so good to see you again!"

The dark-haired man stepped up to the side of the wagon where Jessica was sitting, his grin flashing white against a tanned face. "And it's always good to see you, Jess, honey. I swear you just get prettier every time I see you."

Jessica's lilting laughter set Luke's teeth on edge.

"If I didn't know what a happily married man you are,

James McCalister, I'd accuse you of flirting."

His brown eyes sparkled wickedly. "If I wasn't such a happily married man, you'd be right."

So this was James McCalister. Luke hated the man already.

"And who's this pretty lady?" James asked, taking a step backward to look at Heather, who was sitting on a folded quilt in the back of the wagon.

Jessica's smile was telling as her eyes went to the child. "This is our Heather. Heather, this is a very good friend of mine, Mr. McCalister."

"Call me Mac, sugar," he told the child with a conspiratorial wink that earned him a giggle. "It's a whole lot easier to say. Listen, the other children are over there," he went on, motioning to a group of girls sitting beneath a tree playing with their dolls. "Do you want to go play?"

Heather looked to Jessica, who hesitated uncertainly.

Frannie had gotten down from her wagon and had come up on the group in time to hear the last of the conversation. "Do you mind if I tag along?" she asked the child airily, but the look she gave Jessica said she would make sure no one said anything to hurt the little girl's feelings.

As they watched Frannie and Heather walk off hand in hand, James looked around to find the gossips twittering away harder than ever at the sight of the child. Turning back to Jessica, he shook his head. "You always do liven up a party, Jess, and this time's sure no exception. You've tied more than a few tails in knots, girl." He turned on Luke then, the grin still in place as he offered his hand. "So you're Luke Cameron. Glad to meet you."

Luke was stunned for a moment. He was all set to hate McCalister and wasn't prepared for the cordial greeting. With suspicious reserve he shook the outstretched hand as if it might turn into a rattlesnake at any moment. "Pleasure."

"Sure doesn't sound like it by your voice," James accused laughingly. "But then I guess folks haven't exactly rolled out the red carpet for you, have they?"

"Hardly."

"Don't let it get to you. The ones worth knowin' will take

153

to you soon enough. The others ain't really worth worryin' about. Right, Jess?''

Despite himself Luke found he was starting to like James McCalister. Of course, remembering that Jessica was supposed to be good friends with the man's wife helped too.

Suddenly Luke came out of his thoughts to find McCalister helping Jessica down from the wagon, and he couldn't believe the hot flash of anger he felt at seeing the man's hands around her waist.

"Ruth's in the kitchen," James was saying. "She made me promise to send you in just as soon as you got here. She's been chompin' at the bit to talk to you.''

Jessica hesitated for a moment, looking indecisively at Luke before finally turning toward the house. James watched her for a moment, then turned back to meet the other man's gaze. "Well, you just gonna sit there all day or are you gonna come join the party?''

Luke looked at the smiling man warily. "To be Jessie's friend you sure don't seem concerned that she's married to a gunslinger," he tested. "I could be beatin' her for all you know.''

"You aren't.''

At the confident words Luke's brow raised. "How can you be so sure?''

"I have eyes," James explained. "Soon as these folks started staring, you leaned over and either offered to take Jess back home, or shoot everyone for her. Am I right?''

At Luke's surprised nod, James went on, "That means you care about her. Then, when I sent her off to find Ruth she looked at you like a mama hen being torn away from her one baby chick amidst a pack of wolves. That means she cares for you. And if Jess cares for you, then that means you're all right. She's got an uncanny knack for judging a person's character.'' He grinned. "After all, she did choose Ruth and me as her friends, didn't she?''

The man was pretty observant for a rancher. Eyeing him a little less hostilely now, Luke said, "You know, folks aren't gonna like you welcomin' me here.''

"Like I said, the ones worth knowin' will take to you. I don't give two hoots about what the rest of 'em think. If they don't like who I invite to my party, they know how to leave."

Luke wasn't quite sure what to say to that. It had been a long time since anyone had offered friendship without the incentive of the bounty hanging over his head. This man had nothing to gain by befriending him, however, and much to lose.

"Come on," James was saying. "There's a few men I want you to meet, like Jubal Tucker. Man's from Virginia. Makes the smoothest sour mash you ever tasted. Goes down like silk but it's got a kick like a mule."

Luke jumped down off the wagon and turned the reins over to a hired hand who led the team away to unhitch them. With a little less hostility now, Luke followed his host toward the group of men standing beside the barbecue pit.

"He is a handsome devil," Ruth McCalister said as she leaned against the sink to peer out the window curiously. "I guess that gives me one reason you might have married him." She turned to look back at her friend searchingly. "That is, if I believed you were a shallow henwit that would be swayed by such a thing. Which I don't. That leads me to wonder why you did. Can you imagine my surprise when we got home from our trip last week and I found out—through the gossips, no less—that you of all people had ridden into town and snatched a man you didn't know from Adam off the gallows to marry him? Now, what's going on?"

Someone entered the kitchen to pick up a large bowl of potato salad to take outside, saving Jessica from having to answer for a moment. The reprieve lasted for only a moment, though, and the two women were alone again.

Ruth's gaze never left Jessica. "Well?"

"Well what?"

"Don't you try to be evasive with me, Jessica *Cameron*. I want to know why you married a gunfighter."

"I thought you hated it when people pried," Jessica came back at her friend lightly, stalling.

Ruth recognized the ruse. "This is not prying for curiosity's sake, but concern over a good friend. This is just not the type of thing you do, Jess, so naturally it worries me that you did it."

Jessica busied herself pulling ears of corn out of a large pot of boiling water with a pair of tongs. "It's hard for a woman to run a ranch alone."

"And bulls have feathers!" Ruth shot back with a snort. "This is me you're talking to, Jess. I know you! You could run that ranch blindfolded if you had to. I also know that if you did need help at it you wouldn't have married a *gunfighter*. It leaves me to wonder just what kind of help you need that you did?"

"Are you sure this isn't considered prying?" Jessica asked, trying to laugh her way out of an explanation. "It sounds an awful lot like it to me."

Ruth only crossed her arms stubbornly and stared at her until Jessica finally gave a tired sigh of defeat. After checking the hall to make sure they wouldn't be overheard, she slowly began to tell Ruth what had been happening at the ranch, leaving off her suspicion that Ben may have had something to do with John's death. She wasn't going to throw out accusations like that until she had some solid proof to back them up. But the rest of the story she opened up to her friend, relieved to finally have someone other than Frannie, who worried over her like a mother hen, to confide in.

When Jessica finished talking, Ruth's jaw had fallen open. "Why didn't you come to James and me about this?" she asked with the concerned censure of a friend. "You know we would have helped you."

"I know you would have," Jessica soothed. "But you and James have your own ranch to run. And besides, it could all just be coincidence."

Ruth eyed her friend skeptically. "If you believed that, you wouldn't have married a gunslinger, even given that ridiculous bargain you made."

Jessica bristled. "And just why is it so ridiculous? It benefits both of us."

"Does it? I wonder just how long he'll stick to your *terms*, if he hasn't broken them already." At her friend's guilty blush, Ruth smiled knowingly. "So I'm right? Your terms didn't hold up."

"Yes, they have!" Jessica stated emphatically, too emphatically.

"So you just wish they hadn't."

"Ruth!"

"What? Remember, I know what kind of marriage you had with John. Now you find yourself in close proximity with a handsome, virile man. And I can see it in your eyes whenever you talk about him that you find him attractive, so there's no need even to try to deny it."

"But—he'll be leaving in nine months, if not sooner," Jessica finally put her fear into words.

Ruth reserved her opinion on that until she could meet this gunfighter her friend had married. It could be that Jessica really should stick to the terms of her bargain if the man turned out to be a no-good drifter. Still, she couldn't believe Jess would be attracted to the man unless there was more to him than what his reputation implied. And Jessica was attracted to this Luke Cameron, it was there in her eyes every time she said his name.

Chapter Seventeen

The next few hours were some of the longest of Jessica's life. She helped Ruth carry food to the tables set up out front, while trying to ignore the groups of talking women who grew suspiciously silent whenever she came near. She constantly looked for Heather to assure herself the little girl wasn't being cruelly ostracized. And for some reason she found her eyes frequently slipping to the group of men standing beside the barbecue pit. She wasn't sure what worried her more, that Luke's feelings were going to be hurt or that someone was going to say something he didn't like and he'd show these people firsthand how fast he was at the draw.

He had insisted on wearing the Colts. He had told her it was because of the trouble with Ben, but Jessica was fairly sure it was more to enjoy the shock on people's faces when he showed up with the things strapped to his hips. Thinking of the way the corners of that silky mustache had twitched when she had accused him of just that, Jessica had to smile. He really was incorrigible.

The meal came, and with the hands eating with the rest of the single men, that left only Heather, Frannie, and Zeke to sit with Jessica and Luke at a table that was otherwise conspicuously empty—until James and Ruth made it a point to join them. Jessica had never been so grateful for a friend in all her life. As the meal progressed, she slowly forgot those around them and relaxed to enjoy what turned out to be a lively conversation.

When the meal was over, the men once more gathered by the barbecue pit where the earthenware jug reappeared, then disappeared again mysteriously, depending on the proximity of Reverend Phillips. The women packed away the leftover food while the children played tag in the fading afternoon sun, making for a peaceful interlude before the dancing began.

With the coming of nightfall the children were taken into the house, many of them falling asleep between yawning complaints that they weren't the least bit tired. The older girls, those not yet old enough to attend the dance, moped over their responsibilities as baby-sitters. They looked none too comforted by the assurance that their time would come. Meanwhile, the boys sneaked into the hayloft where they could watch their idols, the cowboys, and find out just how to act when they became men.

The pine-board floor of the huge barn had been swept clean and a platform set up at one end where several men now stood tuning their instruments. A guitar, two fiddles, a banjo, and a harmonica—along with the now empty earthenware jug that Jubal Tucker had taken up—soon filled the barn with lively music. The oak-planked barn floor turned quickly into a dance floor filled with smiling, swaying couples.

From her place standing beside the wall, Jessica tapped her foot in time with the music while her eyes scanned the crowd, stopping now and then on the men from the Circle R. With sisterly pride she noticed, purely unbiased of course, that they were the most handsome of the men here tonight. And speaking of handsome men . . .

Her gaze went to the open double doors once more, but there was still no sign of Luke. He had been talking to James when she came out of the house from tucking Heather into bed. Not having the kind of relationship where she felt at ease enough to join them, she had motioned toward the barn to let Luke know where she would be. She had hoped he would join her, but after the third song ended and another began she realized that he wasn't in any great hurry to rush to her side.

"May I have the pleasure, ma'am?"

Pulled from her thoughts, Jessica found Sam standing before her, waiting. With one last glance at the doors, she gave him

159

a smile and took the arm he offered as he led her onto the floor.

Outside, the sun had disappeared behind the mountains nearly an hour before, and in the darkness left behind Luke stood talking to James McCalister. As the afternoon passed he'd found himself liking McCalister more and more. There was no trace of judgment in the man's eyes, and he met Luke's gaze squarely as they talked, a sure sign the man was trustworthy. He didn't pry either, which was another thing Luke appreciated. It wasn't that he was particularly ashamed of his past, he just felt it was his decision who he did or did not tell about it. As the afternoon had worn on, however, and he got to know McCalister better, Luke began to open up as he hadn't done in years. Of course, the number of times the jug of whiskey had been passed helped a good deal in loosening his tongue.

The other men had already gone inside to join their wives, leaving only Luke and James standing under a group of pines as they watched the well-lit barn. Music and laughter drifted out to them on the night breeze, yet both were hesitant to go inside, each for reasons of his own. Luke knew that when the men joined their wives they would once again turn a cold shoulder to him. That in itself didn't bother him, it was only that in doing so they would be snubbing Jessica as well. He wasn't anxious to rush inside and spend the entire evening watching her try to hide the hurt. For all her outward bravado, she was probably the most tender-hearted woman he had ever known, and Luke knew she had to be hurting at the treatment she had already been subjected to today.

The thought made Luke's fists clench against the urge to go in there right now and pull her into his arms and tell her the whole lot of these people weren't worth one of her tears. The only thing that kept him from doing just that was the knowledge that it was because of him she was being treated this way. He was the one who had forced her to come and endure this censure from her neighbors.

James silently watched the man standing beside him, read-

Thrill to the most sensual, adventure-filled Historical Romances on the market today...

FROM ▉ LEISURE BOOKS

As a home subscriber to Leisure Romance Book Club, you'll enjoy the best in today's BRAND-NEW Historical Romance fiction. For over twenty-five years, Leisure Books has brought you the award-winning, high quality authors you know and love to read. Each Leisure Historical Romance will sweep you away to a world of high adventure...and intimate romance. Discover for yourself all the passion and excitement millions of readers thrill to each and every month.

Save $5.⁰⁰ Each Time You Buy!

Each month, the Leisure Romance Book Club brings you four brand-new titles from Leisure Books, America's foremost publisher of Historical Romances. EACH PACKAGE WILL SAVE YOU $5.00 FROM THE BOOKSTORE PRICE! And you'll never miss a new title with our convenient home delivery service.

Here's how we do it. Each package will carry a FREE 10-DAY EXAMINATION privilege. At the end of that time, if you decide to keep your books, simply pay the low invoice price of $16.96, no shipping or handling charges added. HOME DELIVERY IS ALWAYS FREE. With today's top Historical Romance novels selling for $5.99 and higher, our price SAVES YOU $5.00 with each shipment.

AND YOUR FIRST FOUR-BOOK SHIPMENT IS TOTALLY FREE

IT'S A BARGAIN YOU CAN'T BEAT! A Super $21.96 Value!

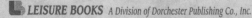

▉ *LEISURE BOOKS* A Division of Dorchester Publishing Co., Inc.

GET YOUR 4 FREE BOOKS NOW—A $21.96 Value!

Mail the Free Book Certificate Today!

Get Four Books Totally FREE — A $21.96 Value!

ing more in his gaze than Luke would have wanted revealed. On a mission from his wife, James had purposely stayed behind as his guests disappeared into the barn. Now he was just where he needed to be: alone with Luke Cameron where he hoped to discreetly ferret out information about the man. Sakes alive, what a man wouldn't do for his wife!

"Jess is a good woman," James began, awkward in the role of snoop.

"Um hmm."

"She's done a lot of growing up in the last six years since we first met her, though sometimes I wonder that she can run a ranch as well as she does yet still seem so naive about some things."

Luke turned with an eyebrow raised questioningly to face the man at his side. "Is this conversation goin' anywhere in particular, McCalister?" he asked, growing wary.

Ruth had told her husband all about the bargain Jessica had made, and her friend's fear that Luke would be leaving at the end of the agreed-upon year. Being a woman, and thus a natural matchmaker, and seeing how Jessica had come to care for her gunfighter, Ruth had insisted that James question the man about his feelings and intentions. Being a man, and of the firm opinion that it was none of their business, for all that he did care for Jessica, James had refused. The fact that he was standing out here now getting ready to stick his nose where it didn't belong showed how well his resolve stood up against the sweet pleadings of his wife. It was plain unfair the advantage women had over their men.

"Jess is a good friend of ours. It's natural Ruth and I would be concerned about her."

Luke understood now. "So that's it?" he asked caustically. "You are worried about poor Jessica bein' married to the evil gunslinger! You know, I was actually beginnin' to believe that bullshit about 'if Jess likes you then you must be okay.' "

"It wasn't bullshit!"

"Yeah? Well, why the questions then?"

James gave a long, disgruntled sigh. "I told her I wasn't any good at this," he muttered under his breath, then looked

Luke squarely in the eyes. "Jess told Ruth about your bargain. My wife is worried Jess'll get to likin' you too much before you leave and she wants me to find out your intentions. I know it's none of my business, I even told Ruth so, but like I said, we both care about Jess. That marriage she had with John didn't prepare her for the feelings a man can stir in a woman. She could really be hurt if your intentions are to entice her into breakin' those terms ya'll agreed on, only to ride out on her later."

Several things in that explanation caught Luke's attention, not the least of which was the statement about "that marriage" Jessica had had with John Randall. His eyes narrowed on James now. "Just what do you mean about her marriage with John not preparin' her for the feelings between a man and a woman? Don't try to tell me she didn't love the man. She goes up to put flowers on his grave practically every day!"

"I didn't say she didn't love John," James corrected, beginning to feel really awkward now. This wasn't a subject he wanted to get into. "They just had an—unusual marriage."

Growing curious now that he could tell that James wanted to hide something, Luke pressed, "Unusual in what way?"

"They were very good friends that loved each other."

"And that's unusual?" Luke asked, perplexed that this was what had made James seem so uncomfortable. "You tellin' me you don't love your wife? Or she's not your friend?"

James growled in frustration, swearing he was going to turn Ruth over his knee for getting him into this situation. "I love my wife very much—most of the time," he added in a disgruntled tone under his breath. "And yes, I consider her my best friend. But she's also more than *just* a friend."

Luke was still puzzled, wondering what the man was trying not to say. Then, ever so slowly, the frown turned to a dawning look of disbelief. "Surely you don't mean to tell me . . ." At the other man's nod, Luke burst out incredulously, "Was the man a eunuch?"

"No, he wasn't," James defended his late friend loyally. "You'd just have to know the story of how they got together

162

to understand their relationship. John told me what happened. Funny thing is, Ruth could never get much out of Jess about her past before she met up with John and Alicia.''

''Alicia?''

''John's wife,'' James explained simply, and couldn't believe the explosion that bit of information touched off.

''His wife? You mean to tell me the bastard already had a wife when he married Jessica?''

''Easy, Luke,'' James cajoled, eyeing the Colts nervously. ''Alicia had died by the time John married Jessica.''

And so the story unfolded, at least what John had told James about his years in the war, and his decision after it was over to see his children born in a land that held a better future. Like so many others he had left behind the bitter memories and ravaged Southland for the shining promise of the West. Luke began to find himself empathizing with the dead man, this same man he had grown to resent over the past weeks of watching Jessica's faithful treks to John's grave with her bouquets of flowers.

''So they left the wagon train and settled here,'' James brought the story up to the building of the Circle R. ''We met Jess one day, and she and Ruth took to each other right off. Over the years we got together now and again and got to be close friends. It didn't take long to realize—well—that theirs wasn't a—*normal* marriage.''

''But you said you thought they loved each other,'' Luke argued, unable to believe there was a man alive who could live with Jessie and not want to share her bed. Wasn't she about to drive him crazy with the ache of wanting her?

''To tell the truth, I don't think he ever got over Alicia. I believe Jess thought a lot of the woman too. They used to talk about her like two friends commiserating in their grief.''

''Maybe,'' Luke allowed, though he was still unconvinced. ''But six years is a helluva long time to commiserate with a woman like Jessica. You can't tell me there weren't times the man was able to get beyond his grief.''

''I don't know if he did or didn't,'' James answered as he gazed thoughtfully toward the lighted barn. ''All I can tell you is that even though she does get me into situations like this when I contemplate tannin' her hide, I truly don't know if I'd ever get over losin' Ruth.''

The statement pricked Luke's conscience. Obviously John Randall had loved his first wife to the point of being devastated by her loss. And James seemed to feel the same about his beloved Ruth. So why was it Luke hadn't felt the same overwhelming emotion for Melinda? He really had cared about her. She was such a sweet, vivacious little thing, for all that reality never seemed to creep in to spoil her world.

But then wasn't that how he had been brought up to see marriage? He would marry a genteel, refined young lady of breeding who would someday become mistress of Riverview. His job would be to keep the ugly realities of life from touching her. Melinda had seemed the perfect choice. The daughter of their closest neighbor to the north, it had been the perfect Southern marriage, one that would someday join two already large plantations into one immense one.

Still, he had cared for Melinda. He had felt a nearly suffocating rage take him as he strained helplessly against those bonds, trying to break free before . . .

Closing his eyes, Luke clenched his teeth together until the too-familiar, haunting vision faded back into the dark recesses of his mind. He hadn't protected his wife. What was worse was that he knew it was his fault that she had gone through that hellish nightmare before finally being murdered. All she had wanted was to live the life she had been brought up to expect, and for all that he had cared for her, Luke knew he had failed her.

There was that word again. *Cared*. Why was it that when he thought of his marriage Luke couldn't associate the word *love* with what he and Melinda had felt for one another? The way James had looked toward the barn earlier made Luke wonder now what it would be like to feel love for a woman, such overwhelming, soul-blending love that her death would leave him as devastated as John Randall had obviously been over losing Alicia.

Was that what worried Ruth? Did she really fear that Jessica could come to feel that way about him? Even as Luke scoffed at the ridiculous notion, he felt a strange catch in his chest. As impossible as the idea seemed, what if Jessica could come to—love him? What if he could live down his past? What if he could stay on here permanently without putting her or Heather in danger?

That was a whole lot of "what ifs" to be hanging his hopes on. The thing was, if there ever was a woman worth gambling such high stakes on, it was Jessica. If there had ever been a woman he could feel the kind of emotion for that McCalister had described, it was Jessie. Hell, if he was honest with himself he was more than halfway there already.

In the silence that continued to stretch out between them, James watched the man across from him carefully. James wasn't sure whether he had helped Jessica's cause by telling Luke the truth about her first marriage, or made matters worse. If the man wasn't what James had judged him to be, then he could sure take advantage of the information James had just given him. From what time he had spent with Luke, though, he had come to the conclusion that he was a decent man who had done what any man would do given the same situation—if the story Jessica had told Ruth was to be believed. Only time would tell the truth, however.

They entered the barn to find a Virginia reel in progress. It didn't take Luke long to spot Jessica, as she was just making her way through the arbor of outstretched hands with Hank as her partner. Luke quickly forced down a flash of what he was suspiciously afraid was jealousy. Besides, he knew by now how Jessica felt about all the men who worked for her.

That thought worried him. Right now she was lucky to have seven decent men working for her who respected women. But there were a lot of men around who would take advantage of a woman like Jessica. She was, by nature, friendly and caring of others. Some men would take that the wrong way, or take advantage of it. If he were to leave when their bargain was up, how long would it be before she ran across just such a human snake?

Luke's entire body stiffened with rage at the thought. Looking up to see Jessica smiling and looking so innocent and vulnerable, he felt a sudden intense urge to protect her, a feeling he knew wasn't going to cease when their "bargained for" year was up.

Chapter Eighteen

Jessica felt Luke's presence long before her eyes finally found him standing in the shadows by the open doors. Actually, she felt his gaze. It wasn't like the uncomfortable feeling of being watched, but more like—and she would admit it was crazy to feel this way—a sudden comforting feeling that something had been missing and now was found again.

Crazy as it was, though, Jessica couldn't help the smile that came to her lips as she found that warm blue gaze. She also couldn't help noticing that every other man seemed to fade into obscurity whenever Luke Cameron stepped into a room. He was without a doubt the most handsome, most totally masculine man she had ever known. The thought that she might be held in those muscular arms soon, even if only for a dance, had her pulse tripping in anticipation.

He had chosen a spot along the far wall where he was partially hidden from the crowd, and guessing the reason for this, Jessica was about to join him when a new arrival stepped through the double doors, causing her to pause. Benjamin Mateland made his usual grand entrance, bellowing out greetings and accepting the fawning admiration of the townspeople who gushed over him as so many do toward the wealthy. Ben had long ago come to expect this as his due. Since the McCalisters were in the very small group who refused to revere him as if he were some higher form of life, Ben usually didn't trouble himself to grace their little soirees with his presence. But tonight he had a purpose, and he saw that purpose standing across the barn watching him as a wary rabbit watches the approaching wolf. And a delicious rabbit she is, too, he thought, hiding a licentious smile at the vision of how much he was going to enjoy gobbling up this tasty prey.

But Ben had become impatient waiting for that gunslinger to get bored and ride out. It was time to do a little pushing, he decided, which was what had brought him here tonight. As he stepped farther into the room, a dozen of his hired hands filed in through the doorway and fanned out behind him. Ben Mateland always made sure the odds were in his favor.

Dragging his eyes away from Jessica, he searched the faces around her, and not finding the one he sought, Ben grinned. Damned gunslinger was obviously too ashamed to show his face around decent folks. Well, that was going to make Ben's plan that much easier to carry out.

Turning to nod meaningfully at his men, who immediately began to spread out into the crowded barn, Ben made his way across the room, stopping in front of Jessica. Only she saw the way his eyes roamed insolently over her, lingering at the lace edging her bodice before he tipped his Stetson in a show of respect for the benefit of those watching.

"Evenin', Ms. Randall. Oh, I'm sorry, it's—ah—Camerell now, isn't it?" he said in a loud, if apologetic, voice. "Forgive my blunder. It's just that it's been such a short time since John passed on it's sometimes hard to remember he's gone."

Jessica was seething by the time he finished. The deceitful, low-down, lying snake-in-the-grass! How dare he act the concerned friend? And he was purposely reminding everyone of how recently she had been widowed, making it sound so heartless of her to have remarried so quickly. The hypocrite! Why, he'd asked her to marry *him* within a month of John's death! Which in all likelihood he had caused!

Her chin came up at the malicious glint in his eyes. "The name is *Cameron*, Mr. Mateland," she corrected smoothly, before adding for his ears alone, "Funny, you haven't had any trouble remembering it on our last two encounters."

The fact that his smile became as brittle as icicles gave her great satisfaction. Luke was right. Irritating certain people was a very enjoyable pastime.

"I haven't seen your husband tonight," Ben gritted out in

a quiet tone through his false smile. "Is there some reason he felt he shouldn't come?"

"You always seem to be concerned over my husband's whereabouts," Jessica pointed out as she saw a familiar tawny-haired figure moving toward them from behind Ben. "I would think you'd have more important things to worry over."

Ben held his smile for the benefit of the group of people standing nearby who were attempting, without much success, to hide the fact that they were straining to catch any word of the conversation. Lowering his voice, he said, "He won't be around forever, Jessica. In fact I wouldn't be surprised if you go home tonight and find him gone."

She played along, fighting an amused smile when Luke stopped just behind Ben. "You really think my husband will leave me? That he's probably already gone?" she asked in a worried tone.

"It wouldn't surprise me. He's an outlaw, Jessica. A killer. If you need a man around, I told you you can come to me." His voice dropped suggestively. "Why don't you let me take you home right now? If he's still there, I'll run that gunslinger off and show you I'm the man to give you what you need."

"As the husband here I don't take too kindly to that notion, Mateland."

Ben whirled to find himself face-to-face with the outlaw. It rankled that he had to look up to meet the ice-blue gaze. "How long you been standin' there eavesdropping, outlaw?" he asked testily, wondering why the hell those no-good hired hands of his hadn't somehow let him know Cameron was sneaking up behind him.

"Long enough to hear what sounded like you propositionin' my wife," Luke answered in a dangerously calm voice. "I hope you're gonna tell me I'm wrong, though. Like I said, I don't take kindly to that notion at all."

The sheer menace lacing those words was enough to wipe away all trace of Jessica's earlier amusement. She hadn't expected Ben to say anything so inflammatory. She'd only thought to let him make a fool of himself going on about Luke not being here, then embarrass him by telling him to turn

169

around and see for himself that her protector was standing directly behind him. Somehow the simple situation had turned volatile. To add to that, she suddenly became aware that their audience was growing.

Ben seemed to realize this as well, for he suddenly took on a look of confusion. "I was only paying my respects to the widow of a dear, departed friend, Mr. Cameron. I can't imagine how you could get such an idea that I would do or say anything disrespectful to John's memory. I'm truly sorry if my merely speaking to your wife angers you so."

Jessica knew Luke was going to call Ben on the lie. She could feel anger radiating from his body like heat from a stoked furnace. She also knew that whatever he said they would have cause to regret. Taking his hand, she squeezed it meaningfully before turning to Ben. "My husband is very protective, Mr. Mateland. I'm sure he just misunderstood your intentions. Now if you'll excuse us, we haven't had the opportunity to dance yet."

Turning to look up at Luke, a silent plea in her eyes as she met his stormy gaze, she said softly, "They're playing my favorite waltz, too."

Every muscle in his body was tensed for a fight, yet Luke couldn't ignore the smaller hand squeezing his. He knew Jessica was trying to avoid an ugly scene. She wasn't the only one who realized how sentiment was running around them. Ben was going to look like the injured party no matter what happened.

With a last menacing glare at Mateland, Luke turned and led Jessica onto the dance floor. "That's three," he gritted out after they had smoothly, if a bit too sweepingly, joined the other couples swirling around the floor.

With a puzzled frown Jessica met his stony gaze. "Three?"

"Three times I've backed down from that bastard for you."

Of all the nerve! "Is that what you call what just happened? And here I thought I was merely avoiding an argument we didn't have a snowball's chance in hell of winning, given our audience!" Her voice dripped with sarcasm as she went on, "But then I forgot, didn't I? You never lose an argument. You

170

always outdraw anyone you disagree with!''

His arm tightened around her waist at the slur. ''Which is exactly why I'm here, Mrs. Cameron,'' Luke reminded, his unrelieved anger at Mateland transferring itself toward Jessica. ''Or maybe you've changed your mind. Maybe you've decided to take Mateland up on his offer!''

''Ohh! If there weren't so many people watching I'd slap your face for that!''

''Go ahead!'' Luke challenged. ''I'm sure these folks would enjoy watchin' when I turn you over my knee and paddle your bottom.''

''You wouldn't dare!''

''Try me.''

She wasn't about to, but neither was Jessica going to admit he intimidated her. ''You're just lucky I don't like to cause a scene!''

At the haughty toss of her head Luke had to grin. Why was it she could get him railing mad at her, but he never could seem to hold on to that anger? Maybe it was because he so enjoyed infuriating her and watching those golden-green eyes flash fire at him. Which was why he couldn't resist goading her just a little bit more. ''Yeah, I guess you bein' facedown across my lap with your skirts tossed back over your head would create quite a scene, wouldn't it?''

''So would my slapping that annoying grin off your face!'' Jessica came right back at him. ''Which is exactly what will happen if you dare lay one finger on me!''

''Careful, Jessie,'' Luke warned, his voice becoming husky at the vision his imagination was creating, ''or I might take that as a challenge. And though I'll admit I might not do it here in front of all these men, there's always later.''

Jessica's confidence faltered, for though she'd known he wouldn't carry out his threat in front of anyone, she wasn't so sure he wouldn't do just as he threatened once they were alone. It would be just like him, the ill-mannered—*outlaw*!

''Well, all I did was prevent an argument we couldn't win,'' she grumbled, bringing them back to the origin of this absurd conversation. ''I'd think you would appreciate me trying to

171

avoid seeing you beaten to a bloody pulp.''

''Ahh, so you did this because you care about me?'' Luke asked, still grinning because he saw through her ploy. ''If I didn't know better I'd think you were trying to placate me.''

She glared at his amusement. ''I don't give a fig about you,'' she claimed in a huff. ''I just don't want to see Ruth's party turn into a brawl.''

He would have been hurt by that if the lie weren't so transparent. As it was, Luke was curious now as to just how much of a lie it was. The music stopped and she tried to pull away, but he refused to let her go. When she finally stopped struggling against his hold and glared up at him, her eyes were shooting sparks of fire that would have reduced a lesser man to cinders.

''The music is over, Mr. Cameron,'' Jessica pointed out frostily. ''You may release me.''

She was so stiff with rage, Luke doubted a tornado could budge her. With a smile meant to infuriate, he tightened his arms. ''I don't think so. I like holdin' you.''

Jessica ignored the way her heart tripped over the words, telling herself that he didn't really mean them. ''You like *irritating* me,'' she corrected. ''And you do a very good job of it.''

''Thank you.''

The scoundrel. He knew she hadn't meant it as a compliment, he just took it as one because he was going to attempt that annoying trick he had of trying to tease her out of her anger. Well, it wasn't going to work this time. It wasn't!

''You think you're going to make me laugh and I'll forget you started this argument with your unfair attack,'' Jessica accused. ''Well, it's not going to work this time, Luke Cameron. You were the one who—''

Luke was looking around them. When his eyes came back to hers they held a suspicious sparkle. ''I think we're about to cause one of those *scenes* you're so set on avoiding,'' he interrupted quietly. ''Would you care to take this outside, away from our audience?''

Glancing around, Jessica realized he was right. It was really pathetic how transparent the eavesdroppers' efforts were to hide the fact that they were trying to move close enough to overhear every word.

With a quicksilver change, Jessica gave a brilliant smile, taking her adversary's arm as if she were having the most wonderful time of her life. "A breath of air is just what I need, dear," she said airily. "How sweet of you to notice."

They walked through the double doors arm in arm, with no one questioning their departure except James McCalister, who wondered at the reason behind Luke's pleased grin.

"You missed your calling, Jessica. The theater can always use such a great actress," Luke complimented as they stepped past the square of golden light cast through the doorway into the velvety blackness beyond. He laughed softly when she tried to jerk her hand from his arm, squeezing his elbow against his side to successfully imprison her wrist.

"Let go of me!" Jessica hissed angrily. "We came out here to finish this argument in private!"

"Is that why we're out here?" Luke asked in feigned surprise. "And here I thought you just needed a breath of air, *dear.*"

"We're out here because I refuse to be cajoled out of being angry at your unwarranted attack on me for simply trying to avoid a fight! *And* for you threatening me!"

Her anger had allowed Luke to lead her around to the secluded side of the barn without her even realizing it. "We're out here to find out the real reason why you wanted to prevent that fight," he corrected softly. "And, Jessica? I don't make *threats*. I've already warned you of that fact."

Too late she noticed how isolated was the spot he had maneuvered her to. It was dark on this side of the barn, and Jessica knew that a wide area holding tack and grain separated this outside wall from the crowded main room where everyone else was. She was alone with Luke, completely at his mercy. Given his earlier threat—no, *warning*—it wasn't a very comforting position she found herself in. Her back was to the wall, and just as sturdy a wall of male chest stood in front of her.

Edging slowly sideways, Jessica tried to act nonchalant in

her attempt at escape. His hand came up to plant itself firmly against the wall beside her head. Swallowing the nervous lump that rose in her throat, she held the smile and began to edge her way in the other direction. He gave a lion's smile that only added to Jessica's rising panic and planted his other hand on the wall on that side, successfully imprisoning her within his arms.

"Uhm—Ruth was expecting me several minutes ago to help with the refreshments," Jessica said quickly, cursing herself when her voice shook. "I'd better get back inside—before she comes looking for me." The last was said with the desperation of a drowning person grasping for a lifeline.

"But we haven't finished our argument yet," Luke pointed out, leaning closer. "You were about to tell me why you wanted to save me from being beaten to a bloody pulp."

"I didn't!" Jessica denied staunchly, trying to ignore the way his nearness made her arms begin to tingle. Dragging her eyes from his firm lips, she met the warm blue gaze. "I told you why I intervened."

"Ah, yes. You didn't want all that blood to ruin Ruth's party. But tell me, if it hadn't been for that, would it have bothered you to see Mateland and his men try to beat me up?"

"Yes!—No!" That broad chest and husky voice were playing havoc with her senses until she couldn't concentrate on what they were talking about anymore. Vaguely Jessica could remember that she was supposed to be angry with him. She just couldn't remember why.

"Which is it, Jessie?"

"What?" she asked in confusion, mesmerized by the shadows playing across the contours of that handsome face. Was it a trick of the moonlight or did the corners of that silky mustache quirk in satisfied amusement?

"Yes, it would have bothered you? Or no, you wouldn't care if I was hurt?" Luke reminded her, trying to hide a satisfied smile. He could read the turmoil of desire in those expressive eyes.

Much as she wanted to lie, Jessica couldn't. But that didn't mean she had to tell him the whole truth either. There was no

The Deal

way she was going to give him that much power over her. "Yes, it would have bothered me," she relented softly. "It would have been my fault, and I couldn't live with anyone being hurt on my account."

It wasn't exactly what Luke had wanted to hear, but the moonlight, the nearness of her body, and the elusive scent of warm lavender were combining to make his own desire more urgent than trying to press a confession from her. One hand moved away from the wall, and Luke fingered a soft wisp of hair that had escaped the pins to fall just in front of her ear. In the process the backs of his fingers grazed the downy soft skin of her cheek, and he watched her eyes melt into liquid gold. Unconsciously her tongue moved to wet her lips in an invitation that he could no longer resist.

Lightning seemed to sizzle through her veins as his lips closed hungrily over hers, melting bone and muscle in its wake. Out of necessity her arms moved to wrap around his neck for the support her knees no longer provided. She felt the groan rumble through his chest as his arms immediately closed around her, crushing her to the cotton-cloaked wall of his muscled flesh. The mother-of-pearl buttons of his shirt front dug into the tender skin of her own chest, but Jessica couldn't work up the desire, or the breath, to complain. She felt like the sand on a beach, with wave after wave of some strange yearning she couldn't put a name to violently washing over her. All she knew for sure was that she couldn't drag herself away from the source of those turbulent sensations. Luke.

His lips pulled away from hers, but her whimper of protest quickly turned to a gasp that caught in her throat as he trailed hot kisses from the spot behind her ear, slowly working his way down the slope of her neck. A flood of new sensations washed through her like a tidal wave, taking away what breath she had clung to. Then his hands were moving up her ribs, his thumbs teasing the soft outer slope of her breasts, and Jessica was sure she'd never breathe again.

Luke was having his own problems remembering where they were. He hadn't meant for things to go this far when he

175

maneuvered Jessica into coming outside with him. A few questions about her feelings, and maybe a kiss or two, was all he had been after. But then experience should have told him how fast he could lose control whenever he touched this woman. And now he had to stop before he passed the point of no return. He meant for their first time together to be something Jessica would cherish, the kind of lovemaking she deserved, not a quick toss on the ground outside a barn that she would later be ashamed of.

Reluctantly Luke pulled away. "Jessie?" he whispered softly, and nearly groaned aloud at the desire that burned clearly in the golden-green eyes that looked dazedly up at him in confused question. "Believe me when I tell you how very much I hate to have to point this out right now, but I don't think we can count on the privacy we need to continue where we're headed."

Slowly the desire drained from her eyes as sanity returned and Jessica realized where they were—and just what she had allowed to happen. *Allowed*? Her arms were still clinging to his neck like a honeysuckle vine! Stepping back, she dropped them quickly to her side, her face flaming hot with embarrassment. "I've got—to go—find Ruth," she stammered out quietly, unable to meet his gaze.

Luke didn't stop her this time as she stepped around him and quickly headed for the front of the barn. She had only gotten a few steps, however, when his soft call reached her.

"Jess?"

She stopped, but wouldn't turn to face him.

"I know you thought you were protecting me in there. Thanks."

Why couldn't he have goaded her with some smug comment that would make her angry? Why did he have to sound so sincerely appreciative that she wanted to turn and race the few steps back to throw herself into his arms and tell him just why she had done what she had? Dear God, why did she have this sick feeling that, against every instinct for survival that screamed out against it, she was falling helplessly, hopelessly, in love with Luke Cameron?

Chapter Nineteen

For the rest of the evening Jessica stayed close to Ruth, or Frannie, or anyone else who would keep her from having to face her husband. Even so, she felt his eyes on her constantly. There was one tense moment when Ben had started in her direction, but Luke had seemed to materialize out of nowhere to block his path. They had exchanged a few words that left Ben red-faced as he stalked out of the barn. She hadn't seen him return, and sincerely hoped he'd collected his men and gone home.

By eleven o'clock Jessica's nerves had had about all they could stand, and to her relief Zeke and Frannie finally mentioned leaving. The Scotsman didn't question her request that he tell Luke, but went off in search of the younger man while the ladies said their farewells to their hosts. Jessica then went to the house to collect a sleeping Heather. The child barely stirred as Luke took her from Jessica and gently laid her on the quilts he had spread out in the back of the wagon, covering her securely against the crisp night air. Snuggling down in the soft nest, she was soon fast asleep once more.

"I'm glad you could come," Ruth said as she hugged Jessica. When she pulled away, a shadow of concern crossed her face. "Are you going to be okay?" •

Jessica knew what her friend was asking. She just didn't have the answer. Was she going to be okay? Or was she in danger of losing her heart to a man who would probably be gone from here in a few short months, never to return?

"I'll be fine," she assured with a smile that didn't fool the other woman one bit.

Ruth squeezed her hand, at a loss as to what to do for her friend. James had told her that he liked Luke and thought he wouldn't do anything to hurt Jess. But then what did James know? He was a man, and men didn't understand how, for some incomprehensible reason, women seemed to be drawn to men who were trouble. And Ruth still felt that Luke Cameron spelled trouble, with a capital T.

"If you need to talk . . ."

"I'll come straight to you," Jessica assured her with a grateful smile. "Don't worry."

Ruth was still worrying as she watched the wagons until they disappeared from sight, her husband's arm around her waist offering little comfort.

Jessica sat as far in her corner of the wagon seat as she could without being in danger of falling off. For some reason, in her worry over trying to avoid Luke after that devastating episode outside the barn, she hadn't even considered that she was going to have to face the half-hour ride home with him alone—in the dark. Hearing the jingle of harnesses from Zeke and Frannie's wagon up ahead offered little comfort. They would soon be pulling off down the drive to their own home, and she and Luke would continue on to the house where they'd again be alone—in the dark.

For an instant Jessica thought about reaching back to shake Heather awake, then mentally chastised herself for being such a coward that she was considering hiding behind a child. What was she so afraid of anyway? Nothing was going to happen that she wouldn't let happen. But then that was the problem. She no longer trusted herself not to let what she feared most happen!

As it turned out, Jessica had nothing to fear. When they arrived at the house, Luke stopped the wagon and jumped down, silently helping her down before he climbed into the back of the wagon to pick Heather up, quilts and all. He took the child into the house and deposited her into her bed upstairs, then went back outside to see to the horses.

Pacing back and forth, Jessica waited nervously for the

sound of his boots on the stairs. They were completely alone except for Heather, who once she finally wound down and went to sleep, slept like the dead. Even the hands weren't around, all of them having chosen to stay at the dance until the last pretty girl went home.

Would Luke come to her room? Would tonight be the night he tried the lock on her door? Jessica crossed to the window to look out at the barn for any sign of his familiar broad-shouldered form. Would he expect to pick up where they had left off outside the McCalisters' barn? A shiver of anticipation ran through her at the thought, even as she told herself she wouldn't open her door for him if he came knocking. It would be emotional suicide if she let him into her room tonight—or any night for that matter. She had to insist that he stick to the terms of their deal.

The front door shut, and Jessica held her breath, waiting. The minutes ticked by and still there was no sound of booted footsteps on the stairs. Finally she cracked her door, just an inch. Everything was dark in the house. Creeping quietly to the head of the stairway, she peeked over the banister. The downstairs was completely dark, with no sound to be heard but the rhythmic tick of Alicia's tall grandfather clock in the parlor.

With a frown Jessica returned to her room and silently shut the door, wondering why she suddenly felt so frustrated.

Luke held Shiloh's reigns loosely, letting the horse follow along with the two beside him. Clayton and Hank were caught up in a discussion about last night's dance, speculating on whether or not Sam was going to work up the courage to ask Reverend Phillips's permission to start courting Lucinda. That left Luke to his own thoughts about last night.

Jessica had made it abundantly clear, first by clinging to Ruth or Frannie's skirts like a frightened child, then later by sitting as far away from him as she possibly could and speaking not one word all the way home, that she regretted what had happened outside that barn. For the rest of the time they spent at the dance, he had watched her as she helped Ruth set

179

out refreshments. Frustrated by the desire that had been stirred to a fever pitch, then left to smolder unquenched, it wasn't any wonder he was wound tighter than a bowstring by the time Mateland started to cross the floor toward her. He'd told Jessie he didn't threaten, but warned. Well, last night he had warned Mateland to get out and never bother Jessie again, or he'd kill him.

Then all the way home Luke had hoped that by some word or gesture Jessica would let him know she might not be averse to letting him stick around after their bargain was over, at least for a little while. But the woman Ruth McCalister was afraid might be falling in love with him had treated him like he had suddenly developed the plague!

"Aw, hell."

Pulled from his thoughts by Hank's exclamation, Luke looked up at Hank, then followed the man's gaze to see what had caused the angry words. Six cows lay just inside the fence, each one shot between the eyes.

"This weren't rustlers," Clayton growled. "They'd've at least took the meat, or cut the fence an' took 'em. Whoever did this did it for the pure meanness of it."

"Wonder who'd've done a thing like this?" Hank asked, and both men looked at Luke expectantly.

It was a rhetorical question, Luke could see it in the eyes of the men as they waited for him to tell them what it seemed they already knew. They were only giving him the chance to confide in them. And why shouldn't he? After what happened to Lee, all the men deserved to know what they were facing by staying on at the Circle R.

"I think y'all already know the answer," Luke replied finally.

Hank leaned over and spat a stream of tobacco juice on the ground before sitting back to look at Luke. "Yeah. We just figure it's about time you an' Ms. Jessica stop actin' like you don't."

"I don't know how much you know about what's goin' on," Luke started, "but Ben Mateland asked Jessica to sell out not long after John died." Both men nodded. "Well, since she refused, he's resorted to tryin' to convince her otherwise."

Clayton straightened at that. "Like how?" he asked, his anger clear. "Besides Lee, and now this?"

"I don't know if she's told me everything," Luke answered. "He came to the house a few days after I came. He thought she was alone so he could frighten her."

"And?" Hank asked.

The look on Luke's face was telling. "And he was wrong."

"We had problems with Mateland and his men before you came," Hank said, as if thinking aloud. "Guess that explains Ms. Jessica's suddenly goin' into town and comin' back marrie—" At Luke's narrowing gaze, Hank seemed to realize how that sounded and he quickly explained. "Come on, Luke. You didn't really think we believed that story about her ridin' into town and seein' you standin' up on the—well, you know—and suddenly decidin' she just had ta marry you. She just ain't like that. And we can all see it ain't your usual marriage."

How could he refute the truth? "I didn't realize we were that obvious," Luke muttered.

"Only to those that see you ever'day," Clayton replied, smiling now. "I hope I ain't steppin' outta line here, Luke, but you been actin' mighty frustrated lately. You been actin' like a starvin' man lookin' at a table full o' food he can't quite reach. An' you been lookin' at Ms. Jessica like she's that table o' food."

"You're steppin' over that line, Clayton," Luke warned with a growl, angry because what the man said was so close to the truth. "What goes on between me and Jessica is nobody's business but our own."

"An' I ain't tryin' to stick my nose in it neither," Clayton quickly assured, eyeing the Colts nervously before he again met Luke's angry gaze. "I'm just tellin' you we've all figured out there's somethin' goin' on."

"We want to help," Hank added. "Ms. Jessica means a lot to all of us, and—well, hell, Luke, you're startin' to grow on us too."

It was said with typical male embarrassment of one man

trying to admit any kind of feelings for another. With that same unease Luke wouldn't admit to them how much it meant to him to hear that they had come to consider him a friend. A person couldn't really understand how strong the need to belong somewhere was until he'd spent years of being forced to be a loner. And Luke had had more than enough of being alone.

But old habits die hard, and he wasn't used to sharing a problem. He was used to solving problems alone. Which is exactly what he meant to do now.

Jessica was sweeping the front porch when Clayton and Hank rode in. They walked their horses into the barn. As the minutes ticked by, she couldn't help glancing in the direction they had come from every few seconds, looking for the familiar form to appear on Shiloh. But as time continued to pass with no sign of Luke, she finally gave up on the sweeping. Leaning the broom against the porch railing, she crossed the yard toward the barn.

Sun poured in through the open doorway, and it took Jessica a moment to spot the men through the tiny particles of hay dust that sparkled golden in the sunlight. They stood in the back of the barn pulling the saddles from their horses, so they didn't hear her approach.

"Hank?"

He looked up at her call questioningly. "Yes, ma'am?"

"Zeke said Lu—Mr. Cameron rode out with you and Clayton to check the fence line."

Hank looked to Clayton, who suddenly busied himself rubbing down his horse. Reluctantly Hank looked back. "He did."

"Then where is he?"

"We—ah—just had a little trouble an' Luke's gone to—ah—see about fixin' it. No need to worry, though, ma'am," he added quickly.

Why was it that whenever someone said those words it usually meant there was a very good reason to worry?

"What kind of trouble?" Jessica asked, striving to remain

calm until she had reason to worry.

"We—had some cows shot. He just wanted to check on—something."

Jessica felt her heart lodge in her throat. "Where did he go, Hank?" she asked, afraid she already knew yet still praying she might be wrong.

Hank looked to Clayton for help, but the other man just ducked his head and brushed harder on his horse's sweat-slick coat. Muttering something under his breath about cowards, Hank turned back to face Jessica, meeting her worried gaze with a sigh of defeat. "He went to the Bar M."

Even expecting as much, Jessica couldn't help her gasp. "And you let him go? Alone?"

Clayton finally intervened. "You bein' a woman, you might not have recognized this as quick as a man would, ma'am, but you don't *let* Luke do anything but whatever he wants to do."

She knew exactly what Clayton meant, but it still didn't ease her fears. "Why go to the Bar M, though? He still can't prove—" She cut herself off quickly.

Hank stepped around his horse and faced her squarely. "We all know Mateland's the one who's behind your problems, ma'am. Luke confirmed it to me an' Clayton this mornin' when we found the cows. He just intends to go have a talk with the man."

"He had a talk with Ben last night, and I just did keep him from stressing his point with those blasted Colts! If Ben says something to make him angry—"

"He won't!" Clayton quickly interrupted, trying to reassure her. "And even if he does, Luke won't really shoot him."

But the words lacked real conviction, and in the silence left behind it was clear from their expressions as they looked at one another that they all knew it.

Chapter Twenty

Luke pulled Shiloh to a halt just outside the massive entry gate. A black wrought-iron arch connected the twin rock pillars holding an enlarged replica of the Bar M brand inside the very crest of the arch. Impressive, Luke thought with a smirk as he urged Shiloh through the entryway. How like Benjamin Mateland to have such a grandiose symbol of the wealth and power he so loved to flaunt. Again Luke had to wonder why the man was so obsessed with getting his hands on a small-time operation like the Circle R.

A split rail fence ran along each side of the long drive that led up to the house, enclosing acres of pasture. At the end of the drive, sitting on a slight rise like a giant pearl, sat Benjamin Mateland's home. The gleaming white house rose two stories in height and looked to be at least seventy feet in length. With black shutters framing full-length windows and a wide porch that ran the length of the front, the house looked more suited to the prewar South than Wyoming ranch land. Another symbol.

After their run-in last night, Luke knew the slaughtered cattle were Ben's way of sending him an invitation. Still, he wouldn't put it past Mateland to be planning an ambush. Luke had dealt with men like this enough in the past to know they protected their own hides first and foremost. Knowing this, he hooked the right side of the tan duster he wore back behind him as he left the relative cover of the fencing, freeing a clear path to the Colt strapped to his thigh.

Out of the corner of his eye he scanned the buildings that sat off to the right of the house, watching for any glint of sun reflecting off a gun barrel. The front door of the house opened then, drawing his attention. It wasn't Mateland that stepped out onto the porch, however, but a burly giant who cradled a shotgun in his arms.

"That's far enough," the man called out as Luke reached the edge of the lawn. "State your business."

Purposely Luke kept coming, not pulling Shiloh to a halt until he reached the bottom of the front steps. "I'm here to see Mateland."

"I'm Russ Fulton, Mr. Mateland's foreman," the man said tightly. "You can tell me what you want."

Luke's gaze was level. "I just did."

Fulton bristled at that. "Mr. Mateland's a busy man. He don't have time to waste—"

"He better make time," Luke cut in coldly, "or else I'm gonna have to leave a callin' card similar to the one he left me this mornin'."

"Mr. Mateland ain't been off this ranch for the last three days 'cept to go to the McCalister place last night. So whatever you're accusin' him of, you're wrong."

"Oh, I've got no doubt he's kept his own hands clean. Men like him always hire someone to do their dirty work for them."

"Someone like you?" Russ sneered, and nearly backed away from the icy blast as the gunslinger's eyes turned so cold that Russ felt an ominous chill race down his spine. He had to force himself not to turn tail and run back into the safety of the house, or to release the sigh of relief that came as he heard the door behind him open. Heavy booted footsteps stopped beside him, bolstering his confidence somewhat, though he still clutched the shotgun in his arms.

"Whatta you want, outlaw?" Ben Mateland asked in a booming voice that had been known to intimidate even the toughest cowhand.

"Nice of you to finally join us," Luke said sarcastically, and saw the older man stiffen at the implication in the words.

"I ain't got time to waste talkin' to every saddletramp that rides onto my land."

"Even when you invite them?"

"I don't know what you're talkin' about, outlaw," Ben answered, though it was clear from the look in his eyes that he knew exactly why Luke had come.

Luke shifted in the saddle, looking almost bored now. "You want to play games, Mateland, or you want to save us both time an' tell me why you asked me here?"

"You got it wrong, outlaw," Ben sneered. "Ain't no way I'd ask trash like you to my home."

Russ Fulton snickered, but Luke didn't show the least sign that he was affected by the remark. "So it's gonna be games. Okay, we'll call this a neighborly visit. We'll say I rode over here to warn you that someone's been shooting at our hands, cutting our fences, and shooting our cattle."

"Tsk, tsk." Ben made the clucking sound as he shook his head in mock dismay at the news. "That's a pure shame. But then things like that tend to happen sometimes when word gets out that a woman's runnin' a ranch."

"Things like that can happen when a man's runnin' a ranch too," Luke came back meaningfully. "Why, you never know. They might just hit the Bar M next."

Ben stiffened angrily at the veiled threat. "I'll shoot anyone that comes messin' around my place!"

"Yeah, I've decided to do the same. I thought it might prevent some bloodshed if *that* word got out."

"You've said your piece, outlaw," Ben gritted out. "Now leave."

"Not just yet," Luke answered. "There's one more thing. I meant what I said last night. I'm gonna take it real personal if you or anyone else bothers Jessica again. You might want to see that word gets out too."

"So that's the way it is, huh, outlaw?" Ben asked, giving a lewd chuckle. "Our little widow is payin' for your gun with that temptin' body of—"

He was looking down the business end of a Colt 45 before he could get the rest of the sentence out of his mouth, which hung slack now in astonishment. It had barely registered that the outlaw's hand was moving before the gun had cleared leather and the lethal bore was leveled on Ben's chest. A fine sweat broke out on his brow, and he felt the icy fingers of fear crawl up his backbone. Beside him, Russ Fulton swallowed audibly.

"You know, my daddy taught me from an early age that a gentleman never allows a lady to be insulted, especially when the lady's his wife," Luke commented with deceptive calm, though his eyes glittered dangerously. "Now, by honor I should shoot you where you stand for that remark, Mateland."

Ben swallowed hard, his knees suddenly beginning to tremble uncontrollably as he stared at the bore of the Colt. He wasn't use to not being the one in control. He was always the one doing the intimidating, and the reversal of roles had him frustrated as well as afraid. Where were the dozens of ranch hands he was paying such exorbitant wages to prevent just such a situation from occurring?

Luke watched Ben's eyes, letting the man stew in his fear for a long moment before he finally went on, "Of course, I might be persuaded to let it pass this time if you were to convince me how sorry you are for insinuating such an ugly thing about Jessica."

What the hell was Fulton waiting for? Ben wondered angrily. The fool had a shotgun in his hands, for heaven's sake!

The soft click of the hammer being drawn back on the Colt got Ben's full attention once more. "You've got five seconds to make up your mind, Mateland," Luke said in a deathly quiet tone. "You can either apologize, or use the time to try to make peace with your maker. It's your choice."

It wasn't a bluff, Ben realized as he met the promise in the icy gaze leveled on him. Luke had judged him well, for though Ben was boiling with impotent rage at having his pride so bruised, he wasn't ready to take the chance with his hide. Grinding his teeth in frustration, he gritted out, "Sorry."

"Surely you can do better than that," Luke pressed, nearly grinning when Mateland's face turned an even deeper shade of red. The man looked as if he were about to drop of apoplexy at any second. "I'm afraid a simple 'sorry' won't be enough."

Ben's chest swelled with a rage that nearly choked him, but

even so he couldn't disregard the Colt. "I meant no offense to the lady," he bit out, tasting each word as if it were bile rising in his throat.

After a weighted pause, the hammer was eased back into place and the barrel of the Colt raised harmlessly toward the sky. "I'll tell her you said so," Luke returned amiably, and grinned.

That grin worked like acid on Ben's lacerated pride and pushed him past good judgment. "Get the hell off my land, outlaw! You ever show your face around here again an' I'll have you shot on sight!"

Eyeing the shotgun Russ Fulton held, Luke looked back at Ben, his eyebrow arched challengingly. "You're welcome to try," he offered, then turned Shiloh to ride away at a leisurely pace that told just how worried he was at the threat.

Trembling with pent-up fury, Ben whirled on his foreman, jerking the shotgun out of the surprised man's arms. "You worthless piece of—Why didn't you shoot him when you saw him going for his gun?!"

"I didn't see him go for it," Russ defended. "All I saw was his gun! By that time it was pointin' square at your chest!"

Even though he knew it was the truth, hearing it didn't improve Ben's disposition. "You should've had this thing leveled on him from the start! What'm I payin' you for anyway?"

"I'm sorry, Mr. Mateland," Russ tried to placate his boss. "I just wasn't expectin' him to have the guts to draw on you here." He couldn't help the note of awe that crept into his voice as he continued, "Hell, I ain't never seen a man alive could move that fast. Have you?"

Ben's fists were still clenched as he growled, "No, and you won't be seein' him alive much longer. That outlaw bit off more than he can chew when he chose to cross me. When I get through with him, he's gonna wish that spineless excuse for a sheriff had hung him!"

He stepped to the edge of the porch, and his eyes narrowed as he watched the horse and rider disappear down the drive. Turning back on his foreman suddenly, Ben growled, "Tell

Cain to get his sorry ass in my office, pronto. It's about time someone around here started earnin' his pay!''

Luke rode slowly, thinking back on his meeting with Mateland, on all his run-ins with the man. His life had sure changed since hooking up with Mrs. Jessica Randall Cameron. Where before he'd never backed down from a fight, he'd now done it three times! And to the same man! The thing was, even though he knew Mateland was behind Jessica's problems, and probably John Randall's murder as well, Luke just couldn't bring himself to shoot Ben. Just knowing would have been enough in the past. For some reason, though, it was going to take finding solid proof this time.

He knew the answer was there if he'd quit running from it. Jessica. He cared about her. And he cared about what she thought of him. The tough gunslinger image was fine for other folks to believe—it had actually kept him from having to face more fights than he had—but he didn't want Jessica to see him as a ruthless killer.

At one time there had been much more to the man Luke Cameron than a gun and a cynical outlook on life. Once, years ago, he had enjoyed friends and laughter. And he'd especially loved the lavish balls his parents had hosted at their plantation, Riverview. Luke could still picture him and his friends as cocky young men standing on one side of the ballroom as they eyed the young ladies, whose mamas in turn eyed the young men speculatively. Ah, those young ladies, with their colorful gowns and their flirtatious laughter that seemed as much a part of the Southern night as the smell of honeysuckle drifting softly on a warm night breeze.

Closing his eyes, Luke could almost feel himself there again, standing on the veranda listening to the soft feminine laughter as he tried to steal a kiss from his latest quarry. He and his friends had always used the same ploy, tempting those ladies with the ''breathtaking view of the moonlight glistening off the Mississippi River.'' More often than not, the young ladies, who were tired of constant surveillance by their overprotective mamas, would, out of a thrilling sense of rebellion, find a way to sneak out onto the veranda. The bolder ones might even allow a kiss or two.

Luke grinned in remembrance. He had also had his face slapped a time or two for his forward manner. Those slaps were never hard enough to discourage, only hard enough to let the man know she was not that kind of girl. This seemed to be a lesson young Southern ladies learned at the same time young Southern gentlemen were learning about "moonlight glistening on the Mississippi."

But then everything had changed. In the spring of 1859 Luke's father had had a heart attack that left him with very little use of his right arm. That one event had brought home the fact that Luke was going to have to settle down and start taking over some of the responsibilities of running Riverview. It was with that prospect in mind that Royce Cameron had suggested Melinda Garner as a wife for his son.

Luke had never really thought of Melinda as a prospective wife, given the six-year age difference. She had always been his friend Thomas's little sister, a sweet enough kid but not what a young man in his late teens, then early twenties, pictured for a wife. But an amazing thing had happened to Thomas's little sister while Luke hadn't been looking one summer. She had turned sixteen, and suddenly she wasn't a little sister anymore. She was a lovely young lady with all the grace and manners any Southern gentleman could ask for in a wife. So, on August 23 of that year Luke married Melinda Garner, to the immense pleasure of both families.

Then the war had come, shattering lives as well as dreams. Luke had signed on in Natchez, never realizing that though he would survive the war, none of those he loved back home would. His parents had died in late '63 when a gang of Yankee deserters had looted and burned Riverview. Then, less than a year later, had come the horrible night when Drake and his men had murdered Melinda. Luke's mind shied away from the all too familiar memories.

That was the answer to what had happened to the old Luke. The cruelties of war had hardened him into the cynical gunslinger whose life would have ended at the end of a rope, if not for Jessie. She had saved his life. But more than that, she had restored his soul. She had made him remember the good times of his past, and the man he had once been, something Luke hadn't let himself remember for a very long time.

Suddenly he was eager to reach home, to see Jessie again. For the first time he let himself believe that they might actually have a chance at a future together. It was the positive, hopeful, eager anticipation for life reminiscent of the old Luke, rather than the hardened man who had almost welcomed the thought of death only a few short weeks ago. He was slowly changing, shedding some of the cynicism that made up the gunfighter Luke, the outlaw Luke—the Luke that would have been anticipating the glint of sunlight off steel up ahead.

As it was, he didn't sense the danger until it was too late, until he had already heard the crack of a rifle firing, until he felt the bullet tear into his chest. Almost as if in a dream he looked down at the red stain slowly blossoming across his shirt. He looked back up, but only heard the sound of hoofbeats rapidly leaving the copse of trees up ahead. He knew it would be useless to try to pursue his assassin. It wasn't going to be long before it would be taking all the strength he could muster simply to stay in the saddle until he could reach home—if he reached home.

Within two miles the road before him began to waver. A few more feet and he slowly slumped forward in the saddle. The ground between Shiloh's hooves wouldn't seem to stay in focus, then suddenly it seemed to be rising up rapidly to meet him. With a sinking feeling he realized he was still several miles from the Circle R, and as he felt himself slipping from the saddle, his last conscious thought was that after years of courting death he finally had a desire to live again—and now he was going to die.

Chapter Twenty-one

Jessica had tried to pretend that everything was normal as she went back to work after talking with Hank and Clayton. That ruse lasted all of an hour before she gave up the pretense and sat down in one of the rocking chairs on the front porch to wait. Alternately she would sit, then pace, then sit again as a myriad of horrible possibilities played out before her eyes, all of which ended with Luke dying because of this deal she had forced him into. Her guilt wouldn't allow her to absolve herself with the thought that he would have been hanged weeks ago if not for her intervention. She had taken advantage of his situation, offering him life only to make him have to lose it anyway, and all for her benefit.

But why did he have to go to Ben's today? It was only a few cows, for goodness sake! It was nothing worth endangering his life over! Guilt goading her, Jessica began to pace once more. Her mind conjured up images of Luke lying in some hidden spot on Mateland's land, his body broken, bloody, and lifeless. And those eyes—sometimes coldly frightening when he was angry, sometimes warm and teasing. The thought of those beautiful eyes closed forever, or worse, staring up at her sightlessly in death, was more than she could stand. Before she realized what she was doing, Jessica was off the porch and striding purposefully across the yard.

Thankfully, Frannie had sensed earlier that something was bothering Jessica, and even though the Scotswoman was somewhat miffed at not having her questions answered, she had finally offered to take Heather to her house to bake cookies. Jessica mentally blessed the older woman now as she pushed open the door to the barn. Seeing Flame poke her head curiously through the stall door didn't help any, for it only brought back memories of the only time Jessica could ever remember seeing Luke look the least bit flustered. It had been when Heather repeated his reason for what he intended to name the mare.

Crossing to the stall, Jessica gently stroked the horse's velvety nose, feeling a sting behind her eyes. "If he's hurt, or . . . I'll never forgive myself," she whispered to the horse, unable to put her worst fear into words. Then to bolster her own confidence she went on, "And if he's not hurt I'll hurt him myself for scaring me like this."

Pulling a rope halter from its hook on the wall, Jessica slipped it over Flame's head, then opened the stall door to lead the mare toward the tack room at the back of the barn.

Luke's first thought when he woke was that surely someone was holding a red-hot brand on his chest. If not, he'd died and gone to hell just as Reverend Phillips had predicted. If that were the case, it would serve him right for so foolishly letting his guard down.

With a groan he finally opened his eyes and was relieved to find Shiloh standing over him. He must still be alive, for surely God wouldn't have sentenced the horse to hell for its owner's stupidity.

Seeing his master rouse, the stallion nuzzled Luke's side.

"Just like—the old—days—huh, boy?" Luke got out, thinking of the time he had awakened much like this, shot and left for dead on a battlefield at Shiloh. He had looked up then to find the silver-gray stallion grazing a few feet away, still saddled. Luke hadn't known how the horse had escaped being captured after the battle, but he wasn't about to look a literal gift horse in the mouth. With his last bit of energy he had pulled himself up onto the miraculously docile stallion and headed the animal south, hoping they would run into Confederate troops rather than Union.

Since that day the gray stallion he had fittingly named Shiloh had been like a talisman for Luke. The animal had outmaneuvered Yankees, outrun bounty hunters, and been the only thing Luke had been able to trust for the last eight years. True to form, the animal stood watch over him now, where another would have wandered back home, leaving him to die.

Rolling to his side, Luke hissed through tightly clenched teeth at the white-hot pain that shot through his shoulder. After taking several shallow breaths to adjust to the searing pain, he looked down to find the entire right side of his shirt and duster soaked with blood. For an instant he could only think how thankful he was that whoever Mateland had sent after him was a lousy shot, for he was sure the man had been aiming for his heart. As it was he could feel the worst of the pain in his shoulder, and since he wasn't dead already that had to mean the bullet hadn't hit anything vital. Now, if he just didn't bleed to death . . .

"Think—we can—do it again?" Luke asked tightly as he reached for the horse's bridle. He got a soft snort that sounded like agreement from the stallion.

Holding on to the gray's leg, Luke put every bit of his waning strength into rising. But he had lost too much blood. The effort only caused his head to begin spinning, and slowly he sank back to the ground, falling again into the yawning black pit of oblivion.

Jessica saw the stallion first, and as her eyes fell to the crumpled heap at the horse's feet, she felt her heart slam into her throat, then seem to stop beating altogether. Spurring the mare into a full gallop that quickly ate up the last several hundred feet, Jessica was off the horse before the animal came to a complete halt. For an instant she had to raise her hand to the bridle of the nervously prancing stallion, calming him so that he wouldn't accidentally step on the man he so faithfully guarded. As soon as she was sure there was no danger of that, Jessica was on her knees beside the unconscious man.

With mounting dread she slowly turned Luke onto his back. A trembling gasp escaped at the sight of so much blood, and she knew with heartbreaking certainty that her worst fears had come to pass. Luke was dead, and it was all her fault.

The Deal

Unconsciously Jessica began rocking back and forth in short, jerking movements as she clenched her teeth against the torrent of tears that threatened, against the awful aching coldness that was gripping her chest. "Oh, God, I'm so sorry," she whispered chokingly, squeezing her arms around her stomach as she leaned forward, nearly laying her head against his bloody, lifeless chest. "I never meant for him to die." Then changing to speak to the man lying on the ground, she went on, "Why did you go, Luke? It was only a bunch of stupid cows! It wasn't worth dying over. *Nothing* is worth losing you!"

Luke woke to the feel of warm rain splashing on his neck. He heard the sound of—not thunder, as he expected, but of weeping; a woman weeping. Opening his eyes with great effort, he saw a mass of honey-brown hair shot through with glistening fire bent over his chest. His eyes moved slowly to the mare that stood beside Shiloh, then back to the woman at his side. "Jess?" he croaked out through a parched throat.

When the weeping only continued, he realized she hadn't heard him so he tried again. "Jessie?"

Slowly her head came up, and as if she were fearful to hope, she hesitantly raised her eyes until she was looking at his face. Caught between disbelief and hope, she gasped, "You're alive!"

"Barely," Luke got out, trying to grin for her benefit. She was white as a sheet, as if she were the one who'd lost so much blood. "How'd you find me?"

Jessica was so relieved to see those eyes open and looking up at her that it took a moment before she realized he had asked a question. "Hank and Clayton told me what happened. When you didn't come home, I decided to come after you."

His eyes searched the road behind her.

"I came alone," she explained at the question in his eyes, and nearly backed away from the fierce scowl he gave her.

"I—told them—to tell you—to stay put!"

"They did," Jessica defended the absent men. "And I did for nearly two hours."

His growl at that sparked her own anger. "It's a lucky thing

195

for you I did disobey your orders, Luke Cameron! You would have bled to death otherwise!"

Unwilling to concede the truth of that, he ground out, "You—could have sent—the men."

Seeing the toll this argument was taking on him, Jessica felt immediately contrite. What was she thinking of, sitting here arguing with the man when he was still in danger of doing exactly what she had feared? From the looks of the fresh blood seeping out of the wound in his shoulder, she knew she'd better do something quick or he was going to die right in front of her eyes.

"You can yell at me all you want later," she admonished. "But for now just shut up and let me get you home where I can try to save your unappreciative hide!"

Tearing the bottom half of her petticoat away, Jessica ripped the hem off, then folded the rest into a thick pad that she placed against the wound. Gently lifting him against her chest, she tied the pad securely in place with the strip of hem.

"Do you think you can help me get you onto your horse?"

Even as Luke nodded in answer, he had to close his eyes for a moment against the dizziness that threatened to send him over the edge into oblivion again. He had to think of Jessie. If he passed out now, the stubborn woman would stay right here by his side, endangering herself should Mateland want to assure himself the job was done. The man could easily decide to leave two corpses to be found rather than one.

That thought gave Luke the incentive needed to open his eyes. He found Jessica's face just above his, her eyes puffy from crying and filled with fear. For a moment it struck him as amusing that he had spent weeks thinking about being in just this position, held in her arms with his cheek pressed intimately against her soft breast, her lips so close he could practically taste them. Unfortunately, now that he was in just such a position he was far too weak to take advantage of it.

"I—ever—told you—I really like—that beauty mark?" he asked, starting to feel a little lightheaded from the loss of blood.

Jessica's hand went up to cover the mark self-consciously.

She knew he had to be losing his senses to say such a thing, which made her that much more determined to get him home as quickly as possible.

"Can you help me, Luke?" she asked again, ignoring his remark. "I don't know if I can lift you."

Again he nodded, and with a soft groan rolled to his knees. Jessica was there to gently lift his left arm around her neck, putting all her strength into helping him as he slowly struggled to his feet.

Breathing heavily from the exertion, Luke leaned against Shiloh for a long moment as he waited for the ground to stop pitching wildly beneath his feet. Only the feel of the woman at his side gave him the strength not to give up and sink back down to the ground as his body cried out to do. But slowly, with more effort than he had ever put into doing anything in his life, he finally managed to climb up into the saddle.

Watching him sway precariously before leaning over the stallion's neck, Jessica was afraid to let go lest he fall. After only a moment's consideration she climbed up behind Luke, wrapping her arms around him securely to take up the reins. At this point she didn't care if their combined weight was too much for the stallion, or if Flame ran off into the hills never to be seen again. All that mattered to her right now was getting Luke home.

"Don't you dare die on me after all this, Luke Cameron!" Jessica warned in a voice made hoarse by fear, and another emotion she wouldn't let herself consider right now. "If you do I swear I'll never forgive you."

Chapter Twenty-two

Zeke was the first one to see the strange procession that rode through the gate to the Circle R, probably because he had gotten his horse saddled the fastest when they finally found out Jessica was gone. He was mounting up when he looked up to see her riding Shiloh in. Anger born of fear mixed with concern as he swung down from his gelding to hurry to her side, calling out to the men in the barn as he went.

Checking Luke over first, Zeke then turned a fatherly frown on Jessica, but at the sight of her ashen face he tempered his words. "You should o' come ta me, girl," he softly scolded. "It scared ten years off my life knowin' ya'd gone out after 'im all by yerself."

"I'm sorry, Zeke," was all Jessica could offer. Truth to tell, she hadn't considered the danger of what she'd done. All she had thought about was that she had to find Luke.

"Well, it's done now," Zeke said as Tim and Billy reached his side. "And I guess it's good fer Luke ya found 'im when ya did. Let's get 'im in the house, boys," he went on to the men at his side. "Easy now. Watch that right shoulder."

It was well over an hour later before Hank returned with Dr. Andrews in tow. In that time Zeke and Billy had gotten an unconscious Luke into bed and Jessica had carefully cut away his shirt, gently cleansing the drying blood from around the wound. She then covered the gaping hole with a clean pad to stanch the bleeding, and with nothing left to do she had spent the next thirty minutes worrying that the doctor wouldn't come.

In those minutes Zeke saw the truth in what Frannie had

been fretting about for the last two days. It was written clearly on the worried face of the young woman sitting on the bedside as she gently tended the injured man. Jessica had fallen in love with her gunslinger. A few weeks ago the thought would have made Zeke run the man off, at gunpoint if necessary. Now he wasn't sure how he felt. He'd gotten to know Luke over the past few weeks, finding there was much more to the man than he'd first thought. And the way he'd seen Luke looking at Jessica lately when he thought no one was watching had Zeke thinking that she wasn't the only one who was trying to hide what she was feeling.

Jessica wouldn't be run out of the room as Dr. Andrews examined Luke's wound, though she did have to bite her lower lip hard when he probed the hole to find the bullet. Tears filled her eyes as she saw Luke flinch, even in his unconscious state, as the scalpel cut into his already torn flesh. She wanted to jerk the doctor away, and could only curb the impulse by reminding herself over and over that this had to be done. Still, she gripped her hands together until her knuckles turned white as she heard Luke moan at the pain the man was inflicting.

Finally the doctor sat back and dropped a lead slug into the bloody water in a basin on the bedside table. Wiping his hands, he cleaned the wound and stitched it up, applying a salve before he bandaged the shoulder.

"Change this dressing each day," he instructed Jessica as he wiped his instruments clean and replaced them in the black satchel at his side. He handed her a jar of yellowish-green salve. "And make sure you cover those stitches with this. It should keep infection from setting in. He's lost a lot of blood, so you need to get liquids into him. Beef broth is best to help him get his strength back. I'll come back in a couple of days to check on him."

Jessica listened intently to every word. "Thank you, Dr. Andrews. I'll do everything you said."

The elderly man looked at her for a moment, seeing the deep concern in her eyes. He then looked to the man on the bed, the condemned gunslinger the whole town was agog over the Widow Randall so suddenly marrying. "Is there anything

I ought to tell the sheriff?'' he asked carefully.

Jessica stiffened in defensive anger. "Until my husband regains consciousness and can tell us what happened, I don't know what I could tell Sheriff Davis,'' she pointed out frostily. "But I think it's obvious someone ambushed him.''

The doctor could well understand her defensive manner, for he had been witness to the townspeople's appalling anticipation of this young man's hanging, and to the condemnation Jessica had faced since marrying the man. Having seen far too much death during the war, though, Elijah Andrews was disinclined to see any man die. And besides, unlike most folks in town, he had believed the young man's story during the trial.

"I just think the sheriff ought to know that someone tried to kill your husband,'' Elijah explained.

Seeing the sincerity in his eyes, Jessica gave a tired sigh. "I'm sorry to snap at you, Doctor. It just scares me, first Lee, and now Luke.''

"Which is exactly why you should take my advice and tell Sheriff Davis. This may be coincidence, but then again I think you're smart enough to realize it may not.''

"Thank you, Dr. Andrews,'' Jessica repeated, more warmly now at his concerned manner. "As soon as Luke can tell us what happened, I'll be sure to report it.''

Zeke saw the doctor out, leaving Jessica alone with Luke for the first time since they had arrived home. She tucked the covers around him, and since he was still unconscious, she allowed herself the luxury of just looking at him. She watched the steady rise and fall of his chest, letting each breath ease the tension from her body. He was alive. And according to the doctor, he had a very good chance of staying that way.

Leaning over, Jessica gently brushed a lock of tawny hair back from his brow, then let her hand move down the side of his face caressingly. Now that the period of crisis was over, she began to tremble at the thought of how differently this all could have turned out.

What would have happened if she had found Luke dead, as she'd first thought? In those few minutes before he had opened his eyes, Jessica had felt more pain than she had ever experienced in her life. Even her mother's death and her father's desertion hadn't made her feel as bereft and totally alone in the world as the thought of Luke's dying had. Jessica was terrified to consider the real reason behind her reaction, even though deep inside she knew what it was. Would admitting it make it any less so?

Giving a short laugh that sounded much like a drowning victim's last gasp for breath, Jessica sank into the chair by the bed. Her eyes remained on Luke's face even as she tried to convince herself she could be wrong. Could it just be gratitude she felt? Loneliness? Infatuation with a knight in shining armor come to slay her dragon?

No. It was none of those things, she finally admitted. What she felt for Luke was something that had grown quietly, without her even realizing what was happening. With every honorable act, every kind gesture, every teasing remark that he made, Jessica had unknowingly walked right into the trap like a lamb to the slaughter. And it *was* a trap she found herself in. She couldn't stop feeling the way she did, even though she knew the pain that was waiting for her at the end of the few short months he had left here. It was going to be like her father all over again. She was going to demean herself by crying and begging him to come back. Only this time Luke would be the man who would ignore her pleas and ride out of her life, and Jessica didn't know if her heart could withstand that devastating break.

Looking at the handsome face so peaceful in sleep, she felt a sharp stab of pain. She was the cause of her own downfall. She had brought him here. But how was she to have known she was going to do something so stupid as to fall in love with her hired gunfighter?

Jessica didn't have long to think about her predicament, however. With the lengthening shadows outside, an uninformed Frances walked through the back door and into the hall with Heather right beside her. Before Jessica could even think to shut the door, the child had broken free and run to the open door of Luke's room to give him the cookies she'd made es-

pecially for him. She frowned at the sight that met her eyes.
"Is Yuke sick?"

Suddenly realizing how the little girl might be affected after having both of her parents shot, Jessica knew she had to handle this carefully. "He's not feeling well," she answered truthfully, patting her lap in invitation, one the troubled child quickly accepted. "Luke got hurt today."

The brown eyes that quickly looked at the man on the bed were clouded with worry. "How?"

This was the part Jessica had been dreading, but she knew Heather was going to find out sooner or later, and she wasn't going to lie to the child. "Someone shot him. But it was only in the shoulder and the doctor said he's going to be fine," she hurried on when she saw the color leave Heather's face. "It's a lot like when Lee was shot. And he's fine now, isn't he?"

The dark little head nodded hesitantly.

"Well then, Luke's going to be fine too," Jessica assured, for her own benefit as well as the child's. "Dr. Andrews said to make sure we feed him well so he'll get his strength back. He's very weak now."

Heather's face brightened at that. "I made him cookies!" she offered, holding up the napkin-wrapped bundle for Jessica's inspection.

"And I'm sure he'll love them. But for now the doctor said we have to give him soup broth. Then, when he's feeling better, he can have your cookies."

At the disappointment on the little face Jessica smiled. "I'll tell you what. Why don't we put these right here?" she said, taking the wrapped cookies to place them on the bedside table. "You know how much Luke loves sweets. We'll leave them here as a bribe to make him eat his broth and get better so he can have them."

Heather grinned, recognizing the ploy from the many times she had been made to clean her plate before she could have dessert. The idea of an adult being made to follow the same rule amused the little girl immensely.

Frannie stepped further into the room then and noticed the strain Jessica was trying hard to hide from the child. She laid her hand on her young friend's shoulder and squeezed comfortingly until the golden-green eyes raised to hers. "Why don't Heather an' me go inta the kitchen an' get a pot o' that soup goin' right now?" she offered. "I'm thinkin' you look like you could use a bowl yerself."

Jessica reached up to squeeze the hand on her shoulder, smiling gratefully at the older woman's perception. "Thank you, Frannie," she said softly. "I don't know what I'd do without you."

"Nonsense," Frances said, clearing her throat as she took Heather's hand. "Come on then, kitten, it's back ta the kitchen with us."

The door closed behind them, and Jessica sank back into the chair with a heavy sigh. Her eyes went to the napkin-wrapped bundle on the table, then to the man who lay so still and pale on the bed. For her sake, as well as for Heather's, she prayed that what she had assured the little girl of was the truth, that Luke was going to be all right.

As the hours wore on, however, and Luke still didn't regain consciousness, Jessica began to pray harder. Surely if everything was as the doctor said, he should have woken by now. It had been nearly eight hours since they brought him in and he hadn't so much as flickered an eyelid. Jessica knew this, for she had been sitting here watching his face practically every second of those eight long hours.

Frances had finally left close to nine o'clock. She had tried to convince Heather to spend the night with her, but the child refused to leave the house. Lacking the strength or confidence to give the little girl what Jessica was fearing more and more might be false hope, she had given in to the child's request to sleep on the couch in the front parlor. Much like herself, Jessica realized the little girl needed to be close to Luke. So Heather slept while Jessica kept vigil at Luke's bedside.

The grandfather clock began striking the hour of midnight, but before it could finish a little barefooted form wrapped in white cotton appeared in the doorway.

"Jess'ca?"

Looking up, Jessica saw her own fear mirrored in the brown

eyes and she held out her arms. The child padded quickly across the floor and crawled up into her lap.

"I scared for Yuke," Heather admitted quietly.

Tucking the cold little feet beneath the quilt that was wrapped around her gave Jessica a moment to get her own fears under control before she tried to reassure the child. "I told you what the doctor said," she offered weakly.

Heather nodded. "But Yuke won't wake up. My mama an' papa didn't wake up." It was so close to what Jessica feared that it was hard to find the words to argue. "This isn't like your mama and papa, though," she tried to explain. "Luke's just sleeping to get better."

Jessica didn't blame Heather for looking confused at that. She knew she wasn't making any sense. But what else could she say? She was just as frightened that Luke wasn't going to wake up.

Not knowing what else to say, Jessica hugged the little girl close, laying her cheek against the soft hair on top of the child's head. The rocking chair creaked softly in the silence as she rocked and let herself draw comfort from the warm little body held so tightly in her arms. Once more, she prayed.

All was quiet for so long that Jessica was sure Heather had fallen asleep. It surprised her when the little girl's quietly voiced question broke the silence. "What's heaven yike, Jess'ca?"

Closing her eyes, Jessica tried to keep her voice even. "I hear it's a very beautiful place."

There was silence for a moment.

"My mama an' papa are there."

Even though it was painful to talk about this right now, given her fears for Luke, Jessica knew Heather needed reassuring. "I'm sure they are, sweetheart."

"An' your mama's there too."

"I believe so."

"Where's your papa?"

That turn in the conversation threw Jessica, and it was a long moment before she could answer. "I don't know."

"You said he yeft you."

And people said children had short memories. "He did."

"Where'd he go? An' why didn't you go wif him?"

Heather had no idea the pain her innocent questions were inflicting. Unconsciously Jessica held her tighter as she stared out into the deep blackness beyond the window, wondering how to explain what had happened enough to appease the child's curiosity without revealing the whole, painful, truth.

"I told you my mama died when I was only six," she began, and at the nod continued. "Well, I guess my papa felt like he couldn't take care of me by himself so he took me to a place where other people could."

"What place?"

"It's called an orphanage. It's where children go who don't have mamas and papas to take care of them."

Heather pushed away to look up at Jessica with a frown of confusion. "Do I hafta go to a orph-nage?"

Jessica pulled the little girl tightly into her arms, not realizing how telling her tone was when she answered adamantly, "No, you don't! You're going to live right here, and I'm going to love you and take care of you!"

With a child's perception Heather asked, "Didn't you yike the orph-nage?"

This was going a lot further than Jessica had intended. Mentally calming herself, she pulled the little girl's head to her shoulder and started rocking once more. "It wasn't so bad," she tried to assure her, though the words were at odds with the slight tremor in her voice. "There were lots of children to play with."

"But didn't you miss your papa?" came the softly muffled question.

As Jessica continued to rock and stare out the window, she slowly began to relive that day in her mind, and she didn't realize how soft her voice became as she spoke. "At first I told myself he would come back for me, that he only meant to leave me there until he got over losing Mama. But as the months passed, and then the years began to pass, I finally accepted the fact that he wasn't coming back."

Lost to the present now, Jessica was no longer even aware

of anyone else as she verbally remembered. "He didn't even say good-bye. He just left me sitting out in that big, empty hallway while he went in to talk to Mrs. Biddle. He tried to sneak out another door, but I saw him through the front window. I didn't know where we were or what was happening, only that he had forgotten me. I ran down the hall, but one of the ladies caught me just outside the door." Her voice caught painfully. "I called to him to come back, but he just kept right on walking away. He didn't even look back."

Jessica jumped at the little hand that came up to touch her cheek, and it suddenly dawned on her what she had done. She had just told someone her most painful secret, the pain she had never admitted to another soul. The brown eyes that looked up at her were troubled, confirming that she had revealed far too much.

"But listen to me." She quickly tried to correct her blunder by laughing now, though it came out sounding strained. "I'm making it sound like the end of the world when it really wasn't. I got along just fine without him. I found I really didn't need him to be happy."

Heather looked ready to question her further, so Jessica quickly spoke up again. "And now it's time for you to go back to sleep, little miss. We've got a very long day ahead of us tomorrow if we intend to make Luke well."

Lifting the child down, Jessica herded her through the doorway toward the parlor before she could object, leaving the bedroom silent.

Carefully Luke opened his eyes just a crack to make sure he was alone. Finding that he was, he opened them further to stare thoughtfully at the empty doorway. He really hadn't been eavesdropping, he told his guilty conscience. He had only been too weak until now to open his eyes and let Jessica know that he was awake.

Actually it had been her voice that awakened him. Of all things, she had been talking about heaven, and for a second he thought he must have died. But then Heather's voice registered and he slowly began to realize he was lying in bed, and from the way his shoulder felt he also realized he couldn't be dead. He truly had been too tired at first to open his eyes. It was only as Jessica continued to speak and he heard the pain in her voice that he chose to quietly eaves—listen.

What he had heard still had Luke battling the indignant rage that had boiled up inside of him as he thought of the lonely, frightened little girl who had been deserted by her father. Now he understood why Jessica wasn't too good at obeying orders. She'd had to learn to take care of herself from the time she was six! That, combined with what James had told him about her time on the wagon train, had Luke wondering how she had escaped becoming as hardened a cynic as he. If anyone deserved to be angry at the injustices of life, she did.

Luke lay there for a long while puzzling over that one. Where a painful past had turned him hard and bitter, one equally as painful, if not more so, had made Jessica into one of the most caring women he had ever known. As he listened to her in the parlor across the hall, singing a soft lullaby to Heather, Luke felt an unaccustomed knot rise in his throat for the little girl who had had no lullabies.

Chapter Twenty-three

Tucking the quilt around a sleeping Heather, Jessica turned down the lamp and made her way out of the darkened parlor just as the grandfather clock struck one. She crossed the hall to return to Luke's room, raking the hair back from her forehead in a way she usually did when she was either very tired or very worried. At this moment she was very much of both.

The quilt still lay in the chair where she had dropped it off her shoulders, and Jessica picked it up now to wrap it around her once more before settling back down into the rocking chair for the long night ahead. With a tired sigh she lay her head back against the high back of the chair as her eyes went to the man lying in bed. Expecting to see the same closed eyelids, she let out a gasp of surprise as she met the ice-blue eyes studying her.

"You're awake!"

"It seems so," Luke got out hoarsely through a throat so dry he could swear someone had driven a herd of cattle through it. "How long have I been out?"

It didn't occur to Jessica to ask just when he had regained consciousness, or if he had overheard her conversation with Heather. "Since early this afternoon. Do you remember what happened?"

"I remember getting shot, then you showin' up to save my hide—again. After that, things get a little fuzzy."

Jessica didn't comment on that first part, but she felt an amazing sense of satisfaction that she had saved his life, even though it was her fault he was out there in the first place.

"Hank went for Dr. Andrews," she explained. "He got the

bullet out and stitched you up. Now you just have to rest and eat so you can get your strength back.''

Luke looked at her for a long, thoughtful moment. "I appreciate what you did," he said finally, then couldn't keep himself from adding, "even though it was foolish."

Her back came up at that. "As foolish as riding over to the Bar M alone to face Ben Mateland?"

"I'm used to that kind of thing," he rasped through his aching throat. "I know what I'm doing."

She made a show of looking at him stretched out on the bed. "Obviously. Then you won't mind telling me why you're the one lying there shot while I'm the one sitting here playing nurse?" Jessica challenged smugly.

Luke glared at her in the face of that logic. "*Playing* nurse is right," he grumbled in place of an argument. "A real nurse—would have gotten me—some water by now rather than—arguing with—a wounded man."

Jessica was suddenly ashamed of herself for standing here arguing when she ought to just feel relieved that he was alive. And he was right. She was a lousy nurse not to have thought that he would be thirsty when he woke. Intending to quickly remedy the oversight, she rose to leave. His words stopped her at the door.

"Where are you going?"

At the urgency in his tone Jessica turned back, her brows knit in a mixture of confusion and surprise. "To the kitchen to get your water. Where did you think?"

Luke relaxed back against the pillows, embarrassed that he had reacted so strongly to the thought that she meant to leave him for the rest of the night. "I just thought you were mad and you were gonna run off an' leave me to fend for myself," he explained gruffly.

Jessica took offense. "You think I'd do that? Leave a wounded man to take care of himself just because I got angry at his high-handed manner?"

His annoyed snort told her what he thought of that assessment, but before he could say anything she cut him off. "Are you still thirsty?"

"Yes."

Her eyes sparkled at the testy tone of his answer, so relieved was she to finally believe he was going to be all right. "Then stop behaving like a sulking child and let me go get your water."

Seeing the smile, Luke figured she was just getting cocky with him flat on his back and weak as a kitten. Still, knowing the reason for her mood, he couldn't help questioning irritably. "And just why are you suddenly so happy?"

"Because you're complaining."

He knew it! "And you like irritating me?" Luke questioned with a scowl that said if that was her intent she was succeeding.

"No."

"Then why?"

Jessica didn't try to hide the smile any longer as she answered, "Because if you feel well enough to argue and complain, then that means Dr. Andrews was right. You are going to be okay."

With that pleased prediction she turned and left the room, leaving Luke to stare at the empty doorway, not sure whether to feel offended, or elated. She had to care somewhat if she was so happy that he was going to be all right. Didn't she?

Of course she did! he told himself staunchly. And for that reason he chose to feel elated.

For the next four days Luke gladly let himself be nursed by the two ladies who seemed to constantly be hovering close by to grant his slightest wish. On the second day of his recovery he forced himself to eat all six cookies while Heather sat perched on the footrail of his bed, watching expectantly. Her pure smile of pleasure made up for the way his stomach threatened to rebel at the solid food.

But two days later Luke was complaining about the lack of anything substantial to eat. He had had broth and dry toast up to his eyeballs, yet Jessica kept coming into his room every three hours like clockwork with that blasted china bowl on the little lap table Zeke had made for her. Luke was tired; tired of china bowls, tired of eating nothing but broth like some ninety-year-old codger with no teeth, and he was especially tired of lying in this bed alone while Jessica hovered over him treating him like he was a helpless, *harmless* old man!

His simmering irritability finally boiled over on the fifth day when the grandfather clock struck the noon hour and he saw Jessica appear in the doorway with that damned china bowl on his tray. That was Luke's breaking point. "Don't you dare come one step closer with that bowl!" he ground out. "I've decided I want a steak!"

Jessica was speechless for a moment, for he had been a model patient up until now. "But Dr. Andrews said—"

"I don't give a horse's ass what he said!" Luke cut her off. "If I was dying right now and you had some magical elixir in that bowl that would give me eternal life, I wouldn't drink it! I haven't used my teeth for so long I don't even know if I remember how to chew!"

She really could sympathize, but Jessica was also afraid not to stick to the doctor's orders to the letter. The only food he had prescribed was broth. To deviate from those orders could mean a setback—or worse. She was clearly torn. "I don't know, Luke. The doctor said—"

"Let me make this simple for you," Luke interrupted again, seeing her turmoil. "I'm going to eat something whether you bring it to me or I have to get out of this bed and go to the bunkhouse and get Billy to fix it for me. Now, you make the choice which it's gonna be."

Jessica stood there, tapping her foot in annoyance as she weighed the choices he had given her. She knew he was stubborn enough to try to do exactly what he threatened if she didn't bring him something. She also knew he'd never make it to the bunkhouse in his weakened condition. Of course, that wouldn't keep the stubborn ox from trying it!

That thought made up her mind. "What about a compromise?" she offered.

"I'm listenin'."

"Though you think you want a steak right now, I can assure you that you'll regret it after going five days with nothing but broth. What if I fix you some eggs and grits, and maybe a slice or two of bacon and a couple of hot, fluffy biscuits dripping with melted butter?''

As Jessica had hoped, her words had Luke's mouth watering.

''Well?'' she asked at his continued silence.

''Well, what are you waiting for? Get to whipping up those eggs and biscuits, Nurse Jessica.'' Luke gave the order with a grin.

Jessica shook her head. ''You're a horrid patient,'' she scolded, trying hard to hide her own smile.

His grin widened. ''Then you ought to hurry up and make me well to get me out of your tender care.'' He seemed to rethink that as he went on. ''Although, come to think of it, I kinda like layin' back in bed, relaxin' and havin' a beautiful woman wait on me hand and foot.'' His grin turned downright devilish as he went on. ''And after you feed me I may just let you give me a backrub,'' he finished, giving her a wink.

Jessica fought the insane urge to blush. ''You're incorrigible.''

''We already established that fact weeks ago. I just haven't been given the opportunity to act on it yet.''

It wasn't the truth and they both knew it. There had been a hundred opportunities if he had wanted to compromise her. He had just been too honorable to take advantage of them.

''And you won't get the chance today either,'' Jessica teased as she turned to leave, only to turn back in the doorway. ''Because if you don't behave yourself, then I won't feed you.''

His frown was contradicted by the amusement lighting his eyes. ''You're a hard woman, Jessie Cameron.''

Unexplainably happy, Jessica's lilting laughter filled the room. ''And you'd better get use to that fact, Luke Cam—''

The enormity of what her words could mean hit them both at the same time, and Jessica's smile faded as all her fears suddenly came back like an unwelcome cloud on a sunny day. ''I'd better get started on your meal,'' she said quietly, and before Luke could question her lightning-quick change of mood, she hurried down the hall.

Luke was left to wonder why she had suddenly become so distressed in the middle of their teasing banter, and he didn't like the answer that came to mind.

That afternoon the visitor arrived that Jessica had been expecting for the past five days. Benjamin Mateland. He rode up imperiously on his buckskin stallion with four of his men following behind. There was such a smug smile of satisfaction on his face as he dismounted and swaggered toward the porch that if Jessica had had any doubts he was behind Luke's being shot they were immediately banished. The man oozed a cocky self-confidence that set her teeth on edge as she quietly opened the front door and stepped out onto the porch before shutting the door just as quietly behind her.

Crossing to the top of the steps, she successfully cut off his approach at the bottom one, using the advantage of making him have to look up at her for this confrontation. Silently, she waited for him to make the first move.

Looking up into the defiant golden-green eyes, Ben frowned. She was supposed to be distraught, or at least scared now that her gunslinger was dead. He at first had hoped to convince her that Cameron had run off, but when he sent that no-account Cain back to retrieve the body, he had come back empty-handed. Ben had ridden out to the spot, and seeing all the blood, he was sure the outlaw couldn't have survived.

After raking his hired gun over the coals for not finishing the job, Ben had slowly begun to realize that the situation might actually be better the way it had turned out. If the man had been found by someone on the Circle R and brought back to Jessica facedown across a saddle, it had probably given her a healthy dose of respect for him, Ben had surmised smugly. That was one of the reasons he had given her a week before this visit, to let her stew in her fear for a while.

It wasn't fear *or* respect he saw in her eyes, however, as she glared down on him now. She looked for all the world as if she would love nothing better than to shoot him where he stood if only she had a gun in her hands. No, this wasn't the way this meeting was supposed to be going at all.

"Afternoon, Ms. Cameron," he said finally, deciding he was going to have to test her mood. Maybe she was more worried than she seemed.

"Mr. Mateland. To what do I owe the pleasure of your visit?" Jessica bit out, managing to make it an obvious insult.

Being of the firm opinion that everyone—especially women—should quake in his presence, Ben naturally stiffened at her show of contempt. "I just came to see how you were doin'. I heard you been havin' a few troubles lately. Wondered if that husband of yours was able to do anything about 'em?"

Jessica's hands clenched within the folds of her skirt. His tone was meant to let her know he had been the one behind Luke being shot. Her voice nearly shook with the anger seething inside when she finally answered him. "I really don't know why you're acting so concerned about my husband, or about my troubles, Mr. Mateland. You and I both know you're not as ignorant on either subject as you pretend to be."

"Why, I have no idea what you mean, Jessica," Ben said innocently, before his tone suddenly turned menacing. "But if you're implying I had anything to do with what's been happening to you, or that outlaw's death, you better think long and hard before you start throwing out accusations."

So he thought Luke had died. For some reason Jessica chose not to disabuse him of that notion. "Is there some reason you're here, Mr. Mateland? Other than to threaten me?" she asked stiffly.

He took one step up, hoping his nearness and size might add intimidation to his words. "I'm here to make one last offer on your place—now that you find yourself alone again." He let his eyes roam over her insolently before he went on. "And who knows? If you're real friendly I might just consider lettin' you stay on here as my—housekeeper."

At the snicker the lewd implication brought from his men, Jessica saw red. "There's about as much chance of that as of hell freezing over!" she spat contemptuously, and was just about to lose the battle against the urge to slap that lascivious leer from his face when the door behind her opened.

The Deal

The change in Benjamin Mateland's expression would have been comical if Jessica weren't so enraged. As it was, she took his look of shock, which changed to disbelief before slowly building to foiled rage, to mean that it was Luke who stood in the doorway. How she wanted to rub Ben's nose in the fact that his attempt at murder hadn't worked this time, yet she knew this situation was too precarious to speak rashly. Luke was still weak. And Mateland did have four men behind him.

"Is there a problem, Jessie?"

His voice was even, but as cold as steel in a blizzard. Jessica could picture in her mind the chilling threat in those ice-blue eyes. Of course, being strong enough to back up that threat was an entirely different story.

"Nothing to worry about," she assured without turning. She kept her eyes focused on Ben's. "Mr. Mateland just heard some misinformation. Somehow a rumor seems to have started that you were killed."

She heard the sound of his boots on the planks of the porch as he stepped up beside her to slip his right arm around her waist. Only Jessica realized how heavily he leaned against her, or that he didn't put any pressure on that arm. She struggled to maintain an even expression while she braced herself to support a good portion of his weight. "Can you imagine that?" she asked lightly.

Luke looked from Jessica to the man who stood on the bottom step glaring up at him. "No. But then I'm sure he was relieved when you told him the rumor wasn't true, and that I'm very much alive. Weren't you, Mateland?" he asked with a smile that did nothing to thaw the icy contempt in his eyes.

"Yeah," Ben played along, his own smile just as brittle. "But then the way the folks around here feel about you, and now Jessica for pairin' up with you, it didn't surprise me none that someone took a notion to shoot you."

"I guess I'm just lucky whoever it was that did it was a lousy shot," Luke taunted, and saw one of the men behind Ben straighten in anger, "or I'd be dead now and Jessie would be left all alone. And I know how much that thought tears you up, Mateland."

It took considerable effort on Ben's part not to pull his gun and do what that good-for-nothing Cain hadn't been able to. The only thing stopping him was that Jessica's hired hands would come running out at the first sign of gunfire and he'd have to shoot them too, and probably Jessica as well. Nobody would think twice about the outlaw's death, but Ben didn't think he could cover up all the others. No, he'd have to bide his time and catch Cameron alone again. And this time he'd personally make sure the outlaw didn't live to tell about it.

"You can't blame me for worryin' over my neighbor," Ben said, turning almost cordial now that he realized everything would still work out as planned. Besides, the more he saw the spirit and fire in Jessica, the more he was getting a taste to keep her. After he got his hands on her land, he fully intended to get his hands on her. After all, she owed him that much for all the trouble she was causing him.

Luke saw the way Mateland was looking at Jessica and his body went rigid with protective rage. Ignoring the pain the move caused, he twisted to push her safely behind him, then spread his feet farther apart to brace himself against the wave of dizziness that threatened. His hand clenched, then relaxed beside the Colt he had strapped on his left hip when he had first heard Mateland's voice out here. He was a split second slower with his left hand, but even at that he was confident he could outdraw Ben. If the man was foolish enough to try.

"You've expressed your concern, Mateland," Luke bit out tightly. "And now that you see there's no need for condolences you can ride out—unless you want to say somethin' else? In that case we're gonna wait until Jessica's safely in the house."

"I'm not going to leave you out here alone!" Jessica whispered the words urgently for his ears alone.

Luke ground his teeth and tried to remind himself she had a reason for being so obstinate. He also wasn't sure he had the strength to wrestle her into the house if it came to that.

"Is that about all you had to say—for now?" he asked the man standing on the step below him.

Ben knew what the outlaw was doing. The man was trying

216

to protect Jessica, which was fine with Ben. In fact, it fit his own plan nicely, so he could feel magnanimous in allowing this confrontation to end peacefully. "That's all I have to say—for now," he repeated those last two words both men understood. He then leaned sideways until he could see Jessica, making her feel like a child hiding behind her parent. He tipped his hat. "Until later, Jessica," he said, and turned to walk to his horse.

Jessica stepped up beside Luke as they watched Mateland and his men ride out. "You know, it really annoys me how dense you men seem to think women are," she said, still watching the disappearing riders.

Luke looked at her profile questioningly. "Excuse me?"

When Jessica turned to face him, her eyes mirrored an anger she wouldn't admit stemmed from fear for him. " 'Is that all for now?' " she mimicked testily. "Did you and Ben really think I was too stupid to understand your little code?"

A tawny brow went up as if in surprise. "Was I accusing you of being stupid? Maybe I just figured if you did understand you might take it better than 'This fool woman refuses to get out of the way, Mateland, so I'd appreciate it if you'd wait 'til some other time to try to kill me again.' "

"What I would appreciate is you not always thinking you have to face my problems alone like some fairy-tale knight out to slay the dragon for the damsel in distress!" Jessica argued. "Ben doesn't fight fairly, as you've already seen. He's not going to face you! He's going to lie in wait like the snake he is and shoot you in the back the first chance he gets!"

"So what do you suggest I do?" Luke asked angrily. "Hide behind you?"

Jessica ground her teeth at the snide tone. "There are eight other men on this ranch to help even up the odds if Ben comes back."

"Eight men who are cowboys, not gunmen," Luke came right back. "You hired me to protect your hide! Remember?"

"I didn't hire you!" Jessica blurted out, then could have kicked herself when she saw his satisfied smirk.

"I'm glad to hear you finally admit it."

"What I meant," Jessica quickly amended, "is that I didn't hire you to ride out alone like a fool and get yourself shot."

But Luke liked her first meaning better. "Admit it, Jessie. You didn't hire me, you married me."

"We made a deal," she corrected, taking a step backward as he took one toward her.

"You bring that up a lot when we're alone," Luke said softly as he noticed her sudden nervousness. "Are you reminding me—or yourself?"

Jessica had gotten used to the helpless, wounded Luke over the last five days and had nearly forgotten this Luke, the one who could make her insides tremble when he looked at her the way he was doing now. "I remind you because you always seem inclined to forget," she said, taking another step backward, which he again matched. "If I could have just hired you, I assure you that's what I would have done."

Luke might have believed her if those golden-green eyes weren't so full of turmoil. Funny, with Mateland she'd had the control and face of a consummate poker player, yet with him her eyes gave away her every thought.

"Deals can be changed if both parties agree, Jessie," he whispered huskily, taking another step forward.

Her retreat backed Jessica against the door. Her knees were threatening to buckle at that husky tone that could so devastate her. He was going to kiss her, she knew, and she also knew that if he did she was going to be lost.

"I think we'd better keep to the terms as they are," she said breathlessly, and as his lips came down to change her mind Jessica's hand found the doorknob pressing into her hip and she turned it, nearly stumbling into the hall as she left Luke to lean into the empty space where she had just been.

"You'd better get back to bed now," she went on from inside the hallway, not meeting his eyes. "It won't do to aggravate your wound by staying up too long."

Luke was frowning darkly. "The only thing aggravating me is an uncooperative female," he muttered as she stepped back a safe distance to clear a path to his room.

Throwing one last frustrated glare her way, he stalked off, slamming the door behind him, only to wince at the pain that act of temper caused his shoulder. Of course, that pain only matched another ache his elusive little wife had caused.

Chapter Twenty-four

For the next three days the routine changed in the house. It took Luke the first day to realize what was going on, but by the end of the day he had caught on to his wife's ploy. He hadn't really questioned Heather's presence with Jessica when she brought in his supper the evening after Ben's visit, or even the next morning when she brought his breakfast tray. The little girl had spent quite a bit of time in his room making sure he "got better." When lunchtime came and Frances brought in his lunch, telling him that Jessica was hanging out laundry, however, Luke began to grow suspicious. When Heather again accompanied the arrival of his supper tray that night, he was fairly certain that Jessica meant to avoid being alone with him again.

Along with his suspicions growing stronger in those three days, Luke was also growing stronger physically. But even though his condition was improving, his disposition was deteriorating. The first few days of having Jessica wait on him had been pleasurable, since he was weak and could do little more than lie flat on his back, but with the return of his health the walls of his room insidiously began to close in on him. His right shoulder was still touchy and pained him if he moved the wrong way, but it was mending. There was really no reason to stay cooped up in the stifling room any longer, especially since Jessica was avoiding spending any time in it with him.

Luke missed that, not only because he was aching to hold her in his arms and sample the sweet taste of her lips, but also because he missed talking to her, sparring with her, teasing her, and seeing her try to hide the blush that would stain her cheeks. He missed his Jessica. And even though he thought the sun rose and set on Heather, Luke was beginning to resent seeing Jessica use the child like some sort of human shield to keep him at arm's length.

So it was that on the morning of the fourth day after Ben's visit, Luke was up before the sun, shaved and dressed to join the living again. He had decided to put an end to Jessica's game. Somehow, after breakfast, he was going to get Heather to go visit with Zeke and Frannie even if he had to bribe her.

But before the child could finish her breakfast so Luke could put his plan in motion, Heather disrupted it. "Jess'ca?"

From in front of the stove where she was taking out a pan of golden-brown biscuits Jessica turned her head. "Yes, sweetheart?"

"Frannie taked me on a picnic when I was at her house yes'erday."

"Frannie took me," Jessica corrected gently. "That sounds very nice. Did you like it?"

"Uh huh. We tak—took a quilt out in the yard and had our san'wiches on it. Have you ever been on a picnic?"

There was the slightest hesitation. "No. Although we did eat outside the wagon when I made the trip out here."

Luke sat staring at her back as she went about her work, answering Heather's questions about that trip as she placed the hot biscuits on a plate. There had been such a poignant note of regret in her answer when she told the little girl she had never been on a simple picnic. Again Luke was reminded of all the little things Jessica had missed growing up without a family, things he remembered fondly but seemed to take for granted.

Suddenly an idea began to form.

"You say you enjoyed that picnic, puss?" he asked, turning his head to look at the child seated beside him.

"Uh huh!"

He grinned at her enthusiasm, reaching over to ruffle the soft hair on top of her head. "You know, I used to love 'em myself. Whatta ya say we see if we can't talk Jessica into

221

goin' on one with us this afternoon?''

"Can we?" the little girl cried, bouncing in her seat and clapping her hands in delight.

His grin widening at the child's obvious pleasure over the idea, Luke turned his gaze on the woman who now faced them. "How 'bout it, Jessica? Would you let Heather and me take you on a real, honest-to-goodness picnic?"

Jessica's eyes were shining with nearly as much anticipation as the four-year-old's, and seeing it Luke felt his heart constrict painfully.

Oh, but it sounded wonderful, Jessica thought as she looked at the handsome man and beaming child who sat waiting expectantly for her answer. And even though she had purposely kept Luke at arm's length the last few days for just this reason, she now allowed herself to indulge in a few short seconds of fantasy. She stripped away the reality of his eventual leaving and let herself see only her family, her husband and child, suggesting something so wonderfully domestic as a picnic. She wanted to go so badly, yet Jessica had to wonder if the more she allowed herself to give in to these wants, the worse it was going to hurt when he left.

With that thought in mind she hesitated. "Well—I'm supposed to wash today," she offered lamely.

Heather's face fell in disappointment. But Luke wasn't going to give up so easily, not after seeing how badly Jessica wanted to go. "The clothes'll still be there tomorrow. Come on, Jessie. We all deserve to get out of this house for a while. I know I've nearly gone crazy staring at those four walls for the last week and a half."

"P'ease, Jess'ca," Heather added her own plea.

Having wanted to go in the first place, Jessica couldn't hold out long against those hopeful brown eyes. She finally smiled, shaking her head as she gave in. "All right! All right! We'll go! But you two will have to tell me what to do. What do we pack besides food and a quilt?"

Heather was bouncing and clapping again. Luke wore a pleased grin that showed straight white teeth beneath the silky mustache, and made tiny little lines crease the corners of his eyes.

"You don't do a thing," he answered, leaning over to put his arm around Heather's shoulders. "This is our treat. Right, puss?" At the child's giggle and nod he went on, "We're gonna take care of everything. All you have to do is go and enjoy yourself. Now eat your breakfast and get out of the kitchen so Heather and I can get to work."

After barely being given time to finish her coffee, Jessica was hustled out of the room, and as she set about straightening the rest of the downstairs she glanced often toward the closed door to the kitchen. There were conspiratorial whispers, punctuated every so often by a childish giggle or muffled male laughter. She was dying to tiptoe to the doorway to try to hear what was being said in those whispers, but she restrained the urge, not having the heart to risk spoiling their surprise. Besides, just the anticipation of the coming picnic had Jessica feeling light enough to float on air.

Finally, after three hours that seemed more like three days, Luke and Heather came upstairs, where Jessica had stayed after getting dressed for their outing, to announce that everything was ready. Heather held a small bouquet of fall flowers, and as soon as the door opened she held them up to Jessica, who couldn't help the mistiness that came to her eyes at the smile on the precious little face.

"These are for you," Heather announced.

Jessica took the bouquet and held them to her nose, breathing deeply. "Umm. They smell wonderful. Did you pick these all by yourself?"

"Uh huh. But Yuke had to tie the ribbon for me."

"They're very pretty," Jessica said, smiling at the pleasure her compliment gave the little girl. "Thank you." Hesitantly she looked to Luke, and the warm look in his eyes further threatened the protective wall she was trying to build around her heart.

"So are you," he said softly. When she looked confused, he went on to clarify. "You're very pretty too."

Against her will Jessica blushed like a sixteen-year-old getting her first compliment. She was so embarrassed by her reaction she wouldn't quite meet his gaze. "Thank you," she whispered.

"Are we gonna go now?" Heather unknowingly broke the mood with her impatient question, causing both adults to snap out of the spell that seemed to have taken hold of them.

Resigning himself to the fact that he was going to have to wait a little longer to have any time alone with Jessica, Luke turned to the child. "We're gonna go right now," he answered, then turned again to the woman standing before him. "Your carriage awaits, milady," he said with a formal bow, then offered her his arm. "Shall we be off?"

At Heather's giggle Jessica swept him an exaggerated curtsy and took his offered arm, playing along. "Why, of course, kind sir. I can't wait to see what surprises you and your cohort here have cooked up."

Jessica was surprised to find the wagon waiting at the front gate, thinking Luke's words had only been in fun. She had expected they might take a quilt down to the creek at best, but it seemed Luke had a different plan in mind. He helped her up to the wagon seat, then turned to help Heather into the back where a pile of quilts lay beside a large covered basket. Untying the reins from the gate post, he climbed up onto the seat and with a click of his tongue and a snap of the reins they set out for Jessica's first picnic.

They traveled for nearly twenty minutes, heading north across Circle R property with Jessica expecting Luke to pull the horses to a halt at any moment. When time continued to pass and they still moved on, she felt her stomach begin to tighten in reaction to the familiar area they were now riding through. She hadn't been able to come out here since her last time nearly six months ago. It was just a mile or so from here that she, Zeke, and Hank had found John's body. Remembering that awful sight, Jessica shivered.

"Cold?" Luke asked solicitously, glancing over at her movement as she pulled her shawl more tightly around her shoulders.

It took a moment to realize why he had asked the question.

Jessica managed to shake her head. "No."

The tone of her answer made him frown, and it was then that he noticed her sudden pallor. "What's wrong, Jessie?"

"Nothing," she answered quickly. Too quickly.

Luke's frown grew heavier, and his eyes left her to roam over the terrain around them before coming back to rest on her once more. "Are you afraid because we're close to Mateland's land?" he asked quietly so that Heather wouldn't overhear. "If that's it, you don't have to worry. I'm gonna stop right up here at a cave I saw a few weeks back when I checked out the boundary between your land and his. I thought you and Heather might like seeing it."

"I—that will be fine," Jessica said unconvincingly.

"If it was fine, you wouldn't be actin' like you're expectin' to see a ghost jump out at you any minute," Luke accused, not realizing how close he came to the truth. "Now, will you please tell me what's botherin' you?"

Jessica was looking at him oddly, but then she realized he couldn't know that his choice of comparisons had been so ironic. She glanced over her shoulder to find Heather caught up in playing with the two dolls Frannie had made for her, then turned back to Luke. Her voice was low and filled with pain as she said, "We—found John just up here."

It was a long moment before Luke spoke as he pushed down the unreasonable jealousy, hating himself for such a petty emotion given what the woman beside him had gone through, and was now going through again in her memory. "I'm sorry, Jessica. I'd never have brought you out here if I'd known. We'll turn around right now and find another—"

"No," she cut him off, laying a restraining hand on his arm as he made to turn the team around. "It's part of my land and I'm going to have to deal with this sooner or later."

He looked at the set expression on her face worriedly. "Well, it can be later."

"No," she answered again, trying to smile reassuringly for her own benefit as well as his. "It might be best this way. We'll just make happy memories here to help ease the bad ones."

"Are you sure?"

At his worried look she nodded. "I'm sure, Luke. Please go on."

Luke reluctantly agreed. "Okay. But point out the spot to me so I won't mistakenly stop too close."

After traveling a few more minutes in silence, Luke felt Jessica go rigid beside him and he followed her gaze to a patch of brush just off the trail. "Is that—"

"Yes," she answered hoarsely. "Whoever killed him tried to hide his body in that thick brush. We probably wouldn't have found him then, but the—buzzards—"

"Ssh," Luke cut her off when her voice cracked on that last. Not even considering the action, he put his arm around her and pulled her head to his shoulder, going on softly, "I know I'm askin' the impossible, but try to put it out of your mind if you can."

But you didn't put something like what she had seen out of your mind. "I can't, Luke. He was such a good man. He didn't deserve to die like that!"

Luke fought to beat down the ugly head of jealousy and tried to comfort her. "So I've heard."

"There was no reason in the world why anyone should have wanted to kill him. Even though I suspect Ben, I still can't think of any plausible reason why he would do it. He'd never seemed interested in our land before John's death. It was only afterward that he started pressuring me to sell." Her tone filled with painful sarcasm now as she went on, "And I won't believe he's concerned about my being a 'woman alone.' Not when the only threat I've faced so far has come from him!"

Luke was wondering about that also. "Was John out here alone when he was killed?"

"Yes. We heard dynamiting that day. Since it came from this direction, John thought it must be Ben blasting stumps to make way for more pasture land. John wanted to make sure none of our cattle were close by to be hurt by the blasting, so he rode out here to have a look."

That sounded a bit strange given all the open range and the acres of wintering pasture Mateland already had. But then some men never had enough no matter how much wealth they accumulated.

"And you say he was shot?" Luke continued his questioning. "He couldn't have just gotten wounded by one of the blasts and tried to make it home? A chunk of splintered wood or a small piece of rock could make a hole a lot like a bullet."

"He was shot," Jessica assured. "Dr. Andrews examined him and found the bullet. Sheriff Davis took it hoping to at least discover what kind of gun was used."

"Any luck?"

Her shoulders sagged. "A revolver, just like most every man in the territory wears. Other than that we know nothing. His money was taken, so everyone automatically suspected outlaws. But with Ben blasting not two miles away, I wonder what kind of outlaws would shoot someone and risk being heard by all the men so close by?"

"That's true," Luke agreed. "Unless they expected the blasts to cover a gunshot. On the other hand, as much as I hate the man—and from experience wouldn't put murder past him—what makes you think Mateland did it?"

"For the same reason I said earlier. He'd never shown any interest in the Circle R until after John died. Since then he's been obsessed to the point of threatening me, trying to get me to sell out. He wants this land for some reason. What I can't understand is why."

"Well, we know he's not happy with me bein' around," Luke offered with a smile that told just how much that fact bothered him. "Now all that's left is to keep pushin' 'til he gets so mad he'll act without thinkin'. That's when we'll find out what he's up to."

Jessica couldn't help her fear at that thought. "Please be careful," she urged him. "I can't help but remember what happened the last time you 'pushed' Ben to anger. The next time you might not be so lucky."

The concern in her eyes gave him reason to hope, and gently he asked, "Would it bother you terribly if he did succeed next time?"

"What a ridiculous question!" she gasped, and out of the

227

corner of her eye she saw Heather's head snap up at her tone. Jessica looked back to smile reassuringly at the child, then turned back to Luke, lowering her voice as she went on. "Of course it would bother me. I couldn't stand the thought that you had been killed trying to solve my problems."

It wasn't the answer he had hoped for, and Luke remained silent, watching her, hoping she would add something—anything that might hint that she'd feel more than just guilt if he were killed. He wanted to think she might at least get a little choked up. Hell! What was he thinking? A lot of good her feelings would do if he had to *die* to bring them out! What he really wanted to know was how she felt about him when he was alive and breathing and could do something about it!

But then what if she didn't have any feelings deeper than friendship for him? What if she believed, like most everyone else, that a gunslinger—even one that meant to retire—made lousy husband material? Could he risk seeing the rejection in her eyes if he were to ask? Oh, knowing his sweet, tender-hearted Jessie, she'd try to be as gentle as possible in explaining why she could never love a killer. But it would be a rejection just the same.

Not knowing whether he could stand to hear the words or not, Luke chose to let any further questions lie for now. He had a few more months to show her there was more to Luke Cameron than a hired gun. He wasn't going to risk that by getting impatient now.

Patience, boy, Bedford Forrest's words echoed from the mist-shrouded battlefields of his memory. *Timing is everything. If the prize is worth having, then it's worth waiting for the right moment to assure yourself you can take it*.

Thinking of the woman who sat beside him, Luke decided if there was ever a prize worth having, Jessica Randall Cameron was it.

Chapter Twenty-five

When they came to the spot Luke had been thinking of, he brought the horses to a halt and pulled back the brake, wrapping the reins around the handle. By the time he jumped down and came around to help Jessica, Heather had already scrambled down by herself and was in the process of searching out the "most perfect" spot for their picnic. Handing Jessica a quilt from the back, Luke lifted the heavy basket out and they joined the little girl.

The place they finally chose was a sunny patch of grass that was sheltered from the north wind by a short mountain ridge that formed a natural boundary of sorts between Jessica's land and Benjamin Mateland's. It was on this side of the mountain that the cave was that Luke had told them about.

Jessica shook out the quilt and was about to start unpacking the picnic basket when Luke's hand on her wrist stopped her. "Unh uh," he admonished. "This is mine and Heather's surprise. Remember? We get to do the unpackin'. You just sit back and let us wait on you."

Feeling a bit strange at this novel role of letting someone else serve her, Jessica sat back and watched as the man and child began to unpack the basket, revealing the treasures they had created for her. Somehow the two of them had fried chicken, and incredible as it seemed, it actually looked edible. There was a bowl of potato salad, a plate with chunks of cheese and pickles, biscuits—these looked suspiciously like the ones left over from breakfast—and a small cake with brown sugar and nuts on top for dessert.

"Okay, it's confession time, you two," Jessica said with a

suspicious smile as she surveyed the meal laid out before her. "You went to Frannie and she cooked up all this delicious-smelling food, didn't she?"

"Hun uh!" Heather protested vehemently at the accusation. "Me an' Yuke done it aw but the bisicks. Didn't we, Yuke?"

"We certainly did!" he agreed, looking highly offended himself.

Jessica couldn't help the laugh that escaped at that look. "I meant no offense," she assured. "It's just that—well—of all the talents I could think of you possessing, I must admit *cooking* wasn't anywhere near the top of the list."

"Living alone on the trail for so many years I got a little tired of beans and bacon. Besides," he admitted somewhat sheepishly, "I dearly loved our cook when I was growing up. I guess those hours I spent in the kitchen watchin' Hattie Mae paid off."

Jessica's smile softened now at thinking of this rugged, disturbingly virile man who sat before her as a little boy. The only part of his past he had ever mentioned was that horrible episode that had happened to him and his wife. But she could see in his eyes as he spoke of the woman Hattie Mae, that he had good memories of his past as well. The thought also made her realize that she knew practically nothing about that past.

She wasn't given a chance to question him immediately, however, for he and Heather were in the process of fixing her a plate piled high with more food than she could possibly eat in two meals. Finally Jessica had to call a halt to their zealous efforts. "Whoa!" she cried out, caught between laughter and distress as Heather put a third piece of chicken on the plate. "If I eat all that, the horses won't be able to pull me back home."

Heather let out a giggle at that image, then dropped the chicken leg on the plate anyway. "You got to eat, Jessica."

"Eat, yes, but you want me to stuff myself like a Thanksgiving turkey. Besides, if I eat that much chicken and potato salad I won't have room for a piece of that delicious-smelling cake you baked."

That seemed to decide the matter, for the little girl immediately plucked the leg off the plate and put it back in the bowl she had taken it from.

"Well, I don't have any such problem," Luke said, handing the plate to Jessica along with one he had fixed for Heather. That done, he picked up the last plate and piled it so high that Jessica and Heather were gaping in amazement before he was through.

"You can't possibly mean to eat all that!" Jessica said with a disbelieving laugh.

"You bet I do. I'm still tryin' to make up for that week when you wouldn't feed me anything but broth. Don't forget, the doctor said I have to eat to regain my strength."

"You're not going to have the strength to move if you eat all that," she claimed, eyeing the overflowing plate with a mixture of awe and disbelief. "No one can eat that much food at one time!"

"Wanna bet on it?"

His eyes were so full of mischief that she should have known better than to let it go any further, especially when that mustache was quirked so tellingly at one corner. But it was such a ridiculous amount of food on the plate, Jessica knew there was no way any human being could eat it all. Maybe that was the reason she so recklessly played along with his game.

"Okay," she accepted daringly. But then a small voice of reason pushed her to ask, "What are the stakes?"

"What do you want if you win?" he asked innocently enough.

Jessica thought for a moment, then looked around her before meeting his gaze once more. She smiled smugly. "You'll cook dinner tomorrow as well."

"I'll tell you what," Luke offered confidently. "I'll go you one better. I'll cook all three meals tomorrow if I lose."

"You're on!" Jessica accepted rashly before he could withdraw the tempting offer. "Let me see," she went on, thinking aloud. "For breakfast I'd like pancakes and sausage, and maybe eggs too. And for lunch I think I'll have—"

"Jessica?" Luke cut in on her. "Before you completely

231

plan this menu, don't you want to know what it's going to cost you if I win?''

The thought was so ludicrous she couldn't even consider it seriously, but she asked the question anyway. "Okay. Let's say miracles do still happen and you somehow manage to get down all that food. What will I owe you?"

Heather had been looking back and forth between them during the entire exchange, enjoying the game, and noticing her now, Luke tempered the answer he would have liked to give to make it more suitable for little ears. "I think I'd like you to serve me breakfast—in bed."

The gleam in his eyes told what his words couldn't, and Jessica felt a tremor race through her body at the implication. With disturbing clarity the memory of that night outside the McCalisters' barn washed over her. Just that look had her remembering how he had made her feel when he held her, kissed her, touched her. And even knowing what she did, that he would someday leave, Jessica couldn't help being drawn into the promise his voice was weaving again.

"All right," she agreed softly. "I'll serve you breakfast in bed if you win."

"But that's not all," Luke countered, his eyes seeming to glow now. "If you're going to get three meals, then I expect more than breakfast."

It was like a moth playing around a dancing flame. Jessica knew this was dangerous, but the temptation was too great to pull away to safety. "What else do you want?" she asked, sounding a bit breathless.

Why couldn't Heather find some butterfly to chase? Luke wondered as he looked into the liquid, golden-green eyes staring back at him. It was one of those moments that was made to pull the lady into your arms and kiss her, gently falling to the quilt as you deepened the kiss into one that would fan the flames of desire that already smoldered in her eyes.

Except for the fact that a four-year-old child sat between them.

"A kiss," he said finally. Then, looking down into Heather's upturned face, he forced himself to grin past his frustration. "Don't you think that's a fair deal, puss? Like the knights of old, the fair maiden must give a kiss to the knight for conquering the evil dragon."

He held his plate aloft with a flourishing gesture that had the little girl giggling, and gave Jessica a chance to bring her rioting emotions under control. She had been so caught up in Luke's spell she had completely forgotten about the child that sat between them, watching their every move avidly.

Bringing her breathing under control, she finally joined the game going on between the other two. "Knights of old went to slay huge dragons that could breathe fire. Your dragon, Sir Luke," she said, pointing to the fried chicken on his plate, "seems to have had fire breathed upon him."

"But I had to catch the wily creature first, then slay him with my bare hands," Luke returned seriously. " 'Twas no easy task, milady."

Jessica looked suitably touched by his supposed plight. "I'm sure it was not Sir Luke, for surely this fearsome creature might have pecked you nearly to death."

Heather was giggling again, and Luke had a hard time keeping a straight face as he placed his hand over his heart. "The danger was great, fair maiden, but I faced it alone to lay the beast before you now. And I would face the same threat of death again for only the promise of a kiss from thee."

Jessica was caught up in the game and Heather's enjoyment of it too much to notice the gleam that had come back into his eyes now, which was probably why she went on so recklessly. "That seems a fair reward for so brave a feat. Don't you think so, Maid Heather? I say if he slays this particular dragon," she said, pointing out the plate, "then he deserves a kiss from both of us fair maids."

Heather nodded her agreement vigorously.

Looking fondly at the child's happy face, Jessica completely missed the satisfied, and somewhat cunning, smile of the man who watched her.

It took nearly half an hour, but Luke managed to eat every bite of food he had piled onto his plate, even wiping the remaining traces of potato salad up with the last bite of biscuit before popping it into his mouth with a dramatic flourish for the benefit of his astounded audience. Laying the plate down, he leaned back on his hands and chewed, smiling at the clapping Heather before he looked to Jessica, his eyes dancing with devilish delight.

"Well, it looks as if I slayed the dragon, milady."

But before Jessica could say a word, Heather launched herself at Luke's chest, nearly toppling him as she threw her little arms around his neck. "You winned, Yuke!" she proclaimed enthusiastically. "Now you get kisses." At that she promptly squeezed his neck tighter and planted a wet kiss on his cheek.

Luke held the child close, feeling his heart contract. She may not be his own by blood, but he had grown to love her over the past weeks as fiercely as he knew any father could love a daughter. It was only one more reason he was determined to convince Jessica that he was going to stay on after his year was up. He couldn't bear the thought of either of them not being in his life.

"Now it's your turn, Jess'ca!" Heather said as she finally pulled away, gaining Luke's attention once more. "You gotta give Yuke a kiss!"

Jessica looked ill at ease as she got up onto her knees to lean over and give him the same kind of kiss Heather had. Before she could, however, Luke's words stopped her.

"I believe I'll wait on this one," he said, looking at Heather so Jessica couldn't read the intent in his eyes. "That way I've got yours to enjoy now and I've still got one from Jessica to look forward to later."

The little girl didn't seem to question that logic, but when Luke finally met Jessica's gaze she was watching him with a mixture of suspicion and worry. Luke couldn't help himself. He grinned.

As the afternoon passed, the combination of good food and warm sunshine made Jessica's eyelids grow heavy as she watched Heather stooping beside a prairie-dog hole to look inside for the furry little animal. Luke knelt beside the child, and knowing the little girl was safe in his care, Jessica told herself that surely she could lie down and rest her eyes for just a moment. That was her last thought before she gave up to the beckoning arms of sleep.

When Luke found Jessica asleep, he held a finger to his lips as he took Heather's hand and led her away from the quilt. "Why don't we let Jessica sleep while we do a little exploring?" he asked quietly, and at the child's silent nod he went to the wagon for the lantern he had brought. He rejoined Heather, and the two made their way to the cave.

"We'll only go a little ways," Luke said as he lit the wick on the lantern and replaced the glass chimney. "If we find anything interesting we'll come back with Jessica when she wakes up."

They weren't far inside before Luke felt a little hand slip into his. Stopping to look down at her, he saw her fear. "We don't have to go any farther if you don't want to," he offered gently. "I just thought you'd like to see inside."

"I do," Heather protested. "I—just yike ho'din' your hand too."

"Are you sure? We can turn around right now if you want to."

With only the slightest hesitation the little girl shook her head before pulling him along deeper into the cave.

"It's always best to face your fears," Luke said proudly at her decision. "Most of the time you find out there was really no need to be afraid after all."

As they moved farther inside, Luke lifted the lantern so they could see better. "Some tribes of Indians used to live in caves long ago. Some would paint pictures on the walls to tell stories about their life."

Heather's hand slipped from his as curiosity overtook fear. She moved a little ahead of Luke, looking at the walls carefully for any sign of the pictures he described. Smiling, Luke followed along behind. He wasn't paying a lot of attention to his surroundings until he noticed how littered with rocks the floor beneath his feet had become. Frowning, he glanced around his feet, not quite able to place the cause of his sudden unease except for the fact that most caves, having solid rock walls, rarely had dirt and rock littering their floor. Rock rarely just broke off from itself unless there was some tremor in the earth, or something like . . .

Luke frowned heavily as he held the lantern higher for a better view of the cave. Or something like someone dynamiting the rock loose, he finished the thought with sudden concern. Could Mateland's blasting nearby have shaken these rocks loose? If it had, then it could also have made cracks in the rock that hadn't given way—yet.

"Come on, Heather," he said, trying to sound calm as he spoke to the little girl who was stooping down dangerously beneath a rock overhang on the other side of the cave. "We need to get back to Jessica now."

"Okay," she answered, rising to come to his side. "I gonna give her this pretty rock when she wakes up," she said, holding out her hand for him to inspect the rock. "Idn't it pretty?"

Luke glanced down into her eyes, smiling, then moved his gaze to her open palm. "Yes, it's very pret—"

The words seemed to die in his throat as he got a good look at the rock she held. The light from the lantern seemed to reflect its golden glow off the rock, and Luke slowly reached to take it from her so he could inspect it more closely. It couldn't be what he'd first thought. There was no way. It was only a trick of the light that made the tiny rock look like . . .

Luke stepped over to inspect the wall of the cave where Heather had been, holding the lantern close as he looked for what he was still telling himself was an impossibility. In the middle of those thoughts a streak of something glittered as he passed the lantern across one area of the wall, and he brought the light back, only to nearly drop it at what he saw. A low whistle escaped as he reached up to run slightly trembling fingers across the glistening streak that ran in a thin line through the rock.

Gold!

Several emotions bombarded Luke in quick succession— shock, disbelief, excitement—before one last emotion finally took over.

"Heather?" he said suddenly, turning to the little girl who had come up to stand beside him. "You like special surprises, don't you?"

She looked a bit confused, but nodded. "Uh huh."

"Well, I think we ought to make this a special surprise for Jessica. One for later, though, so we'll have to keep it a secret for a while. Do you think you're a big enough girl to keep a secret?"

It was just the thing to say, for the little girl straightened to her full height and claimed adamantly, "I big enough!"

"Good girl," he complimented, trying to hide his relief as he took her hand and led her out of the cave. He was positive that what they had just found was gold. And by the size of the vein it could possibly be a small fortune's worth. The last thing he needed was for Jessica to find out about this.

The sun was hanging low in the sky as the wagon pulled under the welcoming arch of the Circle R. Heather had fallen asleep a little ways back, and with Luke seeming to have something on his mind, Jessica had quietly watched the scenery pass. It wasn't exactly the way she had envisioned this picnic ending. When she woke up to find Luke sitting on the quilt beside her, and Heather playing close by, Jessica had hoped she might be able to find out a little more about his past.

But not only had she not gotten to question him about it, she hadn't really been given the opportunity to say anything. Almost as soon as she opened her eyes, Luke was packing up everything and hustling them into the wagon. It had taken some effort to hide her disappointment at the abrupt end to what had thus far been a wonderful picnic, but Jessica accepted his excuse that it was getting late, knowing that Zeke and Frannie would begin to worry about them.

Still, the lateness of the hour didn't explain Luke's quiet mood. And his wasn't a rested, comfortable silence either. He seemed watchful, almost nervous as he drove along, constantly scanning the area around them. This Jessica put down to the fact that he had so recently been ambushed. But surely Ben wouldn't try anything now. Why, he'd have to shoot all three of them if he did!

That thought had put her on edge, and the rest of the way home Jessica kept a sharp eye out for any sign of movement around them. It gave her little time to wonder on the reason why Luke's attitude had changed so drastically during her nap. All she knew was that the sunny mood of their picnic together had been shattered.

Heather didn't so much as stir later when Luke lifted her out of the back of the wagon. He carried her up to her room, where Jessica slipped off the child's shoes and dress and tucked her into bed. They stood there for a long moment watching the little girl sleep until the intimacy of this family scene seemed to hit both of them at nearly the same instant. As if by some sort of mutual, unspoken agreement they each turned away to seek out their separate, lonely rooms.

Chapter Twenty-six

The grandfather clock in the parlor downstairs struck two before Jessica finally gave up trying to convince herself that she had any hope of finding sleep anytime soon. It had been seven hours since she had escaped to the safety of her room. In all those hours, four of which she had spent lying in bed staring at the ceiling, she hadn't been able to get Luke Cameron out of her mind. Sitting up against the headboard of the bed, Jessica hugged her knees to her chest and stared out into the black night beyond the window. Since she had already found it impossible to stop thinking of the man who lay asleep downstairs, she gave up and let her stubborn thoughts have their way. It was a dangerous thing to do, she soon found out, for her imagination manipulated and enhanced memories that were better left locked away in the furthest recesses of her mind.

Even as her arms grew chilled in the cool November night, Jessica's heart grew dangerously warm as she let herself manipulate the memory of the day she had just spent with *her husband* and *their child*. In her mind she and Luke climbed the steps together to put their sleeping daughter to bed. But instead of turning to the isolation of this lonely room, Jessica's mind had Luke put his arm around her waist as they looked down lovingly on Heather. He turned that loving look on her then, and Jessica saw desire melt those icy blue eyes, turning them to twin blue flames. He leaned over to whisper a deliciously wicked suggestion into her ear before playfully pulling her out of Heather's room to the privacy of their own. There he would do all those things to her that he did so well, the things that made her insides tremble and her knees go weak.

And he would do more this time, Jessica thought with a shiver that had nothing to do with the cold. He would make her his wife in fact as well as in name. And in the aftermath he would pull her close into his arms and swear that only death would make him leave her.

It was a beautiful dream, Jessica thought, giving a long sigh at the futility of dreams. After years of the kind of life Luke had led, it was doubtful he could ever settle down in one place, even if he thought he wanted to. And it was just as doubtful that he would want to, especially here where he would be tying himself to a wife and a child if he did. It just wasn't the kind of thing you saw gunfighters do.

Jessica wasn't going to let herself get involved emotionally, anymore than she already had, with a man who was sure to disappear like a wisp of smoke in a few short months. She was just going to have to keep her distance and remember that what they had between them was a business deal, nothing more. Surely she could do that. Whenever she felt herself slipping, she would just picture Luke's back as he rode away on Shiloh, not even looking back when he heard the heartbroken sobs—Heather's, of course.

Another chill caused Jessica to shiver, and even though she shuddered at the very thought of putting her bare feet on that ice-cold floor, she knew it was just as cold in Heather's room. She now left both bedroom doors wide open at night so that the fireplace and cook stove below would send their warmth up the steps. It had worked well so far, but since no supper had been cooked this evening, the house was colder than usual.

With a reluctant grimace Jessica threw back the covers, and before she could chicken out, hopped quickly out of bed. The breath hissed through her teeth as her feet hit the bare pine floor, and she raced to the armoire where she rummaged around in the bottom until her hand finally brushed across what she was searching for. Leaning her shoulder against the oak armoire, she quickly pulled first one, then the other, of a pair of John's thick woolen socks onto her feet. A blissful smile crossed her face for a moment before she pushed away from the armoire and, on feet now protected from the cold, crossed the room, grabbing up a quilt to wrap around her as she went.

She first made a stop in Heather's room, and like any good mother pulled the coverlet up around the little girl's shoulders and tucked the edges securely beneath the mattress. Brushing a kiss on the sleep-flushed little forehead, Jessica quietly left the room and crept downstairs to add another log to the fire.

The parlor was dark but for the soft red glow from the dying fire. The rhythmic tick tock of the cherrywood grandfather clock softly filled the room like the familiar voice of a friend as Jessica crossed to kneel before the fireplace. How many nights had she sat here after John's death, feeling frightened and alone, with only that tall clock to keep her from going insane in the stifling silence? She had spent entire nights sitting in this room, and just as throughout most of her life she had suffered through the fear alone, never saying a word to anyone, never asking for help.

Fiery red sparks danced up into the chimney as Jessica poked at the embers, stirring them up before she laid two small pieces of split logs onto the bed of coals. The logs crackled and slowly began to smolder, and she leaned one shoulder against the rock facing of the fireplace, waiting for them to catch fire.

The glowing coals and flickering firelight began to have a hypnotic effect, and staring into the flames, Jessica felt herself mesmerized into a trancelike state, suspended somewhere just outside the bounds of reality. The tick of the clock, the dancing flames, the enveloping darkness of deepest night all combined to wipe away all perception of reality.

Luke sensed more than heard the presence that woke him. *Woke him?* Hell, he hadn't really gotten a minute's sleep that wasn't disturbed by visions of the woman lying in bed just above him. He didn't have to try hard to remember how she had looked lying in bed that morning they had stayed with Heather. He could still see her hair, that long, thick mass of hair his fingers always seemed to be itching to bury themselves in, not braided as Melinda had always done hers at night, but spilling over the pillow in a wild, unbound mass of pagan beauty.

And that face, flushed in sleep with those thick black lashes teasing him as they concealed the sparkling eyes that he knew could turn to liquid gold with desire. Then there was that tiny beauty mark at the right corner of her lips. It must have been put there for the sole purpose of driving him crazy, for he couldn't look at it without wanting to pull her into his arms and taste those lush, sweet lips.

Shifting restlessly at the path his thoughts were taking him down, *again*, Luke heard the soft scrape of metal in the parlor. It could mean danger.

With the stealth that had become second nature Luke climbed out of bed, pulling one of the Colts from his gunbelt that hung around the bedpost. Quietly he crept toward the door, fully expecting to find that Ben had finally gotten tired of waiting to catch him alone and had sent one of his hired hands over here to simply break in and shoot him in his bed.

The door stood ajar, and Luke pushed it slowly open with his free hand, cringing at the squeak that had surely announced his presence to the intruder. With no further need of stealth he quickly pushed the door open wide. The mirror on the far wall of his room was situated so that after moving to one side a half step he was able to see down the empty hallway. His first thought was that the intruder was after Jessica, and Luke was set to race up the stairs when he heard a faint sigh from the parlor across the hall. With his Colt still at the ready, he quietly stepped to the parlor door to investigate.

Luke's first reaction was relief on finding Jessica safe. Seeing the iron poker lying on the hearth beside her, he realized it had obviously been her who had made the noise. His body relaxed, his hand lowering the Colt to his side as he carefully eased the hammer back in place. He almost spoke, but something in her expression as she gazed sightlessly into the flames made him hold any words he might have said. In appreciative silence he let himself enjoy looking at her.

Wrapped in a quilt, she sat on the hearth, her knees drawn

up to her chest as she leaned one shoulder against the rock front of the fireplace. The flames she watched so avidly cast a rosy, golden glow across her face and seemed to reflect off the mass of hair that tumbled free across her left shoulder. There was a wistful yet almost lonely look in her eyes that tugged at his heart, and Luke wondered what—or *who*—she was thinking of. A tiny, jealous voice in the dark recesses of his mind whispered a name. *John Randall.*

What if McCalister had been wrong about the kind of feelings Jessie had for her late husband? Luke's mind cruelly replayed all the times that his jealousy had made him verbally attack Randall, and how Jessica had so staunchly defended the man with such deep feeling. Had it been loyalty that made her react so—or love? Either way, it was only right that she think about the man sometimes, Luke's conscience told him. After all, John Randall had been her husband. And even though the thought of her remembering another man bugged the hell out of him, Luke had to admit he hoped that every now and then she would think of him, miss him, after he had to leave.

Still, he was here now, and all trace of gallantry suddenly fled in the face of having to stand here and watch her moon over her dead husband when he, himself, was here, and very much alive. And *he* was her husband now, at least for a few more months!

"Jessie?"

It took a moment for the soft word to register through the dreamlike web her thoughts had woven. Even when Jessica looked up she wasn't sure her imagination wasn't tricking her, putting him there in the doorway wearing nothing but snug-fitting denims and a possessive look on his handsome face that could only be a figment of her wishful dreams. He looked so virile, so totally male, as he stood there with the firelight reflecting off his broad chest and casting secretive shadows over his face.

With one shuddering breath her lungs seemed to stop, as if she were drowning. Indeed, that was what it felt like. She was drowning in the desire that just once, for a few brief minutes in her life, what she dreamed of could come true.

At the glazed, almost incoherent look in her eyes, Luke's irritation turned to concern. "Jessie?"

Her name came from the vision once again, more insistent this time, and with a start Jessica realized he wasn't a dream. Her wish had been granted, and suddenly she wasn't sure whether to be grateful, or to run for the safety of her room.

"Are you all right, Jessica?" Luke asked, his concern growing at her continued silence.

"Of course. I—uh—came down to add some wood to the fire," she finally answered haltingly. "I'm sorry I disturbed you."

You've disturbed me since the first minute I laid eyes on you, Luke wanted to say. Instead, he chose to lie. "You didn't disturb me." With a wry grin he lifted the Colt to show her. "I had to get up and check on a noise in the parlor anyway."

She smiled nervously at his quip, then grasping for something to say to distract herself from the intimacy of the moment, Jessica said, "It's colder tonight, don't you think?"

Taking her cue, Luke laid the Colt on a small table by the door and crossed to her side to hold his hands out to the fire. The weather always provided a safe topic. "Yep," he agreed, being careful not to look at her. "First snow won't be too far off, I'll wager."

In her nervousness Jessica laughingly blurted, "You'd wager on anything, wouldn't—"

It hit them at the same time, the unpaid wager from this afternoon. Jessica's words stumbled to a halt, and Luke finally allowed himself to look down at her face. He was sure the heat from the fire wasn't the only thing putting that color in her cheeks. The control of common sense that had held him in check since he first saw her sitting here looking so tempting began to slip.

"I wager when it's a sure bet," he said softly. "And when the prize is one worth winning."

Jessica continued to watch the flames. "So you're pretty sure it's going to snow?"

He smiled. "Nice try, Jessica. But you know that's not the wager either of us were thinking of."

The Deal

Jessica tried to swallow, but there suddenly seemed to be a lump the size of a horse's hoof in her throat. Her eyes darted evasively to the grandfather clock. "Goodness, would you look at the time? We'd both better get some sleep."

He caught her arm as she rose to flee. The quilt slipped away to pile around her feet. "Shame on you, Jessie," he softly chided in that husky growl that always went straight to her knees. "Don't tell me you're one of those people who welshes on a bet?"

She couldn't bring herself to look at him, probably because she was aching to do just what she knew he was asking. And at this moment if she started kissing him, Jessica knew there would be no turning back.

"I have to go back upstairs," she pleaded almost desperately.

But Luke wasn't about to give up this time. "You owe me a kiss, Jessie," he whispered huskily. "And I'm callin' in payment on that debt—right now."

He wouldn't release her arm, though Jessica knew that if she were to really try to escape he would let her go. It wasn't his superior strength that held her captive, but her own desire. And even as she knew she was going to regret this night, she turned toward him, her eyes slowly rising to meet his.

A look of disbelief mingled with desire in his eyes as she gave in to temptation and slowly reached out to touch Luke's chest. Her hands felt cool against the warm, bronzed skin as she slid her palms up the muscled contours leisurely, enjoying every new inch of skin she touched. Slipping her fingers into the silky hair that now hung to his shoulders, she boldly took the half step that brought her thinly clad chest against his naked one.

"I never welsh on a bet, Luke Cameron," Jessica whispered softly, before rising up on the balls of her feet as she pulled his mouth down to meet her kiss.

Luke's heart slammed against his ribs at her tender assault. It was the first time she had been the one to initiate a kiss, and the effect on his body was as swift and raging as a wind-driven prairie fire. His arms came around her waist in a crush-

245

ing vise, yet the moan that escaped her throat wasn't one of pain, but of matching desire finally surrendered.

The soft sound only added fuel to the flames that already threatened to engulf Luke. He held her tightly, half fearing she would pull away like all the times before. Another disappointment like that and he might be rendered useless to any woman, or at the least, driven insane!

With that very real possibility in mind, Luke forced himself to pull away now, even taking an extra step backward for good measure. When he looked down into the desire-glazed eyes that met his gaze, he almost lost the iron hand of control that kept him from crushing her back into his arms. But this time wasn't going to be like all those times before when she had left him aching with want.

"Jessica?"

"Hhmm?"

"Look at me. I've got something to say to you and you'd better listen, 'cause I'm only gonna say it once. Understand?"

She looked confused as she met his almost angry gaze, but nodded nonetheless.

"I'm tired of the games. I'm gonna count to five, and if you're still here when I get through I intend to take up where you left off just now. And, Jessica? I'm gonna give you fair warning right now, kissing isn't all I intend to do to you."

Chapter Twenty-seven

His words hung between them in the heavy silence that followed. Luke usually didn't give ultimatums to the women in his life, but Jessie wasn't a "usual" woman. She had defied him, teased him, and cared about him until his insides were tied in knots with wanting her. It wasn't just the temporary, physical pleasure he wanted either—though he couldn't deny he did want that part of a relationship with her. Unlike the other women who'd drifted in and out of his life over the last few years, Luke wanted Jessica in his *life*, not just in his bed.

Everything hinged on her decision now, and as Luke watched her reaction to his words he almost wished he could take them back. But he had to know. One way or the other he had to find out if he had any hope of a future with her, or whether she still saw him as only the necessary means to an end.

With an inward sigh of resignation, Luke took the first step on this irreversible course he had set for himself. "One."

Jessica jumped slightly, surprised that he actually meant to follow through with his threat. No, she'd forgotten, he didn't make threats, he made promises. Every instinct told her to turn and flee as if the hounds of hell were nipping at her heels, yet no matter how she mentally screamed at her feet to move, they stubbornly stayed rooted to the floor.

"Two."

Was she crazy? Why was she just standing here like a sheep waiting dumbly for slaughter? She knew Luke Cameron well enough to know that his words were no idle threat. If she wasn't out of here by the time he got to five, he was going to make love to her despite any *terms* he had agreed to. But he had cunningly left the ultimate decision to her.

So why weren't her feet moving?

"Three."

Because you don't want to move, her heart answered. *Even though you know it's going to hurt unbearably when he leaves—and he will leave—you can't stand the thought of wondering for the rest of your life what it would have been like to spend just one night in the arms of the man you've so foolishly fallen in love with.*

"Four."

Who was she kidding? She was going to stay because she wanted to, plain and simple. What was the sense in denying herself the few months she did have with Luke? Sure, there would be pain when he left. But wasn't she used to pain by now? What was one more man she loved leaving her? At least she'd be expecting it this time.

"Last chance to run," Luke offered, looking as if he fully expected her to do just that. Which was probably why he looked so shocked by her answer.

"I'm not going to run, Luke."

"You understand what I said before?"

"Yes."

"And you want to see it through?" he asked, still clearly skeptical. At her brief hesitation his eyes narrowed. "I told you what to expect if you stayed, Jessie. I'm not playing this game of tease and run anymore. If that's what you're thinking to do, you better get out of here right now."

In an unconsciously nervous gesture Jessica's tongue darted out to wet her suddenly dry lips. Then, with a deep breath she finally said, "I think you got to four."

Disbelief registered in Luke's eyes for a moment as he digested that. He searched her eyes for any trace of indecision, and finding none, he pulled her to his chest, nearly groaning as her soft curves molded to his body. Sinking the fingers of one hand into the thick hair at her nape, Luke gently tilted her head back. His lips stopped a hairsbreadth away to whisper,

"Five," before their breaths mingled and his mouth hungrily closed over hers.

Jessica felt that same strange tingling run down her arms. She had heard whispers of "passion," but in her innocence she believed that was more a feeling in one's heart, not this unsettling feeling of her insides quaking, or the tingling in other places she had dared never think of.

All trace of Luke's earlier guarded hesitancy vanished in the face of Jessica's sweet response. After weeks of this gnawing want, the urge was strong to pull her to the floor and quickly assuage his hunger. He fought the temptation, however, for a woman like Jessie deserved a considerate lover, not some rutting animal interested only in his own gratification. Before he satisfied his own desire, Luke intended to make sure she wanted him as badly as he wanted her.

Slowly he began his seduction, drinking fully of the sweet wine of her kiss before he finally tore his lips away, unerringly working his way to her ear, where he nipped gently at the tender lobe. A satisfied smile came when he felt her tremble in response, and he continued to work his magic on the sensitive spot.

His mouth was wreaking havoc on her senses. Jessica felt herself losing a grip on reality as she slipped further and further into the hazy world where only sensations existed. Her arms tightened around his neck, her knees threatening to buckle as the tender assault of his lips moved down the column of her neck to the spot where it sloped into her shoulder. A moan escaped her throat as a fresh wave of sensation coursed through her body to join the growing ache at the junction of her thighs.

She was so caught up in what his lips were doing that Jessica had forgotten about Luke's hands, until she felt the cold rush of air as he slipped the top of the nightgown back off her shoulders, trapping her arms as he bared her breasts to his hungry gaze. The modest protest she was about to give turned to a gasp as his warm hand closed over her breast to squeeze gently.

Frightened by the response her body made to his touch,

Jessica jerked away out of reflex. "Luke—I . . ."

The only reason Luke could think that she would pull away was that she meant to run again. With his own desire fired to the boiling point, frustration came swift and sharp. "So you do intend to tease and run again, huh, Jessica?"

She blinked at his sudden anger. "I don't . . . it's just that I've never—"

"Never what?!" he cut her off harshly. "Don't try to tell me you've never been touched. You're a widow. Remember? Are you gonna tell me old John never—" He couldn't voice the words, so he finished with "touched you?"

"No. But—"

"Forget it! I don't want to hear about it!" Luke bit out, amazed at the knife of jealousy that cut through him at hearing her confirm what he already knew had to be fact. Of course, John Randall had made love to her. She was his wife, for crying out loud!

So why was it that hearing her say the words was like having a hot poker rammed through his chest? Because she couldn't bring herself to sully that memory now by letting a murdering gunslinger touch her, that's why. The thought only fueled Luke's anger. "I think you better get out," he said coldly.

With every word he said, Jessica was becoming more confused. "Why? I don't understand."

"Like hell you don't! I'm the one who doesn't understand why you keep teasing me when it's obvious you can't stand my touch. I guess I defile all those precious memories of how it was with good old John, don't I?"

Jessica could only shake her head dumbly at the unexpected words. How could he have come to so wrong a conclusion? "That's not it at all!" she got out when she finally found her tongue. "It's just that—I—"

"You what?" Luke pounced at her hesitation. "You don't mind my kisses but you can't bare for me to touch you? Well, it doesn't work that way, Jessica. I don't know what kind of man John was, but I'm not goin' to kneel at your feet like some gallant knight out of a fairy tale, hopin' you'll allow me the privilege now and then to chastely kiss your lips! I'm a man, Jessie. And when a woman stirs up a man she ought to expect what comes next, or else she better not tease him! So if you can't stand my touch, then you'd better just stay the hell away from me!''

With that he turned his back on her, hoping to dismiss from his mind the picture of her standing there in that white cotton gown looking so innocently seductive that his insides were still roiling with desire. She had pulled the top back over her shoulders, but with his verbal assault she hadn't thought to button the thing back up. Or maybe it was a calculated move meant to tease him further with what she meant to deny him.

It worked.

Jessica chewed at the corner of her lower lip, caught between confusion over his unwarranted assault and anger at the same time. How could he possibly have gotten the idea that she was revolted by his touch when nothing could be further from the truth? But how was she supposed to explain something she didn't understand herself? All these new sensations he was awakening in her body frightened her.

Taking a tentative step forward, she reached out to touch his back, only to feel him stiffen.

"Get out of here, Jessica," he warned quietly, "or I won't be responsible for what happens."

"But I'm not—"

Luke whirled on her so quickly that she gasped and jumped a protective step backward. "Don't you listen? I've never forced a woman, but then I've never had one tease and tempt me the way you have. For your own sake you'd better get out of here while you can."

When it was evident she wasn't going to leave, Luke cursed hotly and turned for the door, intending to put as much distance as possible between himself and this witch who had cast her spell over him. Now he knew why he hadn't been hanged. This was his punishment for taking vengeance into his own hands. Jessica was his hell!

Tears of frustration sprang to her eyes as Jessica watched him walking away. "You're wrong, Luke!" she called out in a choked voice. "You're wrong about everything you said!"

That made him hesitate at the door, though he wouldn't turn to face her as he asked skeptically, "Am I? Then why don't you explain it to me?"

Where was she supposed to begin? How was she supposed to explain these strange sensations without making him think she had lost her mind? But she had to try. She couldn't let him go on believing what he did now.

"John was a wonderful man," she began, only to see his shoulders flinch. She hurried on before he could leave—or worse, grow angrier, as he tended to do for some reason at the mention of John's name. "I don't know how to explain the kind of marriage we had. He was always so good to me. And I loved him dearly, truly I did."

Jessica didn't realize that at the painful words Luke had started to leave again, until she saw his entire body seem to suddenly freeze at her next words. "But he never made me feel—well—the things you do."

Very slowly he turned back to face her, and for a moment Jessica thought it was anger she saw burning in his eyes, though his voice was very calm as he asked, "What do you mean? What *things* do I make you feel?"

She opened her mouth to answer, but shut it again, wishing she had never brought this up. It was bad enough that he was angry with her. If she didn't shut up, he really was going to think she was crazy as well.

But Luke wasn't about to accept silence after having those tantalizing words thrown out at him. He quickly retraced the steps that separated them and took her chin in his hand, gently but firmly forcing her to meet his gaze, hoping he could read the truth in her eyes. "I asked you what you meant, Jessie," he pressed. "What do I make you feel that John didn't?"

She couldn't meet his piercing gaze and closed her eyes in a mixture of confusion and embarrassment. "I—well—I—tingle when you kiss me," she whispered the confession.

Silence followed her words, and unable to stand the suspense any longer, Jessica opened her eyes expecting to see Luke looking at her as if she'd lost her mind—which she was beginning to seriously believe was the truth. He was looking at her all right, but not as if he were questioning her sanity. This look was more that of a mountain lion who had just cornered a tasty rabbit and was savoring the anticipation of devouring it. From the glow in his eyes and the predatory set of his mouth, Jessica almost expected him to lick his lips at any moment. What on earth had she said to bring on such a drastic change in him?

Nervous now, she tried to back away, but his arm had come up behind her at some point to prevent her escape. "Luke— I—"

"What else do I make you feel, Jessie?" he asked in that husky tone that threatened her knees.

After the effect her last confession had on him, Jessica wasn't sure she ought to make any more, so she remained silent.

Testing his hopes, Luke leaned down to brush his lips across her cheek until he found her ear. "What else?" he repeated in a hot whisper, and smiled when he felt her tremble.

A soft moan came from her throat as Jessica instinctively tilted her head to one side to allow him better access to her sensitive neck. Luke took full advantage of the offering, but he wasn't going to accept a moan as her answer. "Say it, Jessie," he whispered against her skin. "Tell me how this makes you feel."

But before she could answer, his lips blazed a hot trail to her shoulder, and when his teeth gently grazed the corded muscle there, Jessica sucked in her breath at the sharp jolt that went through her body like a flash of lightning in a summer storm.

"You like that?" Luke asked, smiling. "Does that make you tingle?"

"Yes," she whispered breathlessly, lost in the storm he was stirring to life within her.

Luke felt his breath catch as he finally accepted what she had been trying to tell him. He stirred her to *desire*, a desire she didn't understand yet because no man before him had awakened her to it. Not even had dear, wonderful John introduced her to passion. The knowledge was like a heady drug after weeks of aching for her but believing she could never want him. And like an addict Luke needed to hear more.

Slowly he brought one hand around to her waist, then up until his thumb lightly brushed the outer slope of her breast teasingly. He felt her shiver of pleasure and his confidence grew—along with his own desire. "What else do you like, my tingling angel?" he asked, letting one finger trace the slope of her breast. "Do you like it when I touch you here?"

With her breath caught in her throat, Jessica could only nod.

His hand moved away, bringing a whimper of protest. "Say the words, Jessie," Luke reminded. "Tell me what you like."

Embarrassment warred with an aching frustration that Jessica couldn't quite understand. All she knew was that she couldn't bear the thought that he meant to stop if she didn't say the words he wanted to hear.

"Please, Luke—I—want you to—touch me."

"Whatever you want, angel," he whispered softly, and moved his hand to close unerringly over her breast. He wasn't sure which of them groaned the loudest as the soft mound swelled instantly to fill his hand. All thought of words or games fled his mind, replaced by one driving need: to make Jessie his wife in the truest sense of the word.

Tearing his gaze away from her passion-flushed face, Luke gauged the distance to his room, wondering if the spell would be broken if he asked Jessica to follow him there. The idea flashed briefly through his mind that he could carry her to his bed, kissing her all the way, but he had to discard that plan. With his luck, the wound in his shoulder would rip open and Jessica would insist on tending it, breaking the spell.

Coming to a decision, Luke pulled away slightly and waited for her to open her eyes. "Stay right here," he ordered, then punctuated the command with a kiss meant to keep her off balance for the few seconds he would be gone. With two swift strides he crossed the room, shutting the door firmly. The soft click of the lock turning resounded like a gunshot in the silent room.

Chapter Twenty-eight

Jessica wasn't sure quite how it happened. One minute her hands had reached out to touch that hard, bronzed chest, and the next minute she was lying on the quilt before the fireplace. Luke was lying on his hip beside her, kissing, touching, bringing her body alive with sensations.

Her arms crept up and around his neck, and her hands slipped into the tawny mane of hair that fell softly on each side of his neck as he leaned over her. He hadn't had it cut since that first day she'd seen him and it now hung to his shoulders. It might have looked feminine on another man, but somehow it had the opposite effect with Luke, only adding to the untamed, almost dangerous aura that seemed to radiate from him.

With each minute that passed, his sensual touch was taking its toll on Jessica, making her lose her inhibitions. Through some wild twist of fate, this man was her husband, and it was that fact that let her conscience give her permission to relax and enjoy what he was doing. Even then it wasn't the legal document that made this act right. In her heart Jessica knew that Luke was the one man who could make her life whole. Her body was only acting now on that knowledge.

Slowly her fingers traced the muscles of his neck, skimming lightly across his shoulders until her hands splayed against the broad expanse of his back. With the savoring anticipation of one denied a coveted treat, Jessica let her hands slide inch by delicious inch down the hard planes of his back, feeling the muscles flex beneath the warm, smooth skin. A groan sounded deep in his chest, and by some feminine instinct Jessica knew that it was brought on by her touch. It was all so new, especially the exhilarating thought that perhaps she could make him feel some of the same sensations he was stirring within her.

Even as she thought that, Luke's hand came between them to the open front of her gown, slipping within. When his hand closed over her bare breast, her murmur of pleasure filled the quiet parlor. He squeezed gently, then lightly rubbed his thumb over the sensitive crest until it puckered beneath his touch.

Jessica was just getting used to this newest assault on her senses when his head lowered and without warning his warm mouth took over where his thumb had left off. The sensation was so devastating that her back arched off the floor, only succeeding in deepening the exquisite torture. The gasp sounded as if it were being wrenched from her throat. "Luke—I—"

"Trust me, love," he whispered, raining moist kisses as he moved his attentions slowly to her other breast.

That silky mustache was tickling her skin deliciously, and a violent tremor went through Jessica as his mouth again found its goal. Her hands slid to his waist, unconsciously pulling him tightly against her as she writhed beneath his sensual assault. She wasn't sure what it was that her body was crying out for, but she knew somehow, instinctively, that it was within Luke's power to give it to her.

But Luke wasn't finished awakening her body yet. His hand left her breast to run the back of his fingertips lightly down her rib cage and across the satin-smooth skin of her stomach, leaving gooseflesh in their wake. Moving his palm to her slim waist, he slowly skimmed his hand over her hip, where he began to bunch the white cotton up to her thighs.

Realizing what he meant to do now, Jessica stiffened for a moment, remembering. This was where the pain came in. Now all these wonderful sensations would be washed away. She felt a sharp sense of disappointment that the pleasurable part of lovemaking was over and now the painful part had to be endured.

Luke could feel the passion he had worked so hard to kindle draining out of her, and he searched his mind for what could have happened to change her so quickly from writhing desire to this state where she lay almost like a marble statue. Leaning back to look into her eyes, he frowned. "Jessie?"

He looked so sincerely concerned that Jessica lowered her gaze, ashamed. He had given her so much pleasure before he got to this part that she suddenly felt selfish now for showing her dread of what she knew was to be his pleasure. "I'm sorry, Luke," she whispered quietly. "It was very nice what you did for me. I—I'm ready now for you to . . ."

When she broke off into silence, Luke gently lifted her chin, forcing her to look him in the eyes. "You make it sound as if you're getting ready to be . . ."

And suddenly he understood. If he was the first one ever to give her a taste of what desire could feel like, then her previous experiences probably had held little pleasure for her. It had obviously even been painful, judging by her words and the tense way she lay beneath him. Mentally he cursed Randall.

Luke forced himself to bite back his anger with the dead man, focusing instead on the woman he held in his arms. "Relax, Jessie," he whispered tenderly, more determined than ever to make this so good for her that it would wipe out all her bad memories. "Do you trust me?"

There was a brief hesitation before Jessica nodded.

He smiled reassuringly. "Then just relax and let me make you tingle again. And, Jessie? Will you try to take my word that it's only going to get better?"

Another nod, but Luke could see in her eyes that she didn't believe him. Well, he was just going to have to prove it to her. It was a task he didn't begrudge in the least.

Leaning over her, Luke brushed his lips over hers and felt them open to him without hesitation. Slowly he began to stoke the fires of passion once more. When his fingers moved to massage the inside of her thigh, she stiffened. "Relax, sweetheart," he reminded in a husky whisper as he teasingly moved his fingers higher with each massaging circle, until they brushed the soft curls that hid the treasure of her womanhood. Sliding his hand up, he listened to her breathing and smiled at the telling, shallow breaths. With infinite gentleness he dipped one finger within the curls.

Jessica stiffened again, but this time it wasn't in fear but in wonder at the hot rush of liquid heat that centered around where Luke was touching her so intimately. Her hips seemed to have a mind of their own as they instinctively arched to meet his caress, and again she felt that ache of wanting something she couldn't quite name.

Feeling her readiness, Luke felt a surge of tenderness race through him that she was offering herself to him so trustingly, even expecting pain. He swore silently that he wouldn't abuse that trust as he slipped off the denims he wore with one hand. Rolling to lie between her thighs, he braced his weight on his knees and forearms so as not to crush her as he looked down into her passion-glazed eyes.

In that moment the words in his heart nearly choked him trying to get out. Only years of self-preservation kept them locked safely there. It was enough that he knew he loved Jessica like he had loved no other person in his life. It wasn't necessary to say the words aloud.

I love you, Jessie Cameron, his heart called out as he sank deeply into her welcoming warmth.

It happened so quickly that Jessica didn't have time to brace herself. Realizing what he had done, she tensed, squeezing her eyes shut as she braced for the wave of pain she knew was coming. When it didn't, her eyes popped open, only to find Luke watching her intently. At her look of confused surprise he grinned. "I told you to trust me," he reminded, and when he moved within her, Jessica gasped.

Her heavy-lidded look of pleasure broke the tight rein of restraint Luke had been holding on his own raging desire. She was so warm, so tight, that he was afraid he wasn't going to be able to hold out long enough to show her the full extent of her newfound pleasure.

But his prolonged assault earlier had prepared Jessica for this moment much better than Luke realized, and she was quickly straining against him, urging him on as she reached for the storm that was building just beyond her grasp. Every nerve in her body seemed centered on reaching that crest. Clutching his shoulders as the tide of desire surged around her, Jessica was sure of only one thing. Luke was at the center of what her body was raging toward.

And suddenly it hit full force. Jessica felt her breath catch and her entire body go taut as waves of mind-numbing sensation washed over her. Lightning sizzled through her body, leaving white-hot sparks in its wake as she cried out in pure ecstasy as the eye of the storm engulfed her. She held on to Luke with a death grip now, afraid to let go lest she go spinning off into oblivion. In the recesses of her mind she heard him call out her name, but she was too caught up in the tidal wave to answer. She was lifted higher, then higher still as the waves of passion carried her along their crests, until finally they began to slowly subside, easing her gently back to earth.

Limp and damp with sweat, Jessica lay curled up on her side, quietly staring into the fire as she thought on what had just happened to her. Was this what Ruth had hinted at when she'd grinned at saying she bet Luke would be a "satisfying" husband? She had always tried to tell Jessica there was so much more to a marriage than what she had shared with John, but she had never understood what her friend meant, until now. Now Jessica understood a lot. She understood those looks that passed between Ruth and James when they thought no one was watching, because that was exactly the look Luke had worn as he gazed down on her in that instant before he made her his wife.

His *wife*. For the first time Jessica actually felt like a wife. Still wearing a soft smile, she slowly drifted into the most restful sleep she had gotten since meeting this disturbing man who fate had thrown into her life.

"Jessie?"

When he received no reply to the soft whisper, Luke eased away from her and rose to his feet. He stood there watching her sleep for a long moment until she stirred, drawing her knees up against the chill. Quietly he stooped to tuck the quilt around her securely. Then turning his head, he looked at the face of the grandfather clock behind him and gave a long sigh. After all the weeks he had spent wanting what they had just shared, why on earth did it have to happen tonight?

Pulling on his denims, Luke sank his hand into his right pocket and pulled out the "rock" Heather had given him to stare at it in the fading glow of the firelight. *Gold.* Enough to make someone very wealthy by the looks of that vein. Enough to transcend budding feelings of love.

With one last, long look at the woman sleeping so peacefully before the fire, Luke stuffed the nugget back into his pocket and went to his room to finish dressing. From under his bed he retrieved the saddlebags he had packed earlier this evening with all of his belongings. He glanced around the room once more to make sure he had left nothing behind, then quietly stepped out into the hallway. It took some effort, but he forced himself not to look at the parlor door. It would be best if he was gone before Jessica woke.

Chapter Twenty-nine

In the smoke-gray light of predawn Benjamin Mateland woke to the flare of a match. The man's back was to him, but Ben recognized the tan Stetson and duster immediately. His pride wouldn't let him call out for help, but that didn't keep him from glancing at the door nervously. Surely someone among all the inept people he paid to protect this place had seen the outlaw come in.

So why the hell had they let him get as far as his bedroom?

Carefully Ben eased the covers back, judging the distance to the door while he darted quick looks at the back still turned to him.

"You wouldn't make it."

Ben swallowed at the words, feeling impotent rage that the outlaw hadn't even felt it necessary to turn around as he gave the warning. He simply finished settling the glass chimney in place and slowly turned. The soft lantern light revealed a small hole surrounded by a telling rust-colored stain on the right shoulder of the duster, and Ben felt his fear rise. Had Cameron come to repay him for the attempt on his life?

Trying to hide his nervousness at the thought, Ben asked gruffly, "What're you doin' here, outlaw?"

"I thought that would be obvious," Luke answered with a grin that succeeded in destroying the other man's composure completely. With malicious enjoyment he let Mateland taste the fear for a moment, a little devil inside even making him hook the right side of his duster back behind his holster to reveal the Colt resting at his hip. The look of fear that caused in Ben seemed just retribution after the way the man had bullied Jessica so many times.

"If you're plannin' on shootin' me, I'll warn you right now there ain't no way you'll make it outta here alive," Ben tried to bluff. "My men'll cut you down before you make it to your horse."

"I've been shot at by a lot better men than you got workin' for you, Mateland," Luke claimed mockingly. "Was that your best marksman who couldn't even kill me in an ambush?"

The goading words made Ben's face go red. He wasn't ready to test the outlaw's words, though. "Listen," he reasoned. "I'll give you a thousand dollars cash money right now to ride outta here."

Luke only smiled, letting the man sweat for a few more seconds before he spoke. "Funny you should mention money," he said, leaning back with deceptive calm to brace his hips against the table behind him. His arms crossed over his chest as he got to the reason of this visit. "Cause that's just what I came to talk about."

That caught Ben's interest. He looked at the outlaw warily, wishing the lantern weren't behind the man. It was downright spooky the way the shadows played across the gunslinger's face making him seem—well—otherworldly. But the man seemed to have come to talk about money. And greed was something Ben Mateland understood well.

He relaxed a bit. "Whatta you want, outlaw?"

"I want to talk about the Circle R, and why you want it so bad. Or could it be there's only a very small part of it you actually want?"

Ben's eyes widened for the briefest instant but it was enough to tell Luke his suspicions were correct.

"I don't know what you're talkin' about."

Luke chuckled. "Yeah, I'm sure you don't. Just like you don't have any idea what really got John Randall killed."

"It was outlaws killed John," Ben sneered as he looked at the man before him pointedly. "Sheriff Davis figured that out after he investigated." When Luke remained silent, Ben went on, "So if that's all you came to talk about . . ."

The Deal

"Yeah, it was," Luke said, pushing himself away from the table. "So I guess I'll be goin'. I'm thinkin' I ought to find those *outlaws* an' see if they're interested in gettin' their hands on the Circle R—and that cave that's so close to the boundary that joins your land."

"Hold it!" Ben's call stopped Luke before he could take two steps toward the door. There was a tense few seconds of silence before, "I'm listenin', outlaw."

Luke turned, the light illuminating the lower half of his face, though the Stetson still cast its shadow over his eyes. "You could have saved yourself a hell of a lot of trouble, Mateland," he said, almost cordially now, "by just bribin' me to begin with."

Ben's eyes narrowed suspiciously. "You tryin' to tell me you don't want that cave?"

"I'm a gunfighter, Mateland, not a miner. I haven't got the time or the inclination to spend weeks, or even months, diggin' in the ground like a prairie dog. Of course, I have heard of some folks blastin' with dynamite to break loose a vein."

Again the man's look gave away his guilt. So he had been right, Luke thought. It hadn't been a need for more pasture that had Mateland blasting that day.

"Is that what happened to Randall?" Luke asked as if it were really of little consequence. "Did he find you blasting on his land instead of your own?"

Ben tensed. "I'd found one of my cows over there a week earlier. She'd dropped a calf in the cave and I heard the bellowin'. When I went in to check on her I found a small nugget. I sent it to Laramie under a fake name, and when I got the assayer's report back I wanted to see if there was enough to fool with buying Randall out."

"So you blasted around the outside hopin' to shake things loose in the cave without anyone knowin' what you were up to," Luke finished for him.

"You saw the vein?"

"Yeah."

"Yet you're here to see me instead of minin' that streak?" Ben went on, getting them back to the reason for this meeting.

263

"You'll understand if that makes me a little suspicious. Just what is it you want?"

"Like I said, I'm not a miner. I figure since you know the size of that vein, you know pretty much what it's worth. I also figure it'd be worth a few thousand—not to mention savin' you some touchy questions if anyone else turns up dead and you buy the Circle R, only to immediately find gold on it—if you were to somehow have someone make Jessica want to sell.

Ben was still understandably wary. "And would you be that someone?"

"If the price is right."

"Go on, outlaw. I'm listenin'."

"I can convince Jessica to sell the ranch. I'll tell her I don't trust you and I'm the one who's gonna meet with you. I give you the deed, you pay me, I leave, and there's nothing she can do. The outlaw swindled her and headed for Mexico just like everyone expected."

Ben looked impressed. "You'd do that to her? You'd leave her with nothing? Damn. If I didn't hate you so bad I'd hire you, Cameron."

"I'm only takin' three thousand as my part," Luke clarified coldly. "You're gonna give Jessica the rest of what the ranch is worth as a goodwill gesture 'cause you're such a fine, up-standin' human bein'—and because if you don't I'm gonna show up in this bedroom again one night, and you'll wish to God you had."

Ben stiffened. "I'll keep my part of the bargain, outlaw. You just make sure you keep yours."

Luke looked skeptical at the promise, but went on, "Can you have the money tonight?"

Ben couldn't suppress the greed in his tone as he asked eagerly, "Can you have the deed that soon?"

"Be at the cave at ten o'clock with the money. I'll have your signed deed. And be there on time. I'll need to get as far away from here as possible before Jessica finds out what happened."

"I'll be there," Ben promised with a pleased grin. "You can count on it."

"Then I guess that concludes our little meeting," Luke said, and without another word he left the room as soundlessly as he had entered it.

Several minutes later Ben heard the soft sound of hoofbeats. He looked out his window to see the horse with its familiar rider galloping at an easy pace down the drive with not a soul on the place except himself the wiser. Gritting his teeth, he glared at the retreating figure, his hand balling into a tight fist.

"You're a fool, Luke Cameron," Ben hissed, but then a slow, malicious grin began to stretch his lips as he continued to speak softly, "But lucky for me you're a greedy fool."

With a smile of pleasurable anticipation Ben returned to the warm comfort of his bed to dream. Soon he was going to be rid of the outlaw, he would have the gold, and he would have Jessica Randall Cameron to make his bed even warmer. With the smile still in place he drifted off to sleep.

Jessica stirred, her eyes slowly drifting open. She frowned at the sight of the parlor fireplace so close in front of her, until memory returned, bringing with it a vivid blush. She must have really been tired to sleep on this hard floor the rest of the night without stirring. But then she remembered such a pleasant sense of lethargy creeping over her in the wake of their lovemaking that she really wasn't surprised she had slept so soundly. She wondered if Luke had felt the same.

Rolling onto her back to see if he had, Jessica frowned at the empty place beside her. Her eyes searched the room, finding it empty as well. The quilt now wrapped snugly around her seemed to prove that he had gotten up at some point during the night and left.

The muted clatter of pans on the stove reached her then, and Jessica felt a surprising sense of relief wash over her. He was just in the kitchen, probably starting breakfast for them. She smiled in self-reproach at how quickly her fears had taken over. For a brief instant she had actually thought that since he had finally gotten what he wanted . . .

Cynthia Strickland

Instantly Jessica chided herself for the thought. Luke wasn't the kind of man to cowardly slip out in the middle of the night. When he left he would tell her.

Straightening her gown, Jessica warmed at the memory of the night past as she fastened the buttons Luke had so expertly unfastened. It was done. She had let down the last barrier and freely given herself to her husband. Surprisingly, the thought didn't bother her one bit. Well, maybe a tiny bit. But at least now she knew for sure what it was like to be possessed by this man who had stolen her heart. Now she only had to wonder whether in the years ahead that knowledge would be a comfort to her, or a source of torture.

Walking down the hall, Jessica fixed a welcoming, albeit shy smile on her face as she reached the doorway to the kitchen. "You really didn't have to . . . Frannie?"

The Scotswoman turned. "And good mornin' ta you too, sleepyhead," she greeted cheerfully.

Jessica frowned in confusion. "But what . . . ?"

"I came in around seven and you weren't up yet so I thought I'd start yer breakfast. You an' Heather must've had a fine time on yer picnic ta sleep so late this mornin'."

The woman still couldn't bring herself to include Luke's name when she spoke of the happenings on the ranch. It was as if by not mentioning him she could somehow keep him from becoming a part of their lives, which was a ridiculous notion in Jessica's way of thinking. She let her friend know that now.

"You know, Frannie, he's not going to magically disappear just because you refuse to say his name."

"One can always hope," the older woman grumbled under her breath before saying aloud, "I suppose ye're goin' ta tell me he was part o' the reason you enjoyed yerself so much that you overslept this mornin'? Somethin' ya've never done before."

Well, Luke was the reason she'd overslept, Jessica thought with a secret smile, but not for the reason Frannie thought. A blush crept over her cheeks as she again remembered the way Luke had awakened her body with his touch. Now she knew

266

what passion was, and it wasn't a feeling in one's heart!

"Jess?"

The word brought Jessica from her musings and back to the conversation. "Yes?"

Frannie was frowning now. "I asked why you were smilin' so. An' why are ya down here in yer nightgown when he could walk through the door at any . . ." She suddenly halted as a horrifying thought occurred. "Oh, no, Jess," she said miserably. "Tell me what I'm thinkin' isn't so!"

Jessica walked over to take two plates down out of the cupboard, giving herself the excuse not to look at her friend. "How could I possibly guess what you're thinking?" she asked airily over her shoulder.

But the Scotswoman wasn't fooled. "Darlin', please tell me ya haven't gone an' given yerself to that—"

The plates clinked loudly as Jessica slammed them down on the cupboard and rounded on her friend. "That's enough!" she said sharply, and at the older woman's wounded look her tone softened somewhat. "Just don't say anything that either one of us might have cause to regret, Frannie. Please."

Frances Furguson's eyes clouded over at what she considered was her answer. "So that's the way of it, is it? Ye're sharin' his bed?"

Jessica gave a long sigh. "I know what you're thinking, Frannie. But I also know what I'm doing. I'm not deluding myself into thinking he's going to stay when our bargain is over." She looked at the other woman beseechingly now. "Please try to understand. I had to know. I would have spent the rest of my life wondering how . . ."

Frances crossed the room to pull her young friend into her arms comfortingly. "Ssh now, darlin'. You know I only worry about ya. I don't want ta see ya hurt." There was a long pause before she could finally get the words out. "You love him, then?"

A nod.

"An' how does he feel?—But listen to me bein' foolish. The man'd have to be a fool not ta love ya back," Frances claimed loyally. "An' much as I can't say I care for 'im, I

267

have ta admit he doesn't strike me as a fool.'' Another hesitation, then, ''But do ya think he'll still be leavin'?''

Jessica pulled away, wiping at the unwanted mist that stung her eyes. ''I'm not going to fool myself,'' she said, giving her friend a resigned smile as she let her thoughts return to last night, and the man who had shown her what true passion—true love—could be like. ''I'd have more luck taming a mountain lion into being a house pet than I would getting Luke Cameron to settle for the confining life of a rancher.''

The picture came clear to her mind of a sleek, tawny mountain lion pacing restlessly back and forth in an iron-barred cage, its ice-blue eyes staring out at her accusingly. Jessica shook her head to clear it of the guilt-ridden image and looked at Frances once more.

''I'll love Luke and enjoy the time that he's here. There's no telling what the future will hold. He may even decide to come through here from time to time.''

''An' you'd be happy with that?'' Francis asked derisively. ''A man who blows in an' out o' here like the wind whenever it strikes his fancy?''

Jessica met her friend's indignant gaze. ''Happy? No. But if that's the only way I can have him I'll take it, because I can't stand the thought of not having him in my life at all.''

Chapter Thirty

James McCalister paused in the process of heaving a forkful of hay over the fence as his keen eyes caught sight of the rider approaching. Automatically he glanced down to where his rifle lay propped against the wagon seat not two feet away, his body tensing warily for the few seconds it took for him to recognize the rider. Relaxing, he pulled the bandana from around his throat and wiped at the sweat that had his hair clinging to his forehead. Propping the metal tines of the pitchfork on the wagon bed, he leaned one arm on the handle as he waited for his visitor. Years of experience kept his face from showing either surprise or curiosity as the man pulled his horse to a halt beside the wagon.

"McCalister."

"Cameron," James returned the greeting. "Heard you were laid up for a spell. Glad to see you up and around again."

Luke's brow went up questioningly. "And how'd you hear about that?"

"You more than anyone ought to know how the folks around here love to talk. Doc Andrews may be a good doctor but he's also as gossipy as an old woman. He was out here about a week ago when one of the hands got his foot stepped on by an overly zealous bull he was tryin' to get in the breedin' pen with a cow. Knowin' Ruth and Jess are friends, Doc wanted to know if your shoulder was still mendin' okay, since none of you had sent for him since he took the bullet out."

James shook his head here. "I like to had to hogtie Ruth to keep her from rushing over there with a gun to check on you two after Doc told her you'd been ambushed. I told her you'd ask if you wanted our help.''

The idea that he was here to do just that made Luke feel uneasy. It had been a long time since he'd obligated himself to anyone. For too many years he'd been taking care of his own problems, not asking any favors of anyone. Now he was having to go against that rule. It wasn't something that came easily.

Seeing the inward battle the other man was fighting, James had a pretty good idea what was going on. "You know, it was a long summer," he said, looking around him thoughtfully before his gaze came back to Luke. "But then there's never really an easy time around here. If it isn't spring thaw threatenin' to flood the rivers, it's summer drought, or storms, or a fire, or a blizzard. Took me a while to get used to ranchin'. Took me a while to get used to not being able to do everything for myself too. But a man learns quick in this kind of life that there comes a time when he needs help from his neighbors. Course, there'll come times when his neighbors need him, so it tends to even out.''

Luke looked at the man suspiciously, wondering if he could read minds. "So what are you sayin', McCalister?"

"I'm sayin' times are gonna come when a man needs help from his friends. And around here all he's got to do is ask and he's got it."

"And what if he's not used to askin'?"

James gave a long sigh. "Look, Luke, I haven't always been a rancher. There was a time when I was a loner and liked it that way. I figured I didn't owe anybody anything and I meant to keep it that way."

"So what happened?"

"Ruth."

The one word drew an understanding chuckle from Luke. "Snared you, huh?"

"More like she shot me right between the eyes," James corrected with a grin of remembrance. "One look and I knew life was never gonna be the same."

"So you settled down to be a rancher?"

James was quiet for a long moment, as if considering his

words carefully. Finally he said, "It wasn't that simple."

"Why? Didn't her daddy approve?" Luke asked the most obvious question.

A snort answered him. "That's puttin' it mildly."

"What was it? Were you a lowly cowboy who fell in love with the ranch owner's daughter or something?"

There was a longer pause this time, then, "I imagine you've heard of the Texas Rangers."

Luke stiffened, his eyes turning suddenly wary. "You were a Ranger?"

This time James's snort was with wry amusement. "Hardly." And at the other man's apparent confusion he went on, "Let's put it this way, I had gotten to be real popular with the Rangers. Or I guess *un*popular was more the case. Seems they took exception to a few bank withdrawals I made."

A dawning look of understanding came over Luke. "Got picky over just whose money it was you were withdrawing, huh?" he asked with a grin.

"It got to the point my face was on more posters in Texas than a politician runnin' for office," James said, shaking his head at the memory. "I was on my way to Mexico when I decided to stop for one more taste of good whiskey before resigning myself to several years of tequila."

He turned thoughtful. "You know, I've wondered more than once what made me step into that mercantile. I was walkin' toward the saloon when all of a sudden something seemed to be drawin' me into that store. And there she stood behind the counter. When she looked up at me and smiled, I swear it felt like a mule kicked me in the gut."

"So where did Daddy come in?" Luke asked, suddenly feeling a great kinship to James McCalister. Too, he wanted to know how a story much like his own could have ended as well as it had.

"He saw me standin' in the doorway starin' at his daughter and he hurried her into the back room. I guess he knew trouble when he saw it."

Luke found he was truly intrigued by the story now. "So what happened?"

"Luckily Ruth has two faults, and they both worked in my favor. For one, she's curious as a cat when somethin', or someone, catches her interest. And two, puttin' something off limits only makes her determined she's gonna find out why."

"And?"

"Would you believe she slipped out the back of the store and headed me off on my way to the saloon? At first I was amused, but it didn't take me long talkin' to her to find out she wasn't some simple miss just lookin' for excitement.

"I stuck around, and she'd slip out to meet me whenever she could. Funny thing was we did a hell of a lot of *talkin'*, which wasn't something I'd done a lot of with women in the past. I guess that's why I didn't realize what was happenin' until it was too late to stop it."

"And what was happenin'?" Luke asked, though he was pretty sure he knew the answer.

James gave a fond smile as he shook his head. "The bank robber was gettin' his heart stolen right outta his chest."

"I bet Daddy loved that," Luke speculated with a laugh. "I'm surprised he didn't fill your hide with buckshot."

"I guess he would have if it hadn't been for Ruth. Before I could say anything, she told him she was going to marry me and he could either accept me or she would leave with me."

Luke felt a twinge of disappointment that struck too close to home. "So she had to choose you over her family and home?" he asked quietly.

"No. Her father grudgingly accepted me."

"But—"

"I know. Why are we in Wyoming, then?"

Luke nodded.

"Ruth knew I couldn't stay in Texas, but I could see it was tearin' her apart to think of leaving her father, since he was a widower and she was his only child. Actually it was his idea for the three of us to come to Wyoming. Ruth and I built this ranch, and her father decided to build the hotel in Langly."

"And you've lived happily ever after," Luke finished, glad that things had worked out well for this man. If only . . .

"It hasn't been a fairy tale," James corrected, breaking into

Luke's thoughts. "Ranching is a lot of hard work. And just between you and me, I've often wondered what kind of life I'd be livin' right now if I hadn't walked into that store. But then I come in from a long, hard day's work and Ruth's takin' supper off the stove. She'll turn and give me that same gut-twistin' smile, and I realize there's nothin' in Mexico or anywhere else that could make me as happy as I am right here."

Luke couldn't control the feelings of envy. But then his situation was a lot different from James MaCalister's. His acts of revenge had built a reputation with more than just lawmen. As long as he was alive Luke was going to have to be looking over his shoulder. Marrying Jessie may have saved him from a noose, but it wouldn't do anything about the up-and-comers looking to make a name for themselves by outdrawing Luke Cameron.

James watched the blue eyes fill with a look of resignation, and he knew Luke believed that things were different for him and Jessica. But James also knew he had said all he could on the matter. He'd told Luke his story, one that he hadn't shared with anyone else, other than his wife and father-in-law. It was up to Jess now to convince the man that things could work out for them if they wanted it badly enough.

"So what was it you came to ask?" James brought them back to the point of Luke's visit.

The favor Luke was about to ask came hard, especially after hearing McCalister talk about how wonderful it was to have a loving wife to come home to. That was a life Luke would probably never have the chance to know, and he couldn't help but feel bitter toward the fates for denying him it.

Still, that didn't change the way he felt about Jessica. That was why he finally swallowed his pride enough to say, "I'm not used to askin' for favors, McCalister, but this one's real important and you're the only one around here I can trust to take care of it for me."

His tone was so serious that James began to worry. "What is it, Luke?"

It hurt to even put it into words. "I've got to go someplace tonight, and it may be that I won't be comin' back. If that's the case, I'm askin' you to look after Jessica and make sure no harm comes to her.''

The question was aching to get out, but James refused to pry into the other man's business. He'd said all he could. ''You have my word,'' he promised solemnly, then couldn't resist adding, ''But I hope it won't be necessary. My guess is Jess would rather have *you* lookin' out for her than me.''

Luke wouldn't comment on that. Anyway, what was the point? He'd made his decision and he was going to see it through. ''I appreciate you doin' this, McCalister,'' he said instead, then turned Shiloh to ride away, leaving the other man to frown at his back in thoughtful silence.

Chapter Thirty-one

It was midway through the afternoon before Jessica finally gave up the pretense that she had her mind on her work and admitted to herself that she was worried. Luke's absence hadn't bothered her much this morning. Even when the noon hour came and went and he still hadn't returned, she continued to tell herself he was only out working. But as the hours continued to tick by at a slow crawl, the goading little voice in the back of her mind refused to be silenced any longer. *He's left*, it said maliciously. *He got what he wanted all along and he's probably halfway to Colorado by now.*

Luke's not like that! her heart argued in his defense. *He wouldn't sneak out of here without so much as a word of good-bye.*

So where is he?

I don't know. But he hasn't left!

If you're so sure, then why haven't you checked his room to see if his things are gone?

Because I trust him!

Like hell you do! You're afraid to find his room is empty. And as if that weren't enough, the malicious voice gave one last, fatal thrust. *Remember standing on the steps of the orphanage? You kept telling yourself your father wouldn't leave you either. Don't you ever learn?*

"I don't," Jessica answered aloud, hating that voice for making her face the truth. She didn't have to check Luke's room. She already knew what she would—or more precisely, what she wouldn't find. Besides, she had already made the mistake of going out to the barn. Shiloh's stall was tellingly empty, and no one on the ranch had seen Luke since yesterday, which meant he had to have left before first light. There was no other explanation in Jessica's mind for him slipping out before sunup and not returning by now. He wasn't going to return!

The sharp pain that knowledge caused sent her into the house. She wasn't sure whether it was the memory of her father's desertion or the fresh pain of Luke's, but she urgently wanted to find Heather. At least there was one person in the world who needed her as much as she needed them.

Jessica spent the rest of the afternoon and into the evening with Heather, letting the little girl's incessant questions and boundless energy work to numb the pain of losing Luke. Only once did the child mention him, when they sat down for supper alone. She seemed to accept Jessica's evasive explanation that he had something he had to do. She couldn't bring herself to tell the little girl that that ''something'' was hightailing it to Mexico. She also didn't have the heart or the strength to try to explain to the child that they would in all likelihood never see him again.

As had become their custom, Jessica tucked Heather into bed, then lay down beside her for their nightly story. It was one of the few fond memories of her own past that Jessica could remember of her mother. Tonight it seemed to offer a special comfort.

''So what's it to be this evening?'' she asked, smoothing a dark curl fondly from the little forehead that lay close to her heart.

''Te' me about the prince. The one that rescues the yitta' princess.''

''Te*ll* and li*ttle*,'' Jessica corrected gently. ''Remember how you have to touch the back of your top teeth with your tongue for the l's?''

''Te-*ll* me the story about the *l*-itt-*le* princess,'' Heather got out, concentrating hard on pressing her tongue against her teeth so that she dragged out each l.

''That's my big girl!'' Jessica praised, and saw Heather's face beam under the compliment. ''Now what shall we name the princess?'' she asked the ritual question.

"Heather!" came the equally ritual reply.

And so the story began.

They were halfway through when Jessica came to the part she knew Heather liked the best. At this point she usually tried to change the ransom the prince brought, but it was always of great value. "And the prince came to the lair of the fierce dragon to ransom the fair Heather. With him he brought a treasure chest filled with priceless jewels from—"

"What's a jew-el?" Heather asked suddenly.

"Well, it's something like a rock, except it's a beautiful color like red or blue or green."

"Oh."

"So the prince brought priceless jewels to the dragon," Jessica went on. "Jewels in every color of the rainbow. Red ones and green ones and—"

"And yellow ones!" Heather cut in.

"And yellow ones," Jessica agreed. "Do you like yellow better than red and blue?"

"Unh huh. One just like I found yesterday in the cave. Do you think it was a jew-el, Jess'ca?"

The look of excitement on the child's face made Jessica smile. "Well, I don't know. Did you bring it home? We'll look at it and see."

"Luke's got it. He said to—" Suddenly Heather slapped her hand over her mouth and her eyes grew wide.

Concerned at the worried look on the girl's face, Jessica asked, "What's wrong, sweetheart?"

"I wasn't s'pose to tell," Heather admitted miserably. "Luke said it was gonna be our secret."

That strange bit of information caused Jessica to frown. "Did he say why he wanted it to be a secret?"

"Hun uh. He just sticked the rock in his pocket and told me not to tell. Do you think he's gonna be mad at me?"

"I'm sure he won't," Jessica soothed distractedly, her mind busily working through this puzzle. "What did the rock look like?"

"It was yellow. And it shined when I held it up to the

277

lantern. He thought it was pretty too,'cause he started lookin' for more of 'em.''

A suspicion that was too outrageous to consider started taking root. But what else could a shiny yellow rock be? And why else would Luke not want Heather to tell her about it, Jessica wondered miserably, unless he knew what it was?

Was that where he had been all day? Was that where he was even now?

''Heather, sweet, let's get your coat on. I have to go someplace and I want you to stay with Frannie while I'm gone.''

A half moon cast its light on the clearing, though the entrance to the cave was cast in deep, ebony shadows. A tiny spot of red rose like a firefly in the darkness, then glowed brighter to reveal Luke's face as he took a draw off his cigarette. From a distance came the sound of approaching hoofbeats, and Luke dropped the cigarette to crush it out under the toe of his boot, leaving the entrance to the cave in total blackness once more. It was just before ten. Luke gave a wry smile, having known this was one meeting Mateland wouldn't be late for.

As he waited for the approaching horsemen, Luke spared a moment to think of Jessica. By now she was surely wondering where he was. He had stayed away from the ranch, trying to tell himself it was easier for both of them if he didn't go back. Still, it tore at his conscience what she must be thinking, given the last moment she had spent with him.

When the riders drew up, Luke reached down to tuck his duster behind his holster on each side before stepping out of the cave. He eyed Benjamin Mateland, then the other riders who had formed a protective semicircle behind their boss.

''Five men?'' Luke scoffed, raising a brow as his gaze met Mateland's again. ''I don't know whether to be offended that you don't trust me, or take it as a compliment to my skill.''

Ben bristled at the mocking tone. ''Let's just call it a precaution against gettin' shot in the back by a murderin' gunslinger,'' he bit out the insult. ''You got the deed?''

The Deal

"Did you bring my money?" Luke answered Ben's question with one of his own.

Jessica had left Flame tied to a tree a few hundred feet back down the trail, intending to come up on the cave quietly in case her suspicions proved correct. She had thought she might find Luke there looking for gold. She hadn't expected to find the group of men gathered in the moonlit clearing. When Benjamin Mateland's voice reached her, her first instinct was to draw the gun she had brought and protect Luke, even if it meant endangering her own life. As the meaning of their words sank in, however, it was all she could do not to gasp at the pain that knifed through her. Surely no bullet could hurt as badly as what those words implied.

At Ben's nod, Russ Fulton pulled the heavy saddlebags from behind him and threw them on the ground just in front of Luke.

"Three thousand, just like we agreed," Ben said with a note of impatience. "Now where's the deed to the Circle R?"

"You'll understand if I want to count my money first?"

"It's all there, outlaw. If you don't trust me, then go ahead and count it. But be quick about it!"

Luke's brow raised in disbelief. "You actually expect me to trust you after you tried to kill me?"

"Yeah, well, you should have told me it would only take a few thousand to buy your loyalty away from your wife. You know, I wonder how Jessica's gonna feel when she wakes up tomorrow to find out that I own the Circle R and you're halfway to Mexico with her money," Ben said with a malicious smile.

What he wouldn't give to punch the smile right off the man's face, Luke thought, grinding his teeth at the sound of his chuckle. Instead he remained outwardly calm. "I'm sure you're gonna enjoy the hell out of telling her you were right about me."

The grin broadened. "You better believe I am, outlaw. Hell, I even feel like it's worth the three thousand dollars for the privilege."

Pain ripped through Jessica like nothing she had ever ex-

279

perienced before at those words. The man she had come to love more than her own life, the man she had so trustingly given her body and soul to not twenty-four hours ago, had just betrayed her for money! How could she have been so blind? she wondered as she watched Luke stoop down to open the saddlebags. Bile rose up in her throat at the sight, and she turned away before she had to watch him count out his thirty pieces of silver.

The ground before her blurred through a veil of tears as Jessica silently made her way back to Flame. She jerked the reins loose, not even bothering to soothe the mare when it shied away from the unaccustomed agitation of its mistress. All Jessica could think of was fleeing from the scene of the nightmare. She swung up into the saddle, giving Flame a kick that sent them galloping down the trail at a dangerous speed.

"You satisfied it's all there?" Ben asked when Luke replaced the last stack of bills and stood up to toss the saddlebags over his shoulder.

"Surprised is more like it," Luke answered, and saw the older man stiffen. "I guess I can understand you bein' so reluctant to part with this, knowin' it would've cost you a lot less if John Randall hadn't come up on you blastin' on his property that day. Tell me, did you shoot him here or did you have one of your men follow him and bushwack him on his way back home like you tried to do me?"

Ben straightened in his saddle, feeling like bragging a little. "I followed him, just like I shoulda been the one to follow you that day. If I had, then you'd be dead too, and all this wouldn't have been necessary." A pleased smile suddenly came to him as he edged his horse to one side, revealing the man directly behind him who had a shotgun pointed at Luke's chest. Ben went on smugly, "But then mistakes can be corrected. Of course, I'll have to move your body. I can't have Davis nosin' around here."

He shook his head in mock sympathy as he went on to explain the story he planned to tell. "Jessica had decided to sell the Circle R to me and go back East. When I got home from making the deal with her, you showed up accusin' me of tryin' to take her away from you. After the McCalisters' dance nobody'll doubt it. I tried to reason with you, but you went for your gun. It's just lucky for me that Russ here was watchin' from the window, expectin' trouble. He had to shoot you before you shot me.''

''You got it all figured out, don't you, Mateland?'' Luke asked with a derisive smile. ''You're gonna get away with two murders, and you're gonna get the gold.''

''*And* I'm gonna get the girl,'' Ben finished his list of accomplishments. ''I'll have the signed deed, and I don't intend to give Jessica one red cent for it.'' His smile turned lascivious. ''So what do you think a woman alone with no home and very little money is gonna do? I may even marry her if she's— good enough.''

His tone left no doubt what he meant by that, and it was the hardest battle Luke had ever fought not to pounce on the man and tear him apart with his bare hands. But he fought the urge, holding on to his composure, waiting.

Ben's tone changed now as his features grew hard. ''Now I want you to be real careful, outlaw, and raise your right hand behind your head. That's right. Now I want you to unbuckle that gunbelt with your left hand. Easy now!''

Luke was growing a bit concerned. What on earth was—

''Hold it, Mateland!''

Ben's surprise was nearly comical as he watched Sheriff Davis materialize out of the shadows above the cave's entrance to climb down and join them.

''Sheriff! What . . . ? It's a good thing you happened by. I was out ridin' with a few of my men an' we—''

''Save it, Ben,'' Davis said, shaking his head at the man's words. ''I didn't just 'happen by.' I been up there all along. I heard everything.''

The import of those words seemed to hit Ben just an instant before it did his men. He looked wildly around him as several more men appeared from the shadows to his left. In desperation he reached for his gun, but the sheriff's warning halted his hand midway there.

''I wouldn't, Ben. I'd hate to have to shoot you, but I will if you force me. Now get down off your horse.'' Then to the hands of the Bar M who sat in silence behind their leader he called out, ''The rest of you men do the same.''

As Ben swung down from his horse, a deputy took the gun from him. Still in shock over how quickly the situation had changed, Ben looked to Luke, who now stood beside the sheriff. It suddenly struck him that the outlaw didn't look the least bit surprised by the lawman's intervention.

''You okay, son?'' Wilford asked.

Luke looked relieved, if somewhat perturbed with the sheriff. ''Yeah, although for a minute there I was wonderin' if you meant to let him kill me too so you'd have two murders to charge him with.''

Wilford chuckled, slapping Luke on the back. ''Naw. I wouldn't do that. Besides, you got him to confess in front of witnesses to killin' John, just like you said you would. I reckon that'll be enough evidence.''

The realization of what had happened hit Ben then. His eyes went wide with surprise for a brief instant before filling with rage. ''You set me up, outlaw!'' he screamed the accusation at Luke.

A fury like nothing he had ever felt before filled Benjamin Mateland as he suddenly realized just what this meant. Like sands through an hourglass he saw the fortune in gold he had worked so hard to attain slipping through his fingers.

And all because of one man. Luke Cameron.

Luke Cameron, who had given Jessica the security and protection to defy all Ben's attempts at frightening her off her land. Luke Cameron, who had sneered at Ben's wealth and power as no one else had ever had the courage to do. Luke Cameron, who had shown Ben the unaccustomed taste of fear, not once but several times. And Luke Cameron, who in this final act had taken away every possession Ben had worked his entire life to attain, and had most likely cost him his life as well.

As he saw his nemesis turning away with the sheriff, Ben's rage exploded into blind fury. He shoved the deputy away from him, grabbing the man's gun as he fell.

"Luke!"

It all seemed to happen within a heartbeat. At the warning call years of instinct took over. Luke swung around, pulling his gun as he dropped to one knee in an instinctively protective pose. In the split second it took to look into the bore of the gun Mateland held, Luke fired.

Like a banshee's wail the ominous sound of two gunshots rent the cold night air. And then, all was silent.

Chapter Thirty-two

In the frozen tableau that followed the gunshots, the very wind seemed to hold its chilled breath. No one moved. No one even blinked as they all stood in silent wonder of what they had just seen. From somewhere, someone had called out a warning. The rest, everyone in the clearing was still trying to digest.

Benjamin Mateland was already pulling the deputy's gun when the shout came, and those with the quickest eye saw Luke whirl, pull his own Colt and fire all in the time it took to blink. In fact, those that had blinked were still unsure of just what had happened. Only the smoking Colt in Luke's hand and the still body of Ben Mateland lying on the ground beside his horse gave irrefutable proof that what they had heard about the gunfighter's speed at the draw was, if anything, understated.

The man who had called out the warning was the first to break the trance that seemed to have settled over those in the clearing as he came forward now. "I'm impressed," he said quietly, offering his hand to help Luke stand.

A look of surprise filled Luke's eyes as he now put a face to the familiar voice that had called the warning that saved his life. Massaging at the ache the quick motion had caused his mending shoulder, he looked at the hand held out to him. With only a second's hesitation he grasped it firmly and let the man help him stand.

"What are you doin' here, McCalister?"

"Sheriff Davis came by the ranch this afternoon lookin' for some men to ride with him tonight," James explained. "When he explained what you had planned, I thought you might need a friend's help—even if you were too stubborn to ask for it yourself." When Luke only looked away silently to where Sheriff Davis knelt beside Ben, James went on, "I guess this is why you asked me to look after your wife if you didn't come back?"

"Well, now you see why it was necessary," Luke defended, but looked even more uncomfortable as he went on haltingly, "I want to—thank you for warning me about what Ben was up to just now."

James shook his head that it was still so hard for this man to accept help from another. "Friends help friends," he reminded simply. "Someday you'll have a chance to return the favor."

"I wish I could repay you, McCalister," Luke said as he watched Davis directing a couple of men to hoist Mateland's body over the saddle of his horse for the trip to the undertaker's. "But I'm not gonna kid myself. I've got about as much of a chance of makin' a life here as a blizzard freezin' hell over."

A deep frown creased James's brow. "What makes you say that? Surely not what just happened here? There's no doubt it was self-defense."

Luke looked around the clearing to find several of the men that had ridden with the sheriff huddled together whispering furiously as they cast covert glances his way. Shaking his head with a weary sigh, he looked back to James once more. "Didn't you see the look on everyone's face? I'm always gonna be 'that gunslinger,' even more so after what happened here tonight. Besides, even if I did want to stay, you know why I can't."

"Are you talkin' about that bargain you made with Jess?"

"I just finished the job she hired me to do," Luke pointed out in a tone that revealed more than he realized.

"And so now you plan to just ride out of here? Despite how I know you feel about her?"

There was no point in trying to deny the truth. "How I feel about Jessica is exactly why I have to leave. Even if she wanted to make things permanent—which she's shown no inclination to do—I couldn't ask her to live the kind of life she'd have with me. You've already seen how most of the people around here treat her for takin' up with me. I can't ask her to live with that humiliation for the rest of her life."

"You mean like I've asked Ruth to live with bein' married to a bank robber who's still wanted by the Texas Rangers?"

"It's not the same thing, McCalister, and you know it."

"Oh no? Don't you think I'm wary of every stranger that passes through, thinkin', 'Could this be a Ranger come to blow my life to hell?' "

Luke wasn't swayed. "You changed your name and moved a thousand miles away. At least the folks around here don't know what you were. I can't ask Jessie to move. And if we stayed here, she'd never be accepted by the good townspeople as long as she's married to me. I can't ask her to live like that just because I . . ."

"Because you love her?" James finished quietly for him.

A resigned sigh was the only answer Luke could give to that. "I can't do it to her," he repeated his decision.

"And do you plan to give Jess a say in this? Or are you going to play the martyr and just ride out of here without a word?"

"I'm not tryin' to play martyr!" Luke growled a denial at the unfair accusation. "Hell, don't you think I'd give my right arm if I could stay here? But I can't ruin her life because of what *I* want!"

James was thoughtful for a moment before he continued. "You know, there's one thing I've always liked about Jess. It's how she doesn't give a hoot in a whirlwind about what a few narrow-minded folks think. She's a lot like Ruth there. Both of 'em live how they want and don't waste a minute worryin' about anyone who criticizes 'em for it."

"I know what you're to tryin' to get at, McCalister, but—"

"I remember when I told Ruth just about the same things you're tellin' me," James went on, cutting off Luke's protest. "I was all set to ride out for Mexico because I knew she deserved better than me. You want to know what my sweet, innocent, ladylike wife said to that?"

286

The Deal

"What?"

"She told me I had a helluva lot of gall makin' a decision like that for her. She told me she was the only one who had the right to decide how she chose to live her life, and that if I had left she would have tracked me down with a gun and brought me back!"

Luke had a hard time summoning up a vision of the petite Ruth standing up to the gruff bank robber. "And you took that from her?" he asked, trying to hide his amusement at the mental picture of the scene.

"You better believe I did!" James answered without the slightest trace of embarrassment. "I figured if the woman wanted me that bad it'd be downright selfish on my part to deny her."

At that Luke sobered. "That's just the point, though, McCalister. Your wife wanted you to stay."

"And you won't know how yours feels until you ask her," James came right back. "But don't you think she deserves the right to make that decision for herself?"

"Who?" Wilford Davis asked as he came up on the conversation.

Luke waved the question away. "How's Mateland?" he asked in the place of an answer.

"Dead. But you don't have to worry, son. It was plain self-defense. After what we heard, I don't think nobody'd say nothin' even if it hadn't been. John Randall was a well-liked man around here."

At the moment that was the last thing Luke needed to hear, for it only served to reaffirm his decision of what he had to do. The best thing for Jessica would be for him to ride out right now and never come back, no matter how the thought seemed to be ripping the very soul out of his body.

"Is that all then?" he asked in a tired, defeated tone.

"All except my thanks for settin' this up."

A tawny brow went up now as Luke remembered back to the scene a few short moments ago. "You sure took your sweet time steppin' in."

Wilford chuckled at the other man's pique. "I had to hear

him confess to all of it,'' he offered in good-natured defense. ''Besides, I knew you could take care of yourself.''

''And if I hadn't?''

''I'd of made sure Jessica heard what you did for her. But what're you mad at?'' the sheriff continued at Luke's dark scowl. ''All's well that ends well. You can go home and tell her what happened here tonight, as well as give her the good news that she's gonna be a very wealthy woman.''

Instead of being excited at the prospect of telling Jessica about the gold, as he knew he should be, Luke found he was reluctant to give her that information. Money had a way of drastically changing a person's feelings about a lot of things. She might have been willing to share a life of hard work on a small ranch with him, but she would undoubtedly feel much differently once she found out about the gold. With that kind of wealth she could sell the ranch and move to one of those fine houses in San Francisco, or Saint Louis. Hell, she could live anywhere in the world she wanted to, from the looks of that vein! She could wear the finest gowns and go to the most lavish parties with the cream of society's wealthy elite.

And she could marry a man she wouldn't be ashamed of, Luke thought with a fierce tightening in his chest—the kind of man she deserved for a husband.

''I said, don't you think it's about time you went home to tell her?'' Wilford asked again, snapping Luke from his thoughts.

He looked at the sheriff, then to James McCalister, who was watching him intently for his decision. Maybe it would be better if he gave Jessica the opportunity to tell him to his face that she really didn't want to have anything more to do with him now that their bargain was met. Maybe it would ease the ache somewhat if he knew for sure rather than having to spend the rest of his life wondering.

With an inward sigh of resignation Luke left the two men and swung up onto Shiloh, turning the stallion back in the direction of the Circle R. As he rode from the clearing, he had to wonder at the uncharacteristically self-destructive inclination that drove him to face Jessica to hear the words he knew were going to hurt like hell.

Jessica counted the chimes absently as the grandfather clock downstairs struck the hour of two. Sniffing softly, she rolled to her side to stare out the window, wiping at the moisture that still clung to her lashes from her latest bout of self-pity. There was nothing to look at through the panes of glass, only a cold, lonely blackness that seemed to mirror the emptiness in her soul.

Another sniff came as she stared sightlessly out the window, her mind replaying with brutal repetition the scene where Luke had stooped to count out his money. She had always thought he might leave when their bargain was met, but never in the last few weeks since she thought she had come to know him had she even considered that Luke might betray her so cruelly.

But much as she wished it weren't so, there was no denying the facts. She had heard his words of betrayal, had seen him accept his payoff from Benjamin Mateland. And the deed? Jessica knew she could prove the document was forged. She just couldn't work herself into the anger she knew she ought to be feeling over the thought that she was going to have to do so. Right now she couldn't feel anything. It was funny how the mind had this means of self-preservation where it could shut down all feeling when subjected to such devastating anguish.

In the midst of wiping at a fresh wave of tears, Jessica's hand suddenly froze. Her ears strained against the silence, wondering if it was only her imagination that had created the sound. But no, it came again, the sound of footsteps in the hallway downstairs. And then they were climbing the steps!

Her first thought was of Benjamin Mateland, and sitting up, Jessica glanced around wildly for anything she might use as a weapon against the intruder. Finding nothing, she was about to throw the covers back and try to make it to her door to slam and lock it when the tall, broad-shouldered shadow filled the doorway. For the briefest instant stark terror made her heart leap into her throat, until he stepped into the room.

The shadowy form was too tall and lean to be Ben, and Jessica probably would have screamed in fear if not for the outline of the familiar duster and Stetson. As it was, she wanted to scream at him anyway, to ask if he had only come back out of some sick desire to torture her shattered heart further.

"Jessie? Are you awake?"

Controlling the urge to burst into tears at the soft tone in his voice, Jessica chose to use anger instead as a shield against the pain he was inflicting. Leaning over, she lit the lantern on the bedside table before turning back to face him, her eyes flashing golden-green fire. "How dare you come back here after what you've done to me?"

The ferocity of her attack took Luke off guard, and he searched his mind for an explanation of her anger. The only possible reason that came to mind was that she regretted giving herself to him the night before. That thought tore viciously at his heart, and almost made him turn to leave without another word. But even though he felt he had the answer to the questions he had come with, Luke couldn't seem to turn away. Not quite yet.

Years of experience had taught him that cold sarcasm was the best camouflage for masking his true feelings, and Luke fell back on that knowledge now. "I'm sorry you feel that way about it," he said, his eyes falling insolently to her breasts where they strained against the white cotton chemise pulled taut against them. "I was under the distinct impression that you enjoyed what I 'did to you' last night just as much as I did."

His inference was clear, and Jessica cursed herself doubly; first that in her despondency she had only had the strength to pull off her denims and flannel shirt and crawl into bed in only a chemise and pantalettes, and secondly she cursed herself for the bolt of heat that shot through her at the way his eyes were caressing her breasts through the thin fabric. It was anger she was feeling, she told herself staunchly; hot, scalding anger at him!

To compensate for her body's betrayal, Jessica's voice came

like an icy wind blowing across a frozen lake as she corrected his lewd assumption. "I'm not talking about that, Mr. Cameron, though right now I consider it almost equally as degrading."

Jessica could see in his eyes that her comment scored a direct hit, for they turned to shards of blue ice. But she was too hur—*furious*, to be intimidated by the thought of stirring up this man's formidable temper. She went on bitingly, "What I was referring to is your despicable lack of even the tiniest shred of decency or honor."

His eyes had narrowed dangerously as each word fell from her lips like venom. The very quietness of his tone as he answered should have set off warning bells in Jessica's head. "Do you want to tell me exactly what in the hell you're talking about?"

She didn't heed the warning. Anger was the only shield she possessed now that allowed her to voice the painful knowledge. "Of course, you wouldn't know yet that I'm already aware of exactly what you are, Mr. Cameron," she bit out, wanting to somehow hurt him as much as he had hurt her. "You're a conscienceless, deceitful, greedy, lying son of a—"

"Jessica!" Luke cut her off icily. "I suggest you quit name-callin' and start explainin' just why your opinion of me has altered so drastically in the last twenty-four hours." And in his hurt he couldn't help adding his own barbs. "Or do you make it a habit to crawl in bed with men you hold such a low opinion of?"

The unknowing reminder of how much she had loved him only a few short hours ago was worse than any physical blow he could have inflicted, and Jessica lashed out against the pain. "You can stop the pretense of offended innocence, Luke! I was at the cave tonight! I saw everything! I *heard* everything!"

She was satisfied to see that render him speechless. "That's right. Heather told me about the gold you found, and I went to the cave to see if that's where you'd been all day. What I saw was you making your deal with Ben Mateland!"

Luke was speechless, not out of guilt, as she supposed, but

Cynthia Strickland

out of confusion. Why, if she'd seen and heard it all as she claimed, was she now attacking him for doing exactly what she'd asked him to do in the first place? Hell, he'd even done it without just shooting the man as he once would have. Was her anger because he hadn't told her about the gold?

Tears burned behind her eyes, but Jessica wasn't about to let him see how his betrayal had hurt her. "You know what the worst part of all this is, though?" she asked, then didn't give him a chance to answer as she went on to tell him. "The worst part is how foolish I feel for defending you to everyone. They told me not to trust you, that you'd only bring me more trouble than I already had. But did I listen? No! I actually told everyone how honorable you were!" Her choked laughter was filled with self-mockery as she asked, "Can you believe that? Do you know how stupid I feel right now, knowing I was so gullible to your lies?!"

"I assume your ravings are about the gold," Luke asked quietly, angry that he had been right about how it would change her feelings. "You think I wasn't going to tell you about it?"

Out of everything he had done, the lies, the deceit, the betrayal, Jessica could only gape in astonishment that he actually seemed to think the blasted gold was what she was most concerned about.

"I guess it's understandable you would think that," she said when she finally found her tongue again, "since money seems to be all that's important to you. Knowing that, I'm surprised you sold out for a measly three thousand when you could have just killed me and had all the gold for yourself!"

That she would even suggest he could do something so reprehensible told Luke all he needed to know. "I thought about it," he bit out sarcastically, not caring now whether she took his words seriously or not, "but I figured I would be the first one folks around here would suspect of doin' you in. The three thousand seemed the safer bet."

He had already turned to leave when her next words stopped him halfway out the door.

"And you never bet on anything unless you're sure you can

292

win. Do you, Mr. Cameron?'' Jessica spat acidly. "How well I'll remember that degrading lesson for the rest of my life!''

He turned slowly, his eyes mere slits of icy fury, and it finally dawned on Jessica too late the stupidity of antagonizing this man when there was no one in the house to call out to for help. With his booted heel he reached back to kick the door shut, then slowly began to retrace his steps toward the bed.

Jessica swallowed audibly. "Get out, Luke,'' she ordered, cursing her voice when it cracked in the middle of the command. When he only kept coming, she scrambled up onto her knees, clutching the sheet to her chest as if it might magically shield her. "I'll scream,'' she warned desperately.

His cold grin made her tremble. "I wouldn't suggest it. The only thing it'll accomplish is upsettin' Heather.''

"She's with Fra—'' Jessica began automatically, then cut herself off quickly at the stupid blunder. The light in his eyes told her she hadn't shut her mouth quickly enough.

"So we're alone in the house,'' Luke said with a wolf's pleasure at finding the rabbit held helpless by a snare. Obviously savoring her predicament, he stopped by the side of the bed. "Just think of the possibilities if you didn't feel so degraded by my touch,'' he went on in a silky drawl as he reached out to trace one finger along the lace trimming the top of her chemise.

Her eyes closed as an uncontrollable tremor shot through her breasts at his touch, and Jessica cursed her rebellious body as her breathing deepened. When she forced her eyes open to meet his, it was to find a cruel smile of satisfaction in those icy eyes.

"Get out of here, Luke,'' she ordered tremulously.

Her claim that she had felt only degradation in what they had shared had cut Luke to the depths of his soul. Some demon drove him now to prove to them both that she wasn't as repulsed as she claimed.

"I only want to apologize for forcing myself on you last night,'' he said, slipping his hand to the back of her neck to massage the muscles there lightly. "I just meant to give you pleasure."

Her breathing had become shallow, as if his hand was gripping her lungs instead of melting the tension from her neck and shoulders. "I—forgive—you," she got out, sounding as if she had just run up a long flight of stairs. "Now—leave."

Instead of doing as she asked, he leaned forward, pulling one knee up onto the bed beside her hip. "But I feel so bad about mistaking your reaction," he whispered, the smoky promise in his eyes mesmerizing her. "I wish you'd told me how repulsed you were by this."

A searing bolt of pure fire shot through her as he leaned forward to whisper those last words against the tender skin just beneath her ear, and Jessica shuddered violently.

"And this," he whispered again as he gently grazed her earlobe with his teeth, melting her bones with the heat.

At some point during the assault his lips were making on her neck, Luke's right hand had moved up her side to rest just below her breast. His fingers moved now to brush the sensitive outer slope, and a groan broke rebelliously from her lips.

"Please—don't do this—Luke," she whispered, helpless to pull away from the exquisite pleasure of his touch, from the too recent memory of the incredible conclusion that waited for her at the end of this sensuous journey that only he was capable of taking her on.

Somehow this act that had started out as a punishing lesson now had Luke caught securely in a web of his own making. "Tell me you don't feel anything," he challenged huskily against her ear as his hand closed gently over her breast. "Tell me you despise my touch and I'll leave you right now."

Jessica couldn't say the words. She hated herself for her weakness, but she hated Luke even more for being able to use it so well against her, even after his betrayal.

His lips were trailing bone-melting heat across her shoulder as his fingers slowly worked their magic on more vulnerable parts of her body. "Tell me," he whispered against her skin. "Tell me you don't want this as much as I do."

A sound that was half moan, half sob escaped Jessica's

throat as she admitted defeat. "I can't," she got out brokenly, and in the next moment Luke was taking her on that magical journey to the eye of the storm.

But the storm passed much too quickly, and in the aftermath Jessica could again think clearly. As she rolled onto her side, the tears of betrayal and shame came bitterly. Lust had driven her to give herself to the man who had sold her out to her enemy only a few short hours ago, and the knowledge tasted like bile in her throat. And it was lust that had driven her, no matter how her heart argued against the point. She did not still love Luke Cameron! She couldn't!

But you do, her heart forced its voice to be heard. *You're just angry because you know you want to beg him to stay, despite everything he's done.*

I hate him! her mind argued fiercely.

Do you? Honestly?

The tears came harder as she admitted the painful truth.

Lying there on his back, staring at the ceiling, Luke knew that a horsewhipping couldn't hurt nearly as bad as listening to Jessica cry over what they had just done. If she'd been angry at him before, she surely despised him now.

"Jessie?"

"Just get out, Luke," she pleaded brokenly. "Please just go away."

Without another word he climbed from the bed and pulled on his denims that had been thrown on the floor in the heat of passion. *Passion?* Luke stood for a long moment looking at the back turned to him so reproachfully. He watched her slim shoulders jerk with each heartwrenching sob, and he knew a desolation he had never known before. His heart wanted to cry out to her, to beg her to return his love. But the impossibility of that, combined with pride, which was the only thing he had left at this moment, kept the words locked firmly inside.

Throwing the blue cotton shirt over one shoulder, he settled the tan Stetson on his head, then leaned down to pick up his boots. His eyes searched the room but found no other trace that he had been here—except the woman he had come to love more than life itself crying tears of degradation.

No man will ever love you as fiercely as I do, Jessie Cameron. Luke's heart spoke the words he couldn't bring himself to utter. Instead he said softly, "Forgive me, Jessica."

And then he was gone.

Chapter Thirty-three

Five months later

Jessica stepped out onto the front porch of what had once been Benjamin Mateland's home and looked around her at the changes the last few weeks had wrought. If she was feeling any elation that her project was nearing completion, it didn't show on her face. In fact, there had been very little sign of any kind of emotion evident in Jessica for the last five months, which worried the two people who stood just behind her. Ruth and Frannie exchanged glances behind her back, their concern evident.

"The renovations are coming along nicely," Ruth said, stepping up to take Jessica's arm. "James tells me the first children should be able to move in next week."

Jessica simply nodded.

When Zeke finally convinced her to check into mining the gold in the cave, they were all stunned at the size and quality of the vein. Instead of spending it on a house in San Francisco or Saint Louis as Luke had imagined, however, Jessica had bought the Bar M. The renovations Ruth spoke of were those needed to turn the grandiose house from a symbol of excess into a home for orphaned children, though everyone had been made aware from the very beginning of the project that the word *orphanage* would not be associated with this place. It was going to be a working ranch where children would grow up as members of a very large family. They would have jobs to do, but Jessica sincerely felt it would give each child a sense of belonging. She was adamant that every child who grew up here would feel loved and wanted.

Zeke and Frannie had taken to the idea immediately, and had pitched in wholeheartedly in getting the work going. And when the hands from the Circle R weren't busy with their chores there, they came to the Bar M, now called the Gold Bar, to lend a hand. Ruth had been invaluable in coordinating the efforts of several of the ladies in the area in making curtains and bed coverings for the many more bedrooms that had been added to the house.

The one sore point in all this had been James. He had come over two days after Luke left to find out how things had gone for the two of them. Jessica had refused to talk about that night at first, but when James pressed her and found out she had asked Luke to leave, he had gotten angry. Being so unfairly attacked, Jessica had told him how despicable Luke was, quoting the exact words she had overheard that night.

Not a day had gone by since that morning that Jessica didn't think about the truth that James had revealed. And not a day went by that she didn't curse Luke for not standing up for himself in the midst of her accusations to tell her that truth himself.

But no, just like the stubborn, proud man he was, he had let her rant and rave and accuse him of crimes he was innocent of, not saying a word in his defense. For those first two days she had fumed over the last words he had spoken to her. *Forgive me, Jessica.* She couldn't believe the audacity of the man, asking her to forgive him for his betrayal. But after hearing the truth of what he had done for her, Jessica now couldn't get those words out of her mind. What had he meant? Forgive him for what?

Jessica chewed at her lower lip as she looked out over the fenced pasture in front of the house. Once again she tried to assuage her guilty conscience. *What was I supposed to have thought, given what I heard him say? How was I supposed to have known it was all a plot Luke came up with to have Ben confess his guilt in front of Sheriff Davis and his men?*

You should have had more faith in him, her heart made her

face the uncomfortable truth. *You should have at least given him a chance to explain before you lambasted him with such horrible accusations.*

And so the familiar argument went, back and forth, just as it had for the last five months, and still it didn't change the most important fact in all this. Evidently Luke hadn't really cared what she thought, or at least he hadn't cared enough to try to explain. No. He had taken off that night without a backward glance. For all she knew, he was in Mexico right now, lying in some dark-haired woman's arms and sipping tequila.

The visual image she had tortured herself with for months brought a familiar, stabbing pain in her chest, and as before Jessica steeled herself against the feeling.

In fact, she had steeled herself against feeling anything in these last months. Only Heather could draw a genuine smile from her, and even then Jessica would forget for a brief instant and want to share the moment with Luke. But then she would remember, and the protective wall of ice she had built around her heart would become that much thicker.

"You know, we ought to be puttin' up the curtains in yer own room upstairs soon, darlin'," Frannie brought her from her thoughts. "You'll want to be stayin' here as soon as the first little ones arrive."

Jessica tried not to shiver at the thought. For months she had been trying to come to grips with the idea of actually spending the night under the same roof her husband's murderer had once slept under. She kept telling herself that it wasn't Benjamin Mateland's home any longer, that it was wonderfully poetic justice that the same money he had been willing to kill for was now being used to turn his house into a home for parentless children.

Still, Jessica felt a coldness run along her arms at the thought of sleeping here. She told herself she would have to get over that soon. But she didn't have to do it tonight, she decided with a tired sigh. Tonight she just wanted to go home and curl up in her own bed, under her own roof.

"I think I'll head on home now," she told Frannie, then gave a ghost of a smile. "I'm sure Heather is *helping* Zeke and the men. Would you mind bringing her home when you come?"

"You know I don't, darlin'," Frannie answered, giving a worried frown. "But are ya sure ya don't want to stay and ride with us? You an' Heather could eat supper at our house an' Zeke could walk ya both home later."

Ruth nodded her agreement with the idea. "Why don't you do that, Jess? You look tired. And besides, you could use a good meal."

"Thanks!" Jessica said with a reproachful laugh.

"I'm just telling you what I see. That dress is hanging on you like you're a little girl playing dress-up in an adult's clothes. When is the last time you ate a decent meal?"

"I eat!"

"You pick!" Frannie accused. "Stirrin' it around on yer plate with yer fork doesn't do a thing towards keepin' meat on yer bones!"

"Will you two stop ganging up on me about this?" Jessica asked, crossing her arms defiantly as she faced them over the familiar argument. "I'll eat when I'm hungry. Right now I'd just like to go home if you don't mind and take a warm bath and go to bed early. Now, can Heather ride with you, Frannie, or should I go get her and take her with me?"

Frances gave a snort, but relented. "You know she can ride with me. I'll feed her supper and then bring her home." She couldn't resist adding, "And I'll bring you a plate as well."

"Thank you," Jessica said, then turned to Ruth. "Will you be coming back tomorrow?"

Ruth shook her head, at a loss as to how to deal with the self-destructive path her friend was traveling. But what could she do? She couldn't force Jessica to eat, *or* to forget Luke Cameron.

"I'll be here. We have to hang the curtains Liza Campbell brought over this afternoon for the young boys' bedrooms."

With a nod, Jessica turned and left for the barn.

"Damn Luke Cameron!" Frances said, causing the woman at her side to turn and look at her in astonishment. "What? Can you tell me you don't feel the same about the man?"

"I'm upset about it, yes. But we have to remember that Jessica also told us what she accused him of. James told me if I had said half the things to him that she said to Luke he would have left me too."

Frances made a rude sound at that. "An' he couldn't tell her what really happened? He couldn't try to understand how she felt at what she believed he'd done?"

"He had no way of knowing Jessica left before it came out that he was setting Ben up," Ruth tried to excuse the absent Luke. "You know how stubborn men are. I'm sure once she started accusing him, then told him to leave, pride wouldn't let him stay around and try to explain."

"So you're not the least bit angry at him?" Frances asked skeptically.

At that moment Jessica rode by on her way down the drive. Ruth watched the gaunt shell of the woman her friend had once been for a long moment. She didn't turn to face the older woman at her side as she answered. "I'm mad as hell at Luke Cameron for having too much pride to set things right, and I'm mad at Jessica for her own stubborn part in this ridiculous misunderstanding. But mostly I think I ache for how much they both have had to suffer because of it."

The sun had disappeared behind the mountains to the west, leaving only streaks of deep red and vibrant magenta streaking the sky as Jessica opened the gate to the small graveyard and stepped inside. A few hundred yards away the house looked pink in the last light of the day. Everything was silent except for the soft twitter of birds as they began to settle down for the night. In the peaceful solitude that she once would have welcomed, Jessica now felt only an aching loneliness. It was what had brought her here in the first place, the need to talk to someone who wouldn't condemn her for feeling as she did, someone who wouldn't insist that she needed to eat, or get more sun because she looked so pale.

"You're the only one I can talk to, John," she said softly as she knelt to place a small bouquet of flowers on the grave. "I can tell you things and not have to defend myself, or listen

301

to why I should just forget him and get on with my "life."

Only the gentle breeze answered.

"I guess I should have known it would happen. Every man I've ever loved has left me; first Papa, and for all you didn't do it intentionally, you left me alone, and now Luke."

Tears burned behind her eyes, but Jessica had become an expert at denying them escape. She bit her lip hard until she forcefully willed the tears down, then went on. "But no more, John. I've made up my mind that I'll never love another man like I came to love Luke. I'll never let another one hurt me like he has."

Looking down at her left hand, Jessica toyed with the ring for a moment, then coming to a decision, she took the gold band off and slipped it on her right hand where it had been before she had entered into this painful episode of her life.

"I know I've got to let go of the memories at some point, John, and I think that time has come. I'll be opening the ranch next week, and those little children don't need a woman who mopes about all the time, languishing over lost love. Much as I haven't appreciated hearing it, I think the time has come to do as Ruth said and get on with my life."

She didn't receive an answer, but she hadn't expected one. It was just comforting to be able to talk to a good friend who would remain silent as she made this painful decision to try to turn loose of her pain and grief.

Standing, Jessica looked down at the headstone once more and smiled softly. "Thank you for listening, my dear friend," she whispered quietly, and after a long moment, turned to leave.

Her hand froze on the latch to the gate.

Sitting on a rise a few hundred yards away was a familiar silver-gray stallion. More familiar still was the broad-shouldered form sitting atop the horse, watching her. In the waning light he was only a shadow, but Jessica knew without a doubt who it was. Her heart soared, then fell to the pit of her stomach, then seemed to stop beating altogether as he kicked the stallion into a canter.

Jessica's first instinct was to run, whether it was toward him or away from him she wasn't quite sure. Finally she decided to simply stand her ground. She silently thanked God for the few moments it took the horse and rider to reach her, for it gave her the opportunity to disguise her rioting emotions behind a cool mask of disinterest.

Luke pulled Shiloh to a halt just outside the short fence. His eyes feasted on the sight of the woman standing before him like a starving man's would food. But unsure of his reception after their last meeting, he kept his tone carefully neutral. "Jessica."

"Luke."

Her returned greeting had the warmth of a January blizzard, and Luke knew he had made a mistake in returning. Nothing had changed. She still hated him. Despite that, there were a few things he meant to say to her before he left again. He at least wanted to set the record straight.

Luke was about to do just that when he looked at her, *really* looked at her this time, and suddenly realized how pale and gaunt she was. "Are you all right?" he asked, unable to hide his concern.

Jessica bristled at the tone. How dare he sound worried when it was his fault she looked so awful? "Of course I'm all right!" she bit out. "Why wouldn't I be? All my problems have been solved. But then you know that, don't you? James came over a couple of days after you left and told me what really happened at the cave that night. If you had gone to the trouble of telling me the truth that night, I could have thanked you before you left."

It came as some surprise to hear that she hadn't known the full truth when she verbally attacked him that night, but Luke's own battered sense of honor wouldn't absolve her of guilt. She should have at least asked him to explain his side of what she had seen. "If you'll remember, you didn't give me much of a chance to say anything before you started throwing out your accusations."

"You could have denied them!"

"What good would it have done?" Luke came right back.

"You believed what you wanted to believe! Once a lowlife outlaw, always a lowlife outlaw, Right?!"

"You know I didn't think that!"

"Oh, didn't you? You thought I sold you out to Mateland!"

"That's the only part I heard! Forgive me if I didn't want to stick around and hear all the despicable details of your supposed betrayal! You had the chance to set me straight later, but you chose not to. You chose to just ride away without a word."

"You told me to get out! Forgive *me* if I didn't want to stick around while you thought up more names to blacken my character!"

Jessica wouldn't meet his gaze, but she still wasn't going to take full responsibility for what had happened. He could have stayed if he had really wanted to. He obviously hadn't, though, just as he didn't mean to stay this time. Well, the sooner he left, the better, in her opinion!

"You know James also told me that you broke the terms of our—agreement by leaving," Jessica informed him. "Aren't you afraid Sheriff Davis will see you and try to hang you again?"

"Not especially. I only came back because for some insane reason I thought you might care to hear where I've been these last months."

Jessica scraped her thumbnail across the rust on the latch. "Where you went is your business. I really couldn't care less."

"I've been in Washington."

"I've heard it's lovely this time of year."

Luke was growing angrier by the second at her flippant attitude. "I didn't go there for the damn weather. I went there to argue my case before a *real* judge. An old friend from my days at West Point helped me convince the man that I was justified in what I did, if not completely within the law. I was granted an official pardon."

"How nice for you."

"Damn it, Jessica!" Luke growled, bringing her head up in surprise so that she finally met his gaze. "I hate it when you get sarcastic like this. If you're still angry with me for some reason, then tell me why and give me hell about it instead of this sugar-coated venom you're spittin' at me!''

Jessica was just as angry as he was. The only difference was she was glaring at him through a veil of unshed tears. ''What do you want from me, Luke?'' she demanded to know. ''Do you want me to tell you how thrilled I am for you? Well, I am. I'm glad you got your pardon. You deserve it.''

''Damn right I do! I deserve to be able to settle somewhere an' not have folks lookin' at me like I'm some lowlife, murderin' scum of the earth. I deserve to clear my family name so I can be proud to give it to a woman when I make her my wife. And I deserve to have that woman proud to take it!''

Jessica felt a tightening in the region of her heart at what his words implied. ''Are you saying you've found someone you want to marry?'' she asked quietly, all trace of her sarcasm gone. ''Is that why you came back? To get our marriage annulled?''

She was looking down at that blasted latch again so Luke couldn't read her eyes, but she looked as if she were braced for a physical blow. The only reason he could think of that she might be upset by the idea of him remarrying was too impossible to believe. Could it be? His heart soared for a brief instant before the strong sense of self-preservation he had acquired over the past few years made him proceed with caution.

''And if I tell you that it is?'' he tested for her response.

The words were an admission to Jessica, and she felt them just as if he had struck her in the face. She went rigid for a moment, then had to turn away from him to hide the tears she could no longer hold at bay. Her shoulders squared as she said in a very quiet voice, ''Okay. I'll take care of it as soon as possible.''

He saw her shoulders tremble, and Luke prayed he wasn't reading his own hopes into her reaction. He wanted her to make the first move that would tell him her feelings, but then he realized from what he had told her just now that she really believed he meant to marry another woman. She would be foolish to admit to any feelings for him now.

Pressing down every instinct that screamed out against it, Luke opened himself up to say, "And as soon as you do, you're gonna marry me."

That brought her back around, and in her shock Jessica forgot to hide the tears that had escaped to trail down her cheeks. "What did you say?"

Relief washed over Luke as he realized he hadn't been imagining her response. Incredible as the idea was, it seemed she might just care for him after all. Maybe happily-ever-afters did come true. He swung down off Shiloh and crossed to the gate to stand before her, wiping a tear from her cheek tenderly. "Try to see my side of this, Jessie. You married a gunslinger because you were afraid of Mateland. I couldn't live like that the rest of my life, feelin' like you were tied to me out of some sense of gratitude. I don't want you like that."

Jessica held her breath, hoping this dream wouldn't end like all the others, hoping that if it were a dream she would never wake up. "How do you want me?" she asked tremulously.

Luke laughed softly, shaking his head. "Just like a woman. You're gonna make me say the words. Aren't you?"

She nodded.

"All right. I love you, Jessie Cameron. I don't know when it happened, but it did. Hell, it was probably from the very first when you whipped off that veil and looked like you would have shot me yourself if you didn't need me so bad."

It was as if the black clouds of five months had suddenly rolled back and the brilliant sunlight poured back into her life. Jessica actually pinched herself, then laughed at the pain when she realized that this time the dream wasn't going to end as it had in the past. Knowing that, she gave the first real smile she had given in a very long time as she admitted happily, "You know, I was mad enough at the time to do just that."

"And now?"

The look in her eyes told Luke what he needed to know as she answered softly, "And now I'm glad I needed you too badly to do it."

"Which proves my point of how desperate you were," Luke stressed, not willing to be distracted quite yet. "But we're gonna do it right this time. *I'm* gonna be the one to do the askin'." He looked down at her bare left hand, then to the gold band she had replaced on her right, then back up to pierce her with a breathtakingly possessive look as he took her left hand. "And I'm gonna put *my* ring on this finger, and you won't be takin' it off for the rest of your life. Understand?"

"And if I say no?" Jessica asked, looking totally serious but for the sparkle lighting her eyes.

Grabbing her under her arms, Luke lifted her over the fence. Even when her feet touched ground once more he only pulled her closer into his arms, which was really a good thing, for his voice took on that husky growl that always made Jessica's knees grow weak. "I was kinda hopin' you might do just that," he claimed, quietly. " 'Cause in that case I get to convince you otherwise."

Still caught in a hazy fog of disbelief, Jessica hardly realized when he lifted her into his arms and started walking toward the house. The sheer intensity of his gaze held her own imprisoned as he traveled down the hallway, silently daring her to speak a word of protest. Up the stairway he climbed, his every step filled with purpose. Without hesitation he crossed the threshold to her room and kicked the door shut behind him, crossing to lay her on the bed.

Breathless, as if she'd run the entire way from the gravesite on the hill instead of being carried, Jessica watched in an almost numb fascination as he straightened and began to unbutton his shirt. The boots came off next, each hitting the wooden floor with a thud of finality. It was only as he reached to unfasten his belt buckle that he paused for the first time, one golden brow raised in question.

"I should warn you I've always been the impatient kind. I was one that'd rip the wrapping paper off to get to the present inside. So if you like that dress the way it is, you might want to get busy on those buttons before I get to 'em."

The words, given with that slight twitch at the corner of his mustache that had so often infuriated her, but that she had missed so terribly these past five months, finally snapped Jessica out of her stupor. Still, elated as she was with his earlier profession of love, it went against her character to give in so mildly to his arrogant words. Tossing her head, she gave him a look of cool challenge. "If you think you can just waltz in here after five months and simply tell me to take my clothes off for you, Luke Cameron, you are sadly mis—''

The rest was cut off by a squeal as Luke made a dive for the bed, catching Jessica beneath him. Braced on his elbows, he gazed down into her eyes, drinking in the way the golden flecks seemed to sparkle like sunlight within their depths. God only knew how he had missed looking into her eyes. He had missed everything about this remarkable woman who had come into his life at the darkest moment, promising him a reprieve he wasn't sure he wanted. Then, before he was even aware it was happening, she had gotten under his skin until now he couldn't imagine having to live without her. That was why he had come back, because he had finally given up trying to be noble and decided he wasn't going to *accept* life without her.

"You asked for this, Jessie Cameron," Luke accused, holding her wrists captive on each side of her head. "I warned you in the jail I wanted you as part of the deal."

Their bodies were pressed together intimately, and it seemed his every movement was calculated to remind her of what was to come. It made coherent thought difficult, but still she made the attempt as she argued, "But you said that was just a test to see how serious I was. You told me you weren't serious."

Jessica saw the flash of a sexy grin before his lips lowered to the sensitive spot behind her ear. The warm rush of his breath made her shiver violently as he whispered an answer against her skin. Caught up in the onslaught of desire, it took her moment before the husky words registered. By then it was too late to take him to task for his admission.

"I lied."

Epilogue

The parlor at the Circle R was filled with people. Frannie and Zeke stood in the center of the room, with Clayton, Hank, Billy, Tim, Lee, Allen, and Sam lined up behind them. The cowboys wore their best clothes and the widest grins anyone could remember seeing on any of them before. Ruth stood just behind Jessica, wiping at the tears that coursed down her cheeks. Standing across from her, James grinned and shook his head, then turned back to listen to the sheriff.

James McCalister took his obligations as best man seriously, for all that he had given Luke quite a bit of ribbing about coming back after he had already broken away to freedom. That particular comment had earned him two elbows in the ribs, one from his wife and one from Jessica, who had threatened more damage if he didn't revise the statement to tell Luke how lucky he was that he had come back.

Now James watched a very different, very demure Jessica as she stood before Wilford Davis in a beautiful gown of cream satin. Heather stood on one side of the bride, watching the proceedings with a smile that threatened to split her little face in two. On Jessica's other side stood Luke, looking uncomfortable in the stiff black suit. James shook his head, grinning as he realized that the groom was also looking at his bride as if he wanted nothing more than to get this service over with and get on to the honeymoon.

"And do you, Jessica, take Luke to be your lawfully wedded husband, to love, honor, and obey him till death do you part?" Wilford asked the familiar question.

Jessica looked at the man standing beside her. His brow

was raised in such obvious doubt at the word "obey" that she almost burst into laughter. "I do," she promised solemnly, but with a spark of amusement in her eyes that left him to wonder how much of that vow she meant to keep.

Wilford looked to Luke. "You have the ring, son?"

Luke nodded, and after taking it from James he turned and took Jessica's left hand to slip the band on her third finger. He refused to let go of her hand as Wilford continued.

"Then by the power vested in me as Justice of the Peace, Wyoming Territory, I now pronounce you husband and wife." And he couldn't help adding with a grin, "For what I hope's gonna be the last time necessary."

There was such deep, abiding love in Jessica's eyes as he looked down into them that Luke could only meet her gaze in wonder. Now he knew what John Randall had felt for Alicia. Now he knew what James had tried to explain of his feelings for Ruth. Luke's life had ceased to hold any meaning those months away from Jessica. If he had thought his life empty in the years after the war, he had quickly realized he hadn't begun to know what empty was until he faced life without Jessica. When he had come back, it was with the hope of someday winning her love. He had never imagined in his wildest hopes that, according to the admission she made when he finally stopped kissing her the day of his return, she had loved him nearly as long as he had loved her.

Looking at the two just staring at each other, Wilford gave a chuckle to break the lengthening silence. "Well, what are you waiting for, son? Go ahead and kiss your bride."

Luke looked at the grinning man, then back to Jessica. With a smile reminiscent of another scene much like this one, he pulled his wife into his arms and repeated those long-ago words, "Don't mind if I do, Sheriff."

And he did just that.

FLAME
CONNIE MASON

"Each new Connie Mason book is a prize!"
—Heather Graham

When her brother is accused of murder, Ashley Webster heads west to clear his name. Although the proud Yankee is prepared to face any hardship on her journey to Fort Bridger, she is horrified to learn that single women aren't welcome on any wagon train. Desperate to cross the plains, Ashley decides to pay the first bachelor willing to pose as her husband. Then the fiery redhead comes across a former Johnny Reb in the St. Joe's jail, and she can't think of any man she'd rather marry in name only. But out on the rugged trail Tanner MacTavish quickly proves too intense, too virile, too dangerous for her peace of mind. And after Tanner steals a passionate kiss, Ashley knows that, even though the Civil War is over, a new battle is brewing—a battle for the heart that she may be only too happy to lose.

_4150-2 $5.99 US/$6.99 CAN

Pure Temptation

Connie Mason

"Each new Connie Mason book is a prize!"
—Heather Graham

Spirits can be so bloody unpredictable, and the specter of
Lady Amelia is the worst of all. Just when one of her ne'er-
do-well descendents thought he could go astray in peace, the
phantom lady always appears to change his wicked ways.

A rogue without peer, Jackson Graystoke wants to make
gaming and carousing in London society his life's work. And
the penniless baronet would gladly curse himself with wine
and women—if Lady Amelia would give him a ghost of a
chance.

Fresh off the boat from Ireland, Moira O'Toole isn't fool
enough to believe in legends or naive enough to trust a rake.
Yet after an accident lands her in Graystoke Manor, she finds
herself haunted, harried, and hopelessly charmed by Black
Jack Graystoke and his exquisite promise of pure temptation.
_4041-7 $5.99 US/$6.99 CAN

THE LION'S BRIDE CONNIE MASON

Winner of the *Romantic Times* Storyteller Of The Year Award!

Lord Lyon of Normandy has saved William the Conqueror from certain death on the battlefield, yet neither his strength nor his skill can defend him against the defiant beauty the king chooses for his wife.

Ariana of Cragmere has lost her lands and her virtue to the mighty warrior, but the willful beauty swears never to surrender her heart.

Saxon countess and Norman knight, Ariana and Lyon are born enemies. And in a land rent asunder by bloody wars and shifting loyalties, they are doomed to misery unless they can vanquish the hatred that divides them—and unite in glorious love.

_3884-6 $5.99 US/$7.99 CAN

SIERRA

Connie Mason

Bestselling Author Of *Wind Rider*

Fresh from finishing school, Sierra Alden is the toast of the Barbary Coast. And everybody knows a proper lady doesn't go traipsing through untamed lands with a perfect stranger, especially one as devilishly handsome as Ramsey Hunter. But Sierra believes the rumors that say that her long-lost brother and sister are living in Denver, and she will imperil her reputation and her heart to find them.

Ram isn't the type of man to let a woman boss him around. Yet from the instant he spies Sierra on the muddy streets of San Francisco, she turns his life upside down. Before long, he is her unwilling guide across the wilderness and her more-than-willing tutor in the ways of love. But sweet words and gentle kisses aren't enough to claim the love of the delicious temptation called Sierra.

_3815-3 $5.99 US/$6.99 CAN

SAVAGE LONGINGS

CASSIE EDWARDS

"Cassie Edwards is a shining talent!"
—Romantic Times

Having been kidnapped by vicious trappers, Snow Deer despairs of ever seeing her people again. Then, from out of the Kansas wilderness comes Charles Cline to rescue the Indian maiden. Strong yet gentle, brave yet tenderhearted, the virile blacksmith is everything Snow Deer desires in a man. And beneath the fierce sun, she burns to succumb to the sweet temptation of his kiss. But the strong-willed Cheyenne princess is torn between the duty that demands she stay with her tribesmen and the passion that promises her unending happiness among white settlers. Only the love in her heart and the courage in her soul can convince Snow Deer that her destiny lies with Charles—and the blissful fulfillment of their savage longings.

_4176-6 $5.99 US/$6.99 CAN

SAVAGE SHADOWS

CASSIE EDWARDS

THE SAVAGE SERIES

"Cassie Edwards is a shining talent!"
—Romantic Times

All her life, Jae has lived in the mysterious region of Texas known as Big Thicket. And even though the wild land is full of ferocious animals and deadly outlaws, the golden-haired beauty never fears for her safety. After all, she could outshoot, outhunt, and outwit most any man in the territory.

Then a rugged rancher comes to take Jae to a home and a father she has never known, and she is alarmed by the dangerous desires he rouses in her innocent heart. Half Comanche, half white, and all man, the hard-bodied stranger threatens Jae's peace of mind even when she holds him at gunpoint. Soon, she has to choose between escaping deeper into the dark recesses of the untamed forest—or surrendering to the secrets of passionate ecstasy in the savage shadows.

_4051-4 $5.99 US/$6.99 CAN

SAVAGE PASSIONS

CASSIE EDWARDS

**Winner Of The *Romantic Times*
Lifetime Achievement Award
For Best Indian Romance Series!**

Living among the virgin forests of frontier Michigan,
Yvonne secretly admires the chieftain of a peaceful Ottawa
tribe. A warrior with great mystical powers and many
secrets, Silver Arrow tempts her with his hard body even
as his dark, seductive eyes set her wary heart afire. But white
men and Indians alike threaten to keep them forever apart.
To fulfill the promise of their passion, Yvonne and Silver
Arrow will need more than mere magic: They'll need the
strength of a love both breathtaking and bold.

_3902-8 $5.99 US/$7.99 CAN

THE **Savage**
S E R I E S

Savage Secrets
Cassie Edwards

Winner Of The *Romantic Times* Reviewers' Choice Award For Best Indian Series

Searching the wilds of the Wyoming Territory for her outlaw brother, Rebecca Veach is captured by the one man who fulfills her heart's desire. But can she give herself to the virile warrior without telling him about her shameful quest?

Blazing Eagle is as strong as the winter wind, yet as gentle as a summer day. And although he wants Becky from the moment he takes her captive, hidden memories of a long-ago tragedy tear him away from the golden-haired vixen.

Strong-willed virgin and Cheyenne chieftain, Becky and Blazing Eagle share a passion that burns hotter than the prairie sun—until savage secrets from their past threaten to destroy them and the love they share.

_3823-4 $5.99 US/$7.99 CAN

Forsaking All Others
GAIL LINK

"Gail Link was born to write romance!"
—Jayne Ann Krentz

Anthony Chambers will inherit half of his Great Uncle Cedric's sprawling Australian homestead on one condition: He must leave England behind and spend a year living at the homestead with his uncle's live-in companion, Annie Ross. Certain the young American is his uncle's mistress, he sets out for Camelot Station eager to meet the scheming tart clever enough to bleed the old man dry, and foolish enough to have a child out of wedlock. But what he finds waiting for him is a softer, gentler woman, a natural beauty who is not intimidated by his arrogant, upper-crust ways. Stubbornly independent, she certainly doesn't fit Tony's idea of the perfect woman—someone he can mold to what he wants. Instead, with her proud spirit and sweet kisses, Annie makes him lose all control, and he wonders if he has the courage to forsake all others and surrender to a love as untamed as the wild Australian landscape.

_4151-0 $5.50 US/$6.50 CAN